Charles Dalton

Life and Times of General Sir Edward Cecil, Viscount Wimbledon

Vol. I

Charles Dalton

Life and Times of General Sir Edward Cecil, Viscount Wimbledon
Vol. I

ISBN/EAN: 9783337059071

Printed in Europe, USA, Canada, Australia, Japan

Cover: Foto ©Raphael Reischuk / pixelio.de

More available books at **www.hansebooks.com**

LIFE AND TIMES

OF

GENERAL SIR EDWARD CECIL,

VISCOUNT WIMBLEDON,

COLONEL OF AN ENGLISH REGIMENT IN THE DUTCH
SERVICE, 1605–1631,

AND

ONE OF HIS MAJESTY'S MOST HONOURABLE PRIVY COUNCIL,
1628–1638.

BY

CHARLES DALTON, F.R.G.S.

IN TWO VOLUMES.

VOL. I.

LONDON:

SAMPSON LOW, MARSTON, SEARLE, & RIVINGTON,

CROWN BUILDINGS, 188, FLEET STREET.

1885.

PREFACE.

—·—

IN these days of universal authorship it is difficult to find a nook or corner in the wide field of English history which has not been thoroughly explored by some past or present writer. There is, however, one plot of ground which has only partially been cultivated by succeeding generations of historians and biographers. This neglected piece of ground was, in the seventeenth century, the camping ground of a large class of Britons known as "soldiers of fortune," whose lives were spent in the Low Countries fighting in the cause of Dutch independence. It was customary at one time for the Home Government, whenever officers were wanted for some special service, to borrow the services of experienced British soldiers of fortune from the Dutch Government for a certain length of time. James I., who may truly be styled the Pacific, rarely troubled any of his military subjects to fight any battles for him, but his son, Charles I., was of a much more bellicose nature, and before he had been two years on the throne he had already despatched two large joint naval and military expeditions to the coast of Spain. The first fleet, which the poet Waller alluded to in one of his poems, was commanded by a soldier of fortune who had served for many years in Holland as colonel of a foot regiment.

The second fleet was also under the command of a soldier
of fortune who had likewise spent the best years of his life
in Holland. These two *çi-devant* colonels were transformed
into admirals for the occasion, and were also dubbed
generals at sea, being invested with supreme naval and
military authority. There being only three instances in
the seventeenth century of soldiers of fortune, who had
served under a foreign flag, being appointed to the high,
but unenviable, position of commander-in-chief of an
English fleet, I have chosen one of these three anomalous
commanders for the subject of the following biography.
The names of these three generals at sea, given chrono-
logically, are Sir Edward Cecil, created Viscount Wimbledon, Robert Bertie, tenth Lord Willoughby de Eresby,
created Earl of Lindsey, and George Monk, created Duke
of Albemarle. Of these three generals at sea, the first
and second were notable failures as admirals. Monk was
as successful on the sea as on land; but then he was
a heaven-born commander, and having served in two
disastrous naval expeditions before he was of age, which
left a vivid and sad remembrance in his mind, he knew
what course to avoid when he himself commanded an
English fleet. The lives of Robert Bertie Earl of Lindsey,
and George Monk Duke of Albemarle, have already
been written. Both have an eulogistic memoir in the
Biographia Britannica, and Monk's life has been written
by that able historian, M. Guizot. There remains therefore only the life of Sir Edward Cecil Viscount Wimbledon,
for me to offer to the reading public.

Although the story of Edward Cecil's life has never
before been written, he has not escaped the notice of
contemporary and after historians. His notable failure
as a general at sea has earned for him a line or two of
contemptuous mention in Clarendon's *History of the*

Rebellion, and after historians, like a flock of helpless sheep, have contented themselves with endorsing this noble historian's remarks, without ever troubling themselves to find out, and to show, how it was that this general at sea failed so lamentably. There is one notable exception to this follow-my-leader class of historians, and this is the able historian of this epoch, Dr. Samuel Rawson Gardiner. The history of the reigns of James I. and Charles I. may, and doubtless will be, rewritten by some aspiring historian in the next century, but I doubt if a more impartial, more reliable, and more unbiassed history of those stirring times will ever supplant, or even equal, Dr. Gardiner's able work. He has shown in his graphic account of the Cadiz expedition in 1625, why that expedition failed, and I can only supplement his account of that expedition by some more details, which occupied too much space to find a place in his valuable work. There is a bright side, as well as a dark side, in every man's character and career, and it is hard if the dark side alone should be displayed to public view. The dark side of Edward Cecil's life has long been known to the readers of English history ; it is my ambition now to show the bright side both of his character and career. It is said that every biographer must either be a flatterer or an apologist. If this is so, then must I appear as an apologist, and not a flatterer, for I have honestly tried not to enhance my subject's qualifications and disguise his failings. I use the word "subject" instead of "hero," as my ideas of the qualifications necessary to constitute a hero are very large, and it appears to me that a man must be a moral as well as a physical hero to deserve that proud appellation.

It is a new departure in biography to write the life of a man who met with greater reverses than successes in his chequered career, but surely it is a more noble aim to try and rescue a man's reputation, as far as historical veracity will allow of, which has been unduly bespattered with dirt by many dead and gone writers whose works still live, than to write a laudatory life of some much over-praised so-called hero. I do not believe in giving an apple to an orchard, or in adding a fresh wreath of laurel to a brow aching with the weight of triumphal honours. If the three years that I have spent in collecting materials for, and in writing, this biography make future historians speak in less condemnation of Edward Cecil, Viscount Wimbledon, when referring to the important expedi-tion placed under his command in 1625, my labours will not have been in vain. As it is, I make no apology to anyone for having written this work, but I do apologise to all those who read it for all the faults, discrepancies, and literary defects which the following pages may contain. I must also beg the reader to read the character of Lord Wimbledon by the light of the age he lived in, and to remember that he lived in an age when society was largely composed of sheep and wolves, and his lordship, who was partial to proverbs, thoroughly believed in the Spanish proverb which says :—" He who makes himself a sheep the wolf eats."

Apart from what a certain class of people speak of slightingly as "the mere accident of birth," Edward Cecil was an historical character. He did not, I own, occupy a high position as an able general, an able speaker, or an able statesman ; but as a soldier, a member of Parliament, and Privy Councillor, he associated on equal terms with the most notable men of his day. As a soldier, he was the contemporary and comrade in arms of such historical characters as Thomas Lord Grey of Wilton, Robert Bertie Lord Willoughby de Eresby, Walter Scott Lord Buccleuch —the "bold Buccleuch" of Sir Walter Scott's stirring

melody—Henry de Vere Earl of Oxford, Henry Wrio-
thesley Earl of Southampton, Edward Sackville Earl of
Dorset, &c. He charged with his troop in the decisive
cavalry charge on Nieuport's bloody field—that hard won
victory which even the victors spoke of with bated breath
and which Dutch ladies loved to represent on tapestry, a
specimen of which is now one of the rarest curiosities in
the Porte de Halle Museum at Brussels. Cecil was the
unsuccessful rival, and for many years the second in command to, the valiant and successful general Sir Horace
Vere, with whom he fought, mined, and raised batteries,
before many of the towns which Maurice of Nassau laid
siege to. At Juliers, where Cecil had a high command as
General of the British contingent, he won honour and
renown, and had such well known men as Sir Edward
Herbert, afterwards created Baron Herbert of Cherbury,
Lord Chandos, Sir Henry Rich, afterwards created Earl
of Holland, Sir Thomas Somerset, afterwards created
Viscount Somerset, and Sir Thomas Howard, afterwards
created Earl of Berkshire, to serve under him as gentlemen
volunteers. When Cecil exchanged camp life for court life
his short sojourns there has an historical interest, as he was
constantly in the company of the chivalrous young Prince
of Wales whose life came to so untimely an end in 1612.
And a melancholy interest attaches itself to Cecil's hurried
journey to Bath, in this same disastrous year, where his
uncle, and kind patron, Robert Cecil Earl of Salisbury,
was seized with that illness which speedily carried him to
the grave.

   As a parliamentary man, Cecil was the contemporary of
Dudley Digges, Robert Philips, Eliot the great patriot, and
many another legislator of whom England may be proud.

   As a Privy Councillor, Lord Wimbledon sat at the
Council Board with such men as Lucius Cary, Viscount

Falkland; William Laud, Archbishop of Canterbury; Thomas Wentworth, Earl of Strafford, and William Juxon, Bishop of London. Wimbledon was one of those Privy Councillors who, on Feb. 17th, 1631, had the privilege of listening to the noble Wentworth (then a Viscount) as he disclosed his propositions to the council concerning the government of Ireland, of which kingdom he was deputy. And it was before Wimbledon, and some other members of the Privy Council, that Oliver Cromwell, on a notable occasion, was brought to answer the charges made against him by the Mayor of Huntingdon.

I have now given a few of the incidents in Edward Cecil's career which, I think, justify me in treating his life historically, and making my biography a history of the Times as well as a record of Cecil's whole life. I make no pretension whatever to any discoveries in the main facts of English history. On the contrary, I have been quite content to extract the main historical facts from well known sources. At the same time I have reviewed these same historical events according to my own ideas, and by no means always in the same light as the authors I have borrowed from. Whenever recourse has been had to the works of a contemporary writer, I have preferred, where possible, to give the extract in his own words. Such extracts as have been translated from Dutch and Spanish writers are given in the exact words of the translators, and have been in no way altered by me.

I have strictly adhered to the old spelling in letters and extracts, only amending the punctuation in the former as well as the involved sentences in many of these letters allows of, and in all cases substituting "the" and "that" for the now obsolete words "y^e" and "y^t." With regard to Lord Wimbledon's letters, many of which I have given in full, I cannot do better than quote the words of Miss

Cooper in her preface to the life of Thomas Wentworth, Earl of Strafford :—" What to us might read like the most fulsome language of servility and flattery, was nothing more than the form of expression common to all in that time."

Nothing remains for me now but the pleasant task of thanking all those to whom I am indebted for any help, however small, in my researches which, though pursued *con amore* and without regard to expense and trouble, have of necessity been arduous, as "works of easy reference" have furnished me with but a small modicum of information regarding the life and doings of a man who has now been dead for nearly 250 years.

I am especially indebted to the Marquis of Salisbury, K.G., for his kind permission to copy all Sir Edward Cecil's letters among the Cecil MSS. at Hatfield. These letters, the foundation of my biography, have been most carefully copied for me by R. T. Gunton, Esq., secretary to the Marquis of Salisbury. I am also especially indebted to the Marquis of Bath for his kindness in lending me an interesting letter of Sir Edward Cecil's, now in his possession at Longleat, for me to copy ; and my thanks are equally due to the Duke of Northumberland, K.G., for his courteous kindness in procuring me a copy of an interesting Cecil document in his possession at Alnwick Castle ; I have also to thank the Dowager Duchess of Northumberland for kind help in the same matter.

I am indebted to the following for their ready help in forwarding my researches :—Miss Amy Yule ; Alexander Turing, Esq., H.B.M. Consul at Rotterdam ; Rev. E. Brine, English chaplain at the Hague ; George Cokayne, Esq. F.S.A., Lancaster Herald ; Dr. S. R. Gardiner, the historian ; Dr. Grosart, F.S.A., the able editor of John Glanville's " *Journal of the Voyage to Cadiz in* 1625 ; " Dr.

Scott, late head-master of Westminster School ; the Rev.
Canon Jackson of Bristol.

I have also received able assistance in copying old letters
and documents, at the Public Record Office, from H. Barr
Tomkins, Esq., Barrister-at-Law, whose experience and
accuracy in making transcripts considerably lightened my
labours in that branch of work.   I may also add that I
have received invariable civility, and ready help whenever
required, at the hands of the officials at the Record Office,
Privy Council Office, and British Museum.

CHARLES DALTON.

32, WEST CROMWELL ROAD,
   SOUTH KENSINGTON.
   September 15th, 1885.

LETTERS IN VOL. I.

LIFE AND TIMES

OF

SIR EDWARD CECIL,

VISCOUNT WIMBLEDON.

CHAPTER I.

1572–1599.

Introduction—The family of Cecil—William Cecil, First Lord Burghley—
Thomas Cecil, Second Lord Burghley and First Earl of Exeter—The travels
of his eldest son, Will Cecil—Letter to Lord Burghley from his grandson
Will Cecil—Marriage of Will Cecil to the Baroness de Ros—Her death—
The Hon. Edward Cecil—Announcement of his birth to William, Lord
Burghley—Westminster School—License for Richard and Edward Cecil to
travel abroad for three years—The civility they received when abroad—
Letter from Florence—The Duke of Bracciano—His visit to London—
Reception by the Queen—Edward Cecil's determination to follow the wars
in the Low Countries—His letter to his uncle, Sir Robert Cecil, from the
Hague.

THE memoirs of a man whose career was one of uninter-
rupted success are not generally so interesting, or instructive
to the reader, as a biography which recounts the struggles
and trials, successes and reverses, of an eventful life. In the
former case you know what to expect, but in the latter you
never know what is going to happen, and so your interest
is kept alive to the end.

Horace Walpole, in his *Royal and Noble Authors*, remarks that there are few memoirs of Edward Cecil,
Viscount Wimbledon. Walpole, in common with some
other writers, mentions that Lord Wimbledon followed the
wars in the Netherlands for many years, and was a general

of great reputation until his miscarriage in the expedition to Cadiz.[1] Most of our historians devote a few lines to the unfortunate expedition to Cadiz in 1625, and mention Lord Wimbledon's name with either sarcasm or opprobrium, not knowing, or not caring to mention, that this same Lord Wimbledon had served for nearly thirty years in the Netherlands, and had won renown in some of the campaigns of those stirring times. It is because historians and biographers have said so little about a man who, whatever his faults may have been, was deservedly reckoned a brave and experienced soldier, and who had raised himself step by step up the military ladder, to the highest military rank, that I have laboured to rescue his name from the oblivion that has so long surrounded it.

Many a face escapes beauty by the possession of one bad feature. Many a character would be considered noble but for one unredeeming trait. Many a general would be reckoned a great commander had he not suffered one signal defeat. A bad feature may improve and soften with age. A character can be improved with care. But a defeat in war is never really forgotten or forgiven, and the defeated commander can seldom retrieve his fame. I say seldom, because it does sometimes happen that the unfortunate commander has the chance of retrieving his reputation and does retrieve it, but if, as is generally the case, he has not the chance, his reputation is never repaired, and what is still worse, his past services and former brave deeds are often forgotten.

---

[1] Walpole's *Royal and Noble Authors*, ii. p. 300. A. Collins, in his *Peerage*, art. *Cecil, Earl of Exeter*, says, Sir Edward Cecil "was one of the most famous generals of his time." Granger says the same, and gives General Cecil a place in his *Biographical Dictionary of England*, i. p. 396. See also honourable mention of Sir E. Cecil in Robert Codrington's *Life and Death of the Illustrious Robert, Earl of Essex*, &c., printed in 1646, and republished in *Harleian Miscellany*, i. pp. 216–239.

Few families can boast of having produced two such illustrious statesmen as William Cecil, the great Lord Burghley, and his illustrious son, Robert Cecil, Earl of Salisbury. If (as I take it to be) the real founder of a family is the one who first brings honour and renown to the name, and raises his family to a high estate, then can we dispense with the genealogists' conflicting statements as to the origin of the Cecils,[1] and merely state that William Cecil, Lord Burghley, was the founder of this noble family. To those, however, who wish for more information, I may state that the Cecils are said to derive their descent from Robert Sitsilt, an assistant to Robert Fitz Hamon in the conquest of Glamorganshire, in the 4th year of King William Rufus. Aubrey, in his *History of Surrey*, says he was in Monmouth Church in 1656, and there was in the window of the church a very old escutcheon, as old as the church, belonging to the family of Sitsilt of Monmouthshire, of which family, he says, was the great Lord Burghley.[2]

The name of this family has been spelt at various times, Sitsilt, Sicelt, Seycil, Seisel, Cicil, &c.[3]

Whatever uncertainty there may be about the descent of Lord Burghley from the Sitsilts[4] of Monmouthshire, it is proved beyond doubt that his grandfather, David Cissil, or Cecil, was the first of his family to settle in Lincolnshire. This David Cecil, of the parish of St. George, Stamford, had a son, Richard Cissel of Burghley, in the parish of St.

---

[1] See an article on " The origin of the noble family of Cecil " in *Notes and Queries*, 6th series, vii. p. 384.

[2] i. p. 15.

[3] Camden's *Remains*, p. 140.

[4] Lord Burghley, who was a great genealogist, drew up several pedigrees of his family with his own hand, and he deduced his descent from the ancient family of Sitsilt. See facsimile of a pedigree in Lord Burghley's handwriting (from the *Hatfield MSS.*) in Dr. Nares' *Life of Lord Burghley*, i. p. 8.

Martin, Stanford Baron, Northamptonshire, who in the
22nd year of Henry VIII. was Groom of the Robes to that
Monarch, and Constable of Warwick Castle.   He left issue
by Jane his wife, daughter and heir to William Heckington,
of Bourn, in Lincolnshire, a son William, "a person," says
Dugdale, " of great learning, singular judgment, admirable
moderation, and comely gravity, who came to be the
chiefest statesman of the age, wherein he lived, unto
whose prudence in council, much is attributed for the
blessing then enjoyed by that prosperous and happy
government throughout the long reign of Queen Elizabeth
of famous memory."[1]

Edward Cecil, the subject of this narrative, had the
honour to be a grandson of this illustrious statesman, his
father being Sir Thomas Cecil, only son of Lord Burghley
by his first marriage with Mary Cheeke, sister to the learned
Sir John Cheeke.   Sir Thomas Cecil served, in the 16th of
Elizabeth, as a volunteer in that expedition into Scotland,
in aid of the Regent of that Kingdom, when the Castle of
Edinburgh was besieged and taken.   He afterwards distinguished himself in the Netherlands, and was made Governor
of the Brill, one of the cautionary towns which the States
of Holland pledged to Queen Elizabeth.[2]

In the memorable year of the Spanish Invasion, 1588, he,
with his half-brother, Sir Robert Cecil, served as volunteers
on board the English fleet.[3]   In 1601, Sir Thomas Cecil,
then Lord Burghley, was installed a Knight of the Garter

---

[1] Arthur Collins' *Life of William, Lord Burghley*, &c.
[2] Rymer's *Fœdera*, xvi. p. 4.
[3] *Brit. Biog.*, iii., art. "Cecil Lord Burghley ;" *Biog. Brit.*, art. "Robert
Cecil ;" Chalmers' *Biog. Dict.*, same life.

at Windsor, and was created 4th May, 1605, Earl of Exeter. This title had been offered to him nearly two years before, but he had declined it. His reasons for so doing are given in a letter from him to Sir John Hubert, dated from Burghley the 12th of Jan. 1603-4 :—

" I am resolvyd to contente myselfe with this estate I have of a Baron. And my present estate of lyvyng, howsoever those of the world hath enlargyd it, I fynde lyttel inough to meyntane the degree I am in. And I am sure they that succede me wyll be less hable to meynteyne it then I am, considerynge ther wyll goo out of the baronage thre yonger broothers lyvyngts."

This nobleman was twice married. He married first, in 1564, Dorothy, daughter and coheir of John Nevill, Lord Latimer,[1] by whom he had five sons and eight daughters, viz :—

I. William Cecil, 2nd Earl of Exeter and 3rd Baron Burghley, born 1566.

2. Sir Richard Cecil, of Wakerley, Northants, Knt., born December 7th, 1570.[2]

3. Sir EDWARD CECIL, Knt.

---

[1] Lord Latimer was son of Sir John Nevill, third Baron Latimer, by his first wife, Dorothy de Vere, daughter and coheir of John, Earl of Oxford (his second wife being Catherine Parr, daughter of Sir Thomas Parr, of Kendal, afterwards married to Henry VIII.). John, fourth and last Lord Latimer, married Lady Lucy Somerset, daughter of Henry, Earl of Worcester. There is a splendid altar monument to Lord Latimer in Well Church, near Bedale, and within two miles of Snape Castle, built by the Nevills, and now a farm-house. Lord Latimer's monument bears a recumbent effigy of that nobleman in armour—his head pillowed on a helmet, his sword by his side, and his hands raised in prayer. A large mural marble tablet by the side of the monu-ment, surmounted by a shield of eighteen quarterings, has the following inscription :—" *Sic transit gloria mundi.* Here lyeth buried S' Jhon Neveil, Knight, laste Lord Lattimor, who died the 23 of Aprill, 1577. Who mared the Lady Lucy th eldest daughter of th Erle of Worseter, and shee lyeth buried in Hackne Church by London, and by hir left 4 daughters and heires whose matches are hereunder expressed."

[2] This birth is recorded in Lord Burghley's *Diary, Harl.* 36.

4. Christopher Cecil, born 1576.

5. Thomas Cecil, born 1579.

1. Catherine Cecil.

2. Lucy Cecil, married Wm. Paulet, Marquis of Winchester and had issue.

3. Mildred Cecil, born 1573, married, first, Sir Thomas Reade, Knt., and, secondly, Sir Edmund Trafford.

4. Mary Cecil, married Edward Denny, Baron Denny and Earl of Norwich.[1]

5. Elizabeth Cecil, married, first, Sir William Newport *alias* Hatton, and, secondly, Lord Chief Justice Sir Edward Coke.

6. Dorothy Cecil, born 1577, married Sir Giles Allington of Horseheath, Cambridgeshire.

7. Frances Cecil, married Nicholas Tufton, first Earl of Thanet, and had issue.

8. Susan Cecil.

William Cecil, the eldest son, will be mentioned occasionally in this narrative, so a few words about him before passing on to his younger brother, Edward, will not be out of place.

At the age of seventeen we find young Will Cecil (as he was generally called) at Paris, having been sent abroad for some years, according to the fashion of that time, to travel and improve his education. That he travelled a good deal is very certain, but in what way he improved his mind is doubtful. An extract from one of his letters from Paris to his grandfather, Lord Burghley, is worthy of a place in these pages, as it shows the same affection for that noble

---

[1] The Earl of Norwich had by this marriage an only daughter and heir Honora, who married Sir James Hay, of Pitcorthie, Co. Fife, created by James I., Viscount Doncaster, and Earl of Carlisle. This nobleman left by Honora, his wife, an only son, who succeeded as second Earl of Carlisle, and at his mother's death succeeded to the barony of Denny. He d. s. p. in 1660.

animal, the horse, which characterised his brother Edward, throughout the latter's military career. This letter[1] is in acknowledgment of "a present of five pounds in Angels and a beautiful bay horse" sent the writer by Lord Burghley :—

"Touching the horse, my good Lord," writes W. Cecil, "no news of like quality could happen more agreeable to my desire and contentátio, then when I hard he was arrived at Paris, much more at the first appearance, when I understood he came from your Lordship, and saw the beauty of his colour, marked his excellent proportion, and perceived the greatnes of his courage, were my senses and mind affected with greater delight then before. But yo[r] L. shall see the incertenty of worldly delights, howe sone my sweet was turned into sower, my mirth into mourninge, and all my joy and delight, into hevines and greef. For my horse had not stood halfe an hower in the stable, but my self and others perceived a great foundringe through out his whole body, which he had gotten by the evil usage of a leud Frenchman, who had the charge of him from Roan[2] hether. For as I am credably informed by honest merchaunts, he came to Roan safly and there was kept six or seven daies; since which hower of his comminge he hath been sic and lame in his whole body, and still remaineth in the hands of the horse-liche without any hope of recovery.[3]

"I thought it discretion and my duety to let yo[r] L. understand in what case I received him, lest if peradventur yet, or herafter, he perishe by occasion of this sicknes it be supposed to be through my default.

"I do most unfanedly assuer yo[r] L. there could no earthly thinge of like value have crossed my joy, more to my greefe and disquietnes, then this misfortune in my horse; wherin I am

---

[1] *Lansdowne MSS.* 104, fo. 168.

[2] Rouen.

[3] Will Cecil appears to have been as unfortunate with his horseflesh as he was in his domestic affairs. Dudley Carleton, in a letter to J. Chamberlain, Dec. 29, 1601, mentions that "Will Cecill was lately robbed at his country house by one of his men of jewels and plate to the value of 2000£, and one of his best geldings."—*S. P. Dom.*

ashamed to show yor L. what very greefe urged me unto, lest yor good L. should condemne me of childishnes and want of dis-cretion. . . . . . At Paris this xxvi of August [1583].

"Your L. most obedient sonn,

"W. CECIL."

Two years later we find Will Cecil paying a secret visit to Rome, and his conduct there gave rise to a suspicion that he had turned Roman Catholic.[1]   Certain it is that his mode of life about this time was highly displeasing to Lord Burghley.   In 1589, the prodigal son having returned home, and amended his way of life, received forgiveness, and was happily married to the only child and heir of Edward Manners, Earl of Rutland.   This lady had succeeded, on her father's decease in 1587, to the ancient barony of de Ros.   A year after his marriage, we find Will Cecil writing to his grandfather, thanking him for consent-ing to be sponsor to his firstborn child, who was to be called William, though the mother had wished him to be called Edward after her father.[2] The young mother lived but a few days, or hours, after her child's birth.   She died on May 11, 1590, leaving her husband a widower at the early age of twenty-four.   And in this forlorn state we must leave Will Cecil and pass on to his brother Edward.

None of the Cecil pedigrees give the true date of Edward Cecil's birth, or state where he was born.[3]   These important

---

[1] Goodman's *Court of James I.*, i. p. 330, note.

[2] W. Cecil to Lord Burghley, 21 May, 1590, *Lansdowne MSS.* 104, f. 71. This child was baptized at Newark Castle on June 4, 1590, and received the name of William.   He succeeded his mother in the barony as sixteenth baron.   His title having been contested by Francis Manners, sixth Earl of Rutland, as heir-general, the barony was confirmed to Wm. Cecil, Lord de Ros, in 1616.

[3] Arthur Collins, in his account of "Cecil, Earl of Exeter," in his *Peerage*, states that Edward Cecil was born in 1571.   Burke and Nichols have copied this vague date. See Burke's *Peerage*, and Nichols' *Progresses of James I.*, ii. p. 441.

links in the biographical chain are supplied by a letter among the State Papers from Thomas Cecil to his illustrious father, Lord Burghley,[1] announcing the birth of his third son, at Burghley House, Stamford, on Feb. 29, 1571–2 :

" My dewty unto yoʳ Lordshipp most humbly considered.   It hath pleasid Almighty God, this present xxixᵗʰ daye of ffebruary, to shewe me his favourable goodnes in sending me, with the saftye as I hoope of my wiffe, a thirde sonne.   My meaning is to require my lorde of Ruttland[2] to be one of the godfathers and the Bishopp of peterborough the other.[3]   As [for] the godmother I am not presently resolvyd of.   And thus requiring yoʳ dailye blessing, booth to me and all youres, I wish that booth in yeares and comfortt you may live to see them the servants of Almighty [God] and a comfortt to yoʳ old age.   And thus most humbly requiring you to beare wᵗʰ this my shortness of writing, hastened therunto for that I would that myne owne letter should be the firste messenger, I end wᵗʰ my dailye prayer for yoʳ safty, ffrom yoʳ l. house of Burghley the xxixᵗʰ of ffebruary 1571 [old style].

" Yoʳ lordshipp's most humble and
" obedient sonne,
" Tho. Cecill."

Addressed :—
" To the right honourable his
very good lorde and father the
lord of Burghley, one of the
lordes of the Quene's Maᵗⁱᵉˢ
most honourable privye councell, &c. &c."
Endorsed :—
" 29 feby. 1571,
Mr. Tho. Cecill to my lord,
his 3ʳᵈ. sonn—born at Burghley."[4]

---

[1] Sir Wm. Cecil had been created Baron Burghley, Feb. 13, 1570–71.

[2] Edward Manners, third Earl of Rutland, K.G., son of Henry, second Earl, by Margaret, dau. of Ralph Nevill, Earl of Westmoreland.

[3] Edmund Scambler, B.D., was made Bishop of Peterborough, Dec. 21, 1560, in the place of David Pole, who had been deprived of the bishopric. In 1584 Bishop Scambler was translated to Norwich.

[4] *S. P. Dom.* 1572.

After reading the above letter it is easy to see that
Edward Cecil was called Edward after his godfather, the
Earl of Rutland.

It is unsatisfactory to have to state that nothing is
known of Edward Cecil's school or university life. It is
more than probable that he was educated at Westminster
School, where his younger brother Christopher[1] was
educated. It never does, however, to deviate from the
beaten track of facts in biography, so this important point
must perforce remain unsettled.[2]

In Lord Burghley's diary, written by himself, we find
that in September, 1594, was granted "a license for
Richard[3] and Edward Cecyll, Sir Thomas Cecyll's sonnes,
to travayle abroad for the space of three years."[4] It is
recorded of the great Lord Burghley, that if anyone came
to the Lords of the Council for a license to travel, he would
first examine him of England ; and if he found him
ignorant, would bid him stay at home and know his
own country first.[5]

The two brothers, Richard and Edward Cecil, travelled
under the most favourable auspices. Their grandfather's

---

[1] In the *Lansdowne MSS.* is a letter in Latin from Christopher Cecil to
his grandfather, Lord Burghley, dated from Westminster School, April vi.,
1591, "thanking for his education." Christopher Cecil was drowned in
Germany—when does not appear, but it must have been before Jan. 12,
1603-4, as Lord Burghley speaks in his letter to Sir John Hubert (already
given) of *three* younger sons' portions.

[2] I am informed by Dr. Scott, late head-master of Westminster School,
that there is no complete list of Westminster scholars during the reign of
Elizabeth among the school records.

[3] Richard Cecil married Elizabeth, dau. of Sir Anthony Cope, Bart., by
whom he had a son, David Cecil, who eventually succeeded as fourth Baron
Burghley and third Earl of Exeter.

[4] Extract from Lord Burghley's MS. *Diary, Harl.* 36. See same diary in
Murdin's *Continuation of Haynes' State Papers*, 1542-1596.

[5] *The Compleat Gentleman*, by Henry Peacham, p. 51.

name was known and reverenced throughout the length and breadth of Europe.

"There were many demonstrations of the reputation many princes had of him," wrote Peck, "as when his lordship's grandchild, Mr Wm Cecill, travayling in Italy, was brought before Cardinal Farnese, a man of great authority. Who, finding Mr Cecill to be the [grand] sonne of the great treasurer of England, lodged him in his owne house, appointed divers gents to attend him and his horses to be at his comandment. Speakinge most reverentlie of his grandfather; and, never left enquiring of the manner of his life, [his] fashion, statue, speach, recreations and such like [matters relating to him]. Delighting to heare and talk of him and, at his departure, gave him presents and money in his purse. The like did the Duke of Florence[1] to M^r. Edward Cecill, a younger brother, and which was an extraordinary favoure the duke gave him leave to ride his own horse, and at his departure gave him gifts of price."[2]

It was during his sojourn at Florence that Edward Cecil wrote to his uncle Sir Robert Cecil. This letter, which is written in Italian, is the earliest letter of Edward Cecil's that has yet been found. It is unfortunately not worth giving, being a mere effusion of gratitude for some favours received from Sir Robert Cecil. Its phraseology, indeed, reminds us of "a letter to an uncle, thanking for a gold watch," given in an old edition of *The Ready Letter Writer*. Edward Cecil had evidently profited by his kinship to Sir Robert Cecil, who was recognised at this time as a rising sun. "Sa bene ella," says young Cecil, in this letter to his uncle, "quant obligo m'ho al cielo e per esser stato favorito da lei, e annoverato fra gli suoi congiunti."[3]

---

[1] Ferdinand de Medicis I., Cardinal-Duke of Florence.
[2] Peck's *Desiderata Curiosa*, i. p. 27.
[3] Letter dated from Florence, Nov. 2, 1596, and addressed, " All Ill^me Sig^r mie Coll^mo il Sig^r Ruberto Cecillio dal consiglio di sua Maiesta sereniss^e"

Amongst those who extended their hospitality to Edward Cecil and his brother, when they were in Italy, was the Duke of Bracciano,[1] chief of the Orsini family, near Rome, and a cousin of the Duke of Florence. When Henry IV. married Marie de Medicis, the Duke of Bracciano accompanied his cousin to France, and came over to England in the winter of 1600–1. He was feasted by Sir Thomas Cecil (now Lord Burghley), as a return for the hospitality shown to his sons in Italy. Queen Elizabeth also graciously entertained him, " and danced," says Chamberlain in a letter to his friend Dudley Carleton, then at the Hague, " both measures and galliards before him to show that she is not so old as some would have her."[2] However unaccustomed the duke may have been to the sight of a princess of nearly threescore years and ten indulging in terpsichorean delights, his courteous nature doubtless made him express his appreciation and delight at the honour shown him. At his departure the Queen sent him a gold cup of six score pounds and a jewel, for which he gave the bearer, Michael Stanhope, an £80 chain.[3]

---

mio zio, Londra."— *Cecil Papers, Hatfield,* 174/13. There is a letter similarly expressed as above, from Richard Cecil to Sir Robert Cecil, among the *S. P. Dom.,* dated from Florence, Oct. 18, 1596.

[1] There is a most curious and startling anecdote regarding a subsequent Duke of Bracciano, given in Wheatley's edition (1884) of *The Historical and Posthumous Memoirs of Sir Nathaniel William Wraxall,* i. p. 186.

[2] Feb. 3, 1601.—*S. P. Dom.*

[3] Aubery du Maurier, in his *Mémoires pour servir à l'histoire de la République des Pays-Bas,* gives an amusing anecdote (which he says was related to his father by Prince Maurice) of a young Dutch gentleman who accompanied the Envoys from the United Provinces on one of their visits to London. When the Envoys were granted an audience by Elizabeth, this young Dutchman accompanied them and gazed so long and admiringly at the Queen that she could not but remark it. She also perceived that he spoke occasionally to a young English gentleman of the Court, never taking his eyes off her all the time. Directly the audience was over, and the Envoys had departed, the Queen summoned the young English courtier she had seen talking to the

Whilst Richard and Edward Cecil were pursuing their travels and studies in Italy, one of them (it will never be known which[1]) had the honour of receiving a letter from the learned Sir Francis Bacon—that king of letter-writers. Though not connected by blood, the families of Sir Thomas Cecil and Francis Bacon were closely connected by marriage—Sir Thomas's stepmother being Bacon's maternal aunt. The two families were also closely connected by friendship ; and from a letter in Bacon's own hand we gather that he wished to be the second husband of the young and beautiful widow, Lady Hatton—one of Edward Cecil's sisters.[2] This fancy, or passion, of the great philosopher's ended, as first loves often do, in nothing, and the bright young widow soon after gave her hand in marriage to the elderly Sir Edward Coke. This ill-assorted union created a nine-days' wonder, and England's most learned judge got a wife who kept him in hot water for the rest of his life.

The next news we have of young Edward Cecil is given by himself in a letter to his uncle, Sir Robert Cecil, in which he informs him he had determined to follow the wars

---

young Dutchman, and asked what he had been saying. On being told of the admiration the Dutch gentleman had expressed to him for her Majesty's beauty, the Queen dismissed the courtier without any remark, but when the Dutch Envoys received the usual gold chains and presents on their departure from London, Elizabeth sent a chain of gold, twice as large and heavy as those sent to the Envoys, to the humble follower in their train who had appeared so dazzled by her incomparable beauty. He wore the chain round his neck all his life. ii. p. 78.

[1] Bacon's letter, which is published in Spedding's *Letters and Life of Bacon* (ii. 38), is unaddressed and undated. It has been endorsed "To Mr Robert Cecil." But as the able editor of *Bacon's Letters* remarks, it could not have been to Robert Cecil, Earl of Salisbury, as he never was in Italy, and the contents of the letter leave no doubt that it was addressed to a young man in Italy, who had written the philosopher a letter in Italian. The date also is ascertained by a reference to the fleet having just sailed for Cadiz, which was in 1596, the year that Richard and Edward Cecil were in Italy.

[2] See *Bacon's Letters*, ii. pp. 53–4.

in the Low Countries, under the command of that great
and worthy general, Sir Francis Vere. This letter is from
the Hague, and is dated February, 1598–9. The *hiatus*
from November, 1596, to February, 1599, is a long one, and
cannot be bridged over comfortably. We may, however,
readily suppose that part of the intervening time had been
spent in travel. It is also pretty certain that Edward
Cecil had been a few months in the Low Countries when
he wrote to his uncle in February, 1599, as when referring
to his length of military service in some of his later letters,
he always appears to date back from 1598. It is also
a curious fact that in a letter from Thomas, Lord Burghley,[1]
to his half-brother Sir Robert Cecil, dated October
30, 1598, the former says, "Your letter for the passports
for my sons is lost ; send the bearer for another, as they are
to depart to-morrow if the wind serves." Might not one of
the writer's sons, who required a passport, be Edward Cecil ?
His former license to travel abroad for three years had
expired in the autumn of 1597. He would require a new
license on leaving England again. The passports Lord
Burghley asked for were not wanted for his eldest son, Will
Cecil, as we find a license granted on June 28, 1599, to
"William Cecil to travel abroad with 2 servants and
3 horses."[2] Edward Cecil being a younger son had his

---

[1] William Cecil, the great Lord Burghley, had died on August 4, 1598,
aged 77.

[2] *S. P. Dom.* June, 1599. Will Cecil's taste for travelling must have been
very great, as he had only recently married (for a second time) Elizabeth Drury,
eldest dau. of Sir Wm. Drury, of Hawsted, Suffolk. She did not accompany
her husband on his travels, as we find her writing to Sir Robert Cecil (her
uncle by marriage) in Jan. 1599–1600, begging him to assure the Queen
that her husband had no intention of going to Rome as had been reported.
"But when I considred what dangerous effects such Reportes may breed in
the thought of a Prince thought (*sic*) of meere malice sugges'ed, I do ounce
agayne humbly besech your furtherance to put it out of her Ma^lie^ head that he
hath or will have anny intencionne of going to roome." This letter is signed
"Elisa Cecill," and endorsed "1599, Jan : M^res^ Cecyll to my M^r^."—*Cecil
Papers, Hatfield,* 68/7.

own way to make in the world and having always had, as his letter to his uncle informs us, "a disposition to follow the wars," he evidently went to the Low Countries to serve under Sir Francis Vere, who returned there in October, 1598,[1] and what he saw of that able general fixed his determination at once, as the following letter informs us :—

MR. EDWARD CECIL TO SIR ROBERT CECIL.

" MAY IT PLEASE Y^r H.,

" To accepete these fewe lines frome mee, as from one, whoe in all duty and affection sendeth them, acknolegin that if there be any one that is bounde to offer his servis to those that beaste deserve it, then I howlde my selfe to have many reasones to present myne to y^r H. The one, by howe much y^r vertues hath made the most parte of men to followe y^r H. as is scene at these dayes. The neaxte, in that the lawe of God and Nature, bindleth mee to honor and respecte y^o, beeyng that y^o are cauled in to so highe a plase, and I of y^r bloude and carry y^r name. My fortune is nowe to followe the warres (having hade allwayes hearetofore a dispositione thereun to : and the rayther of late, by howe much my pore oppinione is establyshed of the great worth of Sr Francis Vere, whome I knowe doth booth highly reverence y^r H., and greatly respecte all those that be longe unto y^o, of wch number I acknowleg my selfe much bounde unto him, and moste of all to y H. (for whose sake I finde it), therefore the profession I have taking upon mee, will that I vowe my selfe to some one that will protect mee (as all men of the like profession doth), and I not knowing to whom my poor servis belongeth more to then to y H., maketh me hope that y H. will wth some littell favoure healpe my poore fortunes forward ; in wch doing, y^o shall not favoure only y^r owne name, but favoure him, whoe will ever acknowlege it wth spending his life, and all

---

Will Cecil's return to England is thus mentioned by Chamberlain in a letter to Dudley Carleton, June 13, 1600 :—" Will Cecill is returned out of Italie and could not find such a mistris as his owne wife in all his travels."—*S. P. Dom.* 1600.

[1] Sir F. Vere sailed from Sandwich on Oct. 27. Vere to Sir. R. Cecil, Nov. 2.—*S. P. Holland.*

he hath, to doe y^r H. servis. I can saye noe more, and to advertis y° wth any nwes, were superfluis to y H. Therefore I only beseeche y^r H. to howlde me in y^r good favour. And I pray the Allmight to all wayes prosper y°; from the Hage, of the 9 of february 99 [n.s.]

"Y^r Ho. :
"in all duty,
"ED. CECIL."[1]

Add. "To the R. H. and his singuler good unkell, S^r Ro. Cecill, K^t, Cheefe Secritarye of Ingland and on of her M^{tis} moste H. prive Counsell at the Corte."

End. "9 Febr. 1598.   M^r Ed. Cecyll to my M^r from the Haghe."

---

[1] *Cecil Papers, Hatfield,* 59/59.

CHAPTER II.

1566–1599.

Struggle for liberty in the Netherlands—The Regent Governess—Arrival of the Duke of Alva—The Council of Blood—William the Silent—Commencement of the Eighty Years' War—Alva's prisoners—Their fate—Assassination of William the Silent—Queen Elizabeth's treaty with the United Provinces—English reinforcements—The Earl of Leicester and his officers—The Prince of Parma—The Cardinal-Archduke—Death of Philip II.—The Admiral of Arragon's Invasion—Maurice of Nassau's defensive strategy—Siege of Bommel—Edward Cecil made Captain of Foot—His letters home—Raising the siege—Expense of the war—A new Anglo-Dutch treaty.

THAT mighty struggle of the Netherlanders against their Spanish rulers and persecutors lasted eighty years. Not eighty years of continual warfare—as occasional treaties of peace gave both sides an opportunity to recruit their shattered forces and finances—but eighty years of firm resistance against the would-be empire of Spain, over a country half of which had revolted from the hated Spanish yoke. The Rise and Progress of the Dutch Republic is one of the most interesting chapters in the history of Europe. "Out of half-submerged morasses," says the talented author of an able work, " in an outlying corner of that vast dominion, a rational and conservative republic is slowly evolved,—born amid blood and fire, but dilating daily through storm and darkness into more colossal proportions. From the hand-breadth of territory, called the province of Holland, rises a power which wages eighty years' warfare with the most potent empire upon earth, and which, during the progress of the struggle, becoming itself a mighty state, and binding about its own slender form a zone of the richest possessions of earth, from pole to tropic, finally dictates its decrees to the empire of Charles." [1]

In 1566, terrible religious riots took place in the Netherlands. More than 400 churches were despoiled by the Reformers. Margaret, Duchess of Parma, the "Regent Governess," as she was styled in the Netherlands, applied to her brother, Philip II. of Spain, for help in this critical state of affairs. Philip not being able to leave his own country, for fear of a rebellion in his absence, decided to send the Duke of Alva with a large force into the Netherlands. Alva, who speedily earned the title of *Castigador de Flamencos*, was a stern bigot, a man after Philip's own heart, and an experienced general, to whom the quality of mercy was unknown. Universal fear fell upon the Netherlanders when they heard of Alva's approach. A general exodus of high and low, rich and poor, ensued. Thousands of refugees sought safety in England, Germany, and Denmark. The regent's proclamation against this emigration merely made matters worse. Alva hastened his march, and those who had determined to stand by their country prepared to receive him with every demonstration of joy, thinking to take the bull by the horns. The general's reply to the congratulations of the deputation which went to Luxembourg to receive him, was plain even to rudeness. "Welcome or not," he said, "it is all one ; here I am." [2]

The arrival of Alva, with an army of 20,000 veterans, was the signal for the departure of the Duchess of Parma. She had, in fact, been superseded. Her power was gone,

---

[1] Motley's *Rise of the Dutch Republic*, preface, p. 1.
[2] Davies' *History of Holland*, i. p. 547.

and her conciliatory measures were ignored by her brother
and his bloodthirsty general.

With the regent (who had governed nine years) departed
the last glimmering ray of hope from the hearts of the
unhappy Netherlanders.   The reign of terror had indeed
begun.   Alva's "Council of Blood" ordered wholesale
executions, and it is said more than 1,800 persons perished
within the space of a few weeks by the hand of the execu-
tioner.[1]   Whilst the Reformers were being butchered by
the merciless Spaniards, preparations were being made for
a mighty struggle against Spanish oppression.   William of
Nassau, Prince of Orange, a man slow to speak, but quick
to act, who was to all intents and purposes outlawed from
his fatherland, convinced that there was no hope of his
returning to his country, invested his brother Lewis with a
commission " to enter the Netherlands with an army for the
purpose of restoring freedom and liberty of conscience to
the inhabitants, and for preserving the provinces for the
king in their former prosperous condition."[2]   This was in
April, 1568.

With Count Lewis of Nassau's "invasion" of the
Netherlands, the eighty years' war may be said to have
commenced.   This first effort of the patriots against their
oppressors ended as might have been expected.   They
gained, indeed, one victory, and then came defeat.   Alva
made this insurrection a reason for causing the noble Counts,
Egmont and Horn, to be barbarously beheaded, hoping to
strike such terror to the hearts of the Netherlanders, that
they would be utterly crushed, and not have the temerity
to rise against their persecutors again.   This judicial
murder did indeed excite terror throughout the kingdom,
but at the same time it caused a spirit of hatred and
vengeance to arise, which only bided its time to burst out

---

[1] Davies, i. p. 553.   [2] *Ibid.* p. 556.

in its full strength. The persecution of the Reformers, by the Spaniards, had the same effect as the persecution of the Christians by the Roman Emperors in the days of old. As the Christians of old were confirmed, strengthened, and united, by the common bond of suffering together in a righteous cause, so were the Dutch Reformers strengthened and united in feeling by the barbarities exercised against them on account of their religious opinions. It often needs adversity to bring out what is noblest and best in man's nature. Adversity had this effect on William of Orange, on whom all the hopes of the Reformers were centred. From henceforth, and to the end of his life, William the Silent showed all the forbearance, the patience, the endurance, and the trust in God of a deeply religious man. A hero and a statesman he had been before, and a valiant commander he was now about to prove himself.

It is not necessary to give a review of the struggle in the Netherlands prior to 1598. Enough has been said to show the nature and aim of the struggle which all Protestant Europe sympathised with; and it only suffices to say, that in 1572 a band of brave Englishmen, commanded by Sir William Morgan, offered their services to Count Lewis of Nassau, to fight in the cause of civil and religious liberty. This band of volunteers was the nucleus of a powerful English force, which afterwards assisted the Netherlanders in their fight for freedom, and greatly contributed to their future success.[1]

It was not until after the assassination of William the Silent, which sad event occurred at Delft in July, 1584,[2] that Queen Elizabeth openly assisted the Dutch.[3]

---

[1] Churchyard's *Civil Wars in the Netherlands*, p. 18.

[2] The Prince of Orange was shot in the Prinsenhof, or palace, by Gérard, on July 10, 1584, and was buried in the New Church, where is a splendid monument, erected to his memory in 1621.

[3] Camden's *Hist. of Queen Elizabeth*, iii. p. 321.

In 1585, Elizabeth concluded a treaty with the States, and agreed to send them 5,000 foot and 1,000 horse, under the command of an English general. These troops were to be paid by her on condition that the general, and two others whom she should appoint, might be admitted into the Council of the States ; that neither party should make peace without the consent of the other ; that the Queen's expenses should be refunded after the conclusion of the war, and that the towns of Flushing, Bergen-op-zoom, and the Brille, with the Castle of Rammekins should be consigned into her hands by way of security.[1]   Each county in England furnished a proportion of the required number of men.   " The Livery Companies of the city of London also provided each a limited number of men for this service," says the compiler of the history of the Third Regiment of Foot, "and the men furnished by the city, having been incorporated into the corps which is now the Third Regiment of Foot, or the Buffs, it was afterwards the practice for this regiment to recruit within the precincts of the city, and to enjoy the exclusive privilege[2] of marching through the city of London, with drums beating and colours flying."[3]   Stow mentions that " on July 23, 1585,

---

[1] Speed's *Hist. of Great Britain*, p. 1173.

[2] This is a mistake, as the marines have the same privilege.   They date their origin from the Third, the Admiral's, or Duke of York's Maritime Regt., levied in 1684 by Charles II. and sent to Holland, where it became altogether a land corps, and ultimately got incorporated with General Monk's Coldstreams. Like the old Holland Regt. (now 3rd Buffs) the Maritime Regt. was raised by the city of London ; hence the privilege, shared with the Buffs, of marching through London with bands playing, colours flying, and bayonets fixed. An authenticated anecdote has it, that a detachment of marines parading down Cheapside, with beat of drum, were silenced by a city magnate, and told that none but the Old Buffs were allowed thus to disturb the "good citizens'" repose.   " Sir, we are marines," replied the officer ; " I did not know it," was the Alderman's rejoinder, " pray continue your route as you best please."   See article in the *Globe* for July 2, 1878.

[3] Cannon's *Records of the 3rd Regt. of Foot*, p. 26.

certain soldiers were pressed in the severall wards of the
citie of London, which souldiers were furnished for the
warres, and cloathed in *red coates*, all at the charges of the
companies and citizens ; set foorth toward the seas on the
13 of August, and were transported over into Holland,
Zealand, &c., as others, the like souldiers out of other
partes of the realme, before had been transported to serve
for the defence of the Lowe Countries, under General Norris
and other approved Captaines." [1]

During the winter Elizabeth sent an additional body of
troops to the Low Countries, which amounted, in 1586, to
8,000 horse and foot.[2]   Robert Dudley, Earl of Leicester,
was appointed to the command of these troops, and his
nephew, Sir Philip Sidney, the pink of chivalry, was
appointed Governor of Flushing.   A number of gallant
Englishmen, of high birth and position, had commands in
the States' army.   Amongst the number may be mentioned
Sir John Norris, Peregrine Bertie Lord Willoughby
de Eresby, the Earl of Essex, Sir Robert Sidney, and
last, but not least, the two brothers, Francis and Horace
Vere.

The actions of the two last named heroes are inscribed
on the brightest page of England's military history, and their
names are synonymous with victory and glory.   In 1586,
we find Francis Vere [3] in command of a company at Bergen-
op-zoom, and when the Spaniards besieged Sluys he was
removed thither, and highly distinguished himself in the
defence of this town.   In the following year Captain Vere
was knighted for his gallantry at the defence of Bergen-op-
zoom, and during the campaign of 1589 he again highly
distinguished himself by his successful defence of Bommel-

---

[1] Stow's *Annals*, p. 709.   [2] Hollinshed's *Chronicle*, iii. p. 1413.
[3] See Dillingham's *Commentaries of Sir Francis Vere*, and the memoir of
Vere in *Biographia Britannica*.

waert, an island formed by the Meuse and Waal in Dutch Guelderland. Ten years later Bommel was again the scene of a struggle between the Spaniards and Netherlanders. At this second siege of Bommel Sir Francis Vere commanded the English forces and was the right hand of Maurice of Nassau, the son of William the Silent, and the most successful general of his time.

Many stirring events had occurred from 1589 to 1599. The expedition to Cadiz in 1596,[1] had taken place, and had been eminently successful. Could it have been otherwise when Howard of Effingham was at the helm, with Raleigh by his side, and such men as Essex and Vere at the prow? Zutphen, Deventer, and Gertruydenberg, in the Low Countries, had been besieged and nobly won by the Dutch and their brave English allies. Alexander Farnese, Prince of Parma, the Spanish Scipio who, of all Philip's generals, could best teach the stubborn foe to yield, had died, worn out with mental and bodily exertion. The Archduke-Cardinal, Albert of Austria, brother of the Emperor Rudolph, had been appointed Governor-General of the Netherlands in 1596, and two years later was married to the Infanta, Clara Eugenia Isabella of Spain, daughter of Philip II. The Netherlands had been graciously ceded by Philip to his daughter just before her marriage with the Archduke Albert. This important event was followed by Philip's illness and death.[2] The horrible nature of this Monarch's last illness is unsurpassed in

---

[1] This may be called the second Cadiz expedition. In April, 1587, the English fleet, under Sir Francis Drake, entered the harbour of Cadiz and destroyed 10,000 tons of shipping, with their contents, in the very face of a dozen great galleys which the nimble English vessels soon drove under their forts for shelter.

[2] He was called, says Voltaire, *the Devil of the South*, because from the centre of Spain, which is the southern part of Europe, he gave disturbance to the dominions of every other Prince.—Nares' *Burghley*, iii. p. 491.

history. The death of Herod Agrippa I. was an awful one and somewhat similar to that of the Spanish king; but Herod's agony was soon over, whereas Philip lingered in indescribable torture for many weeks. Anyone who has seen the picture of " The Dead Prelate," by Juan Valdes Leal, in the chapel of *La Caridad* at Seville,[1] must shudder to think of the state the royal body of Charles the Fifth's royal son was reduced to *before* death.

In the summer of 1598 the Spanish troops in the Netherlands were reinforced, and Don Francis Mendoza, Admiral of Arragon, commander of the forces in the absence of Archduke Albert, threatened the United Provinces with an invasion. In the autumn of this year the admiral crossed the Meuse, at Roermond, with an army of 25,000 foot and 2,000 cavalry, and presented himself before a small town called Orsoy, on the Rhine. "It was his intention," says one of the historians of these events, " to invade the duchies of Cleves, Juliers, and Berg, taking advantage of the supposed madness of the duke, and of the Spanish inclinations of his chief counsellors, who constituted a kind of regency. By obtaining possession of these important provinces—wedged as they were between the territory of the republic, the obedient Netherlands and Germany—an excellent military position would be gained for making war upon the rebellious districts from the east, for crushing Protestantism in the duchies, for holding important passages of the Rhine, and for circumventing the designs of the Protestant sons-in-law and daughters of the old Duke of Cleves. Of course it was the determination of Maurice and the States-General to frustrate these operations."[2]

---

[1] A well-painted but disgusting picture, which Murillo said he could not look at without holding his nose. This criticism from the great master was in itself a compliment to the painter's skill.

[2] Motley's *Hist. of the United Netherlands*, iii. pp. 546-7. Sir Francis

Prince Maurice formed a line of encampments along the Meuse and the Waal, to oppose the designs of the enemy. His small army compelled him to act solely on the defensive, while the Spaniards were ravaging the whole border-land. Orsoy had surrendered without a blow. Burik and Rheinberg capitulated soon after, and Wesel compounded for 120,000 florins. Rees and Emmerick, two of the chief cities of Cleves, surrendered to Mendoza within three days of each other. It was owing solely to the admirable defensive strategy of Maurice of Nassau that the United Provinces (as we may now justly call the revolted provinces) were spared the horrors of Spanish warfare at this time, which converted the inoffensive provinces of Munster, Cleves, and Berg, into a hell, during the winter of 1598–9. "Never before was it written or heard of," said Queen Elizabeth, in speaking of Prince Maurice's successful defensive strategy, " that so great an extent of country could be defended with so few troops, that an invasion of so superior a hostile force could be prevented, especially as it appeared that all the streams and rivers were frozen."

Early in 1599 Mendoza formed the project of making a descent on Bommelwaert, and of capturing the town of Bommel.

Bommel is a frontier town upon the confines of Guelderland, and stands on the river Waal, on the north side of the Dutch island of Bommel. "From the beginning of the Low Country wars," says a Dutch historian, "till

---

Vere refers to the preparations for war in a letter to the Earl of Essex, Lord High Marshal of England, Jan. 1, 1598–9. This letter of Vere's is dated from the Hague, and he informs the earl that the States "are levying certaine newe Troopes of foot and horse, whereof a part shalbee Dutches and the other Frenchmen, and have besides taken order for the reinforcing of all their old Companies, and to raise 5 or 6 Cornetts of Horse of their own nation. . . . His Ex^cie resolveth to departe tomorrowe towards Solderland (*sic*) and there to drawe into some place most of his forces."—*Cecil Papers, Hatfield.*

this day, each party hath laboured to become masters of this town in regard of her situation, especially the United Provinces, because it serves as a rampier [rampart] against the incursions and invasion of their enemies." The same writer goes on to remark that "the siege of Bommel, together with the raising thereof, is one of the notablest exploits of war done in the Low Countries."[1]

As Edward Cecil served at this siege a few remarks concerning it will not be out of place.

On May 5, the Admiral of Arragon having made a bridge of boats across the Meuse, entered the island of Bommel and entrenched himself on both sides the water.[2] Prince Maurice, who had been forewarned some months previously of the admiral's projected descent upon Bommel, had ordered new walls and fortifications to be built round the town of Bommel, and the forts of Voorn and Crevecœur to be enlarged. These works had been begun, but were not yet finished, so that the sudden arrival of the Spaniards created great alarm amongst the inhabitants, many of whom fled from the town. Had the admiral laid siege to the town on his entry into the island, there would have been great danger of his capturing it, as the walls round the town were in a half-finished state. But he awaited the arrival of his remaining forces, who departed from Emmerick May 7, and on their coming the whole Spanish force marched towards Heusden, a very strong place, an hour's distance from the town of Bommel. In the meantime Maurice of Nassau had not been idle. He collected a strong force of horse and foot, and proceeded to Bommel, where he arrived on May 6. On

---

[1] *The Triumphs of Nassau*, art. "Siege of Bommel."
[2] See a tract entitled, "*A true declaration of that which hapened since the enemie's first comming to Bommell, from the besieging of the same until the present moneth of June*, 1599."

the 11th he marched to Heusden with ten companies of foot, and fortified and entrenched that place. The Spanish commander now changed his tactics, and, leaving Heusden alone, assaulted the fort of Crevecœur. This fort, having but a small garrison, was unable to hold out long against the Spaniards, but they made a noble resistance, and were allowed to depart with colours flying and carrying their arms.[1] Prince Maurice caused Bommel to be surrounded by trenches, and the walls were finished. The garrison was augmented, and a good supply of provisions and ammunition sent into the town. The enemy now made show of returning to Heusden, but, changing his course, marched towards Rossem, hoping to enter into the isle of Tiell, to enclose the island of Bommel on all sides ; but Prince Maurice sent ordnance thither and caused batteries to be made, thereby hindering the enemy's passage. On May 14, Count Frederick Van den Berg brought part of the Spanish army before Bommel, having, as the author of the *Triumphs of Nassau* quaintly expresses it, " first run up and down the country, and done nothing but warn those of Bommel and Voorn to fortifie themselves, and given them time to doe it." Prince Maurice garrisoned Bommel with Dutch, French, and Swiss companies ; quartered the English at Haeften, the Guards at Tiell, the Scots, under Colonel Edmonds, at Voorn, and guarded the banks of the river as far as Worcum. A Dutch admiral was likewise ordered to guard the river Waal with fifteen ships. On the night of May 16 the Spaniards made a furious attack upon Bommel, at that part of the town where the fortifications were scarce finished, but they were beaten back with great loss. A few nights after this the garrison returned the Spaniards' assault in kind, and killed many

---

[1] *The Triumphs of Nassau,* art. ". Bommel."

men in the trenches. The troops employed on this occasion were mostly French and English. "Besides those of Bommel," says the narrator of this siege, "the inhabitants of Voorn, Heusden, Gorcum, and other neighbouring towns made incursions upon the enemy, and took daily prisoners and many good horse, and in Bommel alone during this siege more than 400 were sold." On June 3, the Spaniards were obliged to raise the siege and retreat. They retired towards Rossem and there encamped. Their doings there are related in a letter from Edward Cecil to his father. It would appear from a letter written by young Cecil a few weeks earlier to his uncle, Sir Robert Cecil, that he had obtained some great favour from the latter. The endorsement of these letters is fairly conclusive that the favour received from Sir Robert Cecil was the captaincy of an English foot company, which Sir Robert's influence had doubtless obtained for his nephew.

CAPTAIN EDWARD CECIL TO SIR ROBERT CECIL.

" MAY IT PLEASE Y^r HO.,

"I am to reander y^o greate thankes, for y^r extroordinary favoures towardes me (if thankes be not to littell), and howlde my selfe so muche the more bounde to y^r Ho. by howe much they ar above my desertes. I have not as yet had occation to serve y^r Ho., nor have I wanted, in any sorte, a will to performe it, for I howlde it a greate Honore and happines to spende my life for the honer of the Howse, then followe any man living. I accounte y. Ho. the Howse, by cause y^o ar the prinsepaleste parte of the House— and I reccone my selfe the leaste parte of it, by beeyng the unnessessaryist parte. Therefore, by nessesity, I am most bounde to y^r Ho. in all servis. As allso in a nother kinde, a mongste those that doe admire y^r vertues, w^t wch I conclude, rejoysing for the in crease of y^r Ho. greatnes, more then any one. I recommende my selfe and servis to y^r Ho. good favours, not reasting any hower to praye for y^r H. long and happie life. I humbly take my leave.

"Y^r Ho., in all duty,   · E. CECILL.

⸗ "From the Leger at Bumble, this 16 of June 99."[1]

Add. "To the Ri. Ho. and his singular good Unkell S⸢r⸣ Ro. Cecill, Prinsepale Secritary of Ingland."

End. "16 June, 1599, Cap⸢en⸣ Cecyll to my M⸢r⸣ from Bomble.

"Capt⸢a⸣ to be digested."

CAPTAIN E. CECIL TO LORD BURGHLEY.

" MAY IT PLEASE Y⸢r⸣ LO.,

"At this tyme I was in doubte whether I should dereacte my letteres towards the West, or towardes the Northe, to a reive the soner into y⸢r⸣ Lo. handes ; by reason the accustomed tyme of y⸢r⸣ going in to the Cuntry is passed. But to dowe [do] according unto my duty, I will write booth wayes.

"As consarning our Action heare, the Enemy hath lived very quietly, only imploying his time to Bulde a Sconce [fort] upon the River some 2 milles from the Towne of Bumble [Bommel], where he mindeth to leave some 3000 menn in it to keepe the River. His Exselence [Prince Maurice] lyeing nighe against him, did comande 4 of our companyes to goe over to posses some parte of the Enemyes grounde, and in Trenche ourselves in the forme of an Haulfe Moune, knocking in Palisados rounde aboute. The Enemy sending neaxte day, to discover, came the day following w⸢t⸣ soom 2000 to forse the place, [and] gave one [went on, i.e., attacked] very gallantly. The leaders were 6 Spanishe Captaynes and 4 Italiones, which were all slane in the Place. They were ellected [chosen] men to performe each a plase. The [y] were men that had noe charge, but were of a fatione w⸢ch⸣ the Kinge of Spane allowes in paye, as a Captayne, and are most imployed to suche attempes. The [y] cam to the pushe of the Pike, and if the [y] had given on rounde abote the [y] had caryed it. Whereupon wee howlde them men of more resolution then [than] understanding souldiers, w⸢ch⸣ by the effects the [y] did showe in that service ; the [y] loste 500 men—80 leafte dead in the plase—of our men not many were loste. Our Sargant Majore was slane, and a Captayne thrust into the heade w⸢th⸣ a Pike and [an] Ansint

---

[1] *Cecil Papers, Hatfield,* 179/29.

[ancient[1]] shote twice throwe the necke. Sence, his Exselence hath put over to a nother plase, into Brabant not fare of [f], allonge the River side, where on the other side he lieth himselfe. He hath made on the Enemy's side a dipe Trenche on Mille longe [1 mile long] and devided it into 4 sconses, where righte a gainste liese the Enymies Passage to go to his Bridge in to Bumble's-warde [Bommelwaert] to his campe. Upon this passage he hath rased 2 Sconses, having there to the number of 2000 men, whither his Exselence the other daye made over a bridge, from whence he lieth him selfe and passed [over] some 1000 Horse and some 3000 foote, whereof were some 2000 Englishe. S[r] Fras. Vere had the comande of one parte and Count William of Nassaue the other— S[r] Fr. Vere gave one [*i.e.* attacked] upon sconce and the counte upon the other. S[r] Fr. Vere caryed his, where he putte to death many of the Enemye, towke a Captayne or 2, and forsed the reaste to retire. For the other part [y] that the Count comanded the [y] were repulsed, a Captayne or two slane, and many more offeseres and souldiers slane w[ch] were all frenche. This is the last wee have done. Sence, wee heare the Enemye hath beeyne a fore worcum [Worcum] to have surprised it; a plase as fare on the other side of Bumble. But having fauled thereof, theye have returned wth driving some 500 Catell before them, w[ch] was part of there desigment. Wee understande sence that the howle Campe is risone, whither wee longe to prowe [prove].

"S[r] fr. Vere, our Generall, hath desired to recomend his love to y[r] Lo., who maketh mee daly more and more bounde to him. He asked mee the other daye whether I had moved y[r] Lo. a boute the Companye of Horse, and I towlde him I had; whereupon he assured mee I should [have] the comand of all the English horse, if I could com[p]ound with S[r] Ni-parker, and if it would please y[r] Lo. to laye oute the munny, he himselfe would bringe it to pass. I hope y[r] Lo. will consider what a fortune it wil! be to mee, and what an Honer to y[o]. It reasts in y[r] hands this; y[r] Lo. can not doe for one that is more y[r] obliged servant then I am, or on [one] that is more y[r] thankfull sonn, or that more taketh comforte of y[r] happines then I, or on that prayeth more ernesly

---

[1] Apparently the old name for Ensigns.

fór y^r lo. longe life then I doe, wth wch prayer I send in haste having noe more by me. The 13 of July, 99

"Y^r lo. most bounde

"and obedient sonn,

"Ed. Cecill.

" my tyme is so shorte that y^r lo. must pardon my scribline and what ealse is amisse, as a soldier faute."[1]

Add.—" To the Ri. Ho. and his singular good father the Lo. Burghley."

End.—" 13 July, 1599. Cap^{ne} Cecill to my lo. Burghley."

Returning to the Spaniards, we find them at Rossem, a small village within a cannon shot of Voorn. It soon became evident they had a design against the fort of Voorn, so Prince Maurice sent a small force of English and French to Herwaerden, there to entrench themselves in the form of a half moon in view of the enemy. When this was done, the trench was fenced round with palisades. The attack on this entrenchment, and its result, is detailed in the above letter. Colonel Edmonds, a gallant Scot, and Sir Horace Vere, distinguished themselves in the defence.[2] The enemy fought with great fury, and it is related that they were accompanied by some monks, armed with banners and crosses, who encouraged the soldiers by all the means in their power.

There were continual skirmishes between the two hostile forces all July, and on one occasion Colonel Murray was killed.[3] Both camps were very quiet all August and September, being strongly entrenched and keeping good guard. A mutiny, which broke out in the Spanish camp on account of want of pay, caused Mendoza to keep very quiet, and on the approach of winter he

---

[1] *S. P. Holland*, 1599.

[2] *Biographia Britannica*, art. " Horace Vere."

[3] *Davies*, ii. p. 338.

retired into winter quarters. Although unsuccessful in his designs against Bommel and Voorn, he had gained the fort of Crevecœur, and had constructed the strong fort of St. André, at a point commanding both the Waal and Meuse. These two forts were strongly garrisoned before the enemy retired to winter quarters.

The States of the United Provinces had spared no expense in the defence of Bommel. They had furnished the camp with all necessaries, and all that summer kept 280 boats in pay, 379 wagons, 356 draught horses, and 203 bridge masters. This extra expense in boats, wagons, horses, ammunition, provisions, &c., cost the Provinces 120,000 florins.[1] Their finances in consequence having fallen into arrear, they thought it advisable again to reduce their military establishment to a footing better porportional to their means.

In the preceding year (1598) a new treaty had been concluded between England and the United Provinces. By the terms of this treaty the States bound themselves to repay Elizabeth £800,000, and to give security for the payment of this debt. Another equally important clause in this treaty, and the one that most concerns us, was, "That for the future the Queen should be discharged of her engagement to furnish the States with Auxiliaries, and that the English, who now served, or should hereafter serve in the Low Countries, should be paid by the States, take an oath to them, and obey the orders of their Generals."[2]

---

[1] *Davies*, ii. p. 340.   [2] Rymer's *Fœdera*, xvi. p. 340.

CHAPTER III.

1600.

Siege of Fort St. Andrew—Result—Captain Cecil's cavalry ambition—The troop of horse—Difficulties in the way—Sir F. Vere's help—Mr. Gilpin's obstruction—Cecil's invective letter—Gilpin's version—Edward Cecil made Captain of Horse—His gratitude to Sir R. Cecil—The invasion of Flanders—March to Nieuport—Bad tidings—Disaster at Leffingen— Critical position of the States' army—Heroism of Maurice of Nassau— Preparing for battle—Arrival of the Archduke's army—The Sunday battle—Doubtful results—Bravery of the English—Sir Francis Vere— His danger—Maurice's good generalship—The reserve of horse—Charge by Horace Vere, Cecil, and Balen—Rout of the enemy—Different accounts of the battle—After results.

THE commencement of the year 1600 found the States' forces preparing to reduce the forts of Crevecœur and St. André. The latter fort, which had been built by the Spaniards in the preceding year, was a particular eye-sore to Prince Maurice. The Spaniards called it the key to Holland, and no trouble or expense had been spared in its construction and fortification.

The winter of 1599–1600 was unusually long and severe, but the Dutch had great hopes of a short campaign with happy results. News had reached them of a serious mutiny among the soldiers garrisoning Crevecœur and St. André. On February 15 the Archduke had paid each soldier in fort St. André a month's pay, an allowance of two pounds of bread a day, a piece of cloth, and a dollar by way of a bonus, "which," says an old chronicler, "did in no sort content them." They demanded their whole pay for thirty months, and on this not being forthcoming, showed their sense of wrong by throwing one of their captains into the water from the bridge, shot one of their sergeants, and enforced the other captains to keep their houses as prisoners.[1] A general mutiny ensued there and at Crevecœur. It was this news that determined the States of the United Provinces to strike a blow at once for these coveted forts. Prince Maurice commanded eighty foot companies (of which Captain Cecil's was one) to be in readiness before Dort on the 19th and 20th March, with whom he went up the Meuse towards Crevecœur fort, and laid siege to that place on 21st March. The garrison yielded up the fort for a fixed sum on 24th March, and entered the service of the States. It was hoped the strong fort of St. Andrew would also compound, and so save labour and bloodshed. The mutinous garrison, however, refused to treat, hoping that the Archduke's forces would come to their relief shortly and compel Prince Maurice to raise the siege.

The accounts of sieges are so much alike that we forbear to say much about this one, which was carried on with great vigour. Prince Maurice drowned the country, after fortifying himself strongly on the dykes. All hopes of relief were cut off from the St. Andrew soldiers, "who were forced," says an old historian, "to lodge like conies in their rampats in miserie and povertie, suffering extremely, upon hope that they should be relieved, reconciled and paid, doing their best endevors to reconcile themselves with their cannon."[2] The conclusion of this siege is thus related by Anthonis Duyck in his *Journal*:—[3]

---

[1] *Triumphs of Nassau*, art. "Siege of Fort St André." Dudley Carleton to J. Chamberlain, March 2, 1600.—*S. P. Dom.*

[2] Grimston's *History of the Netherlands*, pp. 1230-1.

[3] Translated from the Dutch Journal, ii. p. 600.

" On the 8th of May the weather was pretty good, and everybody was busy securing the approaches. On both sides much firing was going on. The soldiers within the fort perceiving that they were pressed on every side, and that there was no hope of relief, began to fear that in time they would lose the fort as well as the money offered, they therefore, in the afternoon, enquired whether there was anyone sent from his Excellency, and, on receiving an answer in the negative, they asked for some one who was able to speak French. They then said they intended speaking once more to his Excellency, and that they wanted to send him a message, in order that he might despatch a substitute to treat with them; in the meantime they begged for a truce, which was granted. His Excellency went in the afternoon to the trenches, and immediately sent to the fort Captains Cicil,[1] Van der Aa, and Jaxley, for whom three hostages were exchanged. They still persisted in their former request, especially as to the full settlement of their pay, desiring His Excellency to give particular attention to the fact that the fort was a stronghold, and that they were so many brave soldiers who would rather die on the top of each other than not have their pay."

As time was even still more precious to the States than money, they finally agreed to pay the garrison 125,000 guilders for the fort. This was accordingly done, and the mutineers, who made up a strong regiment of 11 companies, entered the service of the States. They were universally styled the "New Gueux" (beggars), from their ragged appearance ; but they soon reclothed themselves, chiefly in buff, and being all old soldiers were a welcome addition to the army of the United Provinces. Count Henry Frederick of Nassau, Maurice's younger brother, was appointed commander of this new regiment.[2]

---

[1] Edward Cecil was doubtless chosen on this occasion on account of his knowledge of French and Italian ; many of the mutineers speaking those languages.

[2] *Davies*, ii. pp. 348–9.

Edward Cecil, in his letter to his father, from Bommel, which has already been given, asks him to advance the necessary money for the purchase of a "Horse Company," which Sir Francis Vere had promised him when the money was forthcoming. Lord Burghley evidently made no difficulty about the money asked for, but Cecil was a young captain and there were many officers who coveted the command of a troop of horse and had prior claims. It required even more interest than the gallant Sir Francis Vere possessed with the States to obtain one of these coveted commands for one of his junior captains. At the time we write of there were very few troops of horse on the strength of the English army in Holland, and these few were commanded by experienced officers of long and distinguished service. It was customary for several of the senior colonels of infantry to have troops of horse also under their command, which they were allowed to dispose of when leaving the service.[1] The system of "purchase" was perfectly well understood, often carried out, and was allowed by the authorities. As long as Queen Elizabeth kept, and paid for, a certain number of horse and foot companies in Holland, her well-known parsimony prevented her from increasing the few troops of horse, even when they were much below their nominal strength. When Sir Robert Sidney, Governor of Flushing, wrote home to request that the troops of horse commanded by him and Sir Nicholas Parker might be reinforced, the Queen flatly refused. A curious account is given by Rowland

---

[1] Sir Horace Vere (Lord Vere of Tilbury) on retiring from the army was permitted " to make the best advantage he could of his 33 companies of foot and his troop of horse in Holland. Mr. Goring had the one and Mr. Wilmot the other."—*Biog. Brit.* art. " Sir H. Vere." The Mr. Goring above-mentioned was the famous Colonel Goring of Civil Wars' notoriety.

White, in a letter[1] to Sir R. Sidney, of his endeavours to obtain the Queen's consent :—

" I made," he writes, " a very fitt Tyme with one that is most inward with 200 (Sir Robert Cecil), and imparted unto hym my sute, and that I would bestow a faire Sute of Hangings to have that effected,[2] and upon hymself, that is the Mover, I would give him two Coach mares for his Wiffe. Within two days I shall know how this Offer is accepted, and thereby gather the successe of my businesse. Your Lordship in a letter unto me, byd me use what meanes I cold, and that you wold make it good as farr as £200 wold come unto . . . . . These Gratuities, my Lord, are honorable and very necessary."

Sir Robert Cecil did his best for Sir R. Sidney, but the Queen remained obstinate. On being told that the re-inforcing the horse would be no expense to her, as the States were willing to cashier (*i.e.*, reduce) two foot companies of fifty men each, she replied that if the States found her foot unserviceable she was pleased to cashier them, but would not turn them into horse. The Earl of Essex, the favoured courtier and intimate friend of Elizabeth, also pleaded for the granting of Sir R. Sidney's request, but to no purpose. All this shows what a coveted prize a troop of horse was in those days, and how few of these prizes the States had to bestow. " If you ever wish to be a soldier," said Sir Francis Vere to Edward Cecil, " get up on horseback."[3] This advice, from the greatest captain of his day, coupled with Cecil's own cavalry ambition, made

---

[1] Dated " Strand, the 13 April, 1597."—Collins' *Letters and Memorials of State*, ii. pp. 37–8.

[2] It is only right to state that Sir R. Cecil declined to accept the " Sute of Hangings," and he " protested much love and willingness to further what might be a pleasure or profit to Sir R. Sidney."—See letter from R. White to Sir R. Sidney, April 16, 1597.—*Ibid.* ii. p. 40.

[3] See " Lord Viscount Wimbledon's *Demonstration of divers Parts of War ; especially of Cavallerye.*—*Royal MSS.* 18 cxxiii. p. 46.

Cecil move heaven and earth to obtain a troop of horse, and when he heard that his claims were opposed by Mr. Gilpin, the English Resident at the Hague, he wrote in a very excited strain to his uncle :—

CAPTAIN E. CECIL TO SIR R. CECIL.

" MAY IT PLEASE Y^r HO.,

" There is noe man living can howld him selfe more bounde to y° then I doe, nor noe man hath more cause to praye for y^r long life then I have. I fiende dayly my obligation to increase towardes y. H., and espetiall amungst those that doe honer and love y° truly. But for those that ar base, ignorant and wicked, it is as hard for those to love y^{rs} or followe y°, wth any faithfullnes, as to alter there owne nature. Of wch condition I have mett wth one (whose name is Mr Gillpine) in my busines aboute the company of S^r Ni. Parkers, one whoe in frinship I never was aquanted wth all. But, I have had good knowlege wth his dispo[s]ition to doe for all those that have caryed failes [false] hartes to y^r H. wch my selfe am wittnes to. When oure Captaynes from heance wente in to Ierland, and by the corespondens he now howldes wth others in Ingland. He bragges much of his friendes in Corte, when he never names y^r H.; he is most covetus, and we thinke heare, he mindeth bribes more then her Ma^u servis, wch maketh him be so fearefull to withstande any thing that the States heare like not of. As for the Injures he hath done me, they ar the greater by reason I never deserved ill at his hand (unless by denyeng him a bribe, wch he begged at my hande). He hath laboured by all meanes to crosse mee in my busines, and to do his beast for the Lieftenant of the companie, whoe is knowne to be a coward, a traeeter, by having served the Enemy long, and not comde oute of England to the companie, but from the Ennemy. He hath, to hinder mee the more, dealte wth Comisares to take advantage of my offesers in these musters, whoe have taken my Clarke oute of his Beade, and put him in to Prison, only to hinder mee wth the States from the Companye of Horse. An accedent was never harde of in these countryes be fore ; Wherefore I though[t] good to lett y^r H. know so much, that y° maye favoure mee heare in as it shall seeme beast to y^r H. And so recommending my humble servis to y°, I will eand as I be gone wth my dayly prayres for y^r long and happie life, wch I will never scease to doe.

" From the Hage, this 10 of Mar., 1599

" Y. H. Ne. [Your Honour's nephew]

- " in all duty,

" ED. CECYLL." [1]

Add. " To the R. Ho. and his singular good unkel S^r Ro. Cecyll, knight, Prinsepale Secritary of Eyngland."

End. " 1599, 10th Mar.—Cap^n Edward Cecyll to my Mr. From the Hagh. An invectyve lre against Mr Gilpen. Rec^d at Richmond the 16th."

This letter calls to mind the familiar Latin quotation—

" Hic moderatur equos qui non moderabitur iræ."

It is only fair to Mr. Gilpin to give his version of this business, and as there was a good deal of ill-feeling and jealousy in regard to this same troop of horse, both Cecil's and Gilpin's letters must be read with all due allowances.

The following is an extract from a letter addressed—

" to his very worthie good friend and kinsman,

Mr. Dudley Carleton, attending on Sir Edward Norreys, Knight.

. . . . " that I crosse Mr Cecill in his sute for the horse-company hath as little grounde as the other ; for I enter-meddle on neyther parte, but leave all to the States disposing. And although he never since his arryvall came or sent unto mee, yet in regarde of the respect I beare to the name, I was of late to see and make him acquainted wth that I had done upon Sir Nicholas Parkers wryting and for his good, seeing how likely his lieutenant was to carry away the company, in consideration of his long service and care of the charge committed to him ; and w^thall requyred Mr Cecill to thinke no other of mee then I deserved ; besydes (without the saying of so much unto him, I meane to try yf the Lieutenant wilbe pswaded to forbeare his sute upon reason-

---

[1] *Cecil Papers, Hatfield*, 68/81.

able conditions, though he might thinke himselfe wronged to receive a repulse after 14 yeares service, and promise made him long ere I dealt with him, by his Ex^{ce} and the chiefe of the States. As for the trouble about the Muster, I knew not thereof, till the clearke and others were emprisoned, and have done what I coulde in favo^r of the porre men. And now I am wryting of Mr. Cecill I will say thus much more, that though I take him to bee a gentleman of sufficient conceipt and qualities, yet can he not phappes sounde the depth of the drift by bringing him to seeke for the saide comp. of horse, w^{ch}, yf it be thoroughly looked into, will appeare not to proceede so much from the good will borne him (what shewe so ever made) as for respect of themselves, that would be rather freed from the continuall pnce [presence] of such an one, wch brings wth it many other considerations, especially to a suspicious humour, and such a nature as can in no sorte abyde to have any long about him of so greate helpes and likely hoods, or that for other worth or desertes might be well thought of besides himselfe, least they should aspire to be raysed as well as he hath (And indeede I knowe not why gent^n that serve, should not carry mindes wth them to seke after preferment). And that this is no supposition will appeare manifestly to any that shall look into and examine the courses helde, and how hath been dealt before wth gentlemen that have caryed mindes worthy of their pfession. But hereof enough, or rather too much, unlesse the subiect were more pleasing. Yo^w see my boldenesse, and I am sure yo^w are wearyed wth my tedious-nesse. I will therefore for the p'nt forbeare yor farther trouble, and ending wth my heartiest commendations commend yo^w to the Almightie. From the Haegh, this 26th of Februarie, 1599.

" Yo^r most assured poore kinsman to my

" power,

" GEO. GILPIN."[1]

Sir Francis Vere made strenuous efforts on behalf of Edward Cecil in the contest for the troop of horse, and it speaks well for Cecil's fitness for the command that such a man as Vere thought him worthy of the appointment.

---

[1] *S.P. Holland.* George Gilpin, Resident at the Hague, died September, 1602.

"Captain Cecyl hath made great means for Sr Nicolas Parker's troops of horse," wrote Carleton to his friend Chamberlain, "and hath driven the bargain with him for £500 ; but the States gave they^r worde before his going over to the Lieutenant, so as a stopp is made, and they know not what to determine. Sr F. Vere hath written that Mr Gilpin hath beene the meanes to hinder Mr Cecill, by wch he hopes to do him a shrewde turne."[1] The States were at last obliged to yield the point, and Edward Cecil was appointed captain of the vacant troop of horse, having paid £500 retiring money to Sir Nicholas Parker.[2] A few weeks after this event Captain Cecil, being at the Hague, took the oath of allegiance[3] as a cavalry officer in the service of the United Provinces, and his appointment was ratified by the Dutch Council of State. The following letter explains whose casting vote obtained this coveted command for Edward Cecil :—

CAPTAIN E. CECIL TO SIR R. CECIL.

" MAY IT PLEASE Y^r HO.,

" I have receved y^r H. letters wth a great deale of favour and grase that it hath pleased y^r H. to take notis of my wrong ; for the wch I reast most bound. Y^r H. letter S^r fra[n]cis Vere would not lett pass, the cause I doubte not but y. H. shall understande by his letters. I did presume to writ my discontented minde oute of a discontented humer, wch caried mee be younde what ealse I woulde have sayde. But I hope y^r H. will consider that in menns nessecety it is naturall to caule upon him that can most ayde him, so I (having receved some wronges wch my patience coulde not suffer) did grounde a stronge faith in y. H. favoure to assist

---

[1] March 2, 1600, *S. P. Dom.*

[2] "The captain of cavalry, Parker, having resigned his troop of horse, the same was given, about this time, to Mr. Edward Cicil, grandson of the late great treasurer Cicil."—*Journal of A. van Duyck*, June 9, 1600.

[3] "Captn Cecyl takes oath as captain of the company of cavalry of Captn Paraguar (*sic*)—*Oath Book*, 1588-1703, p. 16." (Signed, "Ed. Cecyl, June 14, 1600.")

mee. My suing for the companie of Horse hath trubled this State very much; considering S^r fra Vere hath laboured for mee and Mr Gilpine for the Liefftenant. Where upon Mr Gilpine was asked, why he would showe him selfe so against Mr Secritarys Nephew, whoe brought her Ma^t letters (and espetially to howld wth one who had beeyne a Trature). His answer was, he did knowe very well what y^r H. sayd, when her Ma^t lettrs was to be wryten in my be haulfe. I am ignorant how he cometh to his intellygenc; but I am assured he is moste vayne, so that I feare not his prosporing. But I feare that his creadit will make mee leave these countryes, or it be long, wch I did come to, by presuming upon y^r H. favoure, wch I will indevoure by all meanes to deserve, where so ever I shall be come. And wth all affection continue my dayly prayres for y^r H. longe and happie life, as the comforte of

> "Y^r Ho.
> "most diutyfull and affectionatt
> "N. and Se.,
> "Ed. Cecyll."[1]

Add. "To the Ri. Ho. and his singular good Unkell, S^r Ro. Cecyll, Prinsepalle Scecritary of Eingland."

End. "April 1600. Cap^{en} Edward Cecyll to my M^r."

After the acquisition of Fort St. André, Prince Maurice was desirous of pursuing his success along the course of the Meuse, but in consequence of the representations made to the States-General by the Zealanders, who were much harassed by the near vicinity of the enemy, it was determined to invade Flanders. The rendezvous of the troops was

---

[1] *Cecil Papers, Hatfield* 79/15. The command of a troop of horse brought a good deal of extra work to an officer in those days, as Cecil himself shows in his pamphlet on *Divers parts of war, especially of cavalry*, which I shall have occasion to refer to again before long. In this pamphlet he shows forth the hardships of a cavalry officer's life on active service, when food and forage were scarce. "And this myself have endured," he goes on to say, "when I was captain of a troop of horse. For before the battill of Nieuport, our Army then lying in an enemy's country, we were fain to march day and night. . . . I never put off my boots for six weeks together."

appointed at Rammekins, in Walcheren, where nearly 1,000 boats[1] were collected to convey the troops to Ostend. The States' army consisted of 3,000 cavalry and 12,000 infantry, 4 field pieces, and 30 smaller pieces of artillery. The troops were embarked for the purpose of landing at Ostend, but being prevented by contrary winds, the fleet passed up the Scheldt, and the troops disembarked at the Sas de Gand; the fort of Philippine, by which it is defended, having been first captured by Count Ernest of Nassau. The day following, June 23rd, the Prince began his march overland to Nieuport, a small but well fortified town, at the mouth of a branch of the river Yperlee, which forms its harbour.

The army, which was divided into three corps, consisted of Zealanders, Frisians, Hollanders, Walloons, Germans, English, and Scotch. The advance was under the command of Count Ernest of Nassau, the battalia under the command of Count George Solms, and the rear guard, during the march, was entrusted to that experienced soldier, Sir Francis Vere.[2] On the 23rd the troops marched a league and the next day brought them three leagues further. On the 25th they marched to Male, three and a half leagues distant, passing close to the walls of Bruges. It is recorded as a curious fact, that at Male three cows were given for a pot of beer, the States' army being badly supplied with drink.[3] Several writers give a curious description of this march to Nieuport, of the unfriendliness, and even open hostility of the peasantry on the line of march, to the invading army, which had come to conquer or perish in a grand effort against the Spanish usurpers. All writers

---

[1] Motley says, "of war ships, transports, and barges, there were at least 1300." Davies and other writers state the number to have been about 1000.

[2] Motley's *United Netherlands*, iv. p. 7.

[3] *Ibid.* p. 10.

agree in depicting the magnitude of the issues at stake in the impending conflict before Nieuport. And they cannot be too highly portrayed, for the House of Nassau risked its very existence on the issue of the impending struggle. Besides Prince Maurice, there were three other members of the House of Nassau serving in the expedition—his half-brother Frederick Henry, then a lad of 16, and the two brothers of the Frisian Statholder,[1] Ernest and Lewis Gunther. A defeat to the States' army would not only have been a death-blow to the House of Nassau, but it would have extinguished for many a day the growing power of the United Provinces.

It had been confidently hoped by the planners of the invasion of Flanders, that the States' army would steal a march upon the enemy, and be able to relieve Ostend, then being blockaded by the Archduke Albert. Ostend had long been a thorn in the side of the Archduke, and not long before the Infanta had been presented at Ghent with an image of "Flandria," very richly clad, and in the foot of this image was a thorn, signifying Ostend, which she had solemnly promised to pull out.[2] The States-General trusted to the mutinous state of the Archduke's army, and to their unexpected invasion of Flanders, for success in this expedition. But it must be remembered that it had been undertaken against the advice of Prince Maurice, Sir Francis Vere, and other military commanders. The sequel showed how sound the advice was, for the Archduke, having reclaimed his mutinous soldiers, collected a large army from his garrison towns, and, leaving the Infanta at Ghent, marched against the States' army with all possible speed, meaning to overtake them before they had captured

---

[1] Lewis William of Nassau.
[2] D. Carleton to J. Chamberlain, March 2, 1600.—*S. P. Dom.*

all the forts round Ostend. The States' army meanwhile, quite unaware of the rapid approach of the enemy, had, after taking possession of Oudenburg and other important forts near Ostend, arrived at Nieuport on the 1st of July, which town they proceeded to invest. On the evening of that day a messenger, much exhausted and terrified, made his appearance at Count Ernest's tent. He brought the astounding intelligence that the Archduke had captured Oudenburg and all the other forts. " The news " says a learned historian, " was as unexpected as it was alarming. Here was the enemy, who was supposed incapable of mischief for weeks to come, already in the field and planted directly on their communication with Ostend."[1] A council of war was immediately held. Some of the commanders were disposed to disbelieve the news brought by the messenger, but at midnight another messenger, sent directly from the States-General at Ostend, confirmed the startling intelligence. Immediate action of some kind was necessary. Prince Maurice, in order to impede the movements of the enemy and gain time, detached during the night Sir William Edmonds' regiment of Scots foot, a regiment of Zealanders, four squadrons of Dutch cavalry, and two pieces of artillery (which force was already established on the right bank of the Nieuport harbour), under the command of Count Ernest of Nassau. Count Ernest was ordered to march at once in order to seize the bridge at Leffingen, and oppose the advance of the enemy, which would give Prince Maurice time to transport the rest of his army across the haven at low water. The enemy had, however, passed the bridge when Count Ernest arrived there with his small force. To retreat was inglorious ; to proceed seemed utter destruction, as he was outnumbered

---

[1] Motley's *United Netherlands*, iv. p. 14.

eight to one. His orders were to oppose the enemy's advance, and with the valour of his race he determined to obey. He took up a position behind a dyke, upon which he placed his two field pieces, and formed his line of battle exactly across the enemy's path. The result is well-known. At the first onset of the enemy a panic seized the cavalry, and they retreated in a disgraceful manner. The Zealanders followed suit, and the contagion spread even to the Scots, who all turned their backs and fled, helter skelter.

"Had they even kept the line of the downs in the direction of the fort,[1]" says Motley, "many of them might have saved their lives, although none could have escaped disgrace. But the Scots, in an ecstacy of fear, throwing away their arms as they fled, ran through the waters behind the dyke, skimmed over the sands at full speed, and never paused till such as survived the sabre and musket of their swift pursuers had literally drowned themselves in the ocean. Almost every man of them was slain or drowned. All the captains—Stuart, Barclay, Murray, Kilpatrick, Michael, Nesbit—with the rest of the company officers, doing their best to rally the fugitives, were killed. The Zealanders, more cautious in the midst of their panic, or perhaps knowing better the nature of the country, were more successful in saving their necks."[2]

It may truly be said of the Scotch who participated in this unfortunate affair, that "brave men have their moments of fear just in the same way as cowards have their moments of bravery," for no braver men than Edmonds' Scotch soldiers were to be found in the States' army.

Prince Maurice in the meantime had transported the whole of his forces across the haven at Nieuport—no easy task, even at low water—and had placed them in battle array on the beach and downs. They had not been long there, when two troopers, riding *ventre à terre*, arrived in

---

[1] Fort Albert.   [2] Motley, as before, iv. p. 19.

their midst, and announced that the whole army of the Archduke was advancing. These two harbingers of bad news were instantly sent to the rear to deliver their news to Prince Maurice. We know already what a disastrous tale they had to unfold, and history tells us how unflinchingly the son of William the Silent listened to the tidings, and how nobly he acted in this hour of extremest peril. Having forbidden the two messengers, on pain of death, to divulge the news of Count Ernest's defeat to any human being, Prince Maurice sent them, strongly guarded, on board one of the war ships in the harbour. He then calmly gave orders, " that every war ship, transport, barge or wherry, should put to sea at once." The tide being at the flood, the whole fleet stood out to sea. Of his own free will, and without taking anyone into his counsel, Maurice had cut off the sole means of retreat for himself and the whole States' army. The caution of the chess player, the calculations of the mathematician, were forgotten in the natural impulse of the hero. No Alexander could have severed the Gordian knot with more *sang froid.* " No more brave decision," says Motley, " was ever taken by fighting man."

   *   *   *   *   *

On Sunday,[1] the 2nd of July, at 2 P.M., the famous battle of Nieuport commenced.

The States' army was drawn up in battle array among the steep and rugged sand-hills—its left to the sea, and its right towards Nieuport. By direction of Sir Francis Vere, the tops of the sand-hills were crowned with Friesland

---

[1] In the *Curiosities of War* are shown the numerous battles which have been fought on Sundays. This century is fruitful in examples of victories gained on Sundays. In the Peninsular War, the battles of Vimiera, Fuentes d'Onor, Orthes, and Toulouse ; Ciudad Rodrigo was carried by assault on the night of Sunday, Jan. 10, 1812. Waterloo and Inkermann were also fought on Sundays.

musqueteers, while in the hollows were 1,000 English pike-men and 600 musqueteers, supported by the lancers and mounted harquebusiers. By the express orders of Prince Maurice two pieces of cannon had been placed on the highest and most advantageous positions. On the edge of the downs, on the narrow slip of sand above high water mark, was placed a battery of six demi-cannon.[1] The cavalry, under Count Lewis of Nassau, was posted on the right of the downs, in the pastures. Behind the advanced squadrons of horse, were three troops of horse, which Prince Maurice had kept as a reserve force. They were the troops of Captains Balen, Horace Vere, and Edward Cecil.

The battle was commenced by a charge of cavalry, under Count Lewis of Nassau, who led his troops across the pasture land, leaping the ditches in true sportsmanlike fashion. The enemy's cavalry were routed at the first charge, and they turned and fled in all directions, followed by the victorious troopers, whose ardour nearly cost them and their brave leader their lives, as we are told Count Lewis found himself at the head of ten men only, and the enemy between him and his own nation. Fortunately, the quick eye of Prince Maurice had foreseen this contingency and a body of States' carabineers, under Captain Kloet, were speedily sent to the rescue of Count Lewis, who was easily distinguished amongst the enemy by his orange plumes.[2]

In the meantime the States' infantry and the Archduke's

---

[1] Jan. Orlers gives in his interesting work, *La généalogie des illustres Contes de Nassau*, published at Leyden in 1615, a plan of the battle of Nieuport, showing the position of the two contending armies. The men, guns, horses, &c., are all minutely drawn, and the position of each regiment, battery, and troop of horse numbered. Orlers only gives four guns, not six, in the States' battery on the beach. Edward Cecil's troop of horse is given in the plan and numbered *Cecilius, capitaine de chevaux*.

[2] Motley's account of the battle.

had met, and were engaged in a deadly struggle on the downs. "It was," says Motley, in his graphic and soul-stirring account of this battle, "a hot struggle of 20,000 men, pent up in a narrow space, where the very nature of the ground had made artistic evolutions nearly impracticable. The advance, the battalia, even the rearguard on both sides were mixed together pell-mell, and the downs were soon covered at every step with the dead and dying— Briton, Hollander, Spaniard, Italian, Frisian, Frenchman, Walloon, fighting and falling together, and hotly contesting every inch of those barren sands.

"It seemed, said one who fought there, as if the last day of the world had come."[1]

It was during this "bloody bit," as Sir Francis Vere terms it in his account of Nieuport battle, that he received two wounds in his leg.[2] Notwithstanding these hurts, Sir Francis Vere still remained on the field, and fought like a lion. Before the battle commenced, Prince Maurice had placed the chief command of the cavalry and infantry in Sir Francis Vere's hands, reserving to himself the command of the artillery.[3] It was doubtless owing to this fact that Sir Francis Vere took all the credit of the victory at Nieuport to himself and the English, ignoring Prince Maurice altogether.[4] It is, however, clearly proved by Motley, who quotes from many authentic sources, that Maurice of Nassau, and his brave cousin, Count Lewis, were by no means idle spectators of the conflict, and that they both, as well as their own troops, did very much to

---

[1] *Ibid.* iv. p. 34.

[2] Sir F. Vere speaks of "those four holes in my flesh" in his account of the battle. See also Chamberlain to Carleton, July 1/10, 1600, *S. P. Dom.*

[3] The artillery had been placed on wooden platforms, which gave the States' army an advantage over the archduke's, whose artillery, sinking in the sand, was of little use.—*Motley*, iv. p. 41.

[4] Account of Nieuport battle in Vere's *Commentaries.*

ensure a victory. Count Lewis having rallied his cavalry, and obtained the prince's permission to charge the enemy's cavalry, again hurled his devoted squadrons against the Spanish horse. This time, however, they were unable to break the line ; and being exposed to a galling fire from the archduke's infantry, they wavered, and finally retreated. The archduke seized this opportunity to bring up his reserve of infantry, which charged Vere's infantry, who were already wearied with the long-continued life-and-death struggle. Tired human nature could not withstand this fresh influx of strength brought to bear upon them, and so the States' troops fell back, retreating slowly and orderly towards their battery on the beach. To make matters worse, Sir Francis Vere's horse was now shot under him, and he fell under it. Sir Robert Drury,[1] Captain Ogle,[2] and Higham, servant to Sir Robert, providentially saw their gallant leader's perilous position, and the two latter extricated Sir Francis Vere from under his horse, and placed him on the crupper of Sir Robert's horse. Let us now turn to Maurice of Nassau, and see how he comported himself when his army, country, fame, and even life itself, seemed to tremble in the balance.

" He was in the field," wrote a Dutch historian, " and seemed to be the only one not frightened ; and, exhorting, praying, begging, he tried to incite them with the courage of despair, and advised them rather to die fighting than to drown and suffocate all, especially as things were not hopeless. In this manner he rallied some of the cavalry, and hearing that the artillery on the beach

---

[1] Sir Robert Drury of Hawsted, Suffolk.

[2] Captain Ogle (afterwards Sir John Ogle), a distinguished English officer, says in his account of *The last charge at Nieuport battell*, that he assisted Higham to pull Sir Francis Vere from under his dead horse and place him upon Sir Robert Drury's, thereby saving his life, as the enemy was close behind them. Ogle says his clothes were stained with Sir F. Vere's blood, and he wonders at Sir F. Vere never mentioning his (Ogle's) name in connection with this service.—Vere's *Commentaries*, p. 110.

was in great danger, he sent to the rescue, and to charge upon the enemy's infantry the three last regiments of reserve under the command of Balen. They divided themselves in such a way that Balen would charge upon the strand, Vere upon the upper downs, and the regiment of Cicil upon the downs. This latter just arrived upon the downs when the foe had approached the guns, and when the last shots were fired from them, which made such a havoc among the enemy that they abandoned the guns. In passing the downs, Balen ordered his men to ride slowly, in order to ease the horses, but, arriving on the beach, he furiously attacked the infantry, which at that time was there unsupported, charged them on the flank, overthrowing the musketeers, who fired little, because they had been attacking the retreating English, put them to flight, and killed or took prisoners a number of them. The cavalry of Cicil on the downs repulsed the enemy and dispersed part of them ; Vere with his men also overthrew a whole battalion in the upper downs, all of which quite changed the state of affairs, for the English and Frisians, who were retreating along the downs, halted and faced the enemy, while 150 pikemen among the Frisians attacking them made them abandon another down ; and after this the sailors [1] first, and then the gunners, began to cry ' attack, attack ' (*Ian*) ; others, though without cause, began to exclaim, ' victory, victory.' On hearing this, all the troops of his Excellency began to push bravely forward, while the enemy gradually retreated."

The above account is literally translated from Anthony Duyck's *Journal*.[2] This Dutch author has the reputation of being very exact and truthful. Motley has quoted largely from him in his account of Nieuport battle, and Duyck's account tallies with that of other writers. It is well known that no two accounts of a battle are alike, and it is only natural that the Dutch writers should claim a good share of the honour of the victory for their heroic

---

[1] These were Zeeland sailors, " who," says Motley, " had stuck like wax to their cannon during the whole conflict."

[2] Page 674.

prince. It is also only natural that the English, on whom the brunt of the battle most undoubtedly fell, should claim most of the honour for Sir Francis Vere and the English soldiers. Vere has been blamed, and no doubt justly, for his partial account of the fight. He takes the whole credit of defeating an army of 10,000 men to himself and his 1,600 English troops. The Dutch and their leaders are nowhere! No English officers are mentioned in despatches except Sir Horace Vere and Sir R. Drury, to whom Vere owed his life. Such a one-sided account was sure to give offence to many, and we must consider it to be what Motley terms it, "a party pamphlet in an age of pamphleteering." Captain Ogle, who took an active part in the battle, has given us a very good account of the last charge and the events which just preceded the now famous charge by Balen, Horace Vere, and Edward Cecil. Ogle tells us that when the States' infantry and Vere's troops were being borne back by the enemy, slowly yet surely, that he, Captain Fairfax,[1] and Mr. Gilbert, went aside on to the downs to rest a little and to consult what to do; they were presently joined by a small number of their men, and Sir Horace Vere joining them with some of his men, determined them to "turn and make a new head against the enemy."[2] "The vigilant and iudicious eie of Prince Maurice," continues Captain Ogle, "was upon our actions and motions all this while, for (as I have been enformed), he seeing us make head, said to those who stood about him, *Voyez, voyez, les Anglois qui tournent à la charge*, and thereupon gave present order to Dubois (then commissary

---

[1] This was Sir Charles Fairfax, a distinguished officer, who was killed during the siege of Ostend. He was youngest son of Sir Thomas Fairfax of Denton, and brother of Thomas, first Baron Fairfax of Cameron, the father of the great Lord Fairfax.

[2] This partly tallies with Sir F. Vere's account, who says his brother Horace rallied a body of men and made a resolute stand against the enemy.

general for the cavallerie), to advance some of the horse[1]
to be readie to attend and fortifie the events that might
happen upon this growing charge." The three troops of
reserve horse, commanded by Balen,[2] Vere, and Cecil, were
ordered, with those troops that had rallied, to charge the
enemy, who was rapidly bearing down upon the battery on
the beach, behind which the States' troops were fast retiring.
"Much about this time," continues Ogle, "came in the
Horse, namely, the troops of Vere, Cecill, and Ball (*sic*), who,
rushing with violence amongst them (the enemy), so con-
founded and amazed them that they were presently broken
and disjoynted, which being done, the slaughter was great
to them on their side as the execution easie to us on ours.
This rupture also of theirs was not a little furthered by the
Archduke's own troop of Harquebusiers, which, having
advanced somewhat before the grosse on the skirt which
lay between the inland and the higher downs, was so
encountered by Cecill and his troop (who had as then
received order by Dubois from his Excellency to charge),
that they were forced with confusion to seek succour
amongst their foot, Cecill following them in close at their
backs."[3]   Horace Vere and Balen were equally successful

---

[1] Sir F. Vere says he had several times sent to Prince Maurice to send the
horse to their succour (?).

[2] Balen's charge on the beach is mentioned by Vere, who takes the credit
of the arrival of this troop so opportunely to himself.

[3] This charge is referred to by an old writer (in MS. 18 A lxiii. *Royal Lib.*,
Brit. Mus.) as follows : " His Excellency, seeing the whole army in disorder,
comannded his last reserve of horse (which were all English) to make a home
charge ; they put in execution very fortunately his Excellency's direction, and
it was General Cecill's good hap (who was then a Captain of horse) to charge
and rout the Archduke's owne gard of Harcabucas (*sic*), being of black velatt
(*sic*) coatts, and tooke two or three of the Archduke's servants prisoners, and
gott of his owne silver dishes, and I heard his Lieutenant, Captain Bowyer, say,
if his Excellency would have given them leave to follow the execution, he
made no question but they might have taken the Archduke prisoner ; for this
piece of service his Excellency made General Cecill a Colonel of horse."

in their charge, and, as we have already seen from Duyck's and Ogle's accounts, the enemy was completely routed. "This charge," continues Ogle, "(through the hand and favour of God) gave us the day." Ogle accounts for Sir Francis Vere not mentioning Edward Cecil's gallant charge in this manner: he says, Cecil had his order to charge from Prince Maurice and not from Sir F. Vere, who was unaware of the order and likewise not at the charge in person.[1]

"The enemy," wrote Sir Francis Vere in his account of the battle, "lost above one hundred and twenty ensigns (colours), most of his foot slain, not many of his horse lost. On our side, in a manner, the whole loss fell upon English, of which near 800 were hurt and slain, eight captains slain, the rest, all but two, hurt, and most of my inferior officers hurt and slain. In the rest of the army there was no losse at all to speak of, especially among the foot.   .

"I dare not take the whole honour of the victory to the English, 1,600 men ; I will only affirm that they left nothing for the rest of the army to do but to follow the chase." [2]

When Maurice of Nassau at last saw the enemy flying before his pursuing troops he is said to have dismounted from his horse, and, kneeling in the sand, exclaimed, "O God, what are we human creatures to whom Thou hast brought such honour, and to whom Thou hast vouchsafed such a victory !" The Admiral of Arragon, who commanded

---

[1] Vere says, "In this last charge I followed not, for seeing the successe upon the sands, and knowing that my directions in the prosecution of the victory would be executed, I could easily judge that the work of that day was at an end."—*Commentaries*, p. 100, &c. See also Ogle's account in same vol. pp. 106-11.

[2] Vere's account, p. 104. Sir Francis Bacon, in a description of the battle of Nieuport many years after, wrote :—" The services also of Sir Edward Cecil, Sir John Ogle, and divers other brave gentlemen, was eminent."—See Spedding's *Letters and Life of Bacon*, vii. p. 493.

the cavalry, the Count de la Fere, the Count de Salines, and Don Carlo de Zapena, with many others, were taken prisoners. It is said, "there was not any commander of note but was either taken or slain, saving the Archduke (who was wounded in the face), the Duke d'Aumale, and Velasco, Generall of the artillery." [1] " It is the greatest battaile, and best fought," wrote Chamberlain to his friend Dudley Carleton, describing the battle, " that hath been betwixt two disciplined armies in our time in Christendome. There was almost no oddes in number (saving that the States had advantage of about 500 horse), theire foote were about 9000 a peece." [2]

In this battle 3,000 Spaniards were computed to have been slain, and about 600 prisoners were taken.[3]

Edward Cecil sent the following account of this battle to his uncle, Sir Robert Cecil :—

CAPTAIN E. CECIL TO SIR R. CECIL.

" MAY IT PLEASE Y[r] HO.,

" I doubte not at all but y[r] Ho. hath the beast advertisments of all accedentes that doe happene, yet I may doubte whether y[r] Ho. will thinke that I am as desierve of y[r] favours if I showe not my diutye by writing somewhat (considering this occasion), as by writing I take it for a means ; wherefore, allthoughe I have forborne heretofore to write any thing that mighte come to stalle to Ho., yet I have adventered at this tyme, not but that I knowe my ansofisienc to advertis y[r] H. Yet presuming to doe it like a souldier, and as one that was as nighe a wittnes as any other that was in the Battell, y[r] Ho. will not take it for the least advantage tor the good I desier of y[r] favoure. The Battell his Exselenc and the Arche Duke hath foughte was betwxte Nuporte and Ostende ;

---

[1] Chamberlain to Carleton, July 1/10, 1600.—*S. P. Dom.*
[2] *Ibid.*
[3] Captain Scott, in his letter to the Lord Treasurer, dated at Ostend, June 26 / July 6, says, " There were 4000 of the enemy slain and 1000 taken prisoners."—*S. P. Holland.*

wee were planted be for Nuporte, and in the morning wee harde nwes that, that the Arche Duke was coming wth some 12/1000 menn, and some 20 companies of horse to trie his fortune for the Duckedome of flanders, or to lease his fortune there of; wee understoude he was not 5 oures march from us, whereupon our holle Armye marched wth all indevoure to meete him, his Exselence sending the regement of Germans, wch Count Ernestus commanded, and the regements of the Scotes, to hinder the passage, wch were putt all to the sworde, harde by osteand, where there bodis lige there yet to wittnes it, wch made the Enyme march one wth such a furie as was never seene. Then the[y] advansed to meett wth our squaderons of Einghlish, wch all menn can not saye but did gallantly, the Battell induring some 4 oures before S^r fran. vere was shott twise, once in the legge and in the thighe, whom I thinke hath gotten as much honer as a man can gett one earth. One the other side cam up the Arche Duke, La berlott, and Sr William Standly, wch commanders gave great incurregment to the vangarde of Spaniards; that it is not possible for menn to doe better then they; they did make our menn retire very faste till it was the latter eande, that our horse did healpe them, for the were oppressed wth the Enemys horse all the day before. It stowde very doubtefull till the latter eande, and then it wante so muche one oure side that wee performed the exsecution five milles out righte; wee have taken the Admeroute of Arogon, generall of the howle armie, the foure Camp Masters, one cauled lieus de villiar, wch is prisonar to S^r fra. vere, the other gaspar La pieva, another don geronemo de monroye, and Don Allfonsoe de Aunolie, wth many more wch are dead, as S^r william Standly, la bertlott,[1] one Coronell Bostocke, whoe hath now S^r william Standle's regement, but these ar all dead, by many brobabillities; yet there is some doubte; of Einglish wee have lost very nighe a thousande, wee have lost our Sargentmagore, Captayne yaxsly, a very gallant gentlellman, Captayne Hunnewodd, his lieftenant, Ensine, and Sergent, one Captayne Duxburrye, one Captayne Purtene and his lieftenant, Captayne Turrell, his lieftenant, and many more liftenantes, and Captaynes Hurte and can not scape. I have lost some 10 men out of my horse

---

[1] Colonel La Bourlotte was not killed on this occasion, but met his death not long after.

companie, yet I have taken 5 captaynes, one Spaniard, 2 Italions, one wallowne, and one Einglishe Captayne that hath served this 20 years wth Standlie [1] wch his Exselence would have ransomed ; he offers £60 to a souldier of mine, but if it please y^r H. to dispose of him, I will see him forth coming, and expecte y^r H. pleasure. And thus in most humble manner I take my leave, not having time to write more, or to write this in a better hand, for wee ar now marchinge the saye [? waye] to Sluse.

" y^r H. in all diuty,

" ED. CECILL.

" I hope y^r Ho. will pardon the scribbling of a souldier." [2]

Add. " To the R. H. S^r Ro. Cecyll K. Prinsepall Secritary of Einglande, and his Ho. unkell."

End. " June, 1600, Cap^{en} Cecyll to my M^r from the Campe."

Every one must think this letter of Edward Cecil's a very modest one, considering the active part he played in the decisive cavalry charge at Nieuport. His admiration for Sir Francis Vere was genuine, and he entertained to his dying day the greatest reverence and esteem for that great soldier. More than a quarter of a century after, when referring to the battle of Nieuport, Cecil thus eulogises Sir F. Vere :—" Hee was the verie Dyall of the whole Army by whome wee knew when we should fight or not." And again he says, in writing about Sir Francis, " The whole Army both reverenced and stood in awe of him." [3]

Among the British officers killed at Nieuport was a cavalry officer who rode with Edward Cecil in the last

---

[1] Sir William Stanley attended the archduke at Nieuport without command, having disposed of his regiment to his nephew Bostock. A dozen years before, he had betrayed Deventer to the Spaniards and gone over to their side.

[2] *Cecil Papers, Hatfield*, 80/69.

[3] Quoted from a MS. in *Brit. Mus.* (18c xxiii. *Rl. Lib.*) entitled, Lord Viscount Wimbledon's *Demonstration of divers Parts of War ; especially of Cavallerye.*

charge and was slain in Cecil's sight, when they were both pursuing the enemy. This officer was Captain Hamilton, a gallant Scot, who once made, to use Cecil's own words, "the gallantest retreat I ever heard of." Hamilton had been sent out with some Dutch cavalry under Count Lewis of Nassau to skirmish in the enemy's country, the expedition only being to plunder and spoil, and to replenish the count's purse. The Spaniards came down on them in force and made them retreat. As the manner was, they retreated skirmishing, the officers taking it in turns to keep the enemy at bay with a few of their men, whilst the rest of their body retreated. "At last," says Cecil, "it came to Captain Hamilton's turn to make the last retreat, always most difficult and dangerous (which the Dutch loveth not ; therefore left it to him). And because the horses were weary and the enemy was gayning ground upon them, Hamilton fell into the Reere of his men, and so long maintained the skirmish with the pursuing Spaniards that the States' horse had time to make their retreate farr enough. In the end his horse was killed under him, notwithstanding which, hee, leaping over a body, made his retreat on foot and so escaped." [1]

A great victory had been gained by the States' army on Nieuport sands, but the conquest of Flanders was as far off as ever. Three days after the battle, Maurice came before Nieuport, only to find that La Bourlotte [2] had increased the garrison to 3,000 men. Ten days after, the forces of the States retired from before Nieuport and proceeded to the vicinity of Ostend, where they captured a large fort called *Isabella*. Edward Cecil indited the following letter to his uncle from the camp there :—

---

[1] *Ibid.* p. 50.
[2] Colonel La Bourlotte was killed in a skirmish a few days after this.

CAPTAIN E. CECIL TO SIR R. CECIL.

" MAY IT PLEASE Y^r HO.,

" Althoughe I have littell occatione to advertis y^r H. of oure busines heare, considering such messenges as nowe arive wth y^r H. that there ar fewe can better satisfie y° then theye, yet bicause y^r H. shall knowe that y° have a nephewe that woulde be loth y^r H. showlde for git him, and how much he thursteth after y^r favoure, and how much he desiers to doe y° servis. Here wee pore men that laboure for a fortune ar muche incorregged to see so many of oure nobiletye heare [1] wch giveth a grea[t] deall of grase to us and our Campe, wch other wayes is as miserable as maye be, nether affording mans meate or horse meate, wch will forse us to goe seecke some where ealse.

" I have heare to fore trubled y^r H. in the difeculty I founde in obtaning my companie of horse, and was very nighe the going wth out it, but as I beleeved so I founde, wch was that if I gott it not for y^r sake, I looked not for it, as I may very well saye by the favoure I did fiende from the Advocate Barnewell, whoe did mee all the favoure I founde at all, saing that I had good cause to thanke y^r H., and that for y^r sake he would favore mee in any thing he coulde, wherefore I umbly beseeche y^r H. to take notis of that muche, that the Advocat may not only knowe I have acquanted y^r H. wth it, but allsoe that y° doe regarde mee so much for the wch if my life and prayres may deserve it, I shall thinke my selfe happie, and be bounde the more to praye for y° H. long life and hapines ; so in all humblenes I take my leave.

" y^r H. in all diutye,

" ED. CECYLL.

" From the leger before the forte of Isebella." [2]

Add. " To the R. H. and his singular good Unkell Sr R. Cecill knighte, Prinsepall Seccritary of Einglande."

End. " July, 1600. Cap^en Cecyll to my M^r from the Campe in flandres."

---

[1] On July 26 there arrived in an English ship, Lord Cobham, Sir Walter Raleigh, the Earls of Rutland and Northumberland, and Sir H. Pemel.— A. Duyck's *Journal.*

[2] *Cecil Papers, Hatfield,* c. b. 4/30.

The invasion of Flanders having been proved to be a much more serious undertaking than was at first antici- pated, and the States' army being much weakened by recent losses, it was determined to re-embark the troops at once. Accordingly, on August 1, a great part of the infantry was embarked at Ostend, and the ships sailed for Rammekins to await orders there. The remaining ships with the cavalry sailed for Bergen-op-zoom. Besides the eleven companies stationed in the town of Ostend, Prince Maurice left some English companies under Hamond, some of the Frisians under Ripperda, some German and Swiss companies under Husemon, some French battalions under Dussau, some Scotch companies and several Dutch companies ; also the horse troops of Balen, Vere, Cecil, and Arthur, under the command of Balen.[1]

The States' finances being at a low ebb after the Nieuport expedition, the deputies of the States-General wanted to reduce the foreign cavalry and infantry which had not yet returned to their quarters ; Prince Maurice, however, prevented this, not wanting to deprive the country of so many troops, and he retained at the expense of Holland the cavalry commanded by Temple,[2] Cecil, Arthur, La Sale, and Clout, each troop having 80 horses (*bidets*). Also the foot companies of General Vere, Colonel Horace Vere, Captains Fryer, Temple, and La Noue, each com- pany having 150 men ; and the companies of Calisthenes Brook, Harcourt, Tyrrell, Honeywood, Daniel Vere, Ogle, Hamond, Garnet, Holcraft, Forster, Jaxley, Fairfax, Knollys, Cecil, Metckerke (*sic*), Scot, Sutton, Vavasour, Duxberry, Aldrich, Morgan, Beeden, &c., &c., with 115 men in each company.[3]

---

[1] A. Duyck's *Journal*, ii. p. 713.
[2] Sir Oliver Temple.
[3] A. Duyck's *Journal*, ii. p. 737.

It will be seen from the above list of horse and foot that Edward Cecil's foot company still retained his name. It was virtually his company, although commanded by another officer when Cecil was serving with his horse troop. His retaining his foot company bears out what has been previously said, viz., that some of the senior infantry officers had troops of horse under their command. They served with one or the other as occasion allowed. Both Sir Francis Vere and Colonel Horace Vere had their own troops of horse and a certain number of foot companies under their command, which their lieutenant-colonels[1] commanded when they themselves were absent. Although the foot companies were sometimes termed "regiments, they were not really formed into regiments until 1605.

---

[1] Lieut-Colonel Sutton acted as lieut.-colonel to Sir Horace Vere at Nieuport and on other occasions.

CHAPTER IV.

1601–1603.

Marriage of Edward Cecil to Theodosia Noel—Rosebury Topping—The bride's present of sweetmeats to Sir R. Cecil—Preparations for a summer campaign in the Netherlands—Ostend in 1601—Commencement of the siege of Ostend—Rhineberg besieged by Maurice of Nassau—Sir Francis Vere's request for English troops—His arrival at Ostend—Edward Cecil sent there from England in command of troops—Sir Robert Cecil's letter to Lord Burghley—Edward Cecil's letters from Ostend—Sortie of the garrison—Captain Cecil joins his troop at Rhineberg—Siege of Meurs—Edward Cecil returns to England—Strange mode of recruiting—Edward Cecil knighted by Queen Elizabeth—Arrival of Sir Francis Vere in England—Further reinforcements sent to Holland—Sir Edward Cecil made Colonel of Horse—Renewal of hostilities—The Brabant expedition—Siege of Grave—Vere's wound—Great mortality among the troops—Grave surrenders to Prince Maurice—Expedition to Emden—Sir Edward Cecil sent there—Death of Queen Elizabeth.

WE left Edward Cecil at Ostend on August 1, 1600. The next news we have of him is in the following June, when he was in England. It does not appear when he came over from Holland, but it was doubtless in the previous autumn, the campaign being over for that year.

It is easy to tell how Cecil spent some of the early part of the year 1601 as on June 10 he was married at the parish church of Brook, co. Rutland, to Theodosia Noel,[1] daughter of Sir Andrew Noel,[2] of Dalby in Leicestershire,

---

[1] This marriage is given in the Cecil pedigree in Blore's *History of Rutland-shire*. The entry of this marriage is still to be seen in the Brook parish register for 1601, but I am told by the vicar of Oakham that the date of the month in register is now very obscure.

[2] Sir Andrew Noel, of Dalby, Leicestershire, and Brook, co. Rutland, was "thrice sheriff of the latter county." He died at Brook in 1607, and was succeeded by his eldest son, Sir Edward Noel, who was created, in 1617, Baron Noel, and in 1629 (his father-in-law's title) Viscount Campden.

by Mabel, sixth daughter of Sir James Harington[1] of Exton, co. Rutland. Theodosia Noel was apparently seventeen years of age at the time of her marriage, as she was baptized at Brook, Jan. 4, 1584.[2]

It would be well nigh impossible at this distance of time to ferret out any details of Edward Cecil's marriage, or state where the happy pair spent their honeymoon. A marriage in high life, even in the days of the Virgin Queen, who openly frowned on young people bent on entering the happy state, was a ceremony attended with many rejoicings and old world formalities, of which only a few have descended to this prosaic age. The "romance of love" is—and always has been—as common to the high born as to the lowly, and is equally sweet to both. Both choose the choicest spots of Nature's creating in which to plight their vows of life-long fidelity to each other, which are often sealed with some signature, or device, carved on Nature's handi-work, as if to make her a witness of their good faith. Such shallow tokens of constancy unfortunately often survive the love and fidelity of the lovers who make them, and so bear witness to a living lie. This is much more sad than that these emblems should outlive those who left their names and devices on the face of Nature, as "flesh is grass." It is owing, however, to the perennial nature of stone that we are indebted for the following interesting record, given by Ord in his *History*

---

[1] Sir James Harington, of Exton, married Lucy, daughter of Sir William Sidney, of Penshurst, and sister of Sir Henry Sidney, K.G., by whom he had issue eighteen children. Sir James Harington died in 1592, and was succeeded by his eldest son, Sir John Harington, created, in 1603, Baron Harington. His lordship was tutor to the Princess Elizabeth, daughter of James I.

[2] Given in Cecil pedigree, Blore's *Rutlandshire.*

of Cleveland, in his description of Rosebury[1]—a conical-
shaped mountain in Cleveland. "A curious hermitage or
grotto," says this author, "formerly graced the summit of
the rock, but has long since been sacrificed by the ruthless
quarrymen. Here the names, initials, and footmarks, with
various lovers' emblems and devices, were quaintly carved
on the stone. Some of them were in full, with a date
annexed, as ' 1595 Theodocea Cecyll,' ' R. C. 1625.' "[2]

There is no doubt whatever of the above "Theodocea
Cecyll" being Edward Cecil's wife ; indeed there was no
other Theodosia in the Cecil family. The date, however, is
of course completely wrong. The mistake may be accounted
for by supposing the date (even if correctly copied from
the weather-beaten stone (?)) to have belonged to another
name altogether, and not to have been part of Theodosia
Cecil's inscription. The copyist, not knowing when the
lady lived, was quite content with his anachronism.
We also may be entirely wrong in supposing that the
above name was carved on Rosebury Topping in the
year 1601, but as it was a favourite resort with newly
married couples we may naturally conclude that it was
carved soon after her marriage. Supposition must have
a great voice in a far-away record of this sort. The Cecils
had many connections with Yorkshire. Sir Thomas Cecil
(Lord Burghley) was, as we have already seen, married at
Monkton in Yorkshire, to Dorothy Nevill (daughter and
co-heir of Lord Latimer), who inherited the estates of
Well and Snape in the north of the county. Again, the

---

[1] The summit of Rosebury is said to foretell thunder when a white mist
hangs over it :—

  " When Roseberrye Toppinge wears a cappe
  Let Cleveland then beware of a clappe."

[2] Page 424. These old autographs and dates, mentioned by the old Cleveland
historian, have long since vanished, and have been replaced by nineteenth
century autographs which now deface Rosebury's rocky summit.

old Lord Burghley was an intimate friend of Sir Thomas Chaloner, of Guisbro', the great poet, who was sent Ambassador to Spain in 1561 ; and we find Sir William Cecil, as he then was, acting as chief mourner at Sir Thomas Chaloner's funeral at St. Paul's, a few years later.[1] The Chaloner estate lay close to Rosebury Hill. Putting two and two together, therefore, leads to the conclusion that Edward Cecil and his wife were staying at Guisbro' with the Chaloners,[2] when Theodosia left her name so deeply impressed on Rosebury Topping.

Very soon after his marriage Edward Cecil wrote the following letter to his uncle, Sir R. Cecil, but where from does not appear :—

" MAY IT PLEASE Y[r] H.,

" When I laste parted wth y[o] I was resolved to have returned in to the lowe countryes. But to excuse my selfe truly (as I am resolved ever to doe so to y[r] H.), I can confes nothing that hath hindered mee, but beyng a nwe maryed mann. And littell occation I had to be any where this winter, but where I mighte have the pleasantest Garison, considering I howlde my selvfe a commander of horse and not of foote. And now that it drawes nighe that my charge is to com in to the fealde, I woulde be loth that y[r] H. shoulde knowe that I missed an hower of beyng wth them, for my dispositione of the wares was never so earneste as it is wth hope ; and as long as it shall please y[r] H. to favoure my fortunes there in, w[ch] if eyther y[r] blude or a harte woued by all reasons, to be honest and affectionatt to y[o], can deserve, then assure y[r] H. y[o] ar not onely to looke for it of mee, but challenge it by more reasons then y[o] can from any mann living. My wife, may it please y[r] H., as drawing in the same yoake, is as desierus to drawe some of my lode ; and, not knowing in any thing how to showe her diutefullnes, hath presumed to make use of slighte sweat meates that y[r] H. mighte regarde the more her diutefull miende.

---

[1] Ord's *Cleveland*, p. 222.
[2] Rear-Admiral Chaloner, of Longhull, Guisbro', the last male descendant of the family, died in 1884.

And w^(th) all she hath desiered mee that because the ar suche tryfelles, and that sweatt meattes may very well be demineshed, passing many handes, to lett y^r H. know that there is 3 bockes, and 12 porringers, w^(ch) if the may any waye like, y^r H., she will reast a most happie womann. And thus beyng jelius that I may truble y^r H. in y^r greater affares, I will in all humble manner reast, but never reast to praye for y^r longe and happie dayes as the hapines of

" Y^r H.
" Most diutefull and affectionatt
" Nephue and servante,
" ED. CECYLL." [1]

Add. " To the R. H. S^r Ro. Cecyll, Knighte, Prinsepall Scecritary of Eingland.   London.

End. " 1601.   Sr Edward Cecyll to my M^r."

In the month of April, 1601, Sir Francis Vere had been sent over to England by the States to solicit Queen Elizabeth for leave to raise 3,000 men, at the States' charge, for immediate service in the Low Countries. The Queen having agreed to send these reinforcements as soon as their presence was absolutely necessary, Vere returned to Holland.[3]

The States had already settled their plans for the coming campaign. They had projected the capture of the

---

[1] *Cecil Papers, Hatfield*, 90/47.

[2] The endorsement " Sr Edward Cecyll," is of course an anachronism, as Edward Cecil had not yet been knighted. The mistake can be easily accounted for in this way : Sir Robert Cecil's secretary doubtless only endorsed these letters at the end of each year, and as Edward Cecil *was* knighted before the end of 1601, the mistake was easily made.

[3] An amusing anecdote is told of Sir F. Vere's stay at Yarmouth on his return to Holland. Having to wait there for a fair wind, and hearing that his enemy, the Earl of Northumberland, who was also going over to Holland, was in the town, he called upon the Earl and said in his dryest way, that as he was detained by the wind he thought he might as well call on his lordship. His lordship replied that as he was only indebted to the wind for the courtesy, he did not care to see him, and so they parted. Sir R. Cecil to Lord Burghley.—July 15 (?), 1601.—*S. P. Dom.*

eighteen forts which threatened the existence of Ostend—
their only foothold in Flanders. Of these forts the most
considerable were St. Albert, St. Isabella (captured by the
States' troops in the preceding year), St. Clare and Great
Thirst. Ostend, it will be remembered, was the thorn in
Flandria's foot, which the cardinal-archduke had promised
to eradicate. This town and its importance is thus
referred to in the *Records of the 3rd Foot*:—" On the
breaking out of the war between the King of Spain and
the States of the Low Countries, Ostend was a small
village in the earldom of Flanders ; in 1572 it was enclosed
with palisades and wooden gates, to protect it from the
incursions of the Spaniards ; and five years afterwards, the
States, considering the advantageous situation of the place,
fortified it in a more formidable manner. The Prince of
Parma, having reduced a great part of Flanders to obedience, captured Dunkirk and Nieuport in 1583, and afterwards appeared with his army before Ostend, but was
repulsed with loss. From this period Ostend had stood
alone in the provinces subjected to Spain, and the facility
with which it could be relieved by water had enabled it to
resist every attempt of the enemy. The garrison had also
made frequent incursions into the adjacent country, and
had raised heavy contributions to prevent which the States
of Flanders had erected eighteen forts, in which they kept
strong garrisons. The expense of these garrisons had,
however, proved burdensome to the people, and large sums
of money had from time to time been offered to the
Spanish governors to defray the expense of the capture of
Ostend." Archduke Albert had been petitioned by the
States of Flanders to besiege Ostend, and had been offered
300,000 florins a month, as long as the siege lasted,
besides an extra sum of 300,000, of which one third was to
be paid when the place should be invested, one third when

F 2

the breach had been made, and one third after the town had been taken.[1]

The Archduke nothing daunted by his defeat at Nieuport in the previous summer, and anxious to retrieve his military fame in the eyes of his lady, the Infanta Isabella Clara Eugenia of Spain, said that if necessary he was willing to spend eighteen years in reducing Ostend. On the 5th of July he came before the town with a large force and formally began the siege—a siege which was destined to rival the memorable siege of Troy.

Maurice of Nassau, in the meantime, had marched to the Rhine, early in June, and laid siege to Rhineberg with an army of 12,000 men. " It was his purpose," says Motley, " to leave the archduke for the time to break his teeth against the walls of Ostend, while he would himself protect the eastern frontier, over which came regular reinforcements and supplies for the Catholic armies."[2] Maurice had hoped to have diverted the attention of the archduke from Ostend, by laying siege to Rhineberg, which town had been recaptured by the Spaniards in 1598. Ostend, however, was much more important to the Spaniards than Rhineberg, so leaving the latter place to defend itself against the States' army, the archduke brought all his available forces before the little seaport on the coast of Flanders. If Ostend was to be relieved, it must be relieved at once, and the 3,000 men from England, promised by her Majesty, were absolutely necessary for saving the town. So said Sir Francis Vere in his letter to the English Council, which is well worthy of a place here, as it succinctly explains the state of affairs at this crisis.

------

[1] *La Nouvelle Troie, ou, Histoire du siège d'Ostende,* par Henry Haestens, p. 99.
[2] Motley, iv. p. 61.

" MOST HONORABLE. Synce the wrytyng of my lettres of the
9th, I have forborne to trouble y^r H^n, attendyng the good pleasure
of her Matie touchyng the states demande for the ymployement of
the men, the rather for thatt tyll now of late thear was no
occasyon of further advertisment. Butt thennemyes commyng
before Ostende, wth nombres of men and artyllerye compitent for
a siege, thoughe itt is a thyng nott alltogeather unlookead for by
reason thatt from the fyrst thought of goyng before Berch, itt was
heald thatt if the ennemy went nott dyreactlye to the releefe of
thatt place, he would undretake Ostende. W^h was cause also
thatt the States researvead in theas partts 1200 men to be ready
for the renforcement of thatt garnison, w^h ar accordynglye now
gone thether, so as in all the strengthe of thatt towne is about some
2400 men, and they have sent for all the Inglysse compagnyes
from the camp to thrust into Ostende. Theas nombres may
seame sufficient to y^r H^n for the defence of the place, and so no
doubt wth good conduct they myght have been, if they had beenn
all in the garnyson when the enemy came before the towne to
have taken and lodgead themsealves uppon places of advantage,
wth out w^h thear smale nombre would nott geave them leave to
attempt and now is too late, by w^h meanes thear is nothyng leaft
to dispute butt the walle, and in that case y^r H^n may remember
whatt my opinion was, when before your Lordsps I answearead
to questions uppon thatt subjeact, thatt places in thatt estate wear
desperate. W^h, experyence havyng made playne to theas menn,
they ar nott a lyttle troublead, the towne beyng to them of suche
ymportance as in a manner theyr whole well fare depends uppon
the conservatyon thearof. So as I cann asseur y^r H^n if itt wear
nott thatt they ar yeatt in hope of her Matie souccers they would
geave over the siege of Berck rather then abyde this loss, thoughe
itt wear no smale disreputatyon to them, to have so ill forcast
theyr busynes as to be dryven thearunto, butt they would excuse
thatt as they wyll doe the loss of the towne uppon the trust they
reposead of havyng theas menn from Englande. For the w^h they
wryte agayne verye earneastlye. And albeit I knowe y^r H^n, in
theyr wyse-dommes, doe weygh of whatt moment thatt towne is in

every respeact, yeatt I cannott forbear to uttre whatt is thought
hear the loss of thatt place would bryng w^h itt. Fyrst, all the hope
of cleeryng thatt coast is taken away, thennemyes meanes to
annoye us by sea treablead, he is easead of an infinyte chardge the
blockyng thatt place requyread, and his reveneaw by the quietyng
of thatt quarter muche increasead, and this conclusyon is drawn
owt, thatt thennemy in shortt tyme wyll disjoynt this state, wthout
strykyng an offonsyv blowe by land, if they be nott more healpead
by theyr neyghbours, then yeatt thear is any apparence of. On
the other syde itt may please y^r H^n to understande whatt is
conceavead if this soucurs of her Maties arryve in tyme ; thatt itt
wylbe the uttre ruyne of thennemy if he be obstynat, and of
Flandres eyther by his owne forces or owres whatt course soever
he take. If itt shall please her Matie to grawnt the menn, then
itt may also please y^r H^n to consyder whether itt wear nott bettre
to hasten those from the next portts to Ostende, wth all deligence,
and the reast to followe as they may, for whose entrye I hope
thear shalbe a gapp ; as also whether itt wear nott beast armyng
of the menn att the sayed portts, w^h undre y^r H^n correctyon I
should thyncke wear nott amys. The states have been exeedyng
earneast wth me to take uppon me the defence of the place, w^h I
have acceptead, knowyng thatt thearin I could nott butt doe her
Matie service, and am thearfore in good hope she wyll geave itt
good allowance, the rather if itt may be approvead by y^r H^n, and
this I humblye desyre y^r H^n to beleeve thatt my experience hathe
taught me thatt theas ymployements off all other should be
shunnead, by reason thatt commonlye muche travayle and hasarde
in them draweathe no good success, butt I seatt those respects a
syde whear suche a necessitye as this presseathe. The hast of
the messenger is cause thatt I truble y^r H^n wth this blurread lettre
w^h I beseache your H^n to pardonn, and to contyneaw me in your
wontead favor. Riesweek, this 28 June, 1601,

       " Y^r H^n

           " most bounden and affeactyonatt to doe
           " you service,

                        " F. VERE.

    " Itt may please y^r Lordsp. to understande thatt the states have
appoyntead two menn of warr to attend before Yarmouthe and

Lynn, wʰ wear as many as they could spare, most of theyr shyppyng beyng to wafte the heryng fyshers to the northwardes." [1]

No add.

End.—" Sʳ Fra. Vere, 1601."

The English companies, which, Sir Francis Vere says in the above letter had been sent for from Bereke, *i.e.* Rhineberg, to strengthen the garrison of Ostend, numbered twenty-two. Maurice could ill spare these veteran troops at such a time,[2] and only sent eight of the English companies from his camp. To these eight companies were added four additional English companies from the garrisons of Holland, and seven companies of Dutch ; with this force Sir Francis Vere sailed for Ostend, and landed, on 11th July, on the sands opposite the town.

On the receipt of Vere's letter by the Council, immediate steps were taken to send a relieving force to Ostend. Her Majesty ordered 1,000 men to be pressed at once in London, and shipped to Ostend, which consignment of troops was to be followed up by 2,000 more men, as soon as they could be got ready. The command of the 1,000 men raised in London, with 50 other recruits pressed for this service, was given to Captain Edward Cecil, who had volunteered for the service.[3] Edward Cecil's zeal on this

---

[1] *Cecil Papers, Hatfield*, 86/126.

[2] Sir Wm. Brown, deputy-governor of Flushing, in a letter to Sir Robert Sidney, dated July 9, from that town, informs him that a German soldier who escaped out of Berck told Prince Maurice, " they had but ½ lb. of bread a day for each man, that they had eaten all their cattle, and were indeed nothing but skin and bone. The Governor of Berck was wounded and unable to talk. There was a great want of surgeons, and men were lying uncared for in the streets. The garrison was only expected to hold out 8 days longer." The postscript to Sir W. Brown's letter is as follows : " Since the writing hereof the English companies arrived from the campe, and, as I believe by some of them, with no great pleasing countenance to his Excellency."

[3] Edward Cecil appears to have had the temporary rank of colonel on this occasion. " Ostend is besieged, and it is feared will be lost ; to-morrow 1000

occasion, and his departure for Ostend (probably from Yarmouth), are detailed in a letter from Sir Robert Cecil to Lord Burghley, dated July 15 (old style), 1601 :—

" My nephew, Edw. Cecil, is engaged, though contrary to my desire, in a service of importance, but I saw that his emulation in being left behind made him so jealous of his honour, if any other should have the employment, as he cared not to what hazard he put himself (especially after he heard his friend Sir Fras. Vere was engaged), so I could not but give way as follows :—Count Maurice being encamped before Berke, and the Archduke knowing he would not rise resolved to save his own honour—being unwilling to relieve that place by besieging Ostend, hoping to make a diversion or carry the town in fury.   Of this matter her Majesty hath had some providence, when the States acquainted her with their purpose to carry their army as high as Berke ; and knowing what prejudice it would be—even for her own merchants' trade to Middlebourg and other ports of the Low Countries, that the Archduke should be master of all that coast between Calais and Flushing, and should have another haven such as Ostend is, much better for galleys than Dunkirk—she resolved whenever that place was seriously besieged to seek to relieve it ; on this consideration Sir Fras. Vere, being at the Hague, tarried from Berke to be ready.   Whereupon as soon as the Archduke moved towards that siege, he came presently to relieve it, and sent for the English troops from Count Maurice ; but while waiting for them the Archduke invaded the town with his army of 10,000, began his approaches, and placed his cannon to beat the haven and all ships that should pass in.   Nevertheless, on Sunday sevennight, Sir Fras. Vere, with 12 English companies,[1] reached Ostend, in which there were only 2000 men before, but was constrained to take the benefit of the full sea, at which time, induring some shot, he landed with boats in the old town, to the

men are to be shipped thither from hence, and Mr. Cecill is colonel over them."   C. Boulton to Carleton, from London, July 11, 1601.—*S. P. Dom.*— Sir W. Brown also speaks in a subsequent letter of Colonel (*sic*) Cecil.
   [1] Colonel Horace Vere, Captains Ogle and Fairfax, accompanied Sir F. Vere to Ostend.

walls whereof the sea flows every tide, and lost not above three gentlemen. He is there excellently victualled, and well provided with munition; and though before his coming the Archduke had left never a house standing, having before it 100 pieces of artillery, so as those of Ostend had confined themselves from all outworks merely to defend the walls, yet has Sir Fras. Vere gallantly intrenched a piece of ground without the town on the west side and there made an outwork, planted eight cannon, and means for 21 days to dispute that place until more succour arrives—he not liking to be put at first only to defend the town itself, but to hold the enemy as long in play as he can with his other defences. When he sees cause he will quit that trench, and yet doubts not but the winning of that place shall cost the Archduke dear, and he must win it before he can make his assault, where he endeavours to make his breach, because this new intrenchment flanks all those approaches by which his men must enter, this being the good of the town that he cannot in many places plant a battery.

" As soon as Vere was entered, Her Majesty levied 1000 men in London, over which my nephew is commander, who departed last Friday, and they have had a prosperous wind, also honourable waftage by the Queen's fleet in the narrow seas, besides extraordinary cares taken by me that his men might be well and speedily furnished.[1] There is no man more interested in his good success than I am; for men's endeavours are valued by the effects, and if the wind or other accident hinder his relieving the town, it will serve for a good argument to some of former factions, that this was a practise in the uncle to cast employment upon his nephew. . . . A gentleman has just come from Ostend, who met my nephew half seas over,[2] and reports that the States have provided many shallops to land these men, and that his entry is still as safe as when Sir Fras. Vere went in. As soon as his 1000 arrive, the town will be 5000 strong. We have news that Bercke cannot hold out seven days,[3] which being taken, Count Maurice's

---

[1] Stow records in his *Annals* that the city of London furnished 1,000 men ; and the equipment of these levies cost the citizens £3 10s. for each man.

[2] He was obliged to swim to shore, hence his state on landing at Ostend.

[3] The Earl of Northumberland, who served at this siege, wrote from the camp on July 19 to Lord Cobham, and said Berke could not hold out 10 days longer.—*S. P. Dom.*

army will come down into Flanders, and the Archduke will lose his credit with the States of Flanders, who have dearly paid for this siege of Ostend, wherein they have forborn no charge, being so infected by that town, that they are set upon carrying it.

"As soon as Count Maurice comes down Her Majesty will send 2000 more men, making that army 18,000 foot, whereof 6000 English, with which forces, if ever there be good to be done upon Dunkirk, or Sluys, it is now."[1]

Edward Cecil's arrival at Ostend,[2] with the English reinforcements, is told in his own words in a letter to Sir R. Cecil, which is the sequel to Sir Robert's letter to Lord Burghley just given :—

CAPTAIN E. CECIL TO SIR R. CECIL.

" MAY IT PLEASE Y[r] HO.,

"These ar to certefie y[r] [Ho.] that I landed my 2000 me (*sic*) the weddansdaye at nighte, or at leaste the greateste parte, and have this morning delivered above my number, as the Diuche Commisarie hath agreed upone ; and besides I broughte over some 50 wolontaries. Wee landed all well, but some too or tree souldiers that were drowned, and my selfe was put to swimming. For the hope wee have to keepe the Towne, is that wee have so many workes that ar halfe a mille out of the towne, w[ch], as my littell tyme woulde give mee leave, I lerned was to gitt the possestions of such plases as were to muche advantagius to the enyme. S[r] fra Vere and his brother hath taken exceding paines, and espetially that nighte w[ch] wee landed, fering the enemye woulde have gained them at there handes, being not so perfett as the ar nowe this morning, where in wee meane now to dwell in ; he had that daye his quarter master slane, many of his Captaynes hurte, as allsoe the lieftenant to S[r] Horatio vere, whoe is hurte in

---

[1] This letter is published in the *Calendar of State Papers*, domestic series, 1600.

[2] Sir Francis Vere in his letter to Sir Robert Cecil and the Earl of Nottingham, dated from Ostend, July 16/26, mentions the arrival of the troops from England. His letter is thus endorsed, "July 16, 1601. Sir F. Vere to the Lo. Admirall and my M[r]. The 1000 men sent by Capt. Cecyll safely arrived." —*S. P. Holland.*

the foote. Wee accounte our selves some 5000 stronge in the towne, for the eymies streangthe one the Easte side it is not fully knowne, and there cannot a prisoner be gott by no meanes, but at the weste side he is knowne but weake, where Count Fredericke[1] doth commande. The Towne is allsoe muche battered, the enimy having 60 cannones.

"I must crave pardone for my Advertisementes if the prove some what uncertayne; for my diuty is the cause that maketh them so extemporye, my tyme being so shorte. But I hope I shall have noe neade to excuse my diligence, for I have beeyne as carefull as it were for my life (remembring what y^r Ho. sayde, that y^o were carefull that y^r name mighte not be Taxsed wth necligence, espetially in her Maties servis, where in I have noe ambisione but to die in for her sake, following as well my name in lowaltye, as in Name, wch neaxte I desier to deserve towardes y^r Ho. To wch eande I meane to followe this professione, so longe it will please y^r Ho. to favore his intende [? intent], whoe hath rather hope of Honer then riches. For the tymes ar so fitted. And thus wishing in moste humble manner y^r happines as great as can be imagined for y^o and y^r longe life as my hope in this worlde, I reast

" Y^r Ho.,

" in all affectione and servis to be

" commanded,

" ED. CECYLL."[2]

Add. "To the R. H. S^r Ro. Cecyll, Knighte, Prinsepall Secretary of Eynglande.

End. " Cap^{en} Cecyll to my M^r, from Ostende."

A contemporary writer[3] who kept a journal of the siege of Ostend, says that Cecil's 1,500 English troops arrived on the 23rd July—dressed in red coats (*casaques rouges*)—and were indiscriminately distributed amongst the 12 English companies.[4] On the 26th of July the Archduke's soldiers

---

[1] Frederick Van den Berg, cousin to Maurice of Nassau.
[2] *Cecil Papers*, *Hatfield*, 82/107. [3] Haestens.
[4] Sir F. Vere, in a latter to Sir R. Cecil and the Lord Admiral, says, in

fired all day upon one of the outlying fortifications, and in the evening assaulted it in three different places, carried it, and put its defenders to flight, "which," says Haestens, "was very easy to do, as there were only forty of them."

On July 27th the garrison of Ostend made a sortie, and gained the trenches of the enemy, whom they put to flight and pursued to the sand hills, the artillery from the town playing on the enemy with effect all the time. A Spanish soldier, who was taken prisoner, said they had full 600 men killed and wounded.[1] Amongst the killed was Don Diego Idiaquez, a Spanish captain, son of a former Secretary of State to Philip II.

Edward Cecil probably took part in the sortie of the garrison on the 27th, and a day or two after wrote to Sir R. Cecil, giving some interesting details of the state of the town.

Captain E. Cecil to Sir R. Cecil.

" May it please yᵉ Ho.,

"I am at this tyme going in to Holonde, being imployed from Sʳ francis vere a bout the wantes that shoulde be broughte in to this Towne, and frome thence I am going to Berke to my Companie of horse, where my greateste imploymente and charge is. Yet if I can gitt leave to returne to this Towne, I am fully resolved to see what will become of this Towne, in respecte it is leafte to the Truste of oure natione. As for our latte sally wee have made I will not wryte of, presuming that so anciente a souldier as this bearer will relatte substantially to yʳ Ho. But for the certefienge of yʳ Ho. of the state of the enymies campe I presume I can doe it better then this berar (allthoughe shorte of satisfieng yʳ Ho.), yet my redynes to deserve yʳ good favoure is never the less farrder of. I have examined a prisoner that wee

---

speaking of the troops which had just arrived, "They are draughted as itt was from the fyrst desyred by the States and by your Honours approved, amongst the compaynes of my brothers and my Regiment." July 26, *S.P. Holland.*

[1] Haestens, p. 105.

have takene in this last sally, whoe hath delivered to us that the
cheafe commander of there armie is Don Augustin de Missia, the
govener of the Castell of Anwerpe, wch doth commande upone
the side of Nuporte, wch ar to the number of 8000, and one the
other side Counte fredericke doth commande the forses towardes
Brugis, wch ar 4000. And those that doe commande the three
regimantes of Spaniardes, ar Don lius reiliard, Mon. Riwas,[1] and
Don Simon Antonio. And there is arived some seavent^n 100
Spaniardes some towe dayes a goe, and to morrowe the looke for
3000 Italians, that ar camde from Italy. The enimye are in
garde every nighte 3000. The have 30 pease of Artilery planted
and looke for a 100; the generall of the artillery is in Spaine, but
his lieftenant is heare, Sig. Matheo Serrant;[2] the three sergent
majors is cauled Don Louys d'avilla, Baltazar lopus and Don
Gionn Tantoche. The forte of St Clara is yet mutined, and doth
not shout a pease at us. And the Cardenale,[3] is in the Forte of
St Allbertus. Allsoe the prisoner saith that there is gone w^{th}
Counte Herman to the releave of Berke 12 1000;[4] where of there
ar a 1000 900 Spaniardes. There is a companie of Einglishe
one there [s]ide wch one Cap. Flode commandeth; wee have many
of our Einglishe souldiers runn to the Enimye, and wee have takene
2 of our nwe menn running, wch shall be hanged shortly. If wee
coulde have some of the Enimies campe that mighte advertis us
of there intention, it woulde give us muche advantage, wch if y^r
honore have any that come to y°, it will doe us a great deale of
good to knowe same suche thinge. The cannone shott that hath
beeyne made upone this towne hath beeyne counted to be thertine
1000 now at this preasante. I hope y^r Ho. will pardone this
confusednes of my setting downe these cercamstance. For it is
according to this tyme, and may be compared to the raggednes of
this Towne that standeth littell to gether. But I have a stronge
hope of y^r H. good accepting of any thing that comes frome one
that hath all the reasons to love and serve y°, and that y° maye

---

[1] A Spanish general who fought at Nieuport.
[2] Don Matteo Serrano, afterwards Governor of Sluys.
[3] The Cardinal-Archduke Albert.
[4] Twelve thousand.

assuere loveth y° as muche as any servant, and as muche as any blude can, wch shall be for ever or as longe as can laste,

             " Y^r Ho. pore kinsmann,

                   " ED. CECYLL." [1]

Add. " To the R. H. Sr R. Cecyll, K., Prinsepall Scecritare of Eingland.

End. " Cap^en Cecyll to my M^r from Ostende."

This letter informs us that Edward Cecil had received orders to go into Holland at once, on business connected with Ostend, and was to join his troop of horse at Rhineberg, where his duty lay, after the business was transacted. It was evidently his wish to stay longer at Ostend, and take his share in the great drama of war there enacting ; but he had no option in the matter, as all the recruits he brought from England had been draughted into the old English companies, " by which means," says Sir F. Vere in his letter to Sir R. Cecil, " the gentlemen who conducted these men ar for the present unprovided, but I wylbe carefull to ymploye them as opportunytye shall searve, accordynge to their worths."[2] Edward Cecil left Ostend about the last of July. His arrival at Flushing is chronicled by Sir W. Browne, the deputy-governor of that town.[3] His arrival at Rhineberg is also chronicled by Anthony Duyck, in his *Journal*, under the date, August 6th.[4] When Cecil reached Prince Maurice's camp he

[1] *Cecil Papers, Hatfield,* 83/66.
[2] Vere to Cecil and the Lord Admiral, July 26.—*S. P. Holland.*
[3] " I have received a packett of letters from my Lord of Northumberland, and one other from Colonel (*sic*) Cecil, who came on Sunday last from Ostend, since when we have had no newes."—Browne to Cecil, July 21/31.—*S.P. Holland.*
[4] " And to him (Prince Maurice) came Mr. Edwardt Cissel coming from Ostend, reporting that all was still well there, and that the Archduke was drawing nearer to the quarters of General Vere than to the town."—Translated from A. Duyck's *Journal,* iii. p. 121.

found that Rhineberg had capitulated on the 30th July, and the garrison had marched out with the honours of war. Having placed a strong garrison of Dutch troops in the town, Maurice marched to Meurs, a little higher up the Rhine, and laid siege to that place early in August, when it at once capitulated.

After the acquisition of these two fortresses—the keys to the provinces of Juliers and Cleves—Prince Maurice despatched twenty foot companies to Ostend, of which twelve were English and Scotch.[1] Maurice kept the cavalry with his own army, and as, after the taking of Meurs, there seemed to be no further prospect that year of active operations, Edward Cecil, remembering his young bride at home, returned to England, either the end of August or early in September. His hopes of returning to Ostend were probably put an end to by Sir Francis Vere being wounded in the head on 14th August, when he was compelled to temporarily relinquish the command at Ostend, and retire to Zeeland to recruit his health.[2] On the 20th August 2,000 additional troops had arrived from England, so that the besieged were inspired with new confidence. We shall not have occasion to say much more about this memorable siege, which for over three years occupied the attention of the whole of Europe, and cost about a hundred thousand lives.[3] As Edward Cecil was not again sent to Ostend all the thrilling incidents of this life and death struggle have no place in this narrative. But before leaving the subject of this siege, it is necessary to give the reader some idea of the sort of recruits sent by Queen Elizabeth to the United Provinces, during the progress of this struggle, to aid in the defence of Ostend.

---

[1] *Records 3rd Foot*, p. 70.	[2] *Biog. Brit.* art. " Vere."
[3] In the *History of the Siege of Ostend* it is stated that the besieging army lost 72,000 and the garrison 50,000 men.

Among the copies of military warrants in the " King's MSS. of Military and Historical tracts, 1585–1630," preserved at the British Museum, are, " Letters for the Impresse of Idle and Dissolute persons for the service of the Low Countries," dated March, 1601–2, and addressed, " To the High Sheriffe and other the Commissioners for taking the musters in the countie of Norff, and to the rest of the Justices of the Peace of that County."[1]   The Commissioners' Warrant upon the said letters is as follows :—

"Having received Letters from the Honble the Lords and others of Her Maties Privie Counsell for the apprehending and sending to the Port at Yarmouth all Rogues, Vagabonds, idle, dissolute, and masterles persons, which cannot make a good accompt of theire living, being of strong and able body, to be sent over for Her Maties service in the Low Countries.   These are by virtue thereof to command you to make diligent privie search in all places within your Hundred on Saterday at night next, and the day following, for all idle, masterles, and dissolute persons before mentioned, and all other that you can procure to serve voluntarilie, having regard to spare mens servants, and other of honest behaviour, and to bring them before us at Yarmouth upon Wednesday, the 30th of this present March, by 8 of the Clocke in the morning of the ablest of them, then and there to receive further direction, giving to every man 1s. for impresse, where the same shall be repaid you.   And hereof, &c."[2]

However brave these warriors were, both in fighting and plundering friend and foe (and Fleming[3] assures us they did both equally well), it is quite certain they deserted in large numbers whenever they had the chance.   This was only to be expected from men pressed against their will

---

[1] This warrant to the High Sheriff is signed by "Tho. Egerton, C.S.; Tho. Buckhurst ; Nottingham ; Gilb. Shrewsbury ; E. Worcester ; Wm. Knollys ; Ed. Walton ; J. Stanhope ; Ro. Cecill ; J. Fortescu."—*King's MSS.* 265, f. 304.   [2] Fo. 305.
[3] Philippe Fleming, the Dutch clerk and chronicler of the siege of Ostend.

and who had to fight in a cause they took no interest in.
Edward Cecil has told us of some of his " new men " being
caught running to the enemy, for which offence they were
ordered to be hanged. And another English officer writing
from Ostend six months later, to a friend in England, says :
" The soldiers of the new supply that entered the town,
run away as fast as those that were there before, by seven
or eight of a company, of which there have been fewer
English of late—only four or five—because there are not
many in the town, and they not of those that were pressed
in London and packed up in ships, and sent away against
their will."[1]

Now to return to Edward Cecil. His next appearance
on the scene is at Basing, in Hampshire, where the Marquis
of Winchester had a seat. The Marquis had married
Lucy Cecil, daughter of Sir Thomas Cecil, Lord Burghley ;
and her brother, Edward Cecil, had doubtless gone there
on a visit with his bride, on his return from Holland, the
end of August, 1601. On the 5th of September the Queen
being on one of her royal progresses in Hampshire, came
to Basing, and was most sumptuously entertained by Lord
Winchester at his seat. Her Majesty was joined there by
the Duc de Biron, ambassador from Henry IV., who had
been sent to England with the Count d'Auvergne, natural
son of Charles IX., and nearly four hundred noblemen and
gentlemen of quality. Biron was lodged at the Vine, a
princely mansion, belonging to the Lord Sandys.[2] Hunting
and feasting were the order of the day at both Basing
and the Vine, and the Marquis of Winchester's splendid
entertainments involved him in pecuniary difficulties. At

---

[1] Letter to J. B., dated from " The camp, Jan. 29 / Feb. 8, 1601-2."—*S.P. Dom.*

[2] William, 3rd Baron Sandys, had taken part in the Earl of Essex's rebellion, and was in prison at this time.

her departure from Basing on the 14th of September, Elizabeth made ten knights, the largest number she had ever made at one time. Amongst the new knights was " Sir Edward Cecil, second (*sic*) son to the Lord Burleigh."[1] As it was more difficult to obtain knighthood in the reign of Elizabeth than it was to get an earl's patent in the succeeding reign, Sir Edward Cecil had every reason to be proud of the honour conferred on him at the age of thirty.[2]

After the siege of Ostend had lasted eight months, Sir Francis Vere relinquished the command to Colonel Frederick Van Dorp, on March 7th, and went into Holland. In the following month he was sent by the States-General to England to solicit fresh succours.[3] Notwithstanding that the several large detachments of troops sent in the previous autumn to Ostend had dwindled away to a mere handful of men, Elizabeth was again prevailed upon to allow a certain number of her subjects, " whose absence would be a benefit to their native counties," to be pressed for service in the Low Countries. Whether it was that the " rogues and vagabonds," who were " wanted " for service in the Low Countries, managed to keep out of the way, or that the press gangs were not particular in their choice of men, certain it is that they caused men of honest reputation to be pressed against their wills. " There is a press of 1,000 men from the neighbour shires," wrote Chamberlain to Carleton, " and 2,000 from London, to go with Sir Francis Vere. It is so disorderly performed that serving men, country folks, and termers (*sic*) of all sorts, are violently

---

[1] Nichols' *Progresses of Queen Elizabeth*, iv. p. 567, note.

[2] Sir E. Cecil had also the honour of being chosen member for Aldborough in Yorkshire, in the Parliament which met October 27, this year, and which was dissolved on Dec. 19 following.—*Notitia Parliamentaria*, by Browne Willis, iii. p. 149.

[3] *Biog. Brit.* art. " Vere."

carried to the ships, so that it is a grievance at home and a scandal abroad."[1] Was it to be wondered at that of every hundred men pressed in the country, a fourth part ran away before reaching London?[2] Yet there was no lack of gentlemen volunteers from England for the service of the States. It was the great Lord Burghley "who made Holland our stage of war and our school of discipline, where England gained the security and experience of war without its calamity and desolations."[3]

Amongst those who followed Sir Francis Vere to the Low Countries in the spring of this year, were, Lord Grey, Lord North, Sir John Grey, and many young Englishmen of good birth who raised "voluntary companies."[4] Prince Maurice being ready to take the field, and great things being expected from him during the coming campaign, the English officers in the service of the States had all returned to their posts. Sir Edward Cecil had doubtless returned to Holland early in May, and joined his troop of horse at Doesburg,[5] in Guelderland, from whence we have tidings from him.

SIR E. CECIL TO SIR R. CECIL.

' MAY IT PLEASE Yʳ HO.,

. . . . " beyng I am assured that my affectione and diuty is as great towards yᵒ, as any what so ever, I can not chuse (allthough I for beare many tymes in regard of yʳ H. affares), but as often as I can remember it to yʳ H. And wᵗʰ all hope that yʳ H. will showe to accepte my unfaned servis by making mee bounde to yᵒ in those actions, as I may deserve by my professione, where in yʳ

---

[1] John Chamberlain to Dudley Carleton, May 8, 1602.—*S. P. Dom.*
[2] *Ibid.* May 17.
[3] Lloyd's *Memoirs of Lord Burghley.*
[4] Chamberlain to Carleton, May 17.
[5] Doesburg was captured by the English, under Leicester, in 1586. The Admiral of Arragon retook it in 1598, but it soon after was recaptured by Maurice of Nassau, who strongly fortified it.

H. hether to hath diply tied mee and incurraged mee to the warres. For what fortune I have, or shall have, I must acknoledge them to come from yʳ H. and for yʳ sake. And I doubt not but I shall deserve them, by doeing nothing but what shall deserve my name, and living or dieng ever wittnes that I am booth thankfull and faithfull to do yʳ H. honest servis.

"I assuer my selfe that there is littell nwes I can advertis yʳ Ho. that will be news, yet for fatione sake I will not howld from sayng what I knowe at my garyson at Diusborro, in Gillderland. The Enimie doth fortefie at Grave, at Gelldere, at Venloe, and all about these quarters, and ar very gelius of the Burgers of these Townes. He that commandes in these quarters is Count Henricke, the Gallantest Captayne of Horse that the Enymie hath, whose companie is 400. The Enymie is very stronge in these parts, 12,000 at the least, and increase dayly. But the ar not owlde souldiers, onely of the Band of ordinanc[e]. I had order from his Excelence, that every one of my horsemenn should cary a pare of horse shouse and nales, wᶜʰ maketh us beleave that we shall have farr jurnes.

"Wee understand that the Enymie hath sent 3 chife commanders to the Grave van Emdyne,[1] hoping that his Towne and he will come to a greement, and so to intertayne all his souldiers, in the Kinges name. But I am assured they will be trubled to passe the Rine, till our Army be ma[r]ched up hier in to the Country. And I imagine that eyther to morroe or neaxte daye wee shall rise.

"Prince moris [Maurice] hath given mee the Command of all the Einglishe horse.

"His Excelence did show mee a dogg for the Hearne [Heron], wᶜʰ he purposeth so send yʳ H.; the ar very rare and ar not to be gotten in all this country.

"And thus recommending my selfe to yʳ good favour, hoping yᵉ will judge of my desier I hav to serv yʳ H., then how able I reast, but never will reast from prayng the all Mighty for yʳ longe and happie dayes as the onely comforte looked for of

"Yʳ H. most affetionat and diutefull

"nephue and servant,

"ED. CECYLL.

---

[1] The Count of Emden.

"from Diuborroe, this 28 of Maye."[1]

Add. "To the R. Ho. Sr Rob. Cecyll, principall Secritarye of Eingland."

End. "28 May, 1602. Sr Edw. Cecyll to my M^r."

The troops of horse put under the command of Sir Edward Cecil were the three English troops.[2] This command, which virtually made Cecil a colonel of Horse, was given as a reward for his services in the last charge at Nieuport.[3] The bestowal, however just, of a coveted command upon a junior captain of horse, was sure to give offence to many. That fire-eating nobleman, Lord Grey,[4] who had been loth even to be commanded by Sir F. Vere,[5] had solicited the command of the English horse from Prince Maurice, and had letters from the Queen to the States-General. So powerful was his interest that he himself made sure of getting the command of the English horse, and he told Sir William Browne, the deputy-governor of Flushing, that he expected to have 700 or 800 horse under his command.[6]

The two following extracts will show that Edward Cecil was not indebted to Sir Robert Cecil, or Sir Francis Vere, for his cavalry appointment. The first is from a letter

---

[1] *Cecil Papers, Hatfield*, 93/86.
[2] It does not appear who commanded the other two English troops.
[3] See MS. 18 A lxiii. *Royal Lib.*, *Brit. Mus.*, quoted from in chapter iii.
[4] Thomas Lord Grey, of Wilton (15th Baron), went to Ireland with the Earl of Essex, and had a high command there. He afterwards served in the Low Countries as a volunteer, and was present at the battle of Nieuport, where he was wounded in the mouth. Having joined "Raleigh's Conspiracy" in 1603, he was arrested, tried for high treason and sentenced to death. He was never brought to the block, but died a prisoner in the Tower in 1614. It is said that Frederick, Elector Palatine, earnestly intreated James I. in 1613 to pardon Lord Grey, but ineffectually.
[5] Chamberlain to Carleton, May 8, 1602.—*S. P. Dom.*
[6] Sir W. Browne to Sir R. Sidney, May 30, 1602.—Collins, ii. p. 253.

addressed, " To the Right honorable Sir Roberte Cecyll, Knyght, her Majesty's principall secretary."

" I have receyved your Ho. lre concerning the Lo. Grey, and did the very nexte day deale with the States, his Ex^∞, and Barnevelt, according to the order, with all earnestnes. They sayde they woulde consider thereof, and see what coulde be done. His Ex^∞ tolde me the Rutters had their owne commanders already, and that the other were under the Count Lodowicq of Nassaw. How beit yf his Lp. coulde be contented to be as Colonel over certaine troupes of horsse (of wch nature there were divers others already appointed, and amongst them S^r Ed. Cecyll) he woulde doe his best to accomodate him therein. As for any entertainement, or the leavy of a new Company, that belonged to the States, and was by them to be disposed in, wch to further I will continue my uttermoste endeabvors. From Emden nothing, but that the Count procedes in his courses, and the Towne remaynes still irresolute. Wherewith till other occasion I moste humbly take leave, beseching th' Almighty for your Ho. long and prosperous estate."

" Your Hon. most humble

" and bownde,

" GEO. GILPIN.

" Haegh, this 21st of May, 1602."

The next extract is from Sir Francis Vere's letter to Sir Robert Cecil, dated from " Rieswicke, 26 May, 1602," in which Sir Francis makes creditable mention of Edward Cecil's fitness for the command given him ; and any praise from a soldier like Vere is valuable[1] :—

" My Lord Grey is not yeatt come, but his fyrst and recende lett^es delyvred and thynges ar all preparead agaynest his arryval.

---

[1] Vere was very chary of his praise, and held himself (says Dudley Carleton in a letter to his friend Chamberlain) *haut à la main* to all his captains, " which breeds a generall discontentment among them." See a letter among *S.P. Holland*, dated Feb. 15, 1600-1, from Captain Calisthenes Brooke to Sir R. Cecil, complaining of ill-usage by Sir F. Vere.

The command of the Inglyshe compagnyes of horse, was in my absence desposead of by the States and the Prince Maurice to Syr Edwarde Cecyll, from whome I founde them unwylling to w^{th}-draw the chardge, and as I loathe to sollicytt agaynst so good a frende and one so worthy of the commande, w^h in regarde he is Captayne of horse doeth belonge more propperly to him then any other. My Lord shall have a Regyment of theas contry horse, and an honorable entretaignmet towardes the defraying of his chardge, more then I have knowne the estates doe for any adventurer, whearin they sheaw theyr care to content her Ma^{ie}; and Monsr de Barnevelt in perticular hath been very forwarde in the mattre. And I hope that my Lord Grey wyll allowe of my endever though he have nott his desyre accomplyshed in every poynt."[1]

The States having collected an army of 20,000 foot and 5,000 horse, of which force 8,000 were English,[2] were anxious that Prince Maurice should again march into Flanders and relieve Ostend. A bold scheme, and one easily planned and carried out on paper, but not so easy in the performing. The Marquis Ambrose Spinola, an Italian nobleman, and brother of Frederick Spinola,[3] a renowned sea commander in the service of the Spaniards, had, with the King of Spain's leave, levied an army of 8,000 men, chiefly in the Duchy of Milan, for service in the Netherlands. " The Marquis arrived," says Bentivoglio, "just at the time when the Archduke stood most in need of such a recruit. Count Maurice was already marched into the field, and with such forces as the United Provinces till then had never had greater. . . . It was thought that his design was to cross through Brabant, and so advance

---

[1] Vere to Sir R. Cecil, May 26, *S. P. Holland*. Lord Grey once entertained hopes of succeeding Sir Francis Vere in his command in the Low Countries. See a letter from Rowland Whyte to Sir R. Sidney, dated from the Court, May 13, 1600.—Collins, ii. p. 194.

[2] J. Chamberlain to Dudley Carleton, at Paris, June 27, 1602.—*S. P. Dom.*

[3] Killed in a sea fight with the Dutch ships, in May, 1603.

forward to the relief of Ostend, and then to besiege Nieuport again."[1]   Whatever Maurice's plans for the coming campaign were, he wisely kept them to himself. After reviewing the most splendid army he ever had, he crossed the Waal at Nimeguen and the Meuse at Mook. From thence he marched by easy stages along the side of the Meuse to Massyck.   Here an unavoidable delay of five days took place, the cause of which was laid to the English troops.   It appears that on arriving at Massyck, it was found, notwithstanding a general order had been issued by Prince Maurice, before taking the field, for the troops to provide themselves with provisions for ten days at least, that the English troops were quite unprovided with food. A halt was therefore obligatory, until the wants of the troops had been supplied.[2]   From Massyck the States' army marched to St. Truyden and the immediate neighbourhood of Thienen,[3] in the very heart of Brabant, and within a day's march of Brussels.

The Archduke had not been idle all this time.   He had sent Mendoza, the Admiral of Arragon,[4] into Brabant, with a force of 6,000 foot and 4,000 horse, to dispute the march of the States' army to Ostend, whither it was believed they were bound.   This force would have been quite inadequate

---

[1] *The Compleat History of the Warrs of Flanders*, by Cardinal Guido Bentivoglio ; translated from the Italian by the Earl of Monmouth, 1654, part iii. p. 408

[2] Gilpin to Sir R. Cecil, June 27, 1602.—*S. P. Holland.*

[3] " The enemy is reckoned 14,000 foot, and between 3 and 4,000 Horse ; they lye in and near Tienen, or Tielmont, intrenched." Sir W. Brown to Sir R. Sidney, undated.—Collins, ii. p. 256.

[4] Francis Mendoza, Admiral of Arragon, who was taken prisoner at Nieuport, had been subsequently released on parole, the sum of his ransom having been fixed at nearly 100,000 Flemish crowns. This ransom was afterwards foregone by the States, with consent of the Nassau family, on condition that the Admiral should effect the exchange of all prisoners of the Republic, then held in durance by Spain in any part of the world.   This humane plan was carried out, and the Admiral returned to Spain.

to cope with Maurice's troops, had not Spinola arrived on the scene with his Italians at this critical juncture. The Archduke having his hands full in besieging Ostend, despatched Spinola with his contingent to the aid of Mendoza, who was marching towards the States' army, "to discover all their designs, and then to disturb them therein as much as he could."[1] When Maurice arrived with his troops near Thienen, he found his old enemy, the Admiral, strongly entrenched and in great force. Not being able to lure the Admiral into risking "a second Nieuport," and not deeming it prudent to attack Mendoza in his present strong position, the cautious Maurice determined to retrace his steps. Why he went, and where he went, after vainly challenging his foe to give him battle, are plainly set forth in Edward Cecil's narrative of this fruitless march.

SIR E. CECIL TO SIR R. CECIL.

" MAY IT PLEASE Y' HON.,

" Hitherto I coulde not conveniently discharge the dutie where unto affection bindeth mee towards y°. Now, finding this present ocation, I will wth a diutefull and humble remembrence of my selfe, acquant y' H. wth the procedinges of our armye. In the marche wee have had towards the ennemy, wherein, though the exploys are not followed according to the common expectation and desier of us all, yet I thinke not unfitt to informe y° therew^{th}, from the 10 of Jun, that our hole forces did meatte at Nemegame, to this presant daye. Before our departure wee were Mustered at Eltem, to the Number of 20,000 foote and 5,000 horse, and commanded to furnishe oure selves, horse, and menn, for 15 dayes provision w^{th}out farther knowledge of the commaunders dessigne, but to marche towards a village caulled Mouke upon the Mase, where a bridge of bootes (caried for that porpose upon wagines) was presently made to pass over the river as if wee had some meaning to the Grave.[2] But our Army beyng passed over

---

[1] Bentivoglio, part iii. p. 408.
[2] A strongly fortified town on the left bank of the Meuse, besieged and taken by Parma in 1856.

the nexte daye wee leaft it wthin 2 houres march at the righte
hand, marching betwixt the mase and the Peel (sic) in 3 divisions,
under the commaunde of his Excelencie the Grave William[1] and
S^r fra Vere, and wth suche a distanc that wthin halfe an hower
warning at any urgeat ocatione, the mighte have joyned all to
gether, having ever in all oure jurny observed hetherto the like
order.   Thus wee did marche 5 dayes towards Masicke,[2] where
our Army was refreshed and relived wth vittalles, by 5 dayes spasse.
There his Excelence understoude by a Trumpitt that the ennemy
was resolved to meat him in the filde, and that to that eande hee
was gathering all the forces hee could.   They 22th wee parted
from Masicke and marched a longe the river Mase, and leving
Maestricke at the leaft hande wee came the 24 before Tongenne[3]
situated upon a smale river cauled Leker,[4] where hering of the
ennemyes forces gathering about diest,[5] the 26th after some releefe
had out of the sade towne, wee bended our way to St. Trudere,[6]
where wee did arive the 27.   There wee had plane information of
the Enemyes forces, wch were far greater then wee did take them
to be, and by reporte very nighe as stronge as wee, beyng 18,000
foote and 5,000 horse, besides there compaines of ordonnances, so
that there cavallerie was stronger then oures.   But knowing where
wth all the were compounded, to witt for the most parte of Bores
pressed (the fation never used before in these partes), and hearing
how the were intreanched by us, in the way wee meant to take
betwxte Laden[7] and loeuve[8] to enter into there Country. The nexte
daye wth a part of our armie wee cam in Battell by there Treanchis,
when wee beatt in there horse, and after 3 howers standing
in Battell, seeyng how unwilling the [they] were to performe there
promise, wch was to meatt us, and howe harde it was to force such
an Enyme in his treanches, wee did retier the same nighte, every-

---

[1] William of Nassau, brother of Count Lewis, who commanded the cavalry
at Nieuport.
[2] Maaseyck, on the left bank of the Meuse, the birthplace of the brothers
Van Eyck.
[3] Tongeren, the Roman *Adriatica Tongri*, formerly the seat of a bishop.
[4] The Lek?   [5] Diest, a fortress of Brabant.
[6] St. Truyden, a small town, now possessing 11,000 inhabitants and 11
churches.
[7] Landen?   [8] Louvain, the Flemish *Leuven*.

one hoping for some other attempt the next day.   But wherefore soever it was wee proceeded no further.   The causes I doe imagine many.   But cheafly the weaknes of many of our menn, hapned by the jurny wee hade thetherto, having suffered noe distres or want of any thing (untill then), amoungst our friendes wch gave to the chefeste to thinke what might happene, when wee shoulde be in the Enemyes lande, w^{th}out any releafe, but that wee should gett by the sworde and a stronge armye continually troubling and molesting us of all sides, wch wee could neither force to fight nor retire, but at his pleasure wth out great inconvenience iminent unto us, and great uncertaintyes of any good succes.   I thinke, in my smalle knowledge, that w^{th}out urgent necessitye it was not fitt wee shoulde proceede any farther, and that a stronger armye then owers might have been brought that way to bee undoune, w^{th}out any great hasarde of the Enymies forces, and that it was better to imploye oure selves in a more likelyer enterprise of less danger and more benifitt neare home, where our wantes mighte bee supplyed at will, then to continue to linger upon the Enemye that hath better meanes to defend and offend then wee had in his owne country.   Other causes may bee alledged of the regresse from our jurny grounded upon some pollicyes that every statesmann maye suspecte, but few that can rightly hitt one them.   But so it is, that 3 dayes after having receaved some new vitalles from the towne of St Truden wee parted the 30th Junne from thence, in suche intemperat wether, for the exceeding heatt, that many of our souldiers fell dead upon the marche,[1] and cam to a villadge cauled Alleken, where wee stayed the neaxte day, thinking perhappes that the enemye, takeng currage upon our suddayne departe, shoulde forsake his treanches to follow us, as he did, but so farr of a side, that there was noe great feare of any parte.   Thus to make it shorte, wth small jurnes, the Cannone, Trompettes and drommes every morning giving warning of our marching like M. of the fealde that feared not the Enymies forces, after the same order wee went ; wee marched back againe the righteste waye to the Grave, where wee ar arived this morning, the 9 of July, wth a resolution to

---

[1] Meteren mentions the many deaths from the great heat in his *L'histoire des Pays-Bas*, art. " Voyage de Prince Maurice en Brabant au moys de Juin et Juillet, 1602."

beseage the Towne. And thus Fearing that in striving for y^r good opineone, I shall be counted indiscreat amongst so many that doth advertis y° at this tyme, more nigher y^r satisfactione, onely I presume y° wille looke over my weaknes and settell y^r judgement, upon my unfaned desier I have to serve y°. And so in hast out of the littell leasure a pore horse mann hath, I reas[t] in all humilety

> " Y H. most fathfull and affectionat
> " servant as much a[s] nephew,
>   " Ed Cecyll.

" from the leager before the Grave, this 9 of July."[1]

Add. " To the R. Ho. S^r Ro. Cecyll, Prinsepall Scecritary of Eingland.

End. " July, 1602, S^r Ed. Cecill."

Thus ended the " Brabant expedition," from which so much had been expected, and which ended—as great expectations often do end—in smoke. Amongst the many who were disappointed at the ill success of this expedition, was the choleric Elizabeth of England—the firm ally and supporter of the United Provinces. Her disapproval of the cautious Maurice's tactics has been handed down to us by Sir William Browne, the Deputy-Governor of Flushing, who came over to England in the summer of 1602 ; and in one of his letters to Sir R. Sidney, dated from London, 12th Aug.,[2] he gives an interesting account of his interview with Elizabeth :—

---

[1] *Cecil Papers, Hatfield*, 94/15.

[2] This letter is given by Collins in his *Sidney Papers*, ii. but is quite erroneously given under the date of " August, 1601," whereas the interview took place in August, 1602. The mistaken date of this historical letter is very apparent on a close examination of its contents. In the first place, Sir W. Browne was not in England in August, 1601. Among the *S. P. Holland* are letters from him to Sir R. Sidney, dated from " Flushing, August 10 and 11th, 1601." Then again, Sir W. Brown mentions in his letter from England, of " July 7, 1602," that, " My Lady Anne is still very weak," and in the letter which Collins, and other historians, copying from him, have given

"She discoursed of many things," wrote Sir W. Browne, "and particularly of the distaste she had of the States' army returning. It seems that Sir Francis Vere hath lain all the fault upon Count Maurice. I said that 'Count Maurice did protest that this journey was never of his plotting'—'Tush! Brown,' saith she, 'I know more than thou dost. When I heard,' continued the queen, 'that they were at first with their army as high as Nemighem,[1] I knew no good would be done ; but Maurice would serve his own turn, and would, in the end, turn to the Grave.[2] I looked that they should have come down nearer to Ostend or Flanders. That might have startled the enemy, and that they promised me, or else I would not have let them have so many men, to the discontentment of my subjects, as I know, and which, but for the love they bear me, they would not so well digest; and now, forsooth, Maurice is come from his weapon to his spade, for at that he is one of the best in Christendom.'"

It was not to be expected that Maurice would be allowed to reduce the city of Grave without a determined effort on the Archduke's side to relieve the place. It was not long, therefore, before the Admiral of Arragon with a large force, officered by such men as Ambrose Spinola (whose name will be frequently mentioned in this work), Spina, and Simon Antonio, marched to Ruremonde, on the Meuse, and from thence went to Venlo. Having provided his troops with provisions and all necessaries, which were brought up the river to Venlo, the Admiral marched to Grave. When near the camp of the besieging army, the Admiral ordered an attack to be made on his enemy's

---

under the date of "August 12, 1601," Sir W. Brown tells Sir R. Sidney, " My lady Anne mends very well." If other proofs are wanted, they will be found in the Queen's conversation, given in above extract.

[1] Nimeguen, the rendezvous of the States' troops.

[2] Miss Strickland, who gives this letter in her *Queens of England*, under the date of 1601, takes the word " Grave " to mean "landgrave !" and thus entirely destroys the Queen's reference to *the siege of the Grave* by Prince Maurice, iii. p. 558.

quarters. He directed Spina, with 1,000 Italians, to make an attack on one side of the camp, and sent his camp-master, Simon Antonio, with 1,000 Spanish foot to ensure Spina's retreat. At the same time he ordered the Marquis Spinola to march with 2,000 foot against the opposite quarter, and make a feigned attack, to draw the enemy's attention from the quarter attacked by Spina. The attacks were made simultaneously, and both failed. Maurice had made such good use of his spade that his intrenchments were not to be easily carried, and the Admiral retreated in despair.

It was about this time that Sir Francis Vere was badly wounded in the face,[1] and obliged to leave the camp. For some time it was feared his wound would prove fatal, and Sir Robert Sidney,[2] who went to watch the siege operations before Grave, the end of August, begged Sir Robert Cecil to use his interest in obtaining for him Vere's command, if it became vacant by that commander's death.[3] The garrison of Grave seem to have made a brave resistance against their foes; but what could a small garrison do against so large a besieging force, well victualled, well disciplined, and commanded by a leader, whose patience and tenacity of purpose were not to be equalled in Europe. After a sixty days' siege the inevitable result came, and Grave capitulated. The garrison marched out with the honours of war, and the inhabitants had the same fair and

---

[1] "Upon Thursday last, towards noon, Sir Francis Vere, being in the approaches to see the worcks advanced, receaved a muskett shott under the right ey. The bullett went towards the eare and there doth stick. The wound is thought dangerous."—Sir R. Sidney to Sir R. Cecil, Aug. 15, 1602. —*S. P. Holland.*

[2] Younger brother of Sir Philip Sidney. He acquired renown in the Netherlands under his uncle, the Earl of Leicester, and afterwards under Sir F. Vere. Was Governor of Flushing for some years. King James I. created him Baron Sidney in 1603 and Earl of Leicester in 1618.

[3] Sir R. Sidney to Sir R. Cecil, Aug. 26.—*S. P. Holland.*

honourable terms that Maurice always granted on capturing
a town. The following letter from Edward Cecil, who
served at this siege, is interesting, from the fact that it
mentions the flooded state of Prince Maurice's camp.

SIR E. CECIL TO SIR R. CECIL.[1]

" MAY IT PLEASE Y[r] HO.,

" I have receaved y[r] most kinde and favorable letter, wherein it hath pleased y[r] Ho. booth to lett mee know that my Brother
is returned wth that honore, that y° promised mee to doe for him ;
And that I am most bound to y[r] Ho. for the w[ch] I will never be
unthankfull.

" I am most assured y[r] Ho. wantes noe intellygence, and that
myne shall onely serve to showe my diutye ; wherefore I will not
doubte to lett y[r] Ho. knowe, that wee parled upon the 9 of this
month, w[th] the Enemye, and the neaxte day the marched out, w[ch]
made our seage just 2 monthes ; the had all honorable compositione, and a convoye to wayt upon them ; w[th] all, the deserved
well, for if the had but keepd [kept] it 3 dayes longer, wee shoulde
have swme in our Treanches, or have risone w[th]out the Towne, for
al our workes ar over flone, so wee ar drivene out of our quarters
w[th] water, w[ch] will be the occatione that wee goe in to Garisone the
sooner. For now, at this instant, wee ar be twxte going to
Garison or to goe fighte w[th] the Enemye, that ar miended to
beseage there owne mutiners, that lighye [lie] nighe Breadaw,
onder his Excelences favoure, w[ch] Mutinars have offered them
selves (w[ch] ar some 1500 horse and 2000 foote) to serve the states.
But wee ar jeleus to intertayne so great numbers that hath beeyne
our enimes, and fantasticall heades, ungoverned, so that the shall
be much favored and difended, and shall rather lighe upone the
Contry, then in danger any of oure Garisons.[2] And thus hoping

---

[1] *Cecil Papers, Hatfield,* No. 64.
[2] This mutiny amongst the Archduke's troops is described by Motley
(quoting from Meteren, Bentivoglio and Grotius) as " the most extensive, formidable, and methodical of all that had hitherto occurred in the Spanish armies.
The mutineers had seized the city of Hoogstraten, which they strongly fortified,
and levied black mail from the whole country round. Being strong in numbers,
and united among themselves, the mutineers were able to defy the Archduke.
They laughed at his menaces and attempts to subdue them, and when he, in

y^r Ho. will accepe the desier I have to be in y^r favoure, then any
desert in mee, I eand, but never [end] to praye for y^r Ho. longe
and happie life, wch will make happie

        "Y^r Ho. most affectionat and diutefull
        "Nephue and servant,

                                "ED. CECYLL.

"from the Grave, this 14 of September, Sti. Antico."

    Add. "To the Rig. Ho. S^r Ro. Cecyll, Knight, Prinsepale
        Scecritary of Eingland."

    End. "1602. September 14. Sr Edward Cecyll to my M^r."

Grave was taken, but the taking it had cost the lives of
many brave soldiers.[1] Disease—that dreaded camp-
follower—which visits alike the tent of the general and
the private soldier, had claimed more victims among the
States' troops than the bullets and swords of the garrison
had done. It is one of the saddest sequences of war, that
disease, which comes like a thief in the night, should strike
the soldier down in the very hour of victory, when the toils
of the campaign are over, and well-earned rewards and
rest are awaiting him at home. The flooded state of Prince
Maurice's camp, and the exhalations from a badly drained

---

right of his rank as ex-Archbishop of Toledo, excommunicated them with bell,
book and candle in a thundering manifesto, they replied in a denunciatory
manifesto also, which was more true than polite. After this they made overtures to Maurice of Nassau, who gave them leave to take refuge under the
guns of Bergen-op-zoom, should they be hard pressed.—*Motley*, iv. pp. 93–97.
    [1] At a review of the troops by Prince Maurice, on Sept. 21, the following
English and Scotch companies were present, in the strength given after their
names, viz. : The troops of horse of Vere, 78 ; Cecil, 77 ; Darel, 70. Foot
companies of Garnet, 66 ; D. Vere, 63 ; Proud, 76 ; Drury, 73 ; W. Love-
lace, 82 ; Rogers, 44 ; Greville, 54 ; Fairfax, 70 ; Ridgway, 77 ; Ogle, 104 ;
Doyley, 54 ; Woodhouse, 85 ; Wroth, 75 ; Fryer, 50 ; W. Crofts, 89 ; Frost,
59 ; Alleyne, 55 ; H. Vere, 111 ; Sutton, 77 ; Stoddart, 79 ; Carew, 65 ;
Cecil, 79 ; Knollys, 61 ; Harcourt, 78 ; Ed. Vere, 79 ; Wigmore, 64 ;
Vavasour, 67 ; Drake, 89 ; Cokayne, 40 ; Richards, 61 ; Butler, 65 ; Morgan,
56 ; Congreve, 66 ; Fr. Crofts, 64 ; Dutton, 69 ; Edmonds, 160 ; Brogh,
120 ; Henderson, 100 ; Sinclair, 94 : Balfour, 116.—A. Duyck's *Journal*,
iii. p. 482.

country, lower than the level of the sea, during an unusually hot summer, brought on a sickness among the soldiers which "was little better than the plague." [1] The English troops suffered severely, and lost some of their bravest officers. "Many captains are dead in the Low Countries," wrote Chamberlain to Carleton, "as Lile, Clifford, Keyes, Richards, Vavasor, Deacons, Crofts, Drake, and above 4,000 of the 6,000 men that last went over." [2] The same writer also tells us that "Mrs. Bodley has lost her eldest son, Captain Ball, by sickness in the Low Countries," [3] and that "Graf Maurice has been dangerously ill of the plague, the sore breaking out in his neck." [4] George Gilpin, the English Resident at the Hague, died of an ague, in September, at the Hague ; and Sir Robert Drury left the country, while Grave was being besieged, in impaired health. [5] Edward Cecil was fortunate enough to escape the general sickness. We find him ordered on active service again in the month of October, and in command of three troops of horse, which were part of a small force sent on 23d of October to Emden, under the command of Du Bois, a gentleman of Brabant. This force was to help the people of Emden against their tyrannic ruler, Enno, Count of East Friesland.

It appears that this Count Enno, who was a devoted adherent of the Roman Catholic religion, had, under the pretence of aiding the Emperor of Germany in his Turkish wars, raised troops, and imposed heavy taxes on his subjects,—notably one called "chimney money." The

---

[1] Grimston's *Netherlands*, p. 1281.
[2] Chamberlain to Carleton, Nov. 4, 1602.—*S. P. Dom.*
[3] *Ibid.* Oct. 2, 1602.   [4] *Ibid.*
[5] Sir Robert Drury, writing from Paris on Sept. 28 of this year to Sir R. Cecil, says he was detained there " to recover a sickness taken in our fruitless Brabant journey," and obliged to defer his hopes of the baths in Italy till the spring.—*S. P. Dom.*

Count's subjects bitterly resented these taxes, and the citizens of Noorden, a town not far from Emden, refused to install him as their Prince in 1602. In consequence of this refusal, Enno marched there with his troops, took the town, and made the inhabitants pay him 3,000 Rix dollars. He also imposed a tax of five years' "chimney money" on them, and caused the burghers to walk under the gallows "in sign that they had deserved it." Not content with this indignity to the worthies of Noorden, the Count treated the townspeople very cruelly, and threatened to do the same to the citizens of Emden. The Emdeners sent a deputation to the United Provinces, begging for the assistance of the States in their internal troubles. They made it clear to the States-General that Enno had some enterprise in hand for the King of Spain or the Archduke. This consideration induced the States to send some companies of soldiers to Emden in June.[1] During the siege of Grave fresh deputations from Emden arrived in Prince Maurice's camp, soliciting further aid. Grave being taken, and the United Provinces having been informed that Count Enno had fortified Hinta and other villages which commanded the river Ems, and was in league with the Spaniards, whose presence at Emden, and on the borders of Friesland, was very undesirable and prejudicial to the safety of the United Provinces, the States-General determined to send a small force to Emden, to put a stop to the Count's designs against that place, and restore order. Anthony Duyck gives a short account in his *Journal* of the despatch of troops to Emden. The following extracts [2] are all that it is necessary to give :—

---

[1] "The States have put 1200 men into Emden during the jars between the Count and the town."—Chamberlain to Carleton, June 17.—*S. P. Dom.*

[2] Translated from A. Duyck's *Journal*, iii. p. 497.

"On the 23ᵈ of October Captain DuBois was in the Hague. His Excellency spent a considerable time at the State Council, and afterwards also in the States-General, to settle DuBois's share in the conduct of the wars. Twelve companies of foot were to be marched into Friesland, six of these were to be commanded by van Brog, and six by van Calvort. The six stationed at Emden, together with the three companies, which the town had undertaken to provide for, were to remain under the command of the chief-lieutenant of the Frisians, who was on the spot. Besides these the three troops of cavalry of Cissel, Ripperda, and Hasse Brun were sent thither, under the command of Cissel. DuBois was everywhere to command as General-in-chief. It was further agreed that DuBois, on his arrival at Emden, should apply to the town for orders and carry on the war in their name; that he should try to prevent the Count from completing the fortifications, and, if possible, to pull down the works already begun. He was ordered not to plunder or molest the farmers or to force them to flee from their homes, but to levy from them a light contribution. He was also to impose a war tax, to be paid at the town, on so many villages, as to be able to support the army permanently. But in all this he was to use discretion, so that no disgrace or blame might redound to the States through it. If he had to attack any fortified places, and if the town of Emden could not supply him with the amount of cannon required, he was to send for some guns from Friesland. Lastly, he was in all things to take counsel with the deputies of the States that were to accompany him to Emden."

" 4th Nov.

"At Emden General DuBois found provisions and many things not ready. Notwithstanding this he left the town this morning with 19 companies of foot (comprising the 3 companies of the town) and one troop of horse; leaving behind the chief-lieutenant Hettinga with his company, the company of Frans Gerrits, and half the company of van Koorput with the cavalry of Cicil and Ripperda. DuBois marched to a small redoubt at Hinte. From this small redoubt the Count's men fired about 40 shots from small field pieces (*pedereros*), and then left it in hot

H 2

haste. After having occupied the redoubt, DuBois put up for the
night at *Hinte in t'dorp*, where he forthwith began to make some
approaches to the Castle, and put in position two batteries that
same night.

"On the 5th of Nov^r, DuBois opened fire on the Castle early
in the morning. After a few shots the captain in command,
Haen, began to parley. He agreed to surrender the Castle, and
not to serve in the district of Emden for two months on condition
of a free pass for him and his men with their muskets. Here-
upon he marched forth with about 100 men, leaving behind the
rest of their arms and the colours, which were taken to Emden."[1]

Count Enno, who had 4,000 men under his command,
advanced as far as Grevenraeth, in the district of Juliers,
but did not show any disposition to give battle to DuBois,
who, after taking Hinte, laid siege to the fort of Grietziel,
the garrison of which compounded with the States' troops.
The fort of Knocke likewise was yielded up, and Loghen-
horne, which was garrisoned by 700 men and strong in
guns, only stood a few days' siege, and then capitulated on
13th November. Having taken all these forts in three
weeks, DuBois returned to Emden, where he was joyfully
received. The United Provinces informed the electors
and princes of the German Empire that their only object
in making war on Count Enno, was to help the people of
Emden against their oppressor, and at the same time to
secure their own borders, as the Count of East Friesland
was in league with the Spaniards.[2]

It is evident from A. Duyck's *Journal*, that Edward
Cecil was left with his troop of horse in garrison at Emden,
while DuBois was reducing the enemy's forts in the
vicinity. We must leave Cecil at Emden for the present,

---

[1] Pp. 502–503.
[2] Grimston's *Netherlands*, p. 1294.

and turn to a tragedy, which took place a few months after this, in England.

This tragedy was the death of Queen Elizabeth, which took place at Richmond Palace on March 24th, 1602-3. And what a sad death it was ! History records many sad deaths of English monarchs, but few, if any of them, were more melancholy than that of the mighty Elizabeth Tudor, Queen of England and Ireland, defender of the faith, protectress of the United States of the Netherlands, patroness of Shakespeare and Spencer, and the most erudite princess of her day. Remorse, wounded vanity, and sullen despair, were the three attendants at the death-bed of the greatest Queen in Christendom. Remorse was there to keep alive the memory of the unfortunate Earl of Essex ; wounded vanity was the result of the dying Queen's having beheld her natural face in a natural looking-glass, and sullen despair came to haunt the last hours of the last of the Tudors, when she knew many of her courtiers were only waiting for her last sigh to transfer their worship to the son of her murdered kinswoman. For days the mighty Elizabeth lay on the floor of her chamber,

"longing, yet afraid to die,"

until exhausted nature brought death and rest. And so the once glorious sun of the Virgin Queen set in darkness and gloom, and the rising sun, in the person of James Stuart, King of Scots, was hailed with joy by a people who only too soon might have exclaimed :

"But now we've got a worse instead,
For seldom comes a better."

CHAPTER V.

1603-1609.

Two Monarchs—Anglo-French treaty—Court pickings—Grant to Sir Edward
Cecil—Siege of Ostend—Sir F. Vere's retirement—Suitors for colonels—
Invasion of Flanders—Siege of Sluys—Difficulties—Ambrose Spinola—
Maurice's good fortune—He besieges Fort St. Catherine—Lurking bogs—
Retreat turned into victory—Further successes—Isendike invested—The
Spanish mutineers—Spanish attack on Cadsand—Result—Maurice captures
Isendike and Aardenburg—Action at Dam—English bravery—Sluys
invested—The States' ironclad—Details of the siege of Ostend—The
"owldeste Captayne"—Surrender of Sluys—Sickness—Medals—English
treaty of peace with Spain—Sir Edward Cecil made Colonel of an English
regiment—Spinola's tactics—His march to Friesland—Retrograde move-
ment—Action at Broek Castle—Cavalry panic—Bravery of Sir Horace
Vere—Maurice retreats—Lord Salisbury's letter to his nephew—Sir F.
Vere returns to Holland—His letters—Attempt to surprise Sluys—Spinola's
plan for invading Holland—Counter plans—Siege of Groll—Surrender—
Siege of Rhineberg—Maurice arrives at Wesell—Colonel Cecil's redoubt—
His letter to Sidney—Maurice's supineness—Surrender of Rhineberg—
Mutiny — Maurice besieges Groll — Unexpected arrival of Spinola —
Declining to fight—A twelve months' truce—Peace negotiations—Colonel
Cecil's ambition—His letters home—Peace—Sir F. Vere's death—Lord
Exeter's request.

" HE naturally loved not the sight of a soldier nor of
any valiant man." [1]
This character of James I., King of England, is given by
Sir Anthony Weldon, the most scurrilous writer of that
reign, but it is painfully true nevertheless. No one can read
any account of the reign of this Monarch without perceiving
what an enemy he was to all things military. However
odious comparisons may be, it is impossible not to remark

---

[1] *Memoirs of the reigns of Queen Elizabeth, James I., &c.*, by Francis Osborne,
ii. p. 6.

on the extraordinary difference between the rulers of
France and Great Britain in 1603. Henry—justly surnamed the Great—was a soldier, born and bred, who
delighted in wars and rumours of wars—a man who was
as much at home in a palace as in a camp, and who understood the language of the deepest diplomatists as well as he
knew the weak point in his enemy's defences, or the vulner-
able part in a woman's heart. James, the head of a
small but mighty nation, was a scholar and an author, in
whose veins flowed the blood of a line of Kings whose
bravery was to be as much admired as their impolitic and
reckless actions were to be deprecated. Yet was this
King's blood chill in his veins, and so sluggish withal, that
he never let the bonds of friendship, family ties, or popular
feeling, lead him into espousing the weaker cause. His
caution and weakness of character were in themselves his
safest foreign policy, as no wrongs to his subjects, or insults
to himself, could force him into a war. Such was the man
whom the Protestant Netherlanders had to look to for
support when the great Elizabeth was summoned to her
rest.

After making the above remarks, it is almost needless to
say that England's new monarch was unwilling to continue
the policy of his predecessor with regard to assisting the
United Provinces in their struggle against the Spaniards,
and yet he could not absolutely renounce Queen Elizabeth's
policy. " There were pledges he could not break—interests
which he could not neglect." [1] The British troops serving
in the Netherlands being paid by the States, and the officers
having their commissions direct from the States-General,[2]

---

[1] Ranke's *History of England*, i. p. 389.
[2] " All the English Captens have their Commissions direct from the States,
and are sworn to them." Sir W. Browne to Sir R. Sidney, 29 Nov., 1602.—*S. P.
Holland.*

James was quite sätisfied to let them stay there, particularly as the cautionary towns were mortgaged to the English nation, and had English governors. Soon after the accession of James to the English throne, the French King sent the Marquis de Rosny[1] on a special mission to England. The States also sent Barneveld and some of their greatest men to London about the same time. The special object of both these Embassies was to obtain the alliance of England against their common enemy—Spain. It was entirely owing to the subtle diplomacy of the French Ambassador that James agreed to enter into an offensive and defensive alliance with France and the United Provinces. It was arranged that the Spaniards were to be driven out of the Netherlands, and the House of Austria crushed. A treaty to this effect was duly signed and ratified by the Monarchs of France and England ;[2] and Barneveld, with the States' deputies, returned home, well pleased with the result of their mission.[3] It will be seen presently how this treaty was kept.

In all countries, and in all ages, a new *régime* has been looked forward to by those gentlemen of fortune who, having nothing to lose, and everything to gain, by a change of dynasties, run a fair chance of pushing their fortunes on in the world, when an incoming ruler made a clean sweep of all the appointments that lay in his gift. Now, as formerly, selfishness and self-advancement make many welcome a change for the worse, provided that they them-

---

[1] Maximilian de Bethune, Marquis of Rosny, Prime Minister to Henry IV., was afterwards created Duke of Sully.

[2] Sully's *Memoirs*, Eng. edit. 1756, ii., p. 233.

[3] The States' deputies got permission to levy a regiment in Scotland for service in the Low Countries. "His Ma^{ty} hath been pleased to assent to the leavying of the new Regiment in Scotland, for wch purpose there is order already gone to the Lord of Bucklugh, who is to command them." Sir R. Cecil to Winwood, Aug. 12, 1603.—*S. P. Holland.*

selves are no losers by the said change. The interests of country, and the welfare of the plurality of their country-men are quite forgotten by these self-seekers in their own snug shelter, from the security of which they can watch, with a callous indifference, the ravages the storm makes on their native shore.

The accession of the Scottish monarch to the English throne caused the greatest rejoicings in England. The new King's progress to London would have been the most triumphant of triumphant marches, with a never-ending series of costly pageants and entertainments, so dear to the Tudors, who reaped the glory of them, and left all the expense to their loving subjects ; but the sixth Stuart hated crowds and shows, so he issued a proclamation, for-bidding the resort of people on the pretence of the scarcity of provisions.[1] This damper to the loyalty of an en-thusiastic populace, coupled with the King's ungainly and uncourteous manners, which were so different to the "company manners" of good Queen Bess, caused a revulsion of feeling, and James had pretty well lost his popularity, even before his arrival in London.[2] In order to ingratiate himself with his new subjects, James bestowed the cheap honour of knighthood with an unsparing hand. It is stated that within three months after his entrance into the kingdom he had bestowed knighthood on no fewer than 700 persons. Knighthood had been considered a high honour in Elizabeth's reign, she having been very sparing in bestowing that honour, but now men rather avoided than courted the distinction. All titles, indeed, soon lost their former value, as they were not only bestowed in profusion, and in many cases on such unworthy recipients, but they were sold to those who wished to buy them. The

---

[1] Hume's *History of England*, iv. p. 379.   [2] *Ibid.*

prodigality of James was even worse than the parsimony of Elizabeth, for the English saw their titles, estates, and coveted posts bestowed on Scotchmen (foreigners, in their eyes), and they longed for that happy medium course—the " golden mean," which the poet Horace recommends to us— which so few of us ever meet with, but which all who have experienced the extremes of fortune, long and sigh after. Those who came off worst in the general rush for honours and court pickings were military men, for James " naturally loved not the sight of a soldier nor of any valiant man." There being nothing much on the military *tapis* in the Netherlands, in the spring of 1603, excepting the siege of Ostend, which was prosecuted with unabated vigour, the English officers in the service of the United Provinces were able to come over to England to pay their homage to their new Monarch. It does not appear when Sir Edward Cecil came over to England, but he was probably in England most of the year 1603. His uncle, and kind patron, Sir Robert Cecil, was high in favour with King James, and was intrusted with the chief management of the affairs of the nation. The immediate family, and some of the near relatives, of Sir Robert Cecil came in for a few of the posts which the King had in his gift. Sir Edward Cecil was given the grant for life of the office of Keeper of Mortlake Park, Co. Surrey[1], and it appears, from the following letter, that E. Cecil had been appointed a gentleman of His Majesty's Privy Chamber.[2] He also had the honour of being elected Member of Parliament for

---

[1] *Ind. Wt. Bk. S. P. Dom.* p. 21.

[2] I can find no reference to this appointment in any of the State papers or records of that time. Nicholas Carlisle, in his *Gentlemen of the Privy Chamber*, says that James I. took away the salaries of the Gentlemen of the Privy Chamber, "leaving them nothing but Honour, except Diet when in waiting." (p. 90). In 1616 they numbered 24 in number. M. S. *Soc[y] of Antiquaries*, No. 40.

Stamford[1] (his native town), in the first Parliament of
James I., which met at Westminster on March 19th,
1603-4.

SIR E. CECIL TO LORD CECIL.[2]

" MAY IT PLEASE Y[r] LO.,

" I can not chuse, but interrupe y[r] lo. wth my letters (all thouge
I muche reverence y[r] great affares), beyng urged oute of my
diutyfull respecte not to lett my affectione lie in mee still, considering it in creaseth in mee howerly.   And the frute it bringeth
forthe is my harty prayers for y[r] happines.   I have desiered it
longe, and doe desiere to wittnes it wth my beaste bloude, not for
any eande of my profitt, for then woulde I not have followed the
warres wth that desier I doe, w[ch] I ever founde rather to gratte, of
my owne fortune, then make mee better to leve by them.   But
nowe that my love to them is in curraged by y[r] lo. favoure I will
imbrase them, as a true meanes to deserve y[r] good opineone.   I
can not saye to y[r] lo. that I am a Coronell; nor have I receaved
any deniall of the states, in claming my diue as beyng one of there
owldeste Captaynes of our nattione that have continued there
servis ; yet doe I fiende the will make some delaye to showe there
love to our Generall S[r] Francis Vere, w[ch], if it woulde please y[r] lo.
to wryte to M[r] Winwode, to knowe there answere, woulde make
mee moste bounde to y[r] lo. and make my good hope tourne to
happines, of that I looke for.   I have noe resone to looke for more
favoure from y[r] lo. ; yet I hope y[r] lo. will have an honerable care
of mee, that my desier to make mee more able to serve the Kinge
shall not be any cause to make mee lease my place in the Privi-
chambere, w[ch] I howld rather for my grase heare, and my reputatione there, then for any other care.

" For any nwes heare I take it neadless to advertis y[r] lo. of that
y[o] may knowe allredy, that is of the extremitye where in
ostende is at this Instante reducted, beyng out of hope to be
defended any longer, the Enymie beyng redye to pass the Diche,

---

[1] Stamford returned two Members in this Parliament, viz., "Henry Hall,
Esq., and Sir Ed. Cecil." *Parliamentary History*, i. p. 973.
· [2] Sir Robert Cecil had been created Baron Cecil of Essendine, C[o] Rutland,
May 13, 1603.

yet the States doe sende in some 40 companies more then there is, rather to make a good compositione, for those that are wth in, the laste worke the Enymie tooke in of owers, the did put them all to the sworde,[1] that was in it to make the reast be the soner quitted. Wee have loste two Governers[2] of that towne, as y[r] lo. knoweth. And the danger of ostende doth make many of the Zelandars flye booth from flushing and middelborrowe, a pase. Wee make many proffers of risinge, as thoughe wee woulde doe some great enterprise, but I rather thincke the ar pollices to cause the Enemie to devide his forces, and to drawe in leangth the losse of ostend; wth out any furder truble of y[r] lo. I will eande the presente wth my diutefull remembrance unto y[r] lo. And beseache the All mightye to be stowe and continue all those favours one y[e] that can be wished by

" Y[r] lo. unfaned and most diutefull servant, as well as nephue,

" ED. CECYLL.

" from the Hge, the 30th of March, 1604, oulde style. "[3]

Add. " To the Rig. Honorable the Lo. Cecyll, Barone of Essendine, and one of his Ma[u] most Honorable Counsell."

End. " 30 March, 1603, Sir Edward Cecyll to my Lord, from the Haghe."

Ralph Winwood, the English Resident at the Hague, gives the following military news in a letter to Dudley Carleton, written at this time :—

" S[r] Francis Vere hath this last weeke surrendred his charges in the States' hands. Their resolution is not to bestow the title of General upon any other of our nation, neth[r] will they sodainly

---

[1] On April 2, when the Polder ravelin was taken.
[2] These were, the gallant Colonel Peter van Gieselles and Colonel John van Loom, who both met soldiers' deaths.
[3] *Cecil Papers, Hatfield*, 99/70.
[4] Letter dated March 21, 1603-4, and addressed "To my very loving freind Mr. Dudley Carleton, give thease at Essex house." *S. P. Holland.* Winwood's pay as Resident'[is given in the following warrant. "Warrant to pay 40/- per diem to Ralph Winwood, sent to the United Provinces as Councillor for the King in the Council of State. June 5, 1603. Greenwich."

resolve how the troopes shalbe bestowed. S' Horace shall have power to commaund over them all, as heretofore he hath donne in th' absence of his brother, untill they otherwise shall advise, wch perhaps wilbe about michel^{mas}, or the next spring, in regard whereof they have dobled his ent^{r}taynem^{t} from 30^{li} to 60^{li} [£60] the moneth. The company of horse wch S' frances hath likewise resigned the states are desyrous he styll shoulde retayne; but yf he shall refuse that, they have conf^{rr}ed that upon his brother. Here are sutors for Collonels: S' Ed. Cecyll, who hath brought over wth him his lady,[1] S' John Ogle, and Cap^{n} Sutton, who is Lieutenant-Collonel to S' Horace Vere."

The States having determined about this time[2] to re-model their army by forming regiments, which were to be composed of a certain number of companies, united together under a colonel, the senior captains naturally looked forward to obtaining these few coveted commands, and used all their interest when "agitating" for promotion.

It had been definitely settled by the States-General in the spring of this year, that Prince Maurice should lead another invading army into Flanders and strike a blow for the relief of Ostend. This projected step was mainly owing to the advice of the warlike Henry IV., who kept urging the States to seize the Flemish ports, "that they might have something to place as pledges in his hands when he declared war against Spain." It was arranged that a large force should be sent against Sluys—a strongly fortified and important seaport between Cadsand and Bruges, on an arm of the sea. Sluys had been taken by the Spaniards in 1587, after a desperate siege, and had continued ever since in their possession. It was a larger—.

---

[1] This was doubtless the first time Edward Cecil had brought his wife to Holland. Their eldest child, Dorothy Cecil, was born in England. Their second child, Albinia Cecil, was born in Holland, probably about 1604.

[2] Regiments do not appear to have been formed by the States until 1605, and even then the word *regiment* is seldom met with in letters and documents.

and in many respects a more important—place than Ostend. Maurice of Nassau, the commander-in-chief of the States' forces, ordered all his forces to meet him at Willemstad[1] on April 20th. An army of 15,000 foot and 3,000 horse met there, and Counts William, Ernest, Lewis and Adolphus of Nassau accompanied Prince Maurice and his brother Henry Frederick, general of the horse, on this expedition. Maurice had also insisted that a considerable deputation of the States and of the States' Council should accompany the army.[2] On April 25th the whole army sailed for the island of Cadsand, opposite Sluys, where they effected a landing. In two days they had taken possession of the town and all the forts of that island,[3] thus securing an admirable basis of operations before laying siege to Sluys. The siege and capture of Sluys by Maurice of Nassau, form one of the most glorious chapters in the military history of this great commander. No one can read the graphic account by Motley of the difficulties that beset an army besieging Sluys, without fully estimating the military talent of Prince Maurice and the bravery of the besieging army. A short extract about Sluys from the above author will be very applicable at this point.

" A stream of inland water, rising a few leagues to the south of Sluys, divided itself into many branches just before reaching the city, converted the surrounding territory into a miniature archipelago— the islands of which were shifting, treacherous sand-banks at low water, and submerged ones at flood—and then widening and deepening into a considerable estuary, opened for the city a capacious harbour, and an excellent altho' intricate passage to the sea. The city, which was well built and thriving, was so hidden in its

---

[1] A fortress with walls and ramparts, erected by William the Silent in 1583, situated on the *Hollandsch Diep*, as this broad arm of the Maas is called.

[2] Motley, iv. p. 188.

Triumphs of Nassau, art. " Siege of Sluys."

labyrinth of canals and streamlets, that it seemed almost as difficult a matter to find Sluys, as to conquer it. . . . . Besides these natural defences, the place was also protected by fortifications, which were as well constructed as the best of that period. There was a strong rampire and many towers. There was also a detached citadel of great strength looking towards the sea ; and there was a ravelin, called St. Anne's, looking in the direction of Bruges. A mere riband of dry land in that quarter was all of solid earth to be found in the environs of Sluys.[1] . . . . . To master such a plexus of canals, estuaries and dykes, of passages through swamps, of fords at low water which were obliterated at flood tide ; to take possession of a series of redoubts, built on the only firm points of land, with nothing but quaking morass over which to manœuvre troops or plant batteries against them, would be a difficult study, even upon paper. To accomplish it in the presence of a vigilant and anxious foe seemed bewildering enough."[2]

The vigilant and anxious foe was Ambrose Spinola,[3] who, though engaged heart and soul in reducing Ostend— which still held out, though reduced to a pile of ruins, which covered the bones of thousands of its brave defenders— still had time to keep an eye on Sluys and send succours to its assistance. To make that town more difficult of access than nature had already made it, Spinola submerged the country in the vicinity, thus destroying the fair landmarks that Maurice had to guide him. Fortune favours those brave hearts who woo her, and once more she placed the clue to success in Maurice's hand, which he at once availed

---

[1] Motley, ii. p. 248. Dante, in his *Inferno* (xv. 4–6), compares the barrier which separates the river of tears from the desert with the embankments which the Flemings have thrown up between Sluys (or rather the island of Cadsand) and Bruges, to protect the city against the encroachments of the sea.

[2] Motley, iv. p. 190.

[3] Ambrose Spinola, Marquis of Benaffro, Knight of the Order of the Golden Fleece, Councillor of State and War to the King of Spain, and General of his armies in the Netherlands. He was created Duke of Sanseverino when Ostend surrendered.

himself of. A friendly boor offered to guide him and his army through the watery waste, and point out passages where he could cross the waters.[1] On April 28th, the army escorted by the Flemish boor advanced towards Oostburg. "Next morning," says Motley, "a small force of the enemy's infantry and cavalry was seen, showing that there must be foothold in that direction. He sent out a few companies to skirmish with those troops, who fled after a very brief action, and, in flying, showed their pursuers the road." Here was the clue which Prince Maurice wanted. Where troops had come from troops could go, and the States' forces were soon on the road to Sluys. Their progress, however, was soon stopped by the fort of St. Catherine—one of the strongest and best garrisoned of the forts, which guarded Sluys like sentinels. Owing to its position, on what was even at low tide a quaking bog, there was no possibility of establishing batteries. Nine field pieces had been sent for, and brought from Cadsand, by water at high tide, but it was found impossible to plant them. Even the stout heart of the heroic Maurice failed him at the prospect before him, and he ordered a retreat. Now occurred one of those strange accidents—one of those curiosities of war—which occasionally happen, and, when they do, turn the tide of war in quite a different direction to what was at first anticipated. It is recorded by Fleming, the chronicler of Ostend, that the States' artillerymen made such an outcry in the darkness of night, when trying to drag their guns over the morass, where they ran no small risk of losing them for ever, that the garrison of St. Catherine's fort, composed chiefly of irregular troops, were seized with a sudden panic, and evacuated their stronghold under cover of the darkness. Fear, which is

---

[1] Fleming, p. 585, quoted by Motley, p. 190.

more infectious than the most virulent plague, often assumes strange forms and gives rise to the wildest fancies. The garrison of St. Catherine's fort mistook the howls of the States' gunners, who were labouring with their guns over a quaking bog, for shouts of vengeance and triumph at having brought some infernal machine across the quick-sands, which would speedily demolish their fort and render them an easy prey for the bloodthirsty Maurice of Nassau, who had informed them by proclamation that if taken they would be all put to the sword, being irregular troops. They accordingly evacuated the fort that same night, and the States' forces, who had already begun their retreat to Cadsand, retraced their steps, and took possession of the fort. A thing well begun is half done, and this unexpected success inspired Maurice's troops with hopes of victory. The forts of St. Margaret and St. Philip, though strongly garrisoned, offered but little resistance to Maurice's troops, and on May 6 they laid siege to Isendike—a strongly fortified place three leagues to the east of Sluys.

The Archduke had been obliged to divide his forces into three parts. The first division invested Ostend, the second was sent against Prince Maurice, while the third division was employed in quelling the incursions of the mutineers, who numbered 3,000 foot and 1,200 horse. These mutineers have already been referred to in a previous chapter.[1] They had been permitted by Maurice to establish themselves in Grave after the reduction of that place, and they had been as thorns in the side of the Archduke ever since. They carried on a kind of guerilla warfare against the Spaniards, and had been joined by 1,600 of Maurice's horse and " 1,500 musketeers mounted on horsebacke, after a new invention

---

[1] See letter from E. Cecil to Sir R. Cecil from the Grave, dated Sept. 14, 1602, given in Chapter iv.

set upon cuissins, the which were made the winter before in
Holland." [1] The troops sent against Prince Maurice
thought it a good opportunity, when Maurice was before
Isendike, to make a dash for the island of Cadsand, and
capture that most important depôt of provisions and warlike stores, to say nothing of the States' fleet anchored off
the island. An expedition consisting of 2,000 men embarked at Sluys, and dropped down the haven of Sluys
to Cadsand. Half their number landed and nearly over-
powered the small garrison, but, owing to the bravery of a
few companies [2] who held their ground and charged their
enemy so furiously, the Archduke's troops, who were chiefly
composed of Italians, were driven back to their boats with
great loss. Many of the boats were sunk in the channel
and the Italians in them drowned. Had this enterprise
been successful, Sluys would doubtless have been saved for
that year, at least.

On May 10 Isendike was given up, and two days
later the little town of Aardenburg, between Ghent and
Sluys, which was well fortified, surrendered to the States
without striking a blow. [3] After this victory, Maurice's
horse scoured the country, adventuring even to the very
gates of Bruges and Ghent, and brought back great store
of booty, to their great advantage, but to the deprivation of
the country people, who were plundered both by friend and

---

[1] Grimston's *Netherlands*, p. 1306. Also referred to by Sir W. Browne in
a letter to Sidney, dated from Flushing, New Year's day, 1603-4, as follows :
—"For provision of pack sadells most of our Townes have been troubled to
make them, which are to the number of 3000, and great hammers 400. . . .
our Foote, for there Humility, shalbe sett on Horseback, thus much Sir Henry
Carew writes ; I hear by others that the Pack sadells are made that two
musketiers may sit upon one." Collins' *Sidney Papers*.

[2] Motley, quoting from Fleming, says these companies were Scotch.

[3] Aardenburg was garrisoned by German troops, who fled at the coming of
the States' troops, in a most disgraceful manner. *Grimston*, p. 1307.

foe. On May 16 a sharp action took place between
Maurice's cavalry and a strong force of the enemy's cavalry,
an English mile from Dam, a village which commanded
two navigable streams that ran direct to Sluys. The
States' cavalry were worsted, but the infantry coming up
retrieved the fortunes of the day. Sir Horace Vere, at the
head of some English companies, charged with such resolution that he drove the enemy back into his trenches,
and put him to a complete rout.[1] "The enemy received a
foule and disgraceful defeat," wrote Winwood to Northumberland, "423 bodyes have been buryed, as many prisoners,
besides many which were drowned. All fled. . . . Don
Louis de Velasco was the first to turn." The day after
this occurrence fourteen hundred Spaniards were defeated
by the States' troops, who now commanded the two water
highways leading from Dam to Sluys. Before the end of
May Maurice had fought his way to the Swint, or great sea-
channel of Sluys, and then, having all the approaches to the
beleaguered town in his own hands, he proceeded to invest
the city. "He was himself encamped," says Motley, "on
the west side of the Swint ; Charles van der Noot[2] lying
on the south. The submerged meadows, stretching all
around in the vicinity of the haven, he had planted thickly
with gunboats. Scarcely a bird or a fish could go into or
out of the place. Thus the stadholder exhibited to the
Spaniards, who, fifteen miles off towards the west, had been
pounding and burrowing three years long before Ostend
without success, what he understood by a siege." Strenuous
efforts were made by the Spaniards to send supplies into
Sluys, but without success. The siege was only a question
of time now.

---

[1] Winwood to the Earl of Northumberland, May 18, 1604.—*S.P. Holland.*
[2] Governor of Ostend in 1603.

The inevitable result, with a few details of this siege, are given in the two letters from Edward Cecil to his uncle written from before Sluys, which we can now give, having paved the way for them by detailing what had previously taken place.

SIR E. CECIL TO LORD CECIL.[1]

" MAY IT PLEASE y' Lo.,

"I have perceaved by y' letter how ill my footmane hath deserved his charges, and I so favorable a letter; but it shall heance forth make mee love a horsman the better. I understand by a friend that there is a great mann, a bout the king, that hath write to S' Horatio Vere, to have the first advertisment of oure busines heare, and, w'hall, that he is not much y' friend, w'ch out of my diuty I can not but lett y' lo. knowe of.

"As for the present I can say noe more then this bearer can tell y. lo, that is howe wee ar making Haste of our Bridge to pass in to the Towne, w'ch may better be cauled an Ingien then a Bridge. It is made upon mastes of shipes, to suffer the Tide to goe bacward and forward, as it doth there, before the Towne w'th a great force, then is it borded one eyther side, proufe of muskett, w'th a Gallery upon it ; it is ankered faste. Wee look every day to put it over ; there is 50 Cannone mounting for the Battery. Heare ar comde many freanch Gentelmen of accounte, as Mounser de Termes, to see our seage ; as for oure nation, not one, w'ch is much marveled at.

"I have receaved this day a letter out of Ostend of the 5, whereby I understand that the Enyme have made a strong corte of gard upon the Pouldron Bullworke, wherein it is for certayne that the have minded this 8 nights in to it. The enyme that morning were scene marching very strong from there quarter in to the Treanches w'th flieng Collors, w'ch mad them in the Towne thincke the would have blone up the Bulworke, and give a generall assaulte. They had 2 commanders, who cam up to the top of the weste Bulworke to discover what number of menn garded w'th in, the w'ch our menn have this 2 nights quitted, the miends expected

---

[1] *Cecil Papers, Hatfield,* 105/101.

howerly to be blone up.   At hige water the were seene march
backe in to there quarter.   The nwe Towne is all ways garded
wth Diuche and 17 peases of Ordnanc, planted there in.   This
weake wee blue up our miendes in the pouldrome and weaste
Bolwarke ; and this Sonday, his Excelenc hath sente the Corronell
of the wallownes, one Markett,[1] much surpassing many othe
Goveners before him, for Governer of Ostend, and an excelent
miner wth him, a Jerman, w° ^har now moste neadfull.   We have some
3 dayes a goe sent a 1000 menn more in to Ostend, of all
nations, Sr Charles farfaxe commanding our natione.   There is
not one in the Towne that speakes not for to fighte to the laste
mann.   His Excelency towlde mee that he woulde fayne coule the
Towne twise more, as he hathe done allredy, before they should
parly.

"I have looked every day that the states should give mee a
Regiment, beyng the owldeste Captayne of our Nation that lookes
for advancement.   But som hinderanc I fiend by a secon letter
of the Kings for Sr Thomas Knowles,[2] wch is very affectually
wryton for him.   And there is dealing that there should be made
only Lieftennant Corronelles, and sergentmajors, to keepe downe
our Natione.   I desier to be wth they foote, to rise, and I have noe
other patrone but y^r Lo., and others have many.   And I know y^r lo.
can not assuer y^r selfe of a more truar servent then I am, wherefore if y. Lo. doe thincke mee worthy, and that y° desier to have
y^r name live in the warres, then y° must now howlde mee up,
or never.   I would be loth, and ever have beeyne, to truble y^r lo.
much, onely that y^r lo. would wryte y^r letter to Mr Winwod, to
know the States answer for mee, what I shall gayne by the King
letter, that I be not deferred by the pollices of other, to be still
keepte backe.   I shall howlde my selfe much bound to in devore
all I can to deserve y^r favore.   I will not be more tedius to y^r lo.

---

[1] Daniel de Hartaing, Lord of Marquette, colonel of a Walloon regiment,
distinguished himself at the battle of Nieuport.

[2] Sir Thomas Knollys, sixth son of Sir Francis Knollys, K.G., treasurer of
the household to Queen Elizabeth.   Sir Wm. Knollys second son of this Sir
Francis was treasurer of the household to James I., and was afterwards raised
to the peerage as Baron Knollys and Earl of Banbury.   Sir Thomas Knollys
married Odelia de Morada, daughter of John de Morada, Marquis of Bergen,
by whom he had an only daughter.

but to praye for y^r lo.˙longe and happie life, and to give mee meanes to prove my selfe how much I am y^r lo.

"most diutefull servant

and affectionat nephue,

"ED. CECYLL.

"from the leger before the Sluse, this 10 of June."

Add.   "To the Rig^t Honorable the Lo. Cecyll, Lo. Scecrytary of Eingland."

End.   "10 June, 1604.   Sr Edward Cecyll to my Lord from the Campe before Sluce."

SIR E. CECIL TO LORD CECIL.

"MAY IT PLEASE Y^r LORDSHIPE,

"These ar to lett y^r lo. understand, that after a longe and tedius seage, that wee ar M^r of the Towne of Sluse, wch wee had brought to great extremety, a Towne that is not to be wonn wth out famishing.   I can not say that there is a Generall in the worlde that hath takene more care and more paynes, or hath deserved more, then his Excelence hath done in this seage, considering his smale armye.   The enemy hath liene longe by us, to have releeved it.   He hath tryed all wayes, and the laste waye of 3 hath beeyne by the Iland of Casante, where he gave one [attacked] a Redoute there, wee not suspecting him there, for that he did marche all the nighte, towarde Dame.   He founde where he gave one, but a 150 menn, the Enemy having all his Armye there, who did give one, very furius and valliantly, yet was repolsed wth the loss of some 200 of his beaste menn in the place, and those of quallety, as the Marquis of Rentis, and the Sergenmajore of the Mutiners, and one Don phelipo de Taxces, and many more wch I can not name.   They were very nighe the releaving of the

---

[1] A desperate effort was made by Spinola on 16th August to capture Cadsand.   Spinola, who commanded in person, had already recaptured the forts of St. Catherine and St. Philip and had broken through the States' lines at Oostburg.   Maurice hastened to the relief of his troops in the isle of Cadsand and held the position against a larger force than his own.   After a bloody engagement Spinola was obliged to retreat and Sluys surrendered soon after. *Motley*, pp. 197–198.

Towne, by this waye, w^{ch}, till wee were certayne of there repulce, mad our Armye much amased, for oure hopes healde but by a string and now it is by a Chane, for that wee shall hardly be drivene oute of these contries.

" My haste to sende a way this bearer, of purpose to y^r lo., will not lett mee be longer. But to praye God to sende y^o a longe and happie life, and mee occatione to showe howe much I am

" Y^r lo. diutefull and affectionat

" Servant as nephue,

" ED. CECYLL.

" The Towne was givene over upon frida a bout 4 of the clocke in the morning, wth compositione, to leave munition, cannone, and slaves,[1] and to marche wth flieng collors, wth there bollitt in there mouth, and bagage.

" from the Sluse, this 10 of Auguste." [2]

Add. " For his M^d afares. To the Rig^h Honorable the Lo. Cecyll, Lo,. highe Scecritary of Einglande, hast, haste, poste haste, this 10."

End. " 1604. August 10. Sr Edward Cecyll to my Lord from Sluce."

Sluys was won, but, as usual, the sword and sickness had done their work, and the States had to mourn the loss of many a gallant soldier. Among the number was the gallant Count Lewis of Nassau, who died of fever soon after entering the captured town. On September 20, Ostend—or what was *once* Ostend—surrendered to Spinola, after a siege of three years and seventy-seven days. The garrison had held out until all their bastions and redoubts

---

[1] Fifteen hundred galley-slaves, chiefly Turks, who were for the most part sent home in a Barbary ship. Many of them had eaten no bread in Sluys for many weeks, but had fed on old shoes, boots, parchment, and on an herb called *soutenelle*. Dogs, cats, rats, and mice were considered good meat. Meteren, fo. 543, book 25.

[2] Old style of reckoning ; the new style was ten days later. *Cecil Papers*, *Hatfield*, 106/73.

had been carried by assault, and there only remained to them the recently erected citadel called "Little Troy." The States-General had expected Prince Maurice to relieve Ostend after Sluys was taken, but sickness, and tempestuous weather which rendered the roads impassable, prevented his marching against Spinola in time, so Colonel Marquette was obliged to surrender Ostend on honourable terms, and the heroic garrison marched out with the honours of war.[1]

In remembrance of the long siege of Ostend, and the winning of Sluys, silver and copper medals were struck in the United Provinces. The former bore on the *obverse* the town of Ostend, and on the *reverse* the towns of Rhineberg, Grave, Sluys, Aardenburg, and the forts of Isendike and Cadsand, with an inscription to the effect that the siege of Ostend had given only a heap of stones to the enemy, while it had given four towns to the United Provinces. The other medal bore on one side the town of Sluys, with the inscription, *Traxis, duxis, dedit an* 1604, and on the reverse the arms of Zeeland, with the legend, *Beatus populus cujus adjutor deus.*[2]

In the summer of 1604, while British soldiers were adding fresh glory to their nation by their deeds in the Low Countries, the British monarch made a treaty of peace with the King of Spain and the Archduke Albert, notwithstanding all that had been promised, and even ratified, twelve months before. "The peace which was at length brought about," says Ranke, "is remarkable for its indefiniteness. The English promised that they would

---

[1] Spinola entertained the officers at a splendid banquet, to show his appreciation of their gallant defence of Ostend. They also received a great ovation from Prince Maurice and his officers, on their arrival at the States' camp.

[2] *Grimston,* p. 1318.

not support the rebellious subjects and enemies of the King of Spain. The States-General were not interfered with in the enlistment which they had been allowed to begin . . . . similar leave to enlist was granted to the Spaniards also, who, for that purpose, resorted especially to Ireland."[1] The States found out now what a broken reed they had been depending on. They were too hard pressed, however, by their Spanish foe, to be able to quarrel with the nation which held some of their towns, and from which they drew their best troops. From the first they had entertained but small respect for the British Solomon, and thought him fitter to be a preacher than a king.[2] Worldly wisdom, however, prevented them from openly breaking with James;[3] so they swallowed their bitter disappointment as best they could, and centred their hopes for the future on France.

The formation of the English companies in the Netherlands, into regiments, appears to have been a tardy process ; and though it was a step much desired by Sir John Ogle, Sir Edward Cecil, and other old captains, it was opposed by Sir Horace Vere[4] who, as colonel over all the English companies, had supreme and undivided authority in his command. The Scotch companies are generally spoken of at this time as "the Scots regiment "—their colonel being Sir William Edmonds. It is difficult to give the exact date of the formation of the English companies

---

[1] I. p. 391.

[2] Bentivoglio ; *Hist. of the warres of Flanders.*

[3] James allowed the States' envoy in England, Noel de Caron, to have the rank and dignity of an ambassador, which empty honour was all the respect he showed for the feelings of the States.

[4] "Sir Horace Vere workes with his best friends underhand, that there may not be any dealinge of thees troopes into formed Regiments, bycause it would somwhat diminish his greatnes and absolute comaund that he now hath over the troopes generall." Sir John Ogle to Lord Cecil, from Middleborow, Oct. 20, 1604.—*S.P. Holland.*

into regiments, but it appears to have been in the spring of 1605, when Captains Cecil and Ogle [1] were promoted to be colonels. Winwood, in a letter to Lord Cranbourne,[2] dated April 24,[3] says, "Th'englishe troopes are now devyded into regiments,[4] and unto S[r] Horace Vere are added Collonells S[r] Edward Cecyll, S[r] John Ogle, and Cap[ne] Sutton, Lieuetenant collonel to S[r] Horace Vere."

The campaign of 1605 was a failure. The enterprises projected by the States-General, on their army taking the field, failed utterly. An expedition sent in the spring, under Count Ernest of Nassau, to surprise Antwerp, returned without accomplishing anything. Spinola, at the head of a fine army, played a most successful game of hide and seek with his rival, Maurice. Giving out that he was going to attack Grave and Sluys, Spinola kept Maurice and his troops in the east, while he was preparing for a rapid march into Friesland and Groningen. He kept his secret so well, that to the very last Maurice was ignorant of his enemy's design. On July 22, Sir W. Browne, writing to Lord Salisbury, says, "Spinola, according to certen newes com, is marching to beseege Dews-burch.[5] . . . His Excellency departs to-night or to-

----

[1] There are several letters from Sir John Ogle to Lord Cranbourne among the *S.P. Holland* for 1605, begging for his lordship's interest with the States regarding his promotion.

[2] Lord Cecil was created Viscount Cranbourne in August 1604, and Earl of Salisbury, 4 May, 1605.

[3] This letter, which is endorsed "M[r] Wynwood to me," has been wrongly placed among the *S.P. Holland* for 1607. Cecil's promotion to a colonelcy is given in a State Paper in the King's Library at the Hague, in which Sir John Ogle, Sir Edward Cecil and Sir Henry Sutton, are named as those officers selected by his Excellency for promotion, and approved of by the States-General, 2 May, 1605.

[4] Regiments were at this time from 1 to 3,000 strong. Each company carried a colour. Gustavus Adolphus set the example afterwards of reducing regiments to 1,000 men.

[5] Doesburg.

morrow at furthest." Spinola had no intention of stopping to besiege any of the Rhine towns. On August 8 he came before Oldenzaal, which he took in three days, and then proceeded to Lingen, which he invested. Lingen [1] was the stepping-stone to Coeworden, the key to the road to Emden, which was still convulsed with internal troubles. If the two former places were reduced, Emden would be at the mercy of Spinola, and, what was much worse, the high road to Friesland and Groningen would be open for him. Maurice lost no time. He broke up his camp in Flanders, and made forced marches to save Lingen. Before he could arrive there, however, that important place had surrendered to Spinola. That able commander had got the start, and like Philip II. of Spain, he might have boastfully exclaimed, " Time and I against any other two." But strange to say, although Coeworden, the key to Emden and Friesland, was almost within the grasp of Spinola, he stopped short in his onward path to certain victory. " Instead of darting at once upon Coeworden," says Motley, " he paused for nearly a month, during which period he seemed intoxicated with a success so rapidly achieved, and especially with his adroitness in outwitting the great stadholder. On September 14 he made a retrograde movement towards the Rhine, leaving two thousand five hundred men in Lingen." [2]

Maurice, being an experienced chess player, saw at once what a false move his enemy had made, and was quick to take advantage of it. He occupied Coeworden, strongly fortified that place, and, leaving a large garrison there, retired to Wesel. Although the States' troops had been largely reinforced, they were still much inferior in numbers to Spinola's army. That able general had taken up a

---

[1] Lingen is eight leagues from Coeworden.   [2] pp. 218–219.

strong position at Ruhrort, a place on the Rhine, at the mouth of the Ruhr. He waited patiently to be attacked, having every confidence in his position and superior numbers. We are told that Maurice waited a fortnight before making an attack, and only made it when he had discovered a weak point in Spinola's extended lines. The weak point was at Mulheim, a village on the Ruhr, where were stationed some of the enemy's cavalry and infantry, at some distance from their main army. On the opposite bank of the river was Broek Castle, and some hills of considerable elevation. Maurice departed from Wesel in the night of October 8 with a large force of cavalry and infantry, composed of French, Dutch, English and Scotch troops—the English contingent being commanded by Sir Horace Vere.[1] Dividing his force into three parts, he sent a body of cavalry,[2] under Marcellus Bax, to seize Broek Castle and the heights on the other side of the Ruhr. A second body of cavalry,[3] under Count Frederick Henry of Nassau, was sent forward to attack Mulheim and drive the Spaniards across the river, where Bax, with his cavalry, would be waiting to receive them. The infantry under Maurice's command marched straight upon Mulheim. Bax performed his part of the programme very speedily, having met with but little resistance. Count Frederick Henry was not so fortunate. The enemy's outposts were taken by surprise, but they fled into Mulheim and spread the alarm, so that on the States' cavalry coming into the quarter, they were met by three or four troops of cavalry,

---

[1] Sir John Throgmorton, in his letter to Sidney of Oct. $\frac{8}{18}$, says, Sir II. Vere had command "of the 4 Colonels whole companies," which I take to be the private foot companies of Colonels Cecil, Ogle, Vere's own, and Buccleuch's Scotch company.

[2] Eight troops of horse.

[3] *Ibid.*

drawn up to receive them.[1] "These proffering a charge," wrote Sir John Throgmorton to Sidney, "all ours ran cleare away and never stoode to discharge one pistoll shoote ; save onlye Sir John Selby[2] and Sir Archibald Heskins with 2 companyes, did very well, and loste many of their 'Men and Horses.'" While Bax was waiting for the Spaniards whom he was to cut off in their disorderly rout, he was himself attacked by some troops who had crossed the river. At last he saw Prince Henry coming to his rescue with a very small proportion of his troops. All might yet have gone well, had not a fresh troop of cavalry, under Don Louis de Velasco, come on the scene.[3] After a short action, the panic, which had already deprived Henry of Nassau of some of his oldest troops, spread to the remainder, and to those troops commanded by Marcellus Bax, whom they had come to assist. The States' cavalry turned their backs on the foe and fled *en masse*. When Maurice arrived on the banks of the Ruhr, he found what he had once considered the flower of his army in full retreat, and his young brother, with a few staunch followers, fighting against great odds on the opposite bank.[4] Maurice did all he could to stem the flight, but he was on the opposite side of a deep stream and unable to offer his cavalry much assistance. Being now attacked himself by the Spaniards, who were gathering in force on both sides of the river, he ordered a retreat. Spinola,[5] who was now directing the attack in person, had,

---

[1] Bentivoglio, p. 424.

[2] Sir John Selby of Twisell ?

[3] Bentivoglio, p. 424.

[4] Meteren mentions that Prince Henry nearly lost his life in this unequal contest and owed his life to the gallantry of a Dutch trooper.

[5] Spinola had hastened to the scene of action from Ruhrort on hearing of the attack, and resorted to the old stratagem of causing drums to be beaten in all directions to make his enemy think a large force was approaching. Bentivoglio, p. 424.

as a writer expressed it, "grasped up Prince Maurice and his men against the sea-shore, with more than three times their number." The Prince was attempting an orderly retreat, when he was attacked in rear by the Spaniards with great fury. It was at this critical moment that Sir Horace Vere, who commanded the British infantry, desired Prince Maurice to allow him to quit his post in the main body of the army with his troops and attack the enemy. Permission being granted, Vere forded the Ruhr with his troops and charged the Spaniards with great bravery, drove them back a considerable distance, and then retired in good order.[1] This gave the routed Dutch cavalry time to reform and join the main body, where they were told, in very forcible language, by their irate and disappointed commander-in-chief how disgracefully and cowardly they had behaved. As the English were repassing the river the enemy came down upon them in great numbers. The gallant Vere once more threw himself in the breach. Selecting sixty of his veterans he went to the rear, and, on the brink of the river, disputed the passage of the enemy until nearly all his men were killed and his horse shot under him.[2] It lived, however, to carry its gallant rider to the opposite bank of the Ruhr. The States' army was saved, as Spinola himself confessed, by the determined stand made by this English officer.[3] We have positive proof that Edward Cecil was not with the States' troops on the day of the lamentable engagement at Broek Castle. It is necessary, however, to give a short account of this action and the events which preceded it, in order to keep

---

[1] Throgmorton to Sidney; Meteren's account of this action agrees in saying that Vere's troops saved the Dutch army from a great disaster. Meteren also says that Buccleuch, with his Scotch company, greatly distinguished themselves in this retreat.   [2] *Ibid.*

[3] *Biog. Brit.*, art. "Horace Vere."

up the thread of the story, and also to explain the contents
of the letter—or part of a letter—which Lord Salisbury
wrote to his nephew, Edward Cecil, soon after the above
action at Broek Castle. This letter, the rough draft of
which is preserved among the Holland State Papers, is
endorsed, " Mynute to Sʳ Edward Cecyll, Octob. 1605,"
and commences thus :—

" Sʳ, I was very gladd to perceyve by yoʳ lre that you were
absent at the last accident neere Brooke Castell, because the
reputation fell not on that syde where ˙yoᵘ should have beene,
though the losse in bodyes of men was small. That I am farre
from giving over my desire to be advertised of the p'ceedings
there, stands both wᵗʰ the qualitie of my place, considering the k.
my mʳ avoweth himself a confederate, and wᵗʰ my owne particular
disposition, who am alwaies well affected towards them that
p'fess to love the k. and his religion, although I meddle not either
by way of Counsell, or action, to the preiudice of their enemyes
who are now in gen'll termes of amitie wᵗʰ his Maᵗʸ, so as it may
please yoᵘ to understand me in that kind aright concerning the
generall."[1]

Misfortunes seldom come singly. The defeat at Broek
Castle was followed, on October 27, by the loss of the
town of Wachtendonk, after ten days' siege, and on
November 5 Cracow surrendered. Maurice was quite
powerless to save these places, as sickness and losses had
diminished his small army, and in November his troops
went into winter quarters. Edward Cecil writing to Lord
Salisbury, on November 30, from his garrison at Utrecht,
thus refers to the action at Broek Castle.

" Please yʳ lo. to understand the true relation of the action of
Brouke Castell, yʳ lo. shall beast knowe it by this Gentellman,[2] for

---

[1] The remainder of the draft letter is erased.
[2] Probably Sir Thomas Roe, whom Sir John Throgmorton names as
having been severely wounded in his head. Sir T. Roe was a distinguished
diplomatist, and was ambassador at several foreign courts in after years.

that he was a forward wittness in that business, first having charged wth the hors, when Sir Henry Carey[1] was taken prisoner, then after wth the foote, amongst our owne nation, having runn many fortunes that day, his horse beeyng slane, was twise prisoner, hurt in the forhed and shott in the leage, he can tell y[r] lo. howe our foote was commanded that day."[2]

In the summer of 1605 Sir Francis Vere requested leave from the King, through Salisbury, to return to his charge at the Brill, of which town he was governor.[3] His retirement from the States' army early in 1604, seems to have been a voluntary act on his part, and not from any necessity. He had disagreements with the States-General, and Prince Maurice whom he had never liked.[4] From one of Carleton's letters,[5] we gather that Vere had demanded the absolute command of the English troops in the States' service. He virtually and nominally *had* the command, but his troops were at all times under the supreme command of Prince Maurice. Vere's haughty spirit could ill brook control from anyone. He had the confidence in

---

[1] Sir Henry Cary was Master of the Jewels to James I., having succeeded his father, Sir Edward Cary, in that office. Being a volunteer in the States' army he was not permitted to ransom himself at the fixed sum ; he was, however, afterwards exchanged for a Spanish officer. In 1618 he was appointed Comptroller to the King, and in 1620 was created Viscount Falkland. He died in 1633 and was succeeded by his elder son, Lucius Cary, 2nd Lord Falkland, the brilliant and distinguished Royalist leader.

[2] Edward Cecil to Salisbury, *C.P. Hatfield*, 191/89, dated " from my garisonn at Utricke, this 30 of Nov."

[3] Sir F. Vere proclaimed James I. at the Brill in April, 1603. That monarch issued a fresh warrant, re-appointing Vere to be governor of the town of Brill. *Biog. Brit.*

[4] Sir W. Browne gives the following anecdote in a letter to Sidney, dated Nov. 29, 1602, illustrative of Vere's dislike of the Prince :—"I hear that of late Sir F. Vere ryding abroad in his Coach mett his Excellencye's Coach, and passed by without saluting him, and that afterwards he sent his Excuse saying he was sory, and that he saw not his Excellency's Coach because it passed uppon his blynd side ; I hear that his Excellency's answer was that it was a blynd excuse."—*S.P. Holland.*

[5] Carleton to Chamberlain Jan. 15th, 1604.—*S.P. Dom.*

himself that veteran commanders must have to ensure success. He had now arrived at the age when all interference and opposition to his plans were gall and wormwood to him. In plain words, he threw up his command of the English troops in a pet, and returned to his home at Tilbury, in Essex, until his "soldier's humour" should be over. He retained, however, his governorship of the Brill, and Sir Edward Conway acted as governor in Vere's absence. His letter to Salisbury, asking for leave to return to his charge at the Brill, is characteristic, and worth giving.

SIR F. VERE TO THE EARL OF SALISBURY.

" MOST HONORABLE,

" The goyng over of my Ld Lyle awakeneth me in the deewty I owe also to my chardge, whether if itt may stand wth his Matie pleasure I had muche rather goe to doe his Matie thatt lyttle service I can on thatt syde, then to lyve heer lyke a drone, unprofetable every way to his Matie and nothyng to my comfortt or creditt. Heertofor I have made knowne to your Lp my readynes to goe over if I wear commandead, thoughe other wyse in regard of any perticular desyre of my owne I urgead itt note, w^h your Lp perceyvyng in your favor may have forborne heatherto to call uppon me. I saw whatt pollicye and mallyce myght suggeast agaynst my beyng and resedyng thear soddaynly after my leavyng the States, w^h I hope tyme and bettre experience of me hathe sufficyently answearead; and wth all I had somewhatt of the soldyers humor, thatt for a tyme would nott suffre me to brooke so quieat and retyread a lyfe in that actyve state in w^h my intereast had been so great, and my desyre so strong to advaunce the happyness of itt by the wayes of my profession, wch humor I thancke God is now bettre tempread, and I bouth content and desyrous to reast in my guverment and geave the warres the lookyng on tyll my service in them may be heald more necessarye. I thearfore very humbly beeseche yr Lp. out of the asseurance yr Lp. in his great wyse-dome may have of my truthe and weall meanyng bouth to this and that State, favorably to remove those difficutyes yr Lp. shall discover heer, or on the other syde, opposyng this my desyre, thatt so with his Maties and the States good lykyng I may repayer to my chardg wch shall nott be the least of y^{r} Lps. good deedes to me thatt have already bownd me to doe.

> " Y^{r} Lp.
>   " all humble service,
>   " F. VERE.

" Tilbury, this 22 August, 1605." [1]

Add. " To the most hono. the Earle of Salisburye, Pryncypall Secretarye to his Matie."

End. " 22 August, 1605. Sr Francis Vere to my Lord."

Vere arrived at the Brill on December 2, and two days after was present, with the garrison there, at the thanksgiving services which took place in gratitude to God for his Majesty's deliverance from the great conspiracy known as the Gunpowder Plot. From the Brill Vere went to the Hague, where he delivered letters from James to Prince Maurice and the States-General. The substance of these letters was, that his Majesty " would not suffer the United Provinces to fall into utter ruin, and that to prevent further inconveniences to his owne realme he had resolved that from henceforth his subjects should not be let pass so freely to the Archduke's service." [2] Vere was well received by Prince Maurice and the States-General :—

" They gave me a very good welcome," says Vere in his letter [3] to Salisbury, "seemying to be gladd of my retorne into theas partts and of my affectyon to theyr service, which I made appear

---

[1] *Cecil Papers, Hatfield*, 190/24.
[2] Guy Fawkes, having served under the Archduke, had set James more against the Spaniards than all their cruelties to the Protestant Netherlanders had done.
[3] Vere to Salisbury, "from the Haghe, Dec. 15, 1605." *Cecil Papers, Hatfield*, 191/94.

to be as muche as my deewty to my Soveraign myght permitt; but no mentyon was made to me eyther in the assemblye or from his Ex^te, or any of the States in pryvatt, concernyng my retorne to theyr service."

Leaving Sir Francis Vere for the present at his post at the Brill, we must pass on to the spring of 1606, when the States' army again prepared to take the field.

"Never had there been so much sluggishness," says Motley, "as in the preparations for the campaign of 1606. The States' exchequer was lower than it had been for years. The republic was without friends. Left to fight their battle for national existence alone, the Hollanders found themselves perpetually subjected to hostile censure from their late allies, and to friendly advice still more intolerable. There were many brave Englishmen and Frenchmen sharing in the fatigues of the Dutch war of independence, but the governments of Henry and of James were as protective, as severely virtuous, as offensive, and in their secret intrigues with the other belligerent, as mischievous as it was possible for the best-intentioned neutrals to be." [1]

The campaign was opened by an attempted surprise of Sluys by the Spaniards.[2] So badly was the look out kept, and so well did the Spaniards manage their night attack, that they had effected their entrance into the town without any resistance. The guard-houses were to be attacked simultaneously at a given signal. This signal was to be the striking of a certain hour by the town clock. The town clock never did strike. The sacristan had forgotten to wind it up the night before, and this omission of duty on his part saved the sleeping garrison. The watch were aroused, and discovered that their city-gate had

---

[1] p. 237.

[2] Du Terrail, a French engineer, was the leader of this expedition. He had invented a new kind of petard, which he boasted could demolish any city-gate in Holland. Meteren, p. 588.

K 2

been forced. An English captain and sixteen soldiers, quartered near the gate, hearing the report of fire arms rushed to the gateway and assisted in repelling the assailants. The whole garrison was aroused, and turned out half dressed to fight the enemy. Driven to bay the Spanish party threw away their arms, turned and fled. Hundreds were slain trying to force their way through the gateway they had entered by, the breach in which was but small. Many also were killed outside the walls by their pursuers. "The Englishmen, who (beside the watch) were the first that sallied forth against the enemy had the best purses and booty; and whereas most of them went out half naked, they came into the town again with good apparel." So ended the attack on Sluys.

The attack on Sluys took place in June, and it was not until this month that the Marquis Spinola returned to Brussels after a long absence in Spain and Italy. Illness had laid a heavy hand on the young general—hence his tardy return to the Netherlands. His arrival was the signal for immediate action. Not being threatened by another invasion of Flanders, Spinola was at liberty to act on the offensive and carry out his plan for the coming campaign. Having collected a large army together, he divided it into nearly two equal forces, giving the command of one force to Bucquoy and taking the other himself. Spinola's plan was to again invade Friesland. *L'homme propose, mais Dieu dispose.* The summer of 1606 was an exceptionally wet one. The rivers and roads became well nigh impassable and Friesland was for a time turned into a swamp. For that year Friesland was safe from a Spanish invasion. The Commander-in-chief of the Spanish forces was not a man to attempt an impossible

---

[1] Grimston, p. 1357.

feat, merely because he had planned it when he thought it was feasible. Quickly changing his tactics he determined to try and penetrate into the province of Utrecht—the main road to Holland and Zeeland—by crossing the rivers Waal and Yssel. These two rivers formed a natural moat for part of Guelderland, the Veluwe and Betuwe districts[1] (both of which are separated from the mainland by different ramifications of the Rhine), and the fertile province of Utrecht with its ancient capital. It was settled that Bucquoy was to cross the Waal, at a place where that river joins with the Rhine, and seize the town of Nymegen. Spinola was to cross the Yssell at the same time and unite his forces with Bucquoy's, after which all would be easy. Last year's victories had emboldened Spinola as much as they had disheartened Maurice. It was probably partly owing to the late cavalry disaster at Broek Castle that Maurice seemed so unwilling to carry war into the enemy's country, and made him patiently wait for Spinola to open the ball. It must be remembered, moreover, that the States' finances were crippled by years of incessant warfare and the maintaining a large standing army. It was with some difficulty that Maurice collected an army of 15,000 men together, in the neighbourhood of Arnhem, on the Rhine, by the middle of July. Sir Edward Cecil had been sent to Doesburg in May,[2] to command the garrison there, until the army was ready to take the field.

Spinola having crossed the Rhine at Ruhrort on 18th July, Maurice divided his small army into two portions, giving the command of one to Du Bois, an old campaigner, and

---

[1] Veluwe signifies "barren, or unfruitful island;" Betuwe signifies "good island." *Batavia*, the ancient name of Holland, is derived from the latter word.

[2] Ogle to Salisbury, May 12th, 1606. "Syr Edward Cecyll is gone up to Deusborow, there to comaunde till our drawing into field."—*S.P. Holland*.

taking command over the other himself. Du Bois had
orders to oppose Bucquoy's passage across the Waal. He
carried out his orders so well that several attempts made
by Bucquoy to land his troops on the other side of the
Waal, which was unusually swollen by rain this summer,
signally failed. The States' troops guarded the inner side
of the river along the whole length of the Batavian island,
while armed vessels patrolled the stream itself.[1] The
Yssel,[2] from Doesburg (at the union of the Old and New
Yssel) to Campen on the Zuyder Zee, was guarded along
its whole left shore by the States' troops under Maurice,
who had erected temporary forts at regular intervals, to
protect his troops and serve as defences against the enemy.
In vain did Spinola try to force a passage across the Yssel,
first in one place and then in another. Thanks to the
flooded state of the river, and the good look-out kept from
the numerous forts, the Spaniards were unable to effect a
crossing. It was now the end of July, and if anything was
to be done that season it must be effected without further
loss of time. Suddenly leaving the Yssel, Spinola marched
to Lochem,[3] which surrendered at once, having only a
slender garrison. He then marched to the north, and
made a final effort to turn Maurice's position by crossing
the Blackwater and seizing Geeldmuyden on the Zuyder
Zee. The commander of the States' troops in that quarter
gave the Spaniards such a warm reception that they were
obliged to beat a retreat after suffering a heavy loss.

---

[1] Motley, p. 243.

[2] "The New Yssel," says a modern geographer, "is that ramification of
the Rhine which diverges towards the north about three miles above Arnhem.
This channel was constructed 1800 years ago by the Roman general Drusus,
stepson of the Emperor Augustus, as far as Doesborgh, where it unites with the
old Yssel, thus affording direct communication between the Rhine and the
Zuyder Zee."

[3] A small town to the east of Zutphen.

Marching to the south-east, Spinola now laid siege to Groll (Groenlo), a fortified town in the county of Zutphen. This town was well garrisoned, and would doubtless have stood a long siege had not Spinola, maddened by his unsuccessful attempts to break through the chain which guarded the heart of the republic, attacked the place with such fury, piling on his soldiers with the recklessness which had in the end conquered Ostend, that the town surrendered after an eleven days' siege.[1] The possession of Groll seemed hardly worth such a sacrifice of human beings,[2] but it was a foothold for the enemy, and might perhaps serve as a stepping stone for future victories.

Abandoning his schemes of conquest in the provinces beyond the Yssel, which were so near and yet so far, Spinola withdrew to the Rhine, and laid siege to Rhineberg on August 23. "This frontier place," says Motley, "had been tossed to and fro so often between the contending parties in the perpetual warfare, that its inhabitants must have learned to consider themselves rather as a convenient circulating medium for military operations than as burghers who had any part in the ordinary business of life. It had old-fashioned defences of stone, which, during the recent occupation by the States, had been much improved, and had been strengthened with earthworks. Before it was besieged Maurice sent his brother, Frederick Henry, with some picked companies into the place, so that the garrison amounted to three thousand effective men.[3] Spinola, rapid in all his movements, had made a bridge from Ruhrort over the Rhine, somewhat above Rhineberg, and invested

---

[1] The inhabitants of Groll remained in the town when it was taken by Spinola, "as if satisfied with any religion and any government." *Grotius, Hist.* lib. xv. p. 693.

[2] Spinola lost nearly 1,000 men. Davies, ii. p. 399.

[3] p. 244.

the town on all sides, having united his forces with those of
Bucquoy.   The Spaniards had the great advantage of
obtaining supplies from Cologne, and we are told that
" Spinola caused great store of fagots and other furniture
to be brought to Bercke to assaile the trenches over the
Rhine." [1]   In the meantime Prince Maurice, with an army of
15,000 men, which included the English regiments, was
marching to Wesel, with the intention either to fight a
battle or relieve Rhineberg.   Sir John Ogle,[2] writing to
Salisbury from Eltem, Aug. 15/25, says of the defence
of Rhineberg : " I fear Syr Wm Edmonds will return in no
tryumphe from that place, though for his particular men
doubt not but he will deserve honourably."   The same
writer, in a letter to Salisbury, written ten days later from
the camp, near Wesel, says :—

" The enemye is fortyfied on the Lippe, but if he were not I can
not see that the best indgments do fynde it any way convenient to
have attenipted any thinge on that syde, the countrye is so full of
broken wayes and narrow passages. Some of the Captaynes of the
Enemyes camp lay wagers at Wesel that Berk will be lost in ten
dayes, we hope better ; but if he sodeynly gayne that forte wch he
now assayles,[3] I fear we shall come to late to releeve it, perhapps
it will then be found fytt to make to this forte wch we are now
about (of wch Syr Ed. Ceecyll hath the fyrst and mayden-garde, in
the raysinge it), another on this syde the water, and so keep still the
toll of the Rhene. Tyme will shew us. I hear of an enterprize in
hand (but the particulars I know not) that if it take good success

---

[1] *Grimston*, p. 1361.

[2] Frequent mention has been made of this brave officer, who was for many
years colonel of an English regiment in the States' service and governor of
Utrecht, as will hereafter appear, in critical times. Colonel Ogle was fifth
son of Thomas Ogle of Pinchbeck, Lincolnshire, by Jane, daughter of Adlard
Welby, of Gedney, in the same county. He was baptized at Pinchbeck
Feby. 25, 1568-9 ; knighted at Woodstock Dec. 1, 1603. Died in March
1639-40, and was buried in Westminster Abbey on March 17. He left issue
by his wife, who was a Dutch lady. Chester's *Westminster Abbey Registers*.

[3] Probably the Weert fort.

wiil goe ner to turne Hannibal from Rome, and make him look
to his owne countrye.   These men had need pray for a good
year of the next, for if they should remayne upon theyr defensive
condicion still, all the Callenders on this syde say theyr estate is
desperate" [1]

Maurice lost an opportunity of relieving Rhineberg by
waiting for the arrival of a ship-bridge which he had sent
for.   For before he had got his bridge, and raised a redoubt
on each side of the river Rhine to defend the passage, the
garrison of Rhineberg had evacuated the Weert—a strongly
intrenched suburb near the river—and retired within the
town.[2]   This retreat—occasioned by the loss of Colonel
Edmonds—gave Spinola great advantage.   When Maurice's
ship-bridge arrived, he threw a bridge across the Rhine
near Wesel, and erected a redoubt on each side "to keep
the toll of the Rhine," as Sir John Ogle aptly expressed it.
The English regiment, commanded by Colonel Edward
Cecil, was employed, as Meteren tells us, in making earthworks to protect this bridge.[3]   Colonel Cecil was also
employed, as Sir John Ogle has already told us, in raising
a fort on the Rhineberg side of the river, of which he
(Cecil) had the "mayden garde."   A letter from Edward
Cecil to Robert Sidney, Viscount L'Isle, written at this
time, gives some idea of the passive state of Maurice's
army when Rhineberg was being "taken in" before their
eyes.

SIR E. CECIL TO LORD L'ISLE.

" MY WORTHY LORD,

" Your Lordship's kind Letter, and your Choyse to reccom-
mende your Friends to mee, hath made mee full of affection to

---

[1] Sept. 4, *stylo novo.—S.P. Holland.*

[2] A plan of Rhineberg, with the positions occupied by Spinola, Bucquoy,
and the States' army, and the forts raised by Maurice on each side of the
river, &c., is to be found among the *S.P. Holland* for August, 1606.

[3] Fo. 594, book 28.

doe you Servis ; yet I must complane of want of Messengers and
fulfill your Lordship's commandmente to let you know what we
doe heare. It is told wee have not performed so much as we did
expect ourselves ; for wee marched hether wth a Resolucione to
fight a Battel, but wee fiend Spinola so far ingaged in the Seage
of Rinebearke that he will not leave his hopes there to fight with
us. Wee lighe by Wesbell (*sic*), and have made a Bridge over the
Rind. Wee have mustered a fare army, 15,000 Foot and 3,000
Horse, and this night wee are making our passage over the Lipe ;
but what wee shall doe God knoweth, for I fear wee worke to suer
and to leserly. And I am of the Miende that within these tenn
Dayes you shall heare the Towne loste. The Enyme having
gottone all the Outworkes, wheare Coronell Edmons[1] was slane ;
they of the Towne have made a sally of 2,000 menn upon the
Quarter of the Count of Boccoye, his Horse having been oute upon
a convoye, and had the execution of som 400 Menn. I will be
no longer, but to desier some better occasion to showe how much
I am,

> " Your Lordship's most affectionate,
>> " to doe you service,
>>> " Ed. Cecyll.

" From our Armye,
by Wesbell, the last
of August, ould stile, 1606."[2]

The garrison of the beleaguered town made some desperate
sorties and inflicted great loss on the enemy.[3] The French
volunteers[4] who served at the defence of Rhineberg greatly
distinguished themselves, and one of them, Count de la

---

[1] Colonel Sir Wm. Edmonds was killed on Sept. 3d (new style) by a
musket shot in the head. He was a very gallant and experienced officer, who
had risen by merit from the ranks.

[2] Given by Collins in his *Sidney Papers*, ii. p. 317.

[3] "We say here that the enemie hath suffered great loss of men before
Berck." Ogle to Salisbury Sept. 8, also Sept. 14.—*S.P. Holland.*

[4] The Prince de Soubise, the Count de la Fleche, and other Frenchmen of
rank were in Rhineberg.—*Grimston*, p. 1362.

Fleche, was taken prisoner in one of the sorties.[1]　On 13th Sept. (new style) Maurice brought most of his forces over the Lippe, and assailed Spinola's fort at the mouth of that river, which was yielded up. Soon after this a deputation from the States-General came to Maurice's camp, and urged him very strongly to risk a battle with the enemy in order to relieve Rhineberg, which could not possibly hold out much longer. The Prince refused, giving as his reasons for his supineness that Spinola was too strongly intrenched and in too great force. He also declared that a successful battle could at the best only give them the town, while a defeat would put the whole country in danger.[2] These arguments were quite unanswerable, and however disappointing and humiliating this cautious policy was to the States-General, and to Maurice's eager troops, they had to abide by the Prince's decision.

On October 2nd Rhineberg capitulated and the garrison marched out with the honours of war.

Sir Thomas Edmonds, in a letter to the Earl of Shrewsbury, says :—

" The Count Maurice hath laid all the time with an army of 13,000 foot and 3,000 horse within two leagues of Berk, but made no attempt for the succouring of the town, only at the same time of the rendering of Berk he went about to surprise the town of Venlo, which place if he could have carried, would have fully recompensed his other loss, but he failed of that enterprise." [3]

It was at this low state of the tide in the affairs of the United Provinces that an unexpected ally came to the rescue. This ally was *mutiny.* Heavy failures on the Genoa Stock Exchange brought the credit of the Marquis Spinola,

---

[1] *Ibid.* Eighty French gentlemen, many of them of high birth, served at the defence of Rhineberg.
[2] Meteren, p. 594.
[3] Lodge's *Illustration of British History*, iii. p. 191.

which for long had been shaky, to the ground, with a great
crash.   He could no longer raise money to pay his army.
Mutiny ensued as an inevitable consequence, and the fine
army commanded by Spinola dwindled away to nothing.
Once more the mutineers seized the town of Hoogstradt,
and began a guerilla warfare on their own account.
" These miscreants," says Meteren, " were accustomed to go
about with straw in their hats, to signify that they would
immediately set fire to any place where they were refused
contributions, and to send letters to the same effect, burnt
at the corner and headed by a picture of a naked sword.
Neither were they a whit less ready with the execution
than the threat, in case their demands were not instantly
complied with." [1]   Now was the time for Maurice to
retrieve his fame, and win back the places lost to the States
in the last two years.   On October 24 he came before
Lochem, which he speedily retook.   He next besieged
Groll.   "But the rain," says Motley, "which during nearly
the whole campaign had been his potent ally, had of late
been playing him false.   The swollen Yssel, during a brief
period of dry weather, had sunk so low in certain shallows
as not to be navigable for his transports, and after his trains
of artillery and ammunitions had been dragged wearily
overland as far as Groll, the deluge had returned in such
force, that physical necessity, as well as considerations of
humanity, compelled him to defer his intrenching operations
until the weather should moderate." [2]   Delay, however
necessary, is generally fatal when there is anything to be
acquired, as Time works great changes, and makes things
that appeared impossible yesterday quite possible to-day.
Here is an instance.   Spinola, who was thought to be
incapable of giving further trouble that year, by reason of

---

[1] Book xxviii. fol. 596   [2] p. 247.

his army being broken up by open revolt, appeared suddenly before Groll with an army of 8,000 men, raised by super-human efforts out of the wreck of his great army. Wearied with a long march, and in numbers less than half of the States' army, the Spaniards seemed to be an easy prey for Maurice's troops. Maurice had taken up a strong position on hearing of Spinola's advance, and his troops, despite the sickness in their camp, were eager for battle. To their horror and astonishment their commander-in-chief refused the combat, and, giving immediate orders for raising the siege, broke up his camp and withdrew his army ! The troops were most indignant, and it is recorded that the French troops in Maurice's army loudly exclaimed that they must always seek for hiding places from the enemy, if they were to fly before him now when feeble and ex-hausted with cold, wet, and long marches." [1]

The same day that Maurice withdrew from before Groll, Spinola relieved that place. Groll was saved, and the war for that year, and for many years to come, was over.

Many reasons have been given by historians for Maurice's inexplicable conduct on this occasion. Whatever the reason was that made him refuse to fight, when all the odds were in his favour, we may be very sure it was not from cowardice. Had Maurice been fighting for a Crown, and had he been his own free agent, Spinola would not have relieved Groll so easily.

Early in January, 1607, the Archdukes, by means of com-missioners sent to the Hague for the purpose, intimated to the States-General that they would be glad to receive proposals for an armistice. After many negotiations be-tween the States-General and the Archdukes, in which the former upheld their national rights, their liberty, and their

---

[1] Quoted by Davies, ii. p. 401.

readiness to continue the war, if Spain did not recognise
the United Provinces as a free and independent nation,
an armistice was concluded on April 24, by which the
belligerents mutually agreed to a suspension of hostilities for
eight months. It was also agreed that negotiations should
go on between the two contracting parties to settle the
terms of a truce for ten, fifteen, or twenty years, with the
distinct understanding that the Archdukes recognised the
independence of the United Provinces.

However welcome an eight months' truce, with a pro-
bability of peace to follow, might be to the citizens of the
United Provinces, it was by no means palatable to Prince
Maurice, who had been a soldier from his boyhood and to
whom military glory was more dear than anything. "The
Count Maurice is much troubled with this treaty and much
feareth a peace," wrote Sir John Ogle to Salisbury, soon
after the truce was made public.[1]

A long peace, of course, meant a great reduction in the
States' army. Soldiers who lived by war would find the
Netherlands a poor field for fame and fortune, and many
would be thrown out of their employment by being reduced.
This unsatisfactory look out naturally made the English
officers serving in the States' army anxious about their
future, and those who had friends at Court were not likely
to neglect the opportunity of asking for their friends'
help at this crisis in their lives. Colonel Edward Cecil's
military ambition, and desire for advancement, prompted
him at this time to ask his uncle for his interest in obtaining for him the high post of "President of Munster,"
then vacant.

---

[1] Ogle to Salisbury, "from the Haghe, July 13, 1607."—*S.P. Holland.* See
also a speech made by Prince Maurice in the Assembly of the States-General
against granting a peace. Bentivoglio, p. 442.

SIR E. CECIL TO THE EARL OF SALISBURY.

"MAY IT PLEASE YOUR LORDSHIP,

" I have found my harte so resoulved allwaye to honore y°, that I should doe it much ronge in not hoping of y⁻ favore, espetially in a busines that concerneth my howle fortunes, booth in regarde of my reputation and my perticular contentment, considering that as I have taken paynes so many yeares out of my contrye, speante of my owne perticular estate (all to make my selfe able to serve his Maᵗ.), having neclected meanes to inriche my purse, in regarde to yʳ. lo. continuale incoragemente to be advanced. Not fiending any thing to hinder my presant fortune, but as yʳ lo. hath towld mee, that I have not lived in the Contrye wheare I desier to command. It is very true that I never was in Ierland. Yet I have traveled in many Contryes, and sceanc [since] have commanded booth horse and foote, and as a Governer of a Towne,¹ and good commands doe much resemble on a nother, and wᵗʰ yʳ lo. favore and instructions, I can not confess my selfe uncapable of the presedent of Munster. But if yʳ lo. be curyous in regarde y° would not have mee preferred in a contrye wheare others have takene paynes, yʳ lo. will give mee leave to speake thus much for my selfe, that at my going in to the lowe Contryes, the Queene had noe Armye in Ierland. And that my eand [end] was that in going to the beast scoule, I might have the better prefermente; besides I howld it noe diferenc betwixt him that scearves the Kinge and those that venter as much to be able to serve him unless his quallety and command hath beeyne better. Yet I howld the Kings servis to be preferred before all other respects, and if yʳ lo. shall thincke mee worthy of the place I sue for, I can not be to earnest, hoping that as I have the honore to be yʳ nephue and that I doe not presume of it, so it shall be noe hinderance to mee. I can never hope for a better occation. Theare fore I sett up my reaste that if ever yʳ lo. thincke mee worthy of advansment, y° will thincke mee worthy of this ; for that none can come to this plase wᵗʰ out yʳ leading, nor

---

¹ Th:s is ambiguous, but seems to imply that Edward Cecil was, or had been, governor of a town ?

none that is more suerly tyed to praye for y^r lo. longe and happie life as

"Y^r lo. most diutefull and obedient servant

"as well as Nphue,

"ED. CECYLL.

"this present thursdaye."[1]

Add. "To the Rig^h honorable and his singular good lo. the Earle of Salcburye, lo. Scecritary of Eingland, &."

End. "1607. Sir Edward Cecyll to my Lord."

This letter produced no results, and the Presidency of Munster was bestowed on Sir Henry Danvers, who had been created, in 1603, Baron Danvers of Dantsey, in the county Wilts, a distinguished soldier.   Curious to say Lord Danvers was first cousin to Edward Cecil on his mother's side.[2]

The twelve months' armistice was passed in active nego-tiations between the commissioners representing Philip III., King of Spain, and the Archduke, and the commissioners representing the United Provinces of the Netherlands. Conspicuous among the former were the Marquis Spinola, Don Juan de Mancicidor, private secretary to the King of Spain, and President Richardot.   The chief man among the States' envoys, was John of Olden Barneveld—the heart and soul, life and strength, upholder and supporter of his country's rights.   The Spanish commissioners had arrived at the Hague on the last of January, 1607–8, and were sumptuously lodged there.   The negotiations between the rival envoys were stormy and perplexing, and it was long

---

[1] *Cecil Papers, Hatfield*, 12/2.

[2] Henry Lord Danvers was second son of Sir John Danvers of Dantsey, Co. Wilts, by Elizabeth his wife, youngest daughter and co-heir of John Nevill, last Lord Latimer. Lord Danvers served in the Low Country wars under Maurice of Nassau, and was knighted for his services in France. He was Lieut.-General of the horse, under the Earl of Essex, in Ireland, and was created Earl of Danby in 1626. He died s.p. 1643.

doubtful whether it would be peace or renewed war. Another desponding letter concerning the future of the States' army from Edward Cecil to his uncle, written at this time, gives a soldier's view of the anticipated peace—a view doubtless entertained by all the English officers in the States' service.

SIR E. CECIL TO THE EARL OF SALISBURY.

" MAY IT PLEASE Y^r LORDSHIP,

" At my coming to the Hage, I did thincke it strange to fiend the odes [odds] to be on they warres side. But 7 dayes after it was turned like a Cocke pitt mache, and continues so much the stronger, as the Artikell of the Trade to the Indies is passed,[1] wch was all the hope wee souldiers had on our sid that it would not have beeyne. For the greater busines heare I leave to those that should know them better, that ar ordayned to that eand, only I can say thus much, that the pople heare that are protistans ar so indiferent that this 40 years warr have horned them so that they thincke the should live better in warr then in pease. As for the Papists they desier pease upon there knees, so that if it prove pease I shall wishe my selfe a Papist to be the better contented. For our tropes the busines is not as yet handled, only the speake of keeping up of there ammye [army], but the will cassere [cashier] many, and yet howlde on there contrybusion for some 10 years. But if the make pease, I looke for noe other but every yeare the will cassere so many that there Armye will not stand. And as every mann begines to seecke for his beast meanes, so I must confess I have non can healpe mee but y^r lo. wch I know is so honorable, that if for these 10 yeares I have followed the warres I have deserved anything, that y^r lo. will remember mee. If not, I shall thincke my selfe borne in an ill hower, to have spent my tyme, and all I have in the worlde, and to see so many at home,

---

[1] This is a mistake. The rights claimed by the Dutch for their East India trade were violently opposed by the Spaniards all through the year 1608, and the refusal of the Dutch to renounce their India trade nearly brought the negotiations to an untimely end. It was not till February, 1609, that the Dutch commissioners gained their point and secured the India trade to the republic.

wth out paines, profitt so much. I doubte not but y^r lo. is scencible of a mann of my rancke that hath lived like a Coronell, and must come home and live like a younger brother that was comde from the Inns of Corte.

" I feare if my misfortune be so bad, it will conferme many mennes judgements, that thought it safe to stay at home. I have gon farder then I did thincke to have don, therefore I will conclud, and as I have from theye begining only soughte to y^r lo. for my fortune, so will I till the eand of my life, and never cease, but pray dayly for y^r lo. long and happe life as the hope of

" Y^r lo. most humble and most affetionatt

"Nephe and servant,

"ED. CECYL L.

" From uttricke,
      the 12 of Marche."[1]

Add. " To the Rig^h honorable and his very good lo. the Earle of Salsbury, Scecritary of Eingland, and one of his Ma^t most honorable prive Counsell."

End. " 12 Martii, 1607.[2] Sr Edw. Cecill from the Haghe "[?]

No private soldier could be more adverse to peace than was Maurice of Nassau, and he was only won over to the peace party at the eleventh hour, by Barneveld stipulating with the Spanish commissioners, that an army of thirty thousand men should be maintained by the States during the proposed truce with Spain.[3]

---

[1] This is the last letter from Edward Cecil to his uncle that I have been able to find. *Cecil Papers, Hatfield*, 201/122.

[2] March 12, 1608, new style. Two months after this letter was written, Edward Cecil had the misfortune to lose his mother, who died in London, May 22, 1608, and was interred in St. John Baptist's Chapel, Westminster Abbey. See Stanley's *Westminster Abbey*, and Chester's *Registers of Westminster Abbey*, p. 120.

[3] Sir Richard Spencer and Sir Ralph Winwood, who represented the King of Great Britain at the Conference at the Hague, mention, in a letter to Salisbury, dated February 28th, 1607-8, that the negotiators on the Archduke's ·side were particularly anxious for peace, "especially the Marquis (Spinola), whose colo^r as he treateth is observed to come and goe, as the Buisines is in hope to avaunce, or in danger to recule."—*S.P. Holland.*

On April 9, 1609, a truce for twelve years was signed by the deputies of the States-General and the Arch-dukes, and speedily ratified by the States-General and the Archdukes. The King of Spain's signature was still wanting, but that also was obtained after a truly Spanish delay.

The United Provinces had gained a great victory, for they had secured "peace with honour." They had not undergone forty years of incessant war for nothing. Their gigantic struggle was rewarded by the declaration of their independence by the sovereign who claimed them for subjects "by the right of inheritance." They had secured a trade with India which was soon to make their small country one of the richest in Europe, and last, but greatest victory of all, they had established on a firm basis the Protestant religion within their Provinces.

From a list of the States' troops for 1608, we find that Sir Edward Cecil's troop of horse (cuirassiers) was 100 strong, and his private foot company 275 strong; Colonel Horace Vere's being 276, and Colonel Ogle's 200 strong.[1] In 1609 the foot companies of all nations had to be reduced. The reduction seems only to have been in men, and the fair dealing of the States by their foreign troops, which had served them so very faithfully, is shown in the following letter from a Mr. Turner to Lord Salisbury, dated from the Hague, May 20, 1609.[2]

"SIR, Since my former, having mett wth no timely messenger, the proceedinge of the States in the reduction of their Armie, hath given me further matter of relation. Before they sate downe to enacte anythinge touchinge theire Strangers, they caused a

---

[1] *S.P. Holland*, 1608, fo. 239, *et seq.*

[2] The copy of this letter, preserved among the *S.P. Holland* for 1609, has no signature. It is endorsed—"Mr Turner, from the Haige, 20 May, 1609, p. M^r ten (*sic*) 26 May, 1609."

generall muster to be taken of the companies of their owne nation, and reduced them downe to the number of 70; some of them havinge been 200, some 150, and the least 113. This was a kind of prognostication, consequently inducinge the strangers (whome they purposed to deale wth after the same manner) to submitt them selves to the like wth more patience, consideringe they made their owne nation an example of the worst the stranger should suffer. And I thinke the English had stooptd to it, had it not been (that when by speciall order the States came to proceed further) the private companies of the French were ordeined to stand at 100^{ds} and the English at 70^{ies}, this made the English chiefts seeke for redresse. The States at first (without seeminge to understand the emulation between the English and French) begann to dispute the poinct in generall te^{r}rmes of reason, wthout respect to that circumstance, and asked our collonels why they should stand so stiffly for the satisfaction of such demands, consideringe that first they could not be ignorant, the present condition of their states required an ease of their charge, in wch regarde if they cast many of their captaines, the example of all princes in like cases would excuse them. And therefore, since they continued all officers, only discharginge some souldiers wch they must necessarily doe, they had an opinion the couse they tooke would rather be reputed honorable, then any way worthy of mislike. And much the rather for that the deduction of number would not lessen the captains pay (all standing at an equality in that point) unless they hoped to increase it by unlawfull means, wch they would not thincke would be any ground of their pretence. The collonells answered, that the course their Lordships tooke in generall, or for every nation particularly in respect only of itselfe (if it might so barely be understoode), was altogether worthy to be acknowledged honorable; but their order taken wth the English, understood comparatively in respect of the French, did lay some touch of dishonour, or at least neglect of their nation in particular, and therfor requird them for their honours sake, to request their Lordships to remember that the English have deserved as well in their war as the French, and therefore hoped to have as good a condition in their peace. To this the States replyed that whatsoever the French enioyed above the English, it came whollie out of the gratious allowance of their kinge, and was no worke of theirs. Then they insisted, and the collonels departed wth discontentment. The next day, the States sent for them againe, and gave them 50 men a peece more for their owne companies and made their levetenant collonels 100[ths] thinkinge wth this particular pleasure to have satisfyed them. But the Collonels (because it should be seene it was no private respect to themselves, but a regarde in generall to the honor and good of their nation that moved them to speake) prefered a Remonstration to the States givinge them thos fiveties of their owne back againe towards the augmentation of the pravate companies, and comended their cause to their Lordships further consideration, w[ch] at length made them grant 400 more, beside the hundreth that S[r] Horace Vere and S[r] Edward Cecyll returde back to be distributed thorough the nation at that discretion of the chiefes. So that all the Collonels are projected to stand at 200[ths], the Leevtenant Collonels at 100th, and the rest at 90[ies], 80[ies], and 70[ies], accordinge to their chiefs favor or their owne desarte. Only S[r] Thomas Horwell[1] and S[r] Henry Carew[2] who are each of them 100th. This is project of the Collonels; and will stand (if noe new conceipte of the States contradict it) that States continued, will holde 5000 English still in pay. Commissaries are presently to be dispatched away for the guarrisons to performe the deduction.

"Sir Tho. Horewell had his Ex[lies] favour very freely shewed him, in speakinge that his condition (for his honours sake, because he had formerly held place of extraordinarie respect) might be extraordinarylie allowed him. And in that difference of number (I thinke) he shall prevaile.

"I humbli comand my love and service to you, and continue
"Your worship to
be comaunded.

"I beseech excuse my rude hast."

In the autumn of this year, namely on August 28, 1609,

---

[1] Sir Thomas Horwell was one of the 300 gentlemen knighted by James I. on July 23rd, 1603, at Whitehall. Nichols' *Progresses of James I.*
[2] Sir Henry Cary.

died Sir Francis Vere, at his home in Essex, aged 54.[1]   He
had been appointed on June 15th, 1606, Governor of
Portsmouth for life,[2] and while holding that appointment
had greatly improved the fortifications of that important
place.   He was buried in Westminster Abbey, where a
splendid monument, with suitable inscription, was erected
to his memory by his widow.[3]   The epigram given in
Camden's *Remains*,[4] is a more worthy epitaph to this truly
great soldier :—

" When Vere sought Death, arm'd with his sword and sheild,
    Death was afraid to meet him in the Feild ;
    But when his weapon he had laid aside,
    Death like a coward strooke him and he dy'd."

Francis Vere has been often mentioned in these
pages, but not as often as could be wished.   It is left for
some able writer to write his life, and whatever his faults
of temper and character may have been, as a soldier and
leader he was second to none amongst the soldiers of his
time.   The martial Elizabeth recognised his superior
military capacity when she called him "her greatest
captain."   He died too soon, but lived to see the curtain
drop on the first act in the great game of war, in which he
himself had played such a leading part, which was being
enacted in the Low Countries.   "Di che moriva Signor
Francisco Vere ? asked the great general Spinola of Sir
Edward Herbert, some years after Vere's death.   " Per
aver niente à fare," said Herbert.   " E basta per un generale,"
replied Spinola.[5]

---

[1] *Biog. Brit.* art. " Vere."
[2] Grant, June, 1606.—*S.P. Dom.*
[3] Sir F. Vere married Elizabeth Dent, by whom he had several children
who predeceased him.   *Biog. Brit.*
[4] p. 401-5.
[5] Life of Lord Herbert of Cherbury, p. 102.

Two important posts became vacant by Vere's death, viz., the commands at the Brill, in Holland, and at Portsmouth, in England. The Earl of Exeter wrote to his half-brother, Lord Salisbury, three days after Sir Francis Vere's decease, begging him to bestow one of the vacant posts on his (Lord Exeter's) son, Sir Edward Cecil. This letter is couched in the courteous and respectful language used by our forefathers in their letters to both strangers and relatives. The style, however hyperbolical and flattering it may sometimes appear, is more agreeable than some of the matter-of-fact letters of the present day.

LORD EXETER TO LORD SALISBURY.

" MY LORD, occasions dyscover all thynges, and this particular occasio wch is falle by the death of Sir Franncis Vere, wherby two of his offices are voyde, I hope by th'obtayn'g of one of them for my son Edward through yor favour, wherof I doubt not, wyll dyscover the trew affectio of an uncle to a nephew, and the trew honour of yor noble nature to advace them that you shall hold fytt for ether of those places, wherby you shall not oly bynd hym in cheanes of love and trew respect to doe you servyce, but herby advaunce the honour of yor house wch honorable myndes doe for the most part respect, and so my good Lord remebri'g my trew love unto you wch shall the much more be encreased by this occasio, I wyll allwayes rest

"Yo^r trew affectionat
" Brother to coma'd,
" EXETER." [1]

The above letter was delivered to Lord Salisbury by Sir Edward Cecil,[2] who was then in England. It speaks well for Lord Salisbury's upright and fair dealing that he

---

[1] This letter is addressed " To the right honb^{le} my verie good Lo. and D. Brother, the Earle of Salisbury, Lo. High Treasurer of England."

[2] The endorsement of above letter proves this : " Erle of Exeter to my Lo. by Sr Edward Cecill, the last of August, 1609."—*S.P. Dom.*

did not show favour to his own family, at the expense of others who merited advancement for their services to the State.   Lord Arundel of Wardour solicited the captaincy of the Brill, or of Portsmouth, from Salisbury, in consideration of his having spent £18,000 in the service of King James and Mary Queen of Scots,[1] but his claim was also rejected, and the post at the Brill was bestowed on Colonel Sir Horace Vere,[2] who richly merited the preferment. Portsmouth was given to William Herbert, Earl of Pembroke,[3] "one of the most agreeable men of his time."

Blood is thicker than water, and it is only natural for a man to help his family on in the world when he has the opportunity, but an honourable nature will never stoop to injustice, or undue partiality, in order to gratify family pride or the ties of kinship, however close.   And it would have been unjust and partial dealing in the uncle to have bestowed the Presidency of Munster, the governorship of the Brill or of Portsmouth on his nephew, when there were prior claimants for these high posts.   Robert Cecil lived in an age when bribery and jobbery of all kinds were freely exercised in the highest positions.   To his everlasting credit be it spoken, he passed through the ordeal of supreme power with clean hands.   Spanish gold never found its way into his purse, and had his life been spared for ten years longer than it was, the reign of James I. would doubtless have left a brighter page in England's history than it unfortunately did.

---

[1] Lord Arundel to Salisbury, Sept. 8, 1609.—*S.P. Dom.*

[2] Appointed 18th Oct., 7th Jas. I.   *Biog. Brit.*

[3] "Oct. 16, 1609.   Grant to the Earl of Pembroke of the offices of Keeper and Captain of the Town and Isle of Portsmouth, Constable of Porchester Castle, and Lieut. of Southbear Forest for life."—*S.P. Dom.*

CHAPTER VI.

1609-1610.

War clouds—Death of the mad Duke of Cleves—Claimants to his duchies—
Leopold of Austria seizes Juliers—The political situation—Attitude of
France and the United Provinces—The champion of Protestantism—Great
Britain's interest in the Cleves succession—4,000 Britons to be sent to
Juliers—Sir E. Cecil appointed general and commander-in-chief of the
British contingent—His departure from England—Preparations for war in
France and the United Provinces—Assassination of Henry IV.—Anarchy
and confusion in France—Contentions between the French peace and war
parties—Result—Lord Salisbury on the situation—March of the Dutch and
British forces to Cleveland—Arrival before Juliers—The Prince of Anhalt—
Description of Gulich or Juliers—Commencement of the siege—Choosing
positions—Dutch jealousy—Details of the siege—Valour and activity of
the British commander—Sir Edward Herbert—His account of the siege—
Other accounts—Recent adventures of Archduke Leopold—His lack of
means—The broken reed on which he leant for support—The new governor
of Juliers—Journal of the siege—Winwood's letters—His praise of General
Cecil—General Cecil's letter to Henry, Prince of Wales—Difficulties of
the siege—Arrival of the French army—Good artillery practice—Its effect
on the fortifications—A civilian's impatience—The last struggles of the
garrison—Surrender—Terms—Restoration of the disinherited princes—
Further proceedings of Leopold of Austria—Father Baldwin—His capture
—Is sent to London—General Cecil's despatch to the Prince of Wales—
The Cologne conference—Unsatisfactory results.

AT the very time that the two belligerents in the Netherlands were busily employed in burying the war hatchet—
each party to the wished for truce doing their best to bury
it so deep that it would be a difficult task for the one to
dig it up again without giving timely notice to the other—
a storm was brewing, which would, sooner or later, burst
over the Protestant Netherlands, and spread devastation
through Protestant Germany, before the fury of the
tempest should be spent. The first dark cloud on the

horizon of peace was caused by an apparently trivial occurrence. But, as often happens, even now, a trivial occurrence produced the most serious after-results. The cloud no bigger than a man's hand is the first warning of the coming tempest; and no cloud, however small, that overcasts the political horizon can be disregarded by those who study the signs of the times.

In the spring of 1609 died the mad Duke of Cleves without issue. In default of male heirs, the succession was claimed by the representatives of the duke's three deceased sisters, also by the youngest and last surviving sister of the deceased duke. The eldest sister had married Albert Frederick, Elector of Brandenburg and Duke of Prussia. The second sister had married the Count of Neuburg. The third had married the Count of Deux-Ponts; and the fourth, who survived her brother, had married, late in life, the Margrave of Burgau, by whom she had no issue.

The mad duke's duchies were claimed by John Sigismund, Elector of Brandenburg and Duke of Prussia, son of the eldest sister; Philip Lewis, Count of Neuburg, son of the second sister; the Count of Deux-Ponts, and the Margrave of Burgau. These were the four principal claimants, and, as will presently appear, the Elector of Brandenburg was the rightful heir to the duchies.

In 1572, William, Duke of Juliers and Cleves, father of the last duke, settled the succession on the marriage of his eldest daughter to Albert, Elector of Brandenburg, on her and her children, in case of the extinction of the male line in his family. In making this settlement the duke was guided by the example of the first Duke of Cleves, who, in 1418, settled the succession on his eldest son, and on him only, his brothers being excluded from any share in it, and in default of male heirs to him, to his eldest daughter, exclusive of other daughters.[1]   A like anti-Salic settlement was made in 1496, when the only daughter of William, Duke of Juliers and Berg, married John, son of the reigning Duke of Cleves, thus uniting the two territories. These successive decrees had completely cut out many German princes from the right of succession at some future time, however nearly allied in blood to the House of Cleves.   Having shown that John Sigismund, Elector of Brandenburg, was by settlement and birth heir to the duchies on his uncle's decease, it is now necessary to show his superior claims over the three other principal claimants already named.

When the second daughter of the old Duke of Cleves married in 1574 the Count of Neuburg, it was agreed in the marriage contract that the elder sister and her children were at all times to be recognised as the heirs to the duchies, if the male line became extinct.   In 1575, Ann, Countess of Neuburg, and her husband renounced the succession to the duchies, in consideration of an augmentation of their marriage portion.   Her sister Magdalen made the same renunciation on her marriage with the Count of Deux-Ponts four years later.[2]   The youngest sister, Sibylla, who married Charles of Austria, Margrave of Burgau, was not called upon to make this renunciation, partly it is said from her marriage portion not being forthcoming, and partly from her brother's deranged state of mind.   Her claims, however, were nowhere, and caused no uneasiness to the three other competitors.   Whilst these rival claimants were disputing about the succession to the duchies of Cleves and Juliers and the earldoms of La Marck, Berg, Ravensberg and Ravenstein, the Emperor Rudolph, as head of the German Empire, pretended that it

---

[1] Sully's *Memoirs*, iii. pp. 178–9.   [2] *Ibid.*

was his right to hold the duchies until the affair was
decided. Going on the old principle that " might makes
right, " and also that when " rogues fall out honest men get
their due," the Emperor despatched Leopold of Austria,
Bishop of Strasburg, to Juliers to take possession of the
prize. The Prince-Bishop, entering the duchy of Juliers,
seized the capital city and put a strong garrison into it.
This unexpected proceeding convincing the Elector of
Brandenburg and the Count of Neuburg that it would be
better to share the duchies than let them be usurped by
the Emperor, they joined in a league, and taking possession
of the rest of the late duke's dominions, appealed to
France and the United Provinces for aid.

Had the disputed duchies been on the borders of Italy,
or even to the east of Saxony, the wrongs of the German
princes, and the rapacity of the House of Austria, might
not have caused much uneasiness to the King of France.
But the debatable land lay on the frontiers of France, and
the Emperor was a formidable neighbour to have so near.
A Roman Catholic power in Cleves meant destruction to
the United Provinces, which Provinces Henry IV. had
reasons of his own for supporting against Spain and
Austria. It was all important, therefore, to uphold the
Elector of Bradenburg's claims to the duchies, and by so
doing Henry saw his way to humble the House of Austria,
to readjust the balance of power in Europe, bringing
France to the highest position amongst European nations
that she had yet filled. All this Henry hoped to effect by
showing his " disinterested generosity towards persecuted
princes."[1] The United Provinces had no choice but to
uphold the Elector of Brandenburg, and it was of the
utmost importance to them that a Protestant prince with

---

[1] Sully, p. 182.

no Spanish proclivities,[1] should hold the duchies. Here then were two nations, both holding different religions, united together against the Austro-Spanish faction.

James Stuart, King of Great Britain and Ireland, as champion by inheritance of the Protestant faith in Europe, had already been applied to by the disinherited princes, and his alliance, offensive and defensive, asked for by the prince's ambassadors. The champion was quite ready to recognise the fact that either Brandenburg or Neuburg was *de jure* heir to the disputed duchies. He even went so far as to assert that Brandenburg had the best rights of the two claimants, but instead of throwing down his gauntlet and challenging any one to take it up and fight him, who did not believe the Elector of Brandenburg to be the rightful heir to the duchies, he merely offered to bring about a reconciliation between the Emperor and the princes, and so settle the disputed succession in an amicable manner.[2] It is not always an easy matter to reconcile two individuals who were once friends, but have come to loggerheads about some trifling cause, but it is a very difficult thing—if not an impossibility—to reconcile the three claimants to a rich estate, and make two of them give way to one, or even one of them give way to two. The weakest must go to the wall, and he knows it full well, but he does not go of his own free will, or love the hand that sends him there. Neither can he be reconciled to staying there if he thinks he sees his way to reversing the tables and taking a front rank place. In the case of the disputed duchies, the two senior heirs-at-law knew if they renounced their claims now that they renounced them for evermore, as there was another powerful claimant pressing

---

[1] The late Duke of Cleves had privately supported the Spaniards. *Ibid.*
[2] The manifesto of James I. for settling the affairs of Juliers and Cleves, was dated July 15, 1609. Winwood's *Memorials,* iii. pp. 53-4.

to the front, and ready to assert his rights, whom the Emperor openly favoured, in order to make his seizure of Juliers appear an act of justice and on behalf of this claimant, Christian II., the Elector of Saxony.[1]

The efforts of the British peacemaker to reconcile the Emperor to his disobedient vassals totally failed. France and the United Provinces having agreed to send a large army to Juliers to co-operate with the forces of the princes in driving Leopold out of Juliers, and reinstating the two princes, James could not well keep neutral in the coming war, which was really a religious struggle between the Protestants and Roman Catholics. After receiving envoys from France, from the States, and from the princes, and hearing how much the two former nations were going to adventure in the Cleves campaign, the British champion of the Protestant faith ultimately consented to furnish four thousand infantry soldiers to assist the cause of the German princes. Why should Great Britain, it may be asked, who was at peace with all Europe, be drawn into a German quarrel in which she had no concern? France had her own interests to protect, and her own policy of aggrandisement to pursue, in rushing into war. The United Provinces had their whole future safety at stake in the issue of the Cleves succession, but Great Britain seemed removed from all gain and loss, whatever the issue might be. She might have been quite justified in maintaining a

---

[1] "The Emperor Frederick III. did grant unto Albert, Duke of Saxe, in respect of his service against Charles, Duke of Burgundy, and afterwards against the King of Hungary, the Dukedoms of Juliers and Berg, if by death of William, Duke of Juliers and Berg, or by any other means, that dukedom should devolve to the Empire. This grant was afterwards confirmed by the Emperor Maximilian, first to the said Albert, Duke of Saxe, and to his brother Ernest, and to their heirs male." Extract from the claims made by the Elector of Saxony to the duchies of Juliers and Berg, &c.—*S. P. Holland*, 1610.

benign neutrality in these days, but at the time treated of
there was every prospect of a religious war throughout
Northern Europe, which would either establish the Protestant faith on a firm and lasting basis in many countries,
or else turn the balance of power in favour of the Roman
Catholics, and materially check, for many a long day, the
rapid growth of those countries which had lately adopted
the reformed religion. This is why the Cleves succession,
which was a pivot on which mighty events might turn,
was a matter of importance to Great Britain. Added to
this, both France and the United Provinces were largely in
England's debt. James was in fact a French and Dutch
bondholder to a large amount, and though he had not
negotiated the loans or advanced the money, to him was
due both principal and interest, which was a good reason
for his upholding France and the United Provinces. The
grant of 4,000 men for the Cleves expedition was not such
a great concession on the King's part, as these troops were
to be taken from the British regiments then in the States'
service, and were not to be in addition to them. As a
slight balance to this concession, and to make it appear
greater, James agreed to pay these 4,000 men from the
time of their taking the field until their return to their
garrisons.

It is needless to tell of the great preparations made in
France for the coming war, or unfold the mighty designs
of Henry the Great for humbling his enemies, and putting
a stop to Austrian intrusions, as an impending calamity in
France was to put a stop to these great projects, and
completely alter the aspect of affairs.

James, having decided to send 4,000 of the British
troops in the States' service with the expedition to
Cleves, at his own expense, proceeded to make choice of a
general to command these troops. The choice fell on Sir

Edward Cecil.[1]   There was no *London Gazette* in those
days to record military appointments and promotions, but
commissions were given then as now, and Colonel Edward
Cecil's commission as General of the British contingent,
dated April 5, 1610, is given *verbatim* in Rymer's *Fœdera*.[2]
Cecil having been appointed to the command early in the
year 1610, it only remained to select the officers and men
to make up the desired number for active service, and
settle as to their pay when they took the field.   The King
having notified the States-General and his ambassador at
the Hague of his intention to furnish 4,000 men for
the Cleves expedition, the ambassador acted the part
of Adjutant-General, furnishing details of the present pay
of the British troops in the States' service, suggesting
what alterations had better be made, and making all
necessary arrangements according to his instructions.

By his representations to the King, it was decided that
the pay of the soldiers now to be employed should be on
the same footing as heretofore it had been in the States'
service, where the officers' pay was reckoned at thirty-two
days the month, and the soldiers' at forty-two days the
month.[3]   The ordinary pay of a colonel of a regiment in
the States' army was £25 (300 guilders) a month, which
Sir R. Winwood characterises as " slender provision."

To prevent future discontent on the soldiers' part, their

---

[1] I find no mention anywhere of Sir Edward Cecil having personally applied
for this appointment.

[2] " Sciatis igitur quod Nos, de Fide, Probitate Strenuitate et in Re Militari
experientia Dilecti et Fidelis nostri *Edwardi Cecyll* Equitis Aurati, &c., plenius
confidentes, eundem Edwardum, dictorum quater Mille Peditum per *Ordines
Provinciarum* prædictarum Præbendorum, tam Anglorum, quam Scotorum
CAPITANEUM GENERALEM et DUCTOREM fecimus et constituimus."
Extract from Sir E. Cecil's commission, given by Rymer, xvi. pp. 684-5.

[3] These were called "the States' months." See letter from Winwood to
Salisbury, dated February 20th, 1609-10. Winwood's *Memorials*, iii. p. 121.

pay was to be the same as heretofore, but a special scale of
pay was fixed on for the officers, viz :—

Commander-in-chief, per day	£5	0	0
A Colonel, per day	1	0	0
A Lieut.-Colonel	0	6	0
A Sergeant-Major	0	5	0
And the whole 4,000 soldiers with a captain to each company, per day[1]	156	6	8

By the King's express wish, two-thirds of the 4,000 men
were to be English, and the remainder Scotch.

"As for the Commanders," wrote the Lords of the Council to
Winwood, "his Matie holds it fitt, that seeing he bears the
chardges, he may also receave the sole reputation of it, wch he
thinketh may rather be, by having them to subsist of a body by
themselves, and comanded by his owne officers, then by having
them obscured in a mixture wth others, and under the command
of an other; and therefore hath made choice of Sr Edward Cecill
to be comander gnall of these Forces, and to have under him
twoe Lieutenant-Colonells, one for the English and the other for
the Scotts, wth all such other officers as are requisite to a particular
body for the better governement and contentem^t of his people,
when they shall not fynd themselves subordinate to others, but
only subject to the gnall comand of the great Generall of the
whole Army, wch is Christian, Prince of Anhalt." [2]

General Cecil's presence at the Hague being necessary
to help in the selection of officers and men to make up the
desired 4,000 for active service, he received orders the end
of March "to make his speedy repair to the States, where
both the different commands and subordinate places might
be ordered." [3] His departure from England appears to
have been on, or about, April 7th, as Lord Salisbury,

---

[1] From a document among the *S. P. Holland*, 1610.

[2] Letter to Winwood dated March 3rd, signed by the Lord Chancellor,
the Lord Treasurer, the Lord Privy Seal, the Lord Admiral, the Lord Chamberlain, the Earl of Shrewsbury and the Earl of Worcester. Winwood's
Memorials, iii. p. 127.

[3] Salisbury to Winwood, March 28th, 1610. *Memorials*, iii. p. 144.

writing to Winwood under that date, says, "Sir Edward Cecyll besides his Commission hath delivered to him certaine directions to which he is to conforme himselfe, and wherein his Majesty expecteth you shall afford him your best Assistance."[1] James sent a letter to the States-General by General Cecil, assuring them of his affection and good-will towards them, and his readiness to grant them the use of 4,000 of his subjects then in their service, *pour si long-temps que la commodité et l'estat de vos affaires le pourra permettre.* The King goes on to say in this letter that he had specially chosen this gentleman (Sir Edward Cecil) to be commander over the 4,000 men, "tant pour le regard de sa qualité et de la Maison dont il est issu, comme pour son experience et de la preuve qu'il a donnée de sa dévotion au bien de vostre cause ; ce qui, comme nous nous asseurons portera quand à soi sa recommandation envers vous."[2] General Cecil's special rate of pay of £5 per day commenced from April 1st, and he received £300 in advance towards his general expenses.[3]

Sir Edward Cecil arrived at the Hague on April 13th.[4] Before he delivered his Majesty's letter to the States-

---

[1] *Ibid.* iii. 147.

[2] Letter addressed to the "Hautes et Puissantes seigneures nos cheres et bons Amis, &c.," dated "Ce — de Mars, 1610."—*S. P. Holland.*

[3] Warrants. "A warrannt to the Excheq^r to pay to Sr Edward Cecyll, knight, appointed Captain Generall of his Maties forces to be ymploied in the service of Cleve, the some of five pounds by the day from the first day of Aprill last past inclusively, to continue so long as he shall remaine in that charge, and moreover to allow unto him by way of ymprest the some of 300^{li} to be defalk'd upon his Entertaynmt, and such other somes of money for his transportacn as to the Lo. Tres^r shall seeme convenient. Dated at Westm^r, Aprill 12th, 1610." Signet, Docquetts.

Warrant, dated 21st April, 1610, granting 300 li. to Sir E. Cecil, in advance, to be deducted in the future from the allowance of £5 per day "assigned to the Cap.-Gen. of all the forces of the Lord the King about to serve in the duchy of Cleves in the maintenance of the Princes competitors in their posses-sions." Pell's issue Roll, April 21st, 1610.—*S. P. Dom.*

[4] Winwood to Salisbury, April 22d, 1610.—*S. P. Holland.*

General, he, in conjunction with Sir Ralph Winwood, informed Prince Maurice of his Majesty's wishes concerning the British troops, and consulted with him and the English colonels as to the selection of certain companies out of the British regiments, in order to make up the allotted 4,000 men. Sir Horace Vere willingly granted nine companies out of his regiment, and Sir John Ogle, who was absent at Dordrecht, sent word that such companies might be selected out of his regiment as might be necessary for his Majesty's service. The two Scotch colonels being absent, Sir Robert Henderson, lieut.-col. to the Lord Buccleuch, was treated with for as many companies out of the two Scotch regiments as might make up the third part of the 4,000 men, according to the King's directions. It was then agreed by the Prince, General Cecil, and the English colonels, that the 4,000 should consist of General Cecil's whole regiment, nine companies from Sir Horace Vere's regiment ; six from Sir John Ogle's regiment ; nine from Lord Buccleuch's,[1] and Colonel Brogue's Scotch regiments, which made up a total of 3,900 men ; and to make up the full number of 4,000, General Cecil proposed to raise 100 men at his own charge, for the reinforcing of his own company, " to give satisfaction to many young gentlemen whoe doe followe him in this warre," wrote Winwood to Salisbury on April 20th.[2]

General Cecil presented his Majesty's letter to the States-General on April 16th, and Winwood explained all his master's wishes regarding the 4,000 soldiers. The States-General having given their consent to certain

---

[1] Sir Walter Scott, of Buccleuch, was created, 16th of March, 1606, Lord Scott of Buccleuch. He greatly distinguished himself in the border warfare between Scotland and England and afterwards in the Netherlands as colonel of a Scotch regiment. He died in 1611, and was succeeded by his only son, Walter, 2nd Baron and 1st Earl of Buccleuch.

[2] Winwood to Salisbury, April 22d, 1610.

companies being selected from the British regiments in their service, Sir Edward Cecil had the task of forming them into regiments and appointing officers, "both ordinary, as Collonels, Lieut.-Cols., Sergeant-Maiors," wrote Winwood to Salisbury; "and extraordinary, as Sergeant-Maior, Provost, Quartermaster-generall; wch will be necessary and by the States are used." The force was divided into three regiments. The first regiment, consisting of fifteen companies,[1] was commanded by General Cecil,—Philip Pakenham[2] being Lieut.-Colonel, and John Proude,[3] Sergeant-Major. The second regiment, consisting of fourteen companies, was commanded by Lieut.-Colonel Sir Hatton Cheeke, as Colonel—Hollis being Lieut.-Colonel, and Courtenay, Sergeant-Major. The third regiment, which was Scotch, consisting of nineteen companies, was commanded by Lieut.-Colonel Sir Robert Henderson, as Colonel,—Caddell being Lieut.-Colonel and William Balfour, Sergeant-Major.[4]

"My Lo. Generall doth now dayly expect the coming over of the treasurer for his troopes," wrote Winwood to Salisbury, on May 3rd; "in the meantyme, his care is to have all his Companies lodged neere at hand, as now they are, wthout charge to his Mat^{ie}, and to treate with the States, both for provision of waggones and for furnishing of vittayle, not only during the marche into Cleveland, but for the continuance in that service; and yet we fear all care in this point will not be sufficient for preserving the troops (if the French army come downe) from extreme misery of poverty and famine."[5]

This French army which was to eat up all the provisions

---

[1] General Cecil's own company consisted of 300 men.
[2] Afterwards Sir Philip Pakenham.
[3] Afterwards Sir John Proude.
[4] The strength of these three regiments, with the total of their pay per month, and names of officers, made out by direction of Sir R. Winwood, is among the *S. P. Holland* for 1610.
[5] Winwood to Salisbury, from the Hague, May 3, 1610.—*S. P. Holland.*

in and round about the German duchies, was to consist, in addition to the two French regiments in the States' service under Colonel Chatillon, of 20,000 infantry, 4,000 cavalry, 6,000 Swiss, and 50 pieces of ordnance.[1] Early in May the French king had completed most of his preparations, and had sent the following letter to Archduke Albert, preparing him for what was coming :—

"MY BROTHER,

"Not being able to refuse my best allies and confederates the help which they have asked of me against those who wish to trouble them in the succession to the duchies and counties of Cleve, Julich, Mark, Berg, Ravensberg, and Ravenstein, I am advancing towards them with my army. As my road leads me through your country, I desire to notify you thereof, and to know whether or not I am to enter it as a friend or enemy."

Before the Archduke's answer[2] came to this letter, "the great design," as it was called, had been crushed out of existence. On that fatal Friday, May 14th, 1610, the heroic Henry IV., justly surnamed the Great, was foully murdered by the fanatic Ravaillac as he drove through Paris, the day after his Queen's coronation, to witness the preparations for her triumphal entry into Paris on the following Sunday. On the Monday after, Henry was to have left for the frontier to take command of his army.

France was now like a mighty arch from which the keystone had been removed. She shook, swayed from side to side, and then fell to the ground like a house formed out of a pack of cards.

---

[1] Sully, iii. p. 350, *note.*

[2] "The archduke's answer," says Sully, "which did not arrive till after his majesty's death, was to this effect, "My lord, it is in the quality of one of the humblest of your servants that I entreat you will march through my territories, my gates shall be open to you and provisions at your service, relying upon the assurance your majesty will, I hope, be pleased to give, that no act of hostility shall be committed during your march." iii. p. 168.

The grand army waiting at Mezières for Henry to place himself at its head, and the army of the Pyrenees amounting to 12,000 infantry and 2,000 horse, under the Marshal de la Force, were as powerless to move as locomotives waiting for their drivers. Anarchy, confusion and chaos reigned in France ; and Spain and Austria, who had placidly regarded the mighty preparations for war of their deceased enemy, as if ensured of their ultimate safety, had only their once despised enemy, the United Provinces, to guard against.

Henry's death delayed for some time the commencement of the march of the States' troops and the British contingent to Juliers, as the States had to make a serious increase in their expeditionary force, now that there were small hopes of any French succours coming to help them. The last of May Sir Edward Cecil wrote to his friend Sir Julius Cæsar, expressing his hope that the King of Great Britain would grant an additional force in this hour of need to uphold the Protestant cause and check the power of Austria.

SIR EDWARD CECIL TO SIR JULIUS CÆSAR.

" RIGHT HONORABLE,

" I meete wth y^r favors in so many of my occations that I were happie if in this imployment wherein I am, or by any indeavour I could yield y^r ho. some reall testimony of my humble respect and service to y^o, beseeching y^r ho^r continue that noble inclination to mee, for besides the incouragement I have by it, I shall have cause to hope that y^r plentifull and honorable assistanc and good wishes will bring wth them good succes to the action whether I am going. Though by this lamentable accident of the Freanch K. wee ster but wth leaden heeles, if the freanch aydes should fayle ; wee all hope that his Ma^t will iudge the supporting of the Priences an action so full of religion and honor, that he will ioyne wth they states in supplying royally the want of those freanch Levies wthout wch indeed the cause must loose reputation, and the House of Austria be invited to put abrod his homes and brag that our side can not fiend a protecter, noe mann can better iudge of these things than y^r honor, so that it were ill manners to speake more of it. All I will add shalbe a true unfayned hart to doe y^o servic, and be thanckfull to y^r worthy lady for that curtesie I fiend by my wives letter, she afforde her. I desire that my service to her la. and booth y^r worthy dougters may be remembered, and that y^r lo. will ever estime mee

" Y^r Ho.

" most affectionat friend

" and servant,

" ED. CECYLL.

" from the Hage, the
last of Maye."
    " To the Rig^t Honorable
    and his worthy friend S^r
    Julius Cesar, knight, Chan-
    seller of the Exchecker, and
    Counseller to his Matie." [1]

The treaty Henry IV. had made with the German princes after the conference at Halle, was now declared by some of the French Council of State to be null and void, and no longer binding since the maker of it was dead. On June 7th, Cornelis van der Myle, the States' special envoy to Paris, accompanied by Aerssens, the States' ambassador, had an interview with Villeroy, the veteran French Secretary of State, and used all their eloquence in trying to make that wily diplomatist see that France had gone too far to withdraw her promised assistance from the United Provinces and the German princes. Villeroy, as the mouthpiece of the Queen's party —the Spanish party—declared his inability to see that France was bound in honour to hold to the contract made

---

[1] *Add. MSS.* 12507, f. 83.

by the late king. Spanish[1] and Austrian envoys had been cutting the grass from under the feet of the States' envoys and the French war party. Mary de Medicis, the Queen Regent, and most of the Roman Catholic nobility, were for abandoning the German princes, and leaving the States to bear the brunt of the fray. The Huguenots, conspicuous among whom were Bouillon and Sully, were on the side of the war party. The French Ministers were like a house divided against itself, and therefore incapable of a firm and decided policy. To the surprise of everyone they consented at the eleventh hour to send troops to the aid of the disinherited princes. No one was more surprised by this sudden resolution than Lord Salisbury, who sent the following despatch to Sir Edward Cecil on receipt of the intelligence :—

"S[r], I doubt not but that ere this tyme yo[w] have onderstoode the unexpected resolucon of Fraunce, to continue their engagement in the assistance of Cleve w[h] eight thousand foote, and some 12 or 1,400 horse, and that they have chosen the Marshall de la Chastre[2] to be the comaunder of them, to whose choise and direccon it is leafte to take the passages of Trier or Ments, it being not thought fitt that they should goe through anie ptte of the Arch Dukes dominions, all though the Arch Duke had allredy graunted leave for it in the late Kinge his time. This sudden and unexpected resolucon, contrary to so manny strong apprehensions grounded upon the p[re]sent consideracon of their Estate, wherein soe many different and potent humors do nowe showe them sellves, will cleere all those doubts that were caste by the rest of the Confederates concerning the supporting of that action of Cleve ; for though this assistance from France be somewhat inferio[r] to that wch was pmised before at Halle,[3] yet it wilbe

---

[1] The Count de Bucquoy was sent to the funeral of Henry IV., and he openly asked the Queen to countermand the forces to be sent to Juliers.

[2] Claud de la Châtre, Marshal of France, was seventy-three years of age when he accepted the command of this expedition.

[3] "The German princes, of their own accord and in opposition to the

sufficient to divert from the p^rsent, not only from his Matie, but alsoe from the rest of the Confederates, anie newe charge of greater Leavyes, and will add greate countennce and reputacon to the cause it self, when so mightie a State as France, though nowe somewhat destracted by the late assassinate and minoritie of this King, remaineth confident in the associations. It remayneth onely nowe, that in the execution the Princes Possessionaires, wth those that have the charge of the warre, be carefull not to loose the p^rsent opportunitie, before the adversaries gather anie strength, and it will appeare nowe, whether the Archdukes will engage themsellves directlie into the Action for Leopoldus, wch as yet I cannot believe he will doe. Howsoever, there are many apprehensions to the contrary; for yor self I cannot say anie thinge more, but that yo^w must accomodate yor self for the receaving of his Maties troupes into paie, and the disposing of them for this Action, according to the resolucons wch are taken heere, seeing y^or former direccons do lead yo^w to rise when they doe rise, and to march conioyntly wth them. I beseeche God, S^r, to blesse and p'sper yo^w and his Maties subiects under you, as his M^y may receave honor, and y^r cause defense and vigor, whereof God hath made him the great and glorious defender." [1]

Leaving the French contingent under their veteran leader to their tardy preparations for taking the field, and still more tardy march to Juliers, we must return to that little Republic which was going to lead the way in the crusade against the Austrian intruder.

Maurice of Nassau having collected an army of 13,000 foot and 3,000 horse, with 30 pieces of ordnance, arrived at Schenckenschaus, where the troops had their rendezvous,

---

emperor, held an assembly at Hall, in Suabia, to deliberate upon the means of restoring the circles to their former liberty. They met there on the day appointed, to the number of eighteen or twenty. The Venetians, the Prince of Orange, the States of Holland and the Duke of Savoy, who had at last taken a resolution to engage in the common cause, sent deputies thither to represent them. . . . It was publicly deliberated to stop the progress of the House of Austria." Sully, iii. pp. 188-9.

[1] Minute endorsed "June 15, 1610. To Sir Edward Cecyll from my Lord, by Mr Henry Treffrey."—*S. P. Holland.*

early in July. This force included the 4,000 British troops
under Sir Edward Cecil, also the two French regiments
under Colonel Chatillon. It had been definitely arranged
some time before, that his Britannic Majesty's troops were
to march with the States' troops, "not doubting," says
Winwood, " but that their Commander in good discretion
would deferre that respecte wch in right did appertaine
to the Commission of so great a king, and well knowing
that his Generall would be so indicious, not impertinently
to insist upon frivelous and idle puntilles."[1]

On July 16th[2] (new style) the troops began their
march to Juliers. Count William of Nassau, with some
Frisian troops, was left at Schenckenschaus to guard the
frontiers in the absence of the States' army. This was
deemed necessary, notwithstanding the twelve years' truce
with Spain, for had not the late King of Spain repeatedly
declared that *nulla fides est cum hereticis observanda.* Most
of the ordnance, ammunition and stores for the States'
army were sent by river to Dusseldorf, to await the arrival
of the troops there. The army marched in three divisions.
One of the divisions consisted of the 4,000 British troops,
and was commanded by Sir Edward Cecil. Prince
Maurice allowed the British division to have the honour of
marching in the van on the first day of the march, the
Dutch troops, under the Prince, following in the "battalia,"
and the two French regiments in the rear. A small body of
horse, with pioneers, preceded the army, while other troops of
horse flanked the army on either side and guarded the
baggage in the rear. The English, Dutch, and French
divisions took it in turns as to which division should
march in the vanguard, so that all three nations were

---

[1] Winwood to Salisbury, April 22, 1610. *Memorials*, iii. p. 149.
[2] Except when quoting from letters, journals, &c., I have adhered to the *new style* of reckoning, which is ten days later than the *old style*.

contented. It is curious to read nowadays of the short distances covered by an army on the march in the year 1610. "The first daie we marched 4 myles, and quartered in villages by Beber, Cloyster," says Waymouth in his account of this expedition ;[1] "the second we marched some 8 myles. . . . the third we marched some 4 myles, and quartered upon a hill neere Zentem, and over against Wesell." And yet these marches were made by the first general of his day, who must have known every inch of the ground, and had no near enemy to delay his movements.

On July 25th the troops arrived at Neuss[2]—a small town just opposite Dusseldorf—and quartered in corn fields. Here a great review of all the troops was held in honour of the Princes of Brandenburg and Neuburg, who came from Dusseldorf that morning to view the army, "and finding so many old experienced soldiers so well observing order and well apointed, could not but conceive and make shew of great joy for this happie assistance God had sent them."[3] Two days after this event, an untoward accident happened. Two powder wagons blew up, and killed over forty soldiers,[4] besides destroying about thirty wagons and horses that were close by. It is said that Prince Maurice nearly lost his life on this occasion, and there were grave doubts as to whether the two powder wagons had not been purposely set fire to.[5] On the following day the army marched six miles, and quartered

---

[1] "A Journall Relation of the service at the taking in of the towne and castle of Gulicke this present yeare, 1610, with a platt of the town and castle, as it is againe to be fortified, dedicated to the Prince, his Highnes, by George Waymouth." *Royal MSS.* 17B, xxxii.

[2] This town is said to be one of the most ancient in Germany, and has a church dating from the 12th century.

[3] *Journal.*

[4] Crosse, in his continuation of Grimston's *History of the Warres in the Netherlands*, says seventy ; Waymouth only gives forty.

[5] Crosse, p. 1291.

in huts two miles from Juliers.   Here the Prince of Anhalt
joined them with 300 horse and 2,000 foot, besides ordnance
and a great store of provisions and necessaries.

The fortified town of Juliers (German, *Gulich*) is situated
in a fertile plain, at the confluence of the Ellbach and Ruhr,
15 miles north-east of Aix-la-Chapelle, and nearly half way
between Cologne and Maestricht.   The castle, or citadel,
has always been a very strong one, and, according to Zeyler,
is built on piles, which render mining operations difficult.
It was this fortress which Archduke Leopold had seized,
and which the allied forces had now come to wrest from
the tenacious Austrian grip.   It may not seem a great feat
to the modern reader, for an army of nearly 20,000 men,
with 10,000 more troops on the march thither, to lay siege
to, and eventually capture, a small town with a military
garrison of some 2,500 men, however strongly fortified that
small town might be.   It must always be borne in mind that
the art of war was in its infancy in 1610 as compared with
the present day, and consequently artillery was much less
destructive to man, and the work raised by man's hands,
than now.   On the other hand, stone walls, bastions, &c.,
were built as solidly as they are now, and their formidable
height and thickness were serious obstacles to an army which
numbered but very few practical engineers in its ranks.
Added to all this, the fact must never be lost sight of for a
single moment, that the large army which assembled on
the plains of Juliers had every reason to expect the House
of Austria would consider their invasion of the duchies a
casus belli, and that the Archduke Leopold, as representa-
tive of the Emperor of Germany, who considered himself
lord of the soil, would be sent with a large force to relieve
Juliers, and inflict a crushing defeat on the heretics.   It
was also on the cards that the Duke of Saxony (whose
alliance had been secured by the Emperor, when the latter

had recently, for obvious reasons, declared Saxony to be the lawful possessor of the duchies, and promised him his support in obtaining them) would strike a blow to recover what he considered his own property.[1] It was also quite possible that Spain, who set small value on promises made to heretics, would take advantage of the States' army being out of the country, to trump up some reason for breaking the truce.[2] That neither Austria, Spain, or Saxony made an effort to relieve Juliers, and oppose the designs of the allied army, was from no supineness or indifference as to the fate of the debatable land, but merely because the force of circumstances was too strong for them, and Great Britain and France having cast in their lot with the Protestant cause, the Roman Catholic powers did not see their way at present to an advantageous war, so they remained passive, but watchful, spectators, and bided their time.

Waymouth thus describes the fortifications of Juliers :—

" The Castle hath 4 Bulwarkes, and the towne three and one half Bulwarke—everie Bulwarke two Casemates, in every Casemate a sallie ; the wall about the towne and Castle is 16 foote thicke of Bricke, and some 55 foote high from the Bace—the Rampet within the wall of the Castle 120 thicke upon the superficies thereof, of exceeding fast earth, and rammed strong as the wall itself. The towne and castle hath a water ditch, about 200 foot over and 5 or 6 foote deepe of water, with a counterscarpe about the castle 200 foote broade, having a parapett, with a Bankett and a strada coperta 30 foote broade ; likewise two half moones without the Castle, one at each end, or point, of the bulwarkes we attempted, and a raveling between both, in the

---

[1] "The Dukes of Saxony," wrote Salisbury to Winwood, July 23rd, " have undertaken to recover the duchies by war from the *princes possession-aires.*"

[2] "It is thought Spinola might try and relieve Juliers," Winwood to Salisbury, June 15th.

midst of the curtaine against the porte of the Castle ; two ravel-
ings before the two portes of the towne, one half moon before one
bulwark of the town, and another before the half bulwarke . . . .
these works were all stronge, inditiouslie and exactlie made, so
that for the bignes thereof this towne and castle is reputed to be
one of the best fortified by arte that is in Christendom."

On July 29th, the Prince of Anhalt, Prince Maurice,
and General Cecil went and viewed the situation of the
town and castle, and consulted as to the best quarter
for directing the attack. It was resolved that the attack
should be principally bent upon the castle, for being
masters of that, the town must of necessity surrender.
Prince Maurice, in command of two divisions of the army,
took up his quarters, the same day, a mile from the castle,
and began his approaches. Wishing the Dutch and
French troops to have the chief share in the reduction of
Juliers, that the glory of that achievement might fall to
those two nations, Prince Maurice desired General Cecil to
quarter his army in the Maestricht road, and prevent the
town being relieved from that direction. General Cecil
strongly objected to this arrangement, saying very justly
that there was no enemy expected from that quarter, and
while he and his troops were passively waiting for an
enemy who had no intention of coming, the Dutch and
French troops would be doing all the work of the siege,
and the English nation would be for ever disgraced. The
Prince answered these objections by assuring General
Cecil that the Prince of Anhalt was quite content to
quarter his own troops on that side of the town, which
argument the English General quashed by saying that if
the Prince of Anhalt did not understand better what
belonged to his honour and reputation he might lie there
alone if he wished.[1] This reply did not at all please

---

[1] Crosse gives this account of the affair, p. 1296. Waymouth says it was

Prince Maurice,[1] but knowing that to a certain extent the British troops were on this occasion under the immediate command of their own general, and knowing also that they would do their work speedily and thoroughly, he allowed General Cecil to choose his own position, from which he might begin his approaches to the castle with the best advantage. The British troops were accordingly quartered two miles from Prince Maurice's force, but at the same distance (one mile) from the town and castle as the Prince was. The Dutch troops had a whole day's start of the British in making their approaches, and had a famous engineer, Dexter by name, in their quarter. "The Cecilians had only one captain who knew how to work in the earth," says an old historian, "but they made the first breach of all, and were the first that passed over the ditch to the wall."[2]

"The one captain who knew how to work in the earth," was, doubtless, General Cecil himself. He had been brought up in the school of the spade for nearly twelve years, and had assisted at several arduous sieges. "I believe his skill in fortification is his master peece," says an unknown writer in speaking of General Cecil, "for at Gulicke he drew his lines himselfe, and though he began last, he was first in the Rampire, to the honor of our Nation."[3]

the Prince of Anhalt who desired General Cecil to quarter on the side of the town where it was most likely to be relieved, but that General Cecil strongly objected and at last the prince yielded the point.

[1] Crosse, p. 1296.

[2] *Ibid.*

[3] Extracted from *A Discourse of the besieging, defending and relieving of the Towne of Bergen op Zome in the year* 1622. *Royal MSS.* 18A, lxiii. Waymouth confirms the above opinion of General Cecil's skill in fortification, and says in his *Journal,* that he was most part of this siege of Gulick "attending General Cecil, whose hand it pleased him to command in the lineall drawe-ing and describing the manner of his aproaches, batteries, and other workes, by direction from him dailie received."

Enough has already been said to show the reader that
Edward Cecil was a man who chafed under all control, and
whose aim in life was to get to the top of the military
ladder.   In many respects he was well qualified for a
soldier's life, as he was quite willing to take the rough with
the smooth—and in those days there was a good deal more
rough than smooth—and was never so happy as when
marching to battle.   Like all bold men he had plenty of
self-confidence and self-respect, and would not have shrunk
from the most hazardous enterprise committed to his
charge.   A lover of discipline, and a strict upholder of it in
his own regiment, his haughty and independent spirit made
him slow to recognise the fact that a soldier, however high
his rank, has many masters, and must give place to his
senior officer.   Peace and consequent inactivity were gall
and wormwood to Cecil's bellicose and energetic nature,
while active employment in the field brought out all his
good qualities, and he would throw his heart and soul into
his work, in order to bring it to a satisfactory conclusion,
and win distinction.   He only cared for riches in so far as
they helped him to achieve his ends, and brought military
rank, military commands, and military fame, nearer to him.
For years he had been striving (Americans would use the
expressive word *worrying*) to get some command where he
would be his own master, and have a chance of distinguish-
ing himself.   The command in the expedition to Cleves
gave Cecil the chance he had been so long wanting.   Let
us see how he bore himself in this time of probation.

We are told that General Cecil used such diligence
on July 30th, the day he took up his position before
Juliers, that he made his camp, and began his trenches,
which he carried 300 paces towards the castle that night.[1]

---

[1] Waymouth's *Journal.*

The day following, the Prince of Anhalt, tired of waiting for an enemy who came not, came and quartered by General Cecil.

"And that night," says Waymouth, "we made the second and third courts of gaurd and the first Batterie—the 22ᵈ, at night, Generall Cecill, in person, directed the workes and made the fourth court of gaurde and the second Batterie . . . . and the next daie the enemy, with 50 musketeers, sallied out and lodged in dry ditches upon the flanke of our last worke, and these gave fire so hotlie, that our men were hurt as they lay in the trenches. But Generall Cecill commanded a captaine that had the gaurd, to take 60 musketeers and beat them from thence, which accord inglie was done; divers of the enemy being kilde and hurt in their retreate—this daie Generall Cecill riding beyond the trenches to viewe the ground for the next nighte's aproach, within 100 paces of the towne, had his horse kilde under him by a peece of ordinance, which forced him to alighte; yet, after that, he viewed the ground; the castle and the towne all this while continuallie playing upon him with great and small shott . . . . this night and ever after till the Castle and towne was taken in, Generall Cecill was in the trenches and Batteries, at the makeinge of them up, directing in what manner everie thing should be done, which was a great incouragement to all others, seeing their generaȝȝ willing to participate the common hazard."

It may be doubtless thought that Waymouth was a partial writer, and being employed by Sir Edward Cecil, felt himself bound to eulogise that general's conduct. We therefore verify his statements by quoting from other writers, whose veracity will not be questioned.

One of the gentlemen volunteers who came to the English camp before Juliers to learn a lesson in the art of war, was that gallant soldier Sir Edward Herbert, afterwards created Baron Herbert of Cherbury.[1] This gentle-

---

[1] Edward Herbert, 1st Baron Cherbury, was eldest son of Richard Herbert, Esq., of Llyssyn, co. Montgomery, by Magdalen, his wife, daughter of

man, a Herbert of the fighting Herberts, was a man after Sir Edward Cecil's own heart, being chivalrous, brave to recklessness, and a man who delighted in war. Sir Edward Herbert, in his autobiography, thus refers to the siege of Juliers and to his acquaintance with Sir Edward Cecil :—

"It was now the Year of our Lord 1610, when my Lord Shandois[1] and myself resolved to take Shipping for the Low Countrys, and from thence to pass to the City of Juliers, which the Prince of Orange resolved to besiege; making all hast thither we found the Siege newly begun ; the Low Country Army assisted by 4000 English under the command of Sir Edward Cecil . . . . I went and quartered with Sir Edward Cecill, where I was lodged next to him in a Hutt I made there; going yet both by day and night to the Trenches, we making our approaches to the Town on one side and the French on the other.   Our Lines were drawn towards the point of a Bulwark of the Cittadel or Castle, thought to be one of the best Fortifications in Christiandom, and incompassed about with a deep wet ditch.   We lost many men in making these approaches, the town and castle being very well provided both with great and small Shot, and a Garrison in it of about 4000 men besides the Burghers ; Sir Edward Cecill (who was a very active General) used often during this Siege, to go in person in the night time, to try whether he cou'd catch any Sentinells perdues ; and for this purpose still desir'd me to accompany him, in performing wherof both of us did much hazard ourselves, for the first Sentinell retiring to the second, and the second to the third, three Shots were commonly made at us, before we cou'd do anything, tho' afterwards chasing them with our Swords almost home into their Guards, we had some sport in the pursuit of them."[2]

Sir Richard Newport, Knt. Lord Herbert of Cherbury was born in 1581, and married at 15 years of age, his kinswoman, Mary Herbert, daughter and heir of Sir W[m] Herbert, of St. Gillians, co. Monmouth, by whom he had issue two sons and two daughters. Edward Herbert was made a Knight of the Bath at the coronation of James I. and was afterwards sent as ambassador to France. He was raised to the peerage of England as Baron Herbert of Cherbury in 1629. He died in 1648. Burke's *Extinct Peerage*.

[1] Grey Brydges, 5th Baron Chandos, known as the "King of Cotswold.'
[2] *The Life of Edward, Lord Herbert of Cherbury, written by Himself*, p. 75.

The historian of the reign of James I., in referring to the siege of Juliers, says :—

"Sir Edward Cecil, brother (sic) to the Earl of Salisbury, commanded 4000 English at that Siege, whose Conduct gave Life to his soldiers' Valour, and that advanced the glory of his Conduct."[1] Another historian, who records the valour of the British troops at this siege, says, that the soldiers " being animated by the presence of their General (who carried a truncheon in one hand and coyne in the other, to punish the slothful and reward the valiant) they thought nothing too difficult nor dangerous, which might tend to the honor or profit of the service."[2]

Having handed in the above three certificates of Sir Edward Cecil's gallantry and soldierly ability at this siege, we shall forbear for the present to give any more, and proceed now to give the names of the principal gentlemen volunteers who served under Sir Edward Cecil before Juliers. We have already named Sir Edward Herbert and Lord Chandos ; besides these were the Lord St. John,[3] the Lord Walden,[4] Sir Thomas Somerset,[5] Sir Thomas Howard,[6] Sir Henry Rich,[7] Sir Edward Sheffield,[8] Sir

[1] Arthur Wilson's *Life and Reign of James I.* (in Kennett's *History of England*) under year 1610.
[2] W. Crosse, *Hist. of the Netherlands*, p. 1294.
[3] Oliver, 3rd Baron St. John of Bletsloe. He died 1618.
[4] Theophilus Howard, eldest son of the first Earl of Suffolk, summoned to Parliament in the lifetime of his father, as *Lord Howard of Walden*. He was made a Knight of the Garter and appointed Lord Warden of the Cinque Ports. He succeeded his father as 2nd Earl of Suffolk in 1626 and died in 1640.
[5] Sir Thomas Somerset, third son of Edward, 4th Earl of Worcester, was made a Knight of the Bath in 1605, and raised to the peerage of Ireland as Viscount Somerset in 1626. He died in 1651.
[6] Sir Thomas Howard, second son of Thomas, first Earl of Suffolk, was raised to the peerage as Lord Howard of Charlton and Viscount Andover in 1622, and created Earl of Berkshire in 1626. He married Elizabeth Cecil, one of the daughters and co-heirs of Wm. Cecil, 2nd Earl of Exeter, by whom he had nine sons and four daughters.
[7] Sir Henry Rich, second son of Robert, 3rd Lord Rich and 1st Earl of Warwick, by his first wife Lady Penelope Devereux. Sir Henry Rich was created Earl of Holland in 1624. He was beheaded in 1649.
[8] A son of Edmund, 3rd Baron Sheffield and 1st Earl of Mulgrave.

N 2

George Howard, Sir Warham St. Leger,[1] Sir John
Witchard, Mr. Buckhurst, and Captain Brett. Among
the nobles who followed the Prince of Anhalt to Juliers
were, the Duke of Wurtemburg, the Count of Waldeck,
Baron Dona, &c. The Prince of Portugal[2] attached
himself to Prince Maurice of Nassau's division, and learnt
a lesson in the art of war from one of the first masters in
Europe.

We left Leopold of Austria—"that bold and bustling
prelate" as Motley styles the Prince-Bishop—in the
town of Juliers, which he had taken such summary
possession of. But he did not remain there until the allied
forces came before the town to batter the walls down about
his priestly ears. His departure was not caused by
cowardice, as he was one of those fighting prelates who
loved the sword better than the crozier, but by the force of
circumstances. Not having the wherewithal to pay the
troops that had followed him to Juliers, he sent all the
troops that were not required for the immediate defence·of
this place into the province of Liege, " there to live upon the
Spoyle of the Countrey until the season of the yeare should
call them into the field."[3] In consequence of the depredations committed by these marauders, the States-General,
acting in concert with the Dukes of Brandenburg and
Neuburg, sent Prince Henry of Nassau with a large force
of horse to Liege, to co-operate with a force under the

---

[1] This was doubtless Colonel Sir Warham St. Leger, the younger, who for
a short time acted as Vice-President of Munster. His father, known as Sir
Warham St. Leger, the elder, distinguished himself in Ireland, and was Lord
President of Munster in the reign of Queen Elizabeth.

[2] Don Emanuel of Portugal, an outcast and wanderer from his native land,
which was now ruled over by the King of Spain. He had married Amelia of
Nassau.

[3] Winwood to Salisbury, April 22nd, 1610. Winwood's *Memorials*, iii.
pp. 148-9.

Prince of Anhalt, and drive the Leopoldians out of the country. The States' and German troops were fortunate enough to take the Bishop's troops by surprise, and, finding them scattered, inflicted great loss upon them, killing 300, and taking many prisoners, who were taken to Dusseldorf.[1] This disaster to Archduke Leopold happened in April, and as he had no other footholds in the duchies except Juliers and the castle of Bredebent, which had been captured from its rightful owner—Brandenburg—he felt himself awkwardly situated. The Austrian soldiers in Juliers were entertained at the expense of the townspeople, who strongly favoured a ruler of their own religion. But troops are not fed and paid for nothing, and the fighting prelate, being an old soldier, knew that if the sinews of war were not soon forthcoming' his days in the duchies were numbered. Leopold was a man of boundless ambition, and had secret hopes of reaching the Crown of Bohemia on the Emperor's back, and being declared heir to his Imperial Majesty.[2] That feeble prop, the Emperor Rudolph, who at first had strenuously upheld Leopold in all he did, and had been the prime mover in the seizure of Juliers, had been so badgered, worried and blamed about his share in this Cleves business, by all parties concerned, and even by his own subjects, that his weak and unstable character could not bear the strain put upon it. He therefore thought to get out of a dilemma by summoning Leopold back to Prague. On receipt of this most unwelcome summons, Leopold had the effrontery to demand of the Princes, whose capital he had seized, a safe conduct for a free passage for himself, his suite and his baggage, out of the country. The Princes were most anxious to get rid of this "old man of the sea," by hook or

---

[1] *Ibid.*
[2] Teynagel's confession, quoted by Meteren.

by crook, but they naturally refused his request unless
Juliers was delivered up to them.[1]   This ultimatum put a
stop to further negotiations, as there was no intention of
restoring Juliers.   The Bishop took his departure for
Brussels in May, and was made welcome at the court of
Archduke Albert, who furnished him with money.[2]   The
command of the fortress of Juliers was entrusted to
Russenburg, a native of the duchy of Juliers, while the
Bishop of Strasburg was employed in raising money and
recruits elsewhere.   And in this congenial employment we
must for the present leave Leopoldus and continue the
narration of the siege of Juliers.

Russenburg not having had much experience in sieges,
did not, it was said, make as much of his strong defences
as he ought to have done, but he showed no lack of
bravery, and on the first day of the siege had made a sally
with 300 men upon his enemy in their most unprotected
quarter, but they were repulsed with great loss.[3]   The
Cecilians worked so hard at their trenches and batteries,
that by August 5th they had planted all their guns
and brought their approaches so near the half moon, for
which they were making, that they had to begin sapping
" From the 27 to the 30th (old style) we continued sapping
towards the halfe moone," wrote Waymouth, "and finisht
up our Batteries, and planted 4 peices in the 4th Batterie
next the halfe moone ; by this tyme Grave Maurice his
aproach, mett with Generall Cecill's before the halfe
moone ; dureing this tyme the enemy hung over the walls

---

[1] Winwood to Salisbury, May 14th, 1610.   Winwood's *Memorials*, iii.
p. 164.

[2] Trumbull in a letter to Winwood, from Brussels, June 2nd, 1610, says,
" These Provinces have sent 150 waggons laden with Cannon bullets to the
frontier towns, whereof the greatest proportion is to serve for the furnishing
of those places which front upon Juliers."

[3] Crosse, p. 1292.

greate lightes, whereby they saw our men at worke, and did us great harme ;[1] and about the same tyme the Castle made a sallie upon the trenches of the French, who valientlie defended them, yet lost some 60 men."

Sir Ralph Winwood, the British Ambassador to the United Provinces, had been sent to Dusseldorf in May, " in case the Princes and those that have interest in this Busyness shall desyre it."[2] He came to Juliers during the siege, and sent frequent accounts of its progress to Lord Salisbury and to Mr. Trumbull, British Resident at Brussels. Writing to the former on July 27, o. s., from Dusseldorf, he says, in speaking of General Cecil :—

" I cannot sufficiently represent unto your Lp. his industry and dilligence, and how by his example, to stirre up watchfullnes and care in others, he doth descend to the duety of a simple Captaine. If any thing be to be desired in him, it is this, that he would be more respectfull of his person, wᶜh he dothe often hazardᵗy expose to danger ; quem sœpe transit casus aliquando invenit : his horse this weeke was killed under him, by a shotte of a culveryn."

And in a letter to Mr. Trumbull, written a day later, Winwood says :—

" Our siege is far advanced ; our men already are lodged in the Fosse ; and we think (if our skill doth not deceive us) to carry both Town and Castle within 12 days. I am not able to say the Marshall will come ; he may be near to the Passage of the Moselle, but whether he will pass, seeing he is refused the escorte he desired of 6000 Foote and 1200 Horse, may be doubted."

It may readily be supposed that Sir Edward Cecil had very scant time for letter writing, his time being so fully occupied both day and night. He found time, however, to

---

[1] A tract published in 1611, entitled, *Newes out of Cleaveland*, says General Cecil was present all this time, and had his own company there to guard the workmen. The British lost 40 men in killed and wounded.

[2] Salisbury to Winwood, May 19, 1610.

keep his uncle, Lord Salisbury, advertised of the progress of the siege. The Lord Treasurer refers to these letters in his despatches to Winwood;[1] but unfortunately these letters from Juliers are not extant. The three letters written by General Cecil to Henry, Prince of Wales[2], from Juliers, are still preserved, and are interesting relics, both of Edward Cecil and the gallant young Prince, to whom they were addressed. We shall have a good deal to say regarding Henry, Prince of Wales, in a succeeding chapter, as he naturally loved the sight of a soldier and every valiant man. The first letter[3] from General Cecil to the Prince is dated July 29th, old style.

Sir E. Cecil to Henry, Prince of Wales.

" May it please y[r] Highnes,

"I humble beseach y° that I may bepardoned that I have deferred to offer to y[r] Hig[s] the actions of these partes, nothing having happend as yet worthy of y[r] reading. But now we have invested the Town of Guliers, and allredy used such dilligence in our Aproches, that wee have lodged our selves in the poynts of some of there oute workes. And because y[r] Hig. may more perticularly understand how the Seage hath hetherto beeyne caried; I have presumed to present y[r] Hig[s] wth a draft of our Quarter, how wee lighe, and of the Towne and Castell, and of our Aproches to it. The place is exceading strong by arte. The Governer well furnished wth menn and Amunition, yet wee prease him nighly wth our Aproches, that if his exspected reliefe from the Emperer and the Arch Diuke falle him, as wth out doubte it will, the Towne in 3 weakes tyme more will, in all menns iudgement, be rendered in to our hands. And I dare promis it shall apeare to y[r] Hig., that y[r] humble and loyall servants have not gained to them selves the least part of honour and reputation in the cariage of the whole seage.

---

[1] Salisbury to Winwood, Sept. 9, o.s., 1610, *Memorials*, iii. pp. 215-16.

[2] Henry Stuart was created Prince of Wales on June 4, 1610.

[3] This letter, preserved among the *Harleian MSS.* in the British Museum (*Harl.* 7007), has been printed in Dr. Birch's *Life of Henry, Prince of Wales*

"I am only unhappe in one thinge, that the Mutenus and unworthy cariage of S^r Th. Dutton,[1] whom y^r Hig. hath pleased to favore be yonde his meritt, hath from tyme to tyme disturbed the corse of the servis, having even at his first arivall heare braved mee at the heade of the Tropes, daring to tell mee to my face that it seemed his Matie had given mee a Comition to abuse men, when there was nothing in question but the doing of the diuty of a Captayne, wch he ought not to dispute a mongst us, seeing it was the first tyme that even he, or his companie, came into the filde amongst us, and ever since in all meetings hath disputed my commition and Authorety so farr, and wth so much scorne. That though hitherto in respecte of y^r Hig^s, I have contayned my selfe, yet, seeing that now againe in a public assembly he hath contemtably spoken of my commition, and upon Base advantage hurte s^r Hatton Cheek, Coronell, whoe took upon him the defence of it.[1] I most humbly beseach y^r H. to be so farr from giving him countinance heare in, that y^r Hig^s. will be rather pleased to allow of that wch iustice heere shall allott him, the defence of it.[2] I most humbly beseach y^r H. to be so farr from giving him countinance heare in, that y^r Hig^s will be rather pleased to allow of that wch iustice heere shall allott him, presuming that y^r Hig^s Princely iugement will fynd it expedient that I be discharged of such bad members, wch in the heate of his Ma^t servis dare contest wth mee, and be content upon any termes to murder his Commander; I can wishe no greater happines in the world then that y^r Hig. will vouchsafe to be Judge in any thing

---

[1] Sir Thomas Dutton was a great man at Court. Wilson describes him as "a man of a crabbed temper." He died May 16, 1634.

[2] Sir Hatton Cheeke was second son of Sir Henry Cheeke, the eldest son of Sir John Cheeke, tutor to King Edward VI. He was a gallant and distinguished officer. Having been treated with great insolence by Sir Thomas Dutton, his junior officer, he sent that officer a challenge when the siege was over. The duel took place on Calais sands, and they fought with great fury, the seconds having stripped them to their shirts. Sir Hatton Cheeke having only just recovered from a dangerous illness fought at a disadvantage, and received a mortal wound from his adversary, of which he soon died. See account of the siege of Juliers in Arthur Wilson's *Life and reign of James I.* By a letter from Sir Thos. Dutton to Salisbury, dated June 17, 1611, "begging favour for killing his foe in self-defence," it appears that Sir T. Dutton had been deprived of his company in the States' army and had lost the king's favour.—*S. P. Dom.*

that may concerne my Honor, all my studies and indevours tending wholly to this eand, to make my selfe capable of doinge y^r Hig. all humble and loyall service. I fear I have importuned y^r Hig. to longe, but the contiguence of these busines in our profestion is such that I can not but presume of y^r Princely interpretation of them, and the rather that it touches so highly his Ma^t and y^r Hig. servis, to wch there is no man more devoted then [than]

<blockquote>
" Y^r Hig^s
" Most humble and loyall servant,
" ED. CECYLL.
</blockquote>

"From Guliers,
   this 29 of July [1610]."

  "To his Highnes."

There is a great gap between this letter of Sir Edward Cecil's to the Prince and the second he wrote, so we must return to the *Journal* again, as the quaint language and obsolete words therein used make the narrative of this siege somewhat more interesting :—

"The 31st [o.s] grave Maurice and generall Cecill gave order for the Canon to batter the halfe moone which, when they had continued some houre and halfe and made a breach, then generall Cecil commanded Colonel Cheecke that the breach should be assaulted, and men to lodge to maintaine the worke, when it should be taken, and gave him Caveat by any meanes to beware of the Enemyes mynes, of which he was certainely advertised, whereupon Colonel Cheecke, with great iudgment, chose out 12 olde soldiers under the comaund of an Ensigne to be as his forelorne hope, and to make an offer of giving on (*sic*), as if all the grosse had come together, knoweinge that the enemy would be so forewarde to blow up there mynes, and give fire to them at the comeinge on of these fewe ; and then he assaied himselfe to carry the worke afterwards with much ease and little loss ; and this accordingelie took effect, for the Ensigne was no sooner makeing offer with those 12 men to assaulte the worke, but the enemy gave fire to his mynes, and the courage of the Ensigne caried him so farre that he was blown a pike's length from the ground and almost smothered with the earth, but was caried off, and is now well; only one soldier was blowne quite away; upon this, Colonel Cheecke entred the breach with a holberd in his hand and beate the enemy from the worke, and a Coffer (sic) which they had within; whoe seeing their myne and Coffer took no more effect, and that our men so resolutelie lodged themselves, and by Colonel Cheecke's comaundment begane alreadie to turn the earth in defence against them, they retired themselves into the Castle; to which, by reason of the great breach the mynes had made, all the English that gave on (sic) laie open both to there canon and muskett. But here Colonel Cheecke incoraged his soldiers and abode great hazarde, there being above 50 greate shott, besides smale made at the worke, before he could cast up a rampet of any proofe for his defence; which, with the losse and hurte of divers men, he did and maintained it afterward; the Prince of Anholt, and Sednesco, sergeant major generall, under grave Maurice, accompanied with generall Cecill the same daie, being on horseback together to see this service; with a shott the Prince of Anholt's and Sednesco's horses were slaine and Sednesco shott in the thigh, whereof within two daies he died.[1] The first of August generall Cecill begane to make his Batterie on the halfe moone he had taken; the second of August he drewe a line from the third Batterie, and made the 7ᵗʰ Coarte of gaurde; the third of August grave Maurice and generall Cecill begane to make the mayne Batteries close to the mote of the castle, which held us worke on all sides a long tyme, with much danger, the earth being so hard and strong that it was impossible the worke could advance with any speede.[2] On the 4th of August the English, under

---

[1] Crosse states that General Cecil also had a horse shot under him on this occasion, but I think this is a mistake, and that it was on a previous occasion, already mentioned, when Cecil had his horse killed.

[2] Winwood confirms this statement as to the difficulty and danger of the work, in his letter to Salisbury, dated Dusseldorf, this August 4, 1610. He says: " This towne of Juliers through the desperate obstinacy of Russenburg, the Governour, will cost much more labour and blood then was at first expected. The nearer th' approaches doe drawe to the counterscarp, the more stony and rocky they finde the earth; whereby the common souldiar is much consumed, for every night 40 or 50 are lefte dead in the trenches, and yet the workes not much advanced."—S. P. Holland.

grave Maurice, with the waloones, after they had battered with canon, felle on the other halfe moone which was before the Castle, which the enemie defended verie well and threwe 12 granades amongst them, and fell out upon their flankes and put them to retreate, and slewe some 60 of these men. The canon played on this worke all the afternoon, and in the night those under grave Maurice fell on it againe and founde the enemy had left the same, and after they held it ; the 5th, about 11 of the clock, the french, under grave Maurice, after they had batered with the canon some houres, fell on the raveling before the porte of the castle in the midst of the curtaine, and were possessed of it about an hour ; and then the enemy sallied out upon the worke againe and made the french retire and quitt the same with the loss of divers men ; yett att nighte, about 12 o'clocke, the french entred the worke againe, found the enemy had quitt it, and after held the same. This daie, in the evening, generall Cecill drewe downe into the trenches all the shott under his command, whoe discharged three vollies, and twixt everie of them there was a peale of ordinance, in joyfull remembrance of his Majesties blessed deliverance from Gowrie's couspiracie.[1] On the 8th the enemy placed two peeces of ordinance nere the est parte of the towne, which much hurte our men comeing into the trenches, but from our third and fourth Batteries we dismounted them within a day. The 9th the newe french, some ten thousand foote and horse, under the comaund of Mr de Shartois, one of the marchales of ffrance, came to there quarters in villages two myles off Gulicke."

As La Châtre was marching through the diocese of Cologne with his forces, his son-in-law happening by chance to visit the city of Cologne, the Pope's nuncio called upon him, and demonstrated to him that he should not favour or assist heretics, who by their present course of violence were trying to extirpate the Roman Catholic religion. The marshal's son-in-law, whose name is not recorded, gave this loyal answer, "I must obey my king's

---

[1] The Earl of Gowrie's attempt to make James his prisoner took place August 5, 1600.

commands, though it were to lead an army against Rome."[1]

Before the arrival of the French forces the town of Juliers had not been beleagured all round. "In consequence of this the townspeople had made occasional nightly sallies, and had stolen divers wagon horses which were doubtless converted into food. These depredations were now put a stop to by the appearance of the French troops on the scene, who made their approaches on the west side of the town and strengthened all those positions that required it. The days of Juliers were numbered before the French came, and their arrival at the eleventh hour only served to detract from the glory of those who had borne all the burden of this siege. Notwithstanding the large host which encircled Juliers and kept closing in nearer and nearer upon the doomed fortress, the garrison still stood their ground and showed no signs of surrendering. Winwood had come to the States' camp, fully expecting to see the enemy haul down their flag and capitulate, but the end had not yet come and the ambassador could not refrain from expressing his surprise to Salisbury, in a letter written from the camp, on August 12th:—

"What makes the Governour of Juliers to hold out, being w'hout hope of any succours, wee cannot guesse, more then obstinacy and meere malice. The place doth appeare to be exceeding strong, both by arte and nature, and as the Count Maurice doth say, worthy to be compared w'h the cittadell of Antwerp; but the Governour doth shewe not to be his craftsmaister, and the souldiars w'hin to want courage and resolucon, who so slightly did quitte their outworkes, in a manner w'hout resistance or dispute.[2] My next, I hope, will bring w'h them the

---

[1] Crosse, p. 1296.
[2] This seems unjust both as regards the Governor and the garrison.

advertisement of the reddition of the towne and castle, and the returne of his Maties forces into Holland."[1]

"On the 15th," says Waymouth, "the army had on all sides perfited their mayne Batteries to the Castle, which were made upon the enemy's counterscarpe some 40 foot from the mote, with parapetts before them 30 foote thick, and parapetts in the rere of the ordinance with two footeinges to plaie with musketts and defend the ordinance, with traverses of canon proofe at the ends of the Batteries and a parapett for musketteers, all alonge before the curtaine; generall Cecill had two Batteries, each of them with 5 peeces to plaie upon the face of the bulwarke, and one Batterie with 4 peeces to plaie upon the Casematt, and two peeces on a work close to the mote's side, where our galerie went over, to dismount any peece might have bine putt out of the wall by the enemy, to hinder our galerie which we feared, the wall being thereabouts broken; grave Maurice had 4 Batteries, and each with two pieces to plaie upon the face of the bulwarke, and one Batterie with 6 peeces to plaie upon the Casematt; the new French had two Batteries, and each of them with 4 peeces to plaie upon the face of the bulwarke, and one Batterie with six peeces to plaie upon the Casematt; so that there were 50 peece of Canon mounted in Batterie against the Castle. By this tyme, likewise grave Maurice and generall Cecill had sapped under the earth close to the mote; this daie, nere night, the enemy threwe fireworkes into generall Cecill's mayne Batteries, which burnt longe and did much harme before the same could be quenched; the enemy mainetaineinge the same with Canon and muskett the most part of the nighte; but Sr Robert Henderson, Colonell of the Scotts, had the Gaurd that night, who shewed great iudgment both to quench it and to hinder the enemy from attempting it any more; whoe shott wilde fire and granadoes most part of the night. The 17th, his Exelence grave Maurice and generall Cecill battered from their mayne batteries, and dismounted divers peeces of the enemy. The new French began a day after; and generall Cecill made such expedition that before night we had dismounted the ordinance in the Casematt which flanked the side

---

[1] *S.P. Holland.*

where our galery was to goe over. This night we filled the mote with risewood, or faggots, and made it fitt for our galerie to goe over, and the 18th before morninge had gott the first stone out of the wall of the bullwarke; and generall Cecill set men presentlie on worke to myne, and others to make up the galerie; this daie there was a Battle of horse sett for there exercise."[1]

The natural impatience of a civilian, who had no act or part in the military operations he came to witness, was exhibited by Sir Ralph Winwood in no small degree.

Writing to Lord Salisbury " from Hanbacke, by the camp before Juliers, the 16 of August," he almost apologises for the siege not being yet over.

" I can assure your Lp.," he writes, "that it is not long of Generall Cecil that this Siege of Juliers continueth so long, whose industry and painfullnes hath bredde envie in many, and those not of the least note, w[ch] they cannot conceale, but open'ly professe; they do much mervayle why he should make so greate haste to the ende of this siege, w[ch] w[t]hall doth ende his command. Wee looke every day when the Governour should speake, but he is obstinate and desperate, and, as it seemes, hath vowed not to survive the government of Juliers." [2]

The governor evidently thought he might not survive the siege, as on August 28th (new style) he sent his little son to Prince Maurice's camp with a request that the boy might be sent to a place of safety, which request the Prince immediately granted.[3]

Early in the morning of the 29th the British had mined through the wall of the castle. The garrison had set fire to a barrel of pitch upon the wall, intending to throw it over and burn down the gallery underneath, but such a hot musketry fire was kept up by some English companies, that the enemy lacked the courage to approach and throw

[1] *Journal*, as before. [2] *S. P. Holland*, 1610. [3] Crosse, p. 1294.

over the tar barrel, so it burnt itself out. Another similar attempt was made that night, which Crosse thus quaintly refers to :—"They thought fitt to fire these ill neighbours out of their nests, and to this purpose they threw down in the dead of night a basket full of wild fire balls upon the connex or roof of the gallery. But those who were appointed to attend such events prevented the mischiefe and threw the basket into the water, forcing the chaine from those who held it, which was some 8 or 9 fadoms long."[1]

Upon the 30th the men working in the British mine cut into a mine of the enemy's, and, being about to take the powder out, the mine exploded and ten men were killed. The mine was filled again by the British, who closed it and then fired it, inflicting some loss on the enemy. After this the enemy's passage was blocked up, and a new gallery begun by the Cecilians.[2] Prince Maurice had mined into the castle nearly as soon as General Cecil, and went forward with two more galleries, and the French had begun four galleries. The end was now very near, as on the 31st the enemy's artillery in the casemates and shoulders of the bulwarks had been dismounted, and a breach had been effected in the face of the bulwark, which in a few hours would have been large enough to be assaulted. The governor seeing all further resistance was useless, and that there was no hope of succours coming to his assistance, sounded a parley. Sir Edward Cecil immediately sent off a letter to the Prince of Wales, who was much interested in this siege, conveying the pleasing intelligence.

---

[1] Crosse, p. 1294.
[2] *Journal*.

SIR E. CECIL TO HENRY, PRINCE OF WALES.

" MAY IT PLEASE Y^r HIGHNES,

" I am so full of that grate and high favor wch y^r H. hath voutchsafed to cast upon me by y^r owne princely hand, that it hath given a nwe life and incoragement to all my in devours, and in it hath brought me into a fare large field, of y^r H. instice and equity, wherein I dare fore ever safly walke, seyng I have y^r H. warrant for it, and I hope God will add such blessinge to y^r H. favore to mee that I shall gather strength and abilities in my profession, to be able in y^r happiest dayes to become a pore instrument in some remorrkable and princely undertakings of y^r owne. 'Tis the happines after wch I thurste, and in wch I will easily lay doune my life.

" Touching the actions of this sieage, whereof y^r Hi. is pleased to be advertised. This day our labour is groinge towards end, for the Gouverner hath cauld to parly, demanded conditions, and wth in a daye or tow wee looke to have troopes in the towne. Wee were so happely advanst in our approches since I wryt my last to y^r H., that wee had longe since taking from them there outworkes, passed over the ditch of the Castell wth 4 galleries, and were lodged at the foote of there ramper, where wee have made 2 great mynes, wch to morrow would have beyne redy to fier, and the Cannon in our Eiglish approches had allredy playde wth that fury upon the face of the Bulwerke that a great breache was made ; and certaynely, wthin 2 dayes wee should have beyne entered upon that place, yet the Gouverner had made shew of new defencies wthin by cuttinge of the bulwerke nighe the shoulder, having purpose to dispute that as his last retrayt ; but wee prest him so neare, that he durst not attend any assault, nor give us leave to see the operation of our mien, wch wee much desiered, that wee might have had a true experience how pouder would worke in so high and so thick a wall, the like beyng noe where to befound, booth in that and in all other perfection of fortification, as I will make apeare by the particularitie, when I shall have that great happines to kiss y^r H. hands, and render account of all that hath passed heare, till wch tyme and for ever I will offer up my humble prayers for yᴿ H. continuall happines, and ever lastingly approve my selfe

           " Yᴿ Hig.
              " Most humble and devoted
                 " servant,
                     " ED. CECYLL.

" From the Seage of Giuliers,
this 21 of August [1610].
       " To his Highnes." [1]

On the 1st September (new style) Juliers was sur-rendered to the allied forces. Favourable terms were granted to the garrison and townspeople. No change was to be made in the liberty of Roman Catholic worship, and all ecclesiasticals were to be allowed free enjoyment of their goods, rents, and revenues. The garrison were to march out of the fortress with drums beating, matches burning, bullets in their mouths, and colours flying, taking their weapons, horses, and moveable goods with them. The artillery, warlike stores, provisions, and "engines of warre," the garrison were to leave behind them, "without altering or spoiling anything after the agreemente made, or laying any kindled match, or other fiery instrument to sett the powder on fire, upon condition that if any such thing be found the agreemente shall be voide."[2]

On the 2nd September the Dukes of Brandenburg and Neuburg entered the town with some of the troops, and after all things had been performed according to the agreement, there marched out of the south port twenty-one companies, numbering 1,300 men, and 300 sick and wounded in wagons, who took the road for Maestricht. Good store of powder and shot were found in the town, and thirty-three cannon. It was computed the enemy lost

---

[1] *Harl.* 7007, published by Birch.   [2] *Journal.*

about 800 men during the siege, and the allies nearly
2,000, whereof General Cecil lost 500.[1] On the same day,
there departed out of the Castle of Bredebent 800 soldiers
to whom were granted the same terms as to their friends
in Juliers. Frederick Pithan, Sergeant-Major-General to
Prince Maurice, was appointed governor of Juliers, in the
interest of the possessory princes.

Thus was brought to a successful termination an arduous
though short campaign. " The honour of the Conduct of
this seige," wrote Winwood to Salisbury, "no man will detract
from the Count Maurice, who is the *Maistre ouvrier* in that
mestier. But that this seige hath had so happy an end
himself will and doth attribute it to the Dilligence and
Judgement of Sir Edward Cecyll."[2]

A few days after the surrender of Juliers, the French
troops under their veteran leader returned to France. On
September 16th the British and Dutch troops began their
march to Schenkenschaus, where they arrived on September
24th, and the army was then dissolved.

Before passing on to other matters, it is necessary to say
something more about the Archduke Leopold, who had
been the acting partner in the Austrian firm of Rudolph,
Leopold, and Co. We left the Archduke at Brussels, busy
collecting money, and trying to induce Archduke Albert
to adventure something in this Cleves speculation. From
Brussels the active bishop went to his bishopric of

---

[1] It is very strange after reading the various accounts of the siege of Juliers
to see the following statement in Motley's *John of Barneveld*, i. p. 292 :—
" Thus without the loss of a single life, the Republic, guided by her consummate statesmen and unrivalled general, had gained an immense victory."
Winwood, Arthur Wilson, Sir Edward Herbert, and Waymouth, the
chronicler of this siege, on whose authority I have stated the number of
killed and wounded as above, all agree as to the great loss suffered by the
besiegers.

[2] August 22nd, o.s., 1610.—*Memorials*, iii. p. 210.

Strasburg, from which he had long been absent. His return now was not to hold an ordination, or make a pastoral tour through his diocese, but to collect his Alsatian regiments together, and have them ready in case of need. From Strasburg he returned to Prague, where he found his senior sleeping partner, Rudolph, averse to forwarding more funds for what seemed at present a hopeless venture. Leopold's failure in this endeavour accounted for his non-appearance before Juliers, with a force at his back, to relieve that place. When he heard of the capitulation of Juliers, he vented his anger on the head of the governor, Russenburg, whose soldierly ability he so underrated, that when Russenburg offered his services to the Duke of Saxony they were rejected.[1] The Bishop-Archduke made one more effort to recover the duchies. He offered to take the Duke of Saxony into partnership, and unite their joint forces in a crusade against the Protestant Princes. But Saxony had no money to spare, so this scheme fell through like the rest.[2] And in this forlorn state we must bid adieu to Leopoldus.

There was one captive taken by the allied forces whose capture was very pleasing to King James. This was Baldwin, the Jesuit, who was captured in the Palatinate, and, being delivered to two British officers, was sent to London in September. Sir Edward Cecil took advantage of his officers' departure for England to send a letter to his patron—Henry, Prince of Wales :—

"MAY IT PLEASE Y[r] HIGHNES,

    "I presumed latly to advertise y[r] Hig., by M[r] Harbert, of the taking of Juliers, and by him I sent a plant (*sic*) of it, and all the approches, as they were when the Towne was rendered, and

---

[1] Dickenson to Winwood, Dec. 20, 1610.—*Memorials*, p. 243.
[2] Winwood to Trumbull, Jan. 11, 1610-11. *Ibid.* p. 251.

of the iust proportion of one intier Bulwarke of the Castell, that y. Hig. might be pleased by that to iudge how excellent a plase the whole must be. The desier I had to dispach that messenger wth speed, robed me of all tyme to present every thing then in that full perfection to y[r] Hig. as my duity and y[r] owne rare Princly iudgement in the profession of Armes might worthily expect; and now that our Army is so nearly returned, and I so overprest wth a longing desier to come over and be made happy by kissing y[r] Hig. handes, I humbly beseeach y[r] Hig. to allow mee to be the messenger of all the perticularites my self, having made an assembly of the best observations I could to offer to y[r] Hig. viw at my returne, and such as I was unwillinge any hand should be honored in bering them to y[r] Hig. but my owne. Tomorrowe the Tropes will be disperced from Skinkskaus in to there Garrisons, and when I have accompayned Count Mauris to the Hage to see the tropes receaved by the states in there former conditions, I purpose my returne to render an account to his Ma[u] and y[r] Hig. of all my poore endevours in this imployment. This bearer, Cap. Deuhurst, is ioyned wth S[r] John Barlace for the safe delivery of that Arch Jesuit, father Baldwin,[1] into his Ma[tes] hands, and to assuer ourselves of the Garison of Rhyneberke and other of the Arch[des] fronters in these partes, w[h] might have atemted his recovery, wee stayed him till now that the Army marched, and so have shipt him wth all safety for England,[2] where I hope he will

---

[1] Winwood, in a letter to Salisbury at this time, mentions that Father Baldwin was captured at Dusseldorf. On his arrival in England he was imprisoned in the Tower, and we find from a royal warrant issued at Hampton Court on October 8, 1610, that £120 was given to Sir John Borlase and Capt. Barnaby Dewhurst " for conveying Baldwin, the Jesuit, from Dusseldorf, in Cleveland, to London." Baldwin was believed to have joined the conspiracy of Fawkes when the latter was in Flanders, and though nothing conclusive seems to have been proved against him, he remained for long a prisoner in the Tower. Baldwin had many friends among the Roman Catholics, one of whom, Mary Lady Lovell, wrote to Salisbury from Ghent, on Nov. 23, 1610, assuring his Lordship that Baldwin was innocent of all conspiracy. She advises Salisbury in this letter against allowing Baldwin to be executed, as it might set the people against him (Salisbury). Sir Henry Wotton tried to bring about, in 1618, an exchange between Baldwin and Molle, Lord Roos's tutor, who had been imprisoned by the Inquisition at Rome. Molle, however, was not released, and was kept a prisoner for thirty years, until death released him in the 81st year of his age.

[2] Winwood records that Baldwin was guarded by an escort of 45 harque-

discover many rare and hidden practises he hath beeyne busied in against the state. I have never held much discorse wth him, yet I observe him to be naturally of a wonderful pryde, and full of passion in any thing he speaketh of, and rather a generall understander of politike matters then a sound mann in controverses of Religion. I dare presume to comber y^r Hig. noe longer, begging humbly pardon that I have adventured to wryt this much. I doe only add my continuall prayres to make y^r Hig. everlastingly happy, and me occation to show how much I am

" Y^r Hig^s

" most loyall and humble servant,

" ED. CECYLL.

" From Skinckscanc,
this 14 of Septem., 1610." [1]

History does not tell us how the chivalrous young Prince Henry received General Cecil on his return to England ;[2] but King James expressed his appreciation of the good work done by his soldiers and their general before Juliers in a letter to his minister, soon after the events had taken place. An ambassador, after the manner and fashion of this peace-loving King, was to be sent on a mission of reconciliation—he was to try and reconcile the irate Emperor of Germany to the victorious Princes of Cleves. "Ye shall thairfore knowe," wrote the King to Salisbury, "that my ambassadoure can doe me no bettir service than in assisting to the treatie of this reconciliation,

---

busiers à cheval, and Sir Edward Cecil's *own troop of horse.* Winwood to Salisbury, Aug. 23, 1610.—*Memorials,* iii. p. 211. This troop of horse formed part of the cavalry force sent to Juliers with Prince Maurice, under the command of Prince Henry, General of the Horse.

[1] This letter has never been published before. The original (a holograph) is in the possession of the Marquis of Bath, at Longleat, to whose kindness I am indebted for a copy of it.

[2] We have it on Cecil's own authority that he was recompensed for his good service at Juliers, both by the King of Great Britain and by the States. See letter from Lord Wimbledon to the Duke of Buckingham, dated March 15, 1626."—*S.P. Dom.*

quharin he maye have as goode occasion to emploie his tongue and his pen (and I wish it maye be with as goode successe) as generall cecill and his soldiers have done thaire swordis and thaire mattokis."[1]

The treaty of reconciliation which the King refers to in the above letter, was the "Treaty of Cologne." Sir Ralph Winwood was sent to that city early in October, to assist at a Conference, in which the Emperor and the Protestant princes of Germany were all represented by their respective commissioners. The Emperor's representatives demanded that the victorious Princes of Juliers and Cleves should possess their duchies as vassals of the Emperor; that the Duke of Saxony should he recognised by them as a rightful claimant, *and that the differences amongst the competitors should be determined solely by the judgment of the Emperor.*[2] This Imperial dictum would have led as a matter of course to a fresh quarrel in the duchies. It is not surprising, therefore, that the delegates of the Protestant princes replied to the Emperor's overtures, by saying that though their masters were quite willing to possess the duchies in the name of the Emperor, they utterly refused to admit the Duke of Saxony's claim, or to share the duchies with him. This *fiat* put a stop, for the present, to further negotiations, and Sir Ralph Winwood, seeing the matter was not likely to be settled until the Greek Kalends, returned to Dusseldorf, from whence he went to the Hague.[3]

It is useless and needless to prosecute these rival claims any further, for they never were properly adjusted and settled. The Emperor Rudolph and the Duke of Saxony soon passed away, and the world knew them no more; but

---

[1] King James to Salisbury, *Cecil Papers, Hatfield.*
[2] Winwood to Trumbull, Oct. 8, 1610, from Cologne.—*Memorials,* iii. p. 226.
[3] *Ibid.*

the successor of the former invested the successor of the
latter with the disputed duchies, and the matter was as
remote from settlement as ever. Thus it generally is with
claims, and always will be until the end of time. As
regards the Princes of Brandenburg and Neuburg, it suffices
now to add that they quietly shared the duchies between
them. We cannot finish this chapter better than by quoting
the far-seeing opinion of Sir Ralph Winwood regarding
these two Kings of Sparta, as one might almost term them.
"If the *Princes Possedants*," wrote Winwood to Trumbull,[1]
" can be so wise to live together in Amity and good Concord,
and govern their countreys with Justice and good Pollicie,
they shall have small reason to fear either the Power of the
Emperor or the Practises of the House of Saxony."[2]

---

[1] Wm. Trumbull succeeded Sir Thomas Edmonds as envoy to Brussels in
Sept. 1609. He stayed there fifteen years, and was afterwards made Clerk of
the Council. He died in London, Sept. 1635.

[2] Jan. 11th, old style, 1610–11.—*Memorials*, iii. p. 323.

CHAPTER VII.

1611–1614.

State of England under the rule of James I.—Henry, Prince of Wales—The Cecilians—An embassy from Denmark—Edward Cecil's mission to Holland —Illness and death of Lord Salisbury—His character—The sudden rise of Robert Carr—The pastimes of the Prince of Wales—Alliances proposed for him and his sister Elizabeth—Betrothal of Elizabeth to the Elector Palatine—Illness and death of the Prince of Wales—Marriage of Princess Elizabeth—Sir Edward and Lady Cecil accompany Elizabeth to Germany—The journey—Arrival at Gaulstein in the Palatinate—The British Commissioners take their departure—Elizabeth's dilemma on Cecil's departure—Her triumphal entry into Heidelberg—The Essex divorce case—Sir Thomas Overbury's advice to Lord Rochester—Imprisonment of Overbury in the Tower—Found dead—Marriage of the Earl of Somerset to Lady Frances Howard—Temporary triumph of guilt—The Electress gives birth to a son at Heidelberg—Great rejoicings—General Cecil and his wife are sent on a mission to Heidelberg by James I.—A new Parliament—Short and unsatisfactory session—The phantom campaign of 1614 in the Low Countries.

THE reign of James I. of England was not a glorious one.[1] The most ardent admirers of that monarch must admit that much, and he has his admirers and supporters like all other kings and queens. A peaceful reign is often, and ought to be, a prosperous one, but no one can say England was in a prosperous state when Charles the Martyr ascended the tottering throne of his father. The exchequer was empty. The people were suffering from the large subsidies they had been called on to furnish during the late King's reign. Trade was crippled and unfairly handicapped by the granting of monopolies. The decrees of the

---

[1] " His reign in England was a continual course of mean practises." Bishop Burnet's *History of his own time*, i. p. 29.

Court of the Star Chamber had rendered justice a thing of the past. Discontent was rampant. A strong feeling against the divine right of kings prevailed. Men were beginning to think for themselves, and to assert their rights as they had never thought of asserting them in the days of Elizabeth. Were not these threatening clouds which darkened the horizon on the accession of Charles I., mainly due to the mismanagement of State affairs and the abuse of kingly power by the royal James? The great French Revolution was undoubtedly brought about by the tyranny, oppression, and licentious lives of Louis XIV., Louis XV., and their nobility. Louis XV. had foreseen, with a callous indifference, the retribution that was inevitably to come, sooner or later, and yet he made no attempt to ameliorate the condition of his down-trodden subjects or curb the licentious lives of his courtiers and his own. *Après nous le déluge* was the far-seeing expression of the monarch, who, when young, had been called Louis the *Well-beloved*, but whose manner of life in old age had turned the love of his subjects into deadly hate. The sins of the fathers are visited upon the sons unto the third and fourth generation. Louis XVI., the innocent and well-meaning successor to his grandfather's throne, suffered for his ancestors' crimes. And did not Charles I. in like manner suffer for his father's faults? We use the words faults in the latter case, as we have no wish to compare James to Louis XV., though the sequels to both reigns have a strange analogy. As kings went in the seventeenth century, James was by no means a bad man. He was a kind and faithful husband, an indulgent father, and an upholder of religion. Many of his faults were those of his education and country. Others were the results of his constitutional timidity. Had James lived and died in a humble position of life, he would probably have done nothing to disgrace his position. But the cynicism of fate raised him to a position he was in most respects totally unfitted for. As King of England he was the square man in the round hole, and, not being able to govern, he let himself be governed. It too often happens that a weak king lets himself be governed by unscrupulous men who make capital out of his weakness, and carry him along by sheer strength of will through what his own better nature, if left to itself, might have refused to do. It is the want of moral firmness which turns weak kings into bad ones. Edward II., Richard II., and Henry VI., are good examples of weak kings. The two first abdicated their power into the hands of unworthy favourites, who were the ultimate ruin of them. Henry VI., whose chief fault was weakness of character, would have been shaken off his throne long before he was, had it not been for the master mind and strong right arm of Margaret of Anjou. James lived in much less troublous times, but his manner of ruling in the latter part of his reign paved the way for anarchy and rebellion. For the first nine years of his reign England prospered well enough, as the reins of government were in the experienced hands of Robert Cecil, Earl of Salisbury, who understood the British Constitution so thoroughly, and had the good of his country so much at heart. It is in the last year of this great statesman's life that this chapter opens.

Sir Edward Cecil does not appear to have gone over to the Low Countries in the year 1611. Now that the piping times of peace reigned in the United Provinces, soldiering was but a dull trade, and Court life, of which Edward Cecil had had but a very small share during the last twelve years, possessed many attractions for the hero of Juliers. One of the greatest attractions at Court to him, as to all military men, was the young Prince of Wales, who took the keenest interest in all things military. The Cecilians, as

may be supposed, had many friends at Court, notwithstanding the envy and jealousy with which the Lord
Treasurer was regarded by many avaricious courtiers and
needy office seekers. Lord Salisbury's only son, William
Cecil, Viscount Cranbourne,[1] was in constant attendance
upon the Prince of Wales, with whom he was in great
favour.[2] Lord Cranbourne also much frequented the
company of his cousin, Edward Cecil, between whom a
friendship sprang up which appears to have continued
many years. Chamberlain, in one of his chatty letters to
Dudley Carleton, written in 1611, says :—" My Lord of
Cranbourne used me well. . . . Sir Edward Cecil is continually about him, very much to my Lord Treasurer's
liking." [3]   In the following March we find both Sir Edward
Cecil and Lord Cranbourne tilting with the Prince · on
Shrove Tuesday.

---

[1] Wm Cecil, Viscount Cranbourne, only son of the Lord Treasurer, by his
marriage with Elizabeth Brooke, sister of the unfortunate Henry Brooke,
Lord Cobham, was born about the year 1590. He was educated at
Westminster School and St. John's College, Cambridge. In Feb. 1608,
we find his tutor, Thomas Cecil, writing to Lord Salisbury about his son's
progress in learning. "The Course Mr Dean of Westminster commended
unto us," writes Thomas Cecil, "wee doe take—and 'tis the best (I thinke)
wee can take. His Lordship of himselfe is readye to heare, willinge to learne,
forward to conferr wth my selfe and other younge gentlemen wch learne w^{th}
him. So that wee shall (I dought not) gett some learninge. But it comes
to a man, as diseases leave him, by little and little, like deawe, not like a
tempest. Mountaynes of promises often tymes bringe fo·rth but mole-hills
of perfourmaunces, yet thus muche I dare promis, love, duety, dilligence."
Cecil Papers, Hatfield, 817.

Lord Cranbourne succeeded as second Earl of Salisbury, in May, 1612. He
married in Dec., 1608, Catherine, youngest daughter of Thomas Howard,
Earl of Suffolk, and was succeeded in 1668 by his grandson, James Cecil, son
of Charles, Viscount Cranbourne, by Jane, daughter and coheir of James
Maxwell, Earl of Dirleton.

[2] Chamberlain in a letter to Carleton, dated Jan. 29th, 1611–2, speaking of
the Prince's sports, says :—" In all which exercises the Lord Cranbourne
attending him, keeping an honourable table all the while they were at
Greenwich, and grows daily into his favour."—*S. P. Dom.*

[3] Novr 6, 1611.—*S. P. Dom.*

"The Prince, with Viscount Rochester, Sir Thomas Somerset, Sir Thomas Howard, Sir Edward Cecil, and one Ramsey, on his side," wrote Chamberlain to Carleton, "ran a match at the ring, for a supper, against the Duke of Lenox, the Lord Walden, the Lord Cranbourne, the Lord Chandos, the Lord Hay, and Mr. Henry Howard. The Prince won, and the supper and plays were made at the Marquis of Winchester's house on the Tuesday after."[1]

The same writer tells us in this letter how the London "prentices" enjoyed themselves on this Shrove Tuesday :—

"Our prentices," he says, " were very unruly on Shrove Tuesday, and pulled down a house or two, of good fellowship, in which service two or three of them came short home."

The marriage of James I. with Anne of Denmark had brought about very friendly relations between Great Britain and Denmark. Queen Anne was devoted to her brother, Christian IV., King of Denmark, who paid several visits to the English court. In 1611, there being war between Denmark and Sweden, the former country sent an embassy to London soliciting aid.

" There is an ambassador from Denmark soliciting for aid for those wars," writes Chamberlain to Carleton, "and some forces, are said, shall be sent under the conduct of Lord Willoughby and Sir Edward Cecil, and a Regiment of Scots under the Lord Dingwall, with another of Irish under the Earl of Clanrickard. Yet I will not believe that such men will adventure themselves upon so poor conditions as are yet propounded, for they may go on warfare upon their own cost."[2]

However anxious Sir Edward Cecil was to be actively employed in the profession he belonged to, the Danish

---

[1] March 11, 1611-2.—*S. P. Dom.*
[2] From London, Feb. 26, 1611-2.—*S. P. Dom.*

command just referred to did not hold out sufficient in-
ducements to him to throw up his command in the Low
Countries. A subsequent letter by the above writer, informs us that Lord Willoughby[1] sold land to set forth
himself on his journey to Denmark, whither he was to
convey 4,000 men *if he could raise them.*[2] The same letter
also tells of a peaceful mission which Sir Edward Cecil had
been sent on by the Prince of Wales :—

"Sir Edward Cecil is gone over into the Low Countries to
supply the prince's place of godfather to a child of the Count
Ernestus of Nassau of [at] Arnheim, and carried with him a great
present of plate, because the lady is daughter to the Queen's
sister."[3]

Before Edward Cecil went to Holland, his uncle and
kind patron, the Earl of Salisbury, who had for some time
been in failing health, worn out before his time by his
arduous duties, was taken seriously ill with a tertian ague.
Rallying to a certain extent from this illness, Lord Salisbury went, on April 27th, to Bath, to take the waters there.
No waters, however, could shake off the hand of Death who
had laid his relentless grasp on that great statesman.

"On Sunday the news was very doubtful and almost desperate,"
wrote Chamberlain to Carleton about the third week in May,[4]

---

[1] Robert, 11th Baron Willoughby de Eresby, created Earl of Lindsey in
1626. At the commencement of the Civil Wars he was nominated Commander-in-chief of the King's forces, and fell at Edgehill, Oct. 23, 1642, at
the head of a division of the royal army.

[2] Chamberlain to Carleton, March, 25, 1611-2.—*S. P. Dom.*

[3] The wife of Count Ernest of Nassau, was Sophia Hedwig of Brunswick,
daughter of the Duchess of Brunswick Wolfenbuttel, *née* Elizabeth of
Denmark. There is a letter from Sir Edward Conway, deputy-governor of
the Brill, to Henry, Prince of Wales (printed in the Appendix to Birch's
Life of Henry, Prince of Wales), referring to the festivities which took place at
this christening at Arnhem.

[4] This letter, which is given in *The Court and Times of James I.*, is not
dated. i. p. 168.

"so that my Lord Cranbourne was sent for to Audley End and came all night and next day by horses ; and he and Sir Edward Cecil arrived at the Bath and found my Lord somewhat revived, insomuch that yesterday he would needs remove from the Bath to a house six miles off, belonging to Sir Francis Manners in right of his wife, and they say will homewards as fast as his strength will give him leave."

But Robert Cecil never lived to return home, and died on Sunday, 24th May, in the parsonage house at Marlborough, aged 62, having kept his mind clear to the very last.[1] His son was with him at the end,[2] but it does not appear if Edward Cecil was also present. Lord Salisbury was interred at Hatfield early in June, and there were present as mourners :—

" The Lord Privy Seal, the Lord Chamberlain, Lord Worcester, Lord Pembroke, Lord Exeter, young Lord St. John, Lord Clifford,[3] Lord Burghley, Lord Denny, Lord Hay,[4] Sir Edward Cecil, the Master of the Rolls, the Chancellor of the Exchequer, M[r] Attorney and M[r] Solicitor General."[5]

Like all truly great men, Robert Cecil, Earl of Salisbury, has been severely handled by many writers, who have depicted his character in a very unfavourable light. It has been acknowledged by Walpole and other writers, that

---

[1] Chamberlain to Carleton, May 27th, 1612.—*S. P. Dom.*
[2] *Ibid.*
[3] Henry Clifford, Earl of Cumberland, married in his father's lifetime, July 25th, 1610, Lady Frances Cecil, daughter to the Earl of Salisbury, by whom he had divers children. He died Dec. 11th, 1643, at York, and his widow died there, Feb. 14, in the following year.
[4] Lord Hay was sent by King James to Bath, with a valuable diamond ring for Lord Salisbury, a short time before the Lord Treasurer's death, as a token of his Majesty's regard for his minister. The King also sent this message with the ring : " That the favor and affection he bore him was, and should be ever, as the form and matter of that ring, endless, pure and most perfect." *Biog. Brit.* art. " Robert Cecil."
[5] Chamberlain to Carleton, June 11th, 1612.—*S. P. Dom.*

Dr. Birch has given the most fair and impartial view of this great man's character, drawn " from fuller and more impartial light than the ignorance or envy of his own time would allow ; and which may, therefore, be opposed to the prejudiced representations of Weldon, Wilson, Osborn, and the secret-hunting historiographers of that age, as well as to the partial estimate of his character drawn by Turneur." [1]

Before referring to the last-named writer's character of Lord Salisbury, it will be best to give a short extract from Birch's review of Cecil's character :—

" He was properly a sole Minister, though not under the denomination of a favourite, his Master having a much greater awe of than love for him ; and he drew all business, both foreign and domestic, into his own hands, and suffered no Ministers to be employed abroad but who were his dependents, and with whom he kept a most constant and exact correspondence ; but the men whom he preferred to such employments justified his choice, and did credit to the use he made of his power." [2]

With regard to the eulogy by Turneur mentioned above, the title page of his pamphlet chiefly concerns us, as it mentions Edward Cecil's wife, and shows that a bond of friendship existed between her and Lord Salisbury :—

"The character of Robert, Earle of Salisburye, Lord High Treasurer of Englande, &c., by Mr Wm Turneur, and dedicated to the most understandinge and the most worthye Ladye the Ladi Theodosia Cecyll." [3]

England, after Cecil's death, was like a ship deprived of her captain. There were many applicants and aspirants for the vacant post, but James, for reasons of his own, kept the

---

[1] Walpole's *Royal and Noble Authors*. ii. p. 146.
[2] Birch's *Historical view of the negotiations between the Courts of England, France, and Brussels*, p. 348.
[3] *Harl.* 36.

post open for two years.[1]   The king was like a schoolboy
who has just done with school, and feels dazed with his
sudden independence.   Being left to his own guidance,
James, who was surrounded by flatterers and venal
sycophants, chose out the most worthless of them all as the
man he especially delighted to honour.   This was Robert
Carr, a handsome Scot, who had been created, in 1611,
Viscount Rochester, and had been a rising favourite for
some time before Cecil's death, though that wise statesman
had done his best to check the king's foolish prodigality towards him, seeing what disastrous results would ensue from it.

"The Viscount Rochester groweth potent in affairs here ; and
therefore you shall do wisely to respect him thereafter," wrote Sir
Thomas Lake, Secretary of State, from the Court at Ampthill, to
his friend Sir Thos. Edmonds, two months after the great Cecil's
death.   "He hath now the Signets delivered to him, which since
the Lord Treasurer's death have remained with me by way of
custody, as they did in his sickness, and have done often before
in his absence.   But this maketh much discussion here, what his
Lordship's ends may be."[2]

Leaving Viscount Rochester to bask in the king's favour,
and attain his ends by fair means and foul, we must return
to a more pleasing person—Henry, Prince of Wales.   This
chivalrous young prince was, after Lord Salisbury's death,
Sir Edward Cecil's kindest patron at Court.   This is not
surprising when we consider how devoted this prince was to
all soldiers and sailors.   Sir Charles Cornwallis, in his *Life
of Prince Henry*, gives a graphic description of his mode
of life :— [3]

---

[1] Lord Suffolk was then appointed Lord Treasurer.   *Court and Times*, 1.
p. 335.
[2] Quoted in Birch's *Historical view*, &c., p. 349.
[3] *Life and Death of Henry, Prince of Wales*. pp. 20-1.

" He did also practise tilting, charging on horsebacke with pistols after the manner of the wars with all other the like inventions.   Now also delighting to conferre both with his owne and other strangers, and great Captaines, of all manner of wars, battailles, furniture, armes by sea and land, disciplines, orders, marches, alarmes, watches, stratagems, ambuscades, approaches, scalings, fortifications, incampings, and having now and then battailes of headmen appointed, both on horse and foot, in a long table, whereby he might in a manner view the right ordering of a battaile, how every troope did ride and assist another, as also the placing of the light horsemen, vauntgaurd, maine battaille with the assisting wings, and rerewards, &c., which are out of my element to speake of."

Prince Henry had an experienced French riding-master, named St. Antoine, who had been sent over in the suite of the Duke of Sully, when that ambassador came to congratulate James on his accession to the Crown of England in 1603.   It was St Antoine who communicated to the French ambassador, La Broderie, the young prince's desire for a suit of armour, well-gilt and enamelled, with pistols and sword.   Henry IV. sent Prince Henry a beautiful suit of armour, which is now in the Tower.[1]   The prince also caused another suit of armour to be made for himself, which Sir Edward Cecil had orders for procuring ; but where it was made, or after what fashion, does not appear.   It was doubtless ordered just before the prince became ill, and he never lived to see it.   We presume this to be the case from the following warrant :—

" March 31, 1613.   A warrant to the Exchequer to pay to Sir Edward Cecill, Knt., the sum of 330^{li} being the remayns of 480^{li}

---

[1] Note from *England as seen by foreigners in the days of Elizabeth and James I.*, by W. B. Rye.   James I. said of armour " that he could not but greatly praise armour, as it not only protected the wearer, but also prevented him from injuring any other person."   Quoted by Sir S. Meyrick in his *Ancient Armour*, iii. p. 73.

due for an armour which the late Prince Henry caused to be made for himself. Subscribed and procured by Windebank by order from M[r] Chase of the Exchequer."[1]

Early in 1612, and for some time previously, James had been looking out for a suitable princess for his son and heir. Both the king and queen are said to have been anxious to marry their son to a Spanish infanta, and for political reasons this projected alliance was promoted by the anti-Protestant party. Prince Henry showed himself very averse to wedding a princess of the Roman Catholic religion, and he had a strong supporter in the Lord Treasurer Cecil, who said that the gallant Prince of Wales could find blooming roses everywhere, and did not need to search for an olive.[2]   A husband was also required for that charming princess, Elizabeth Stuart, sole surviving daughter of James I. There was quite a contest between Protestants and Roman Catholics as to who should carry off this pearl.[3]   The Duke of Savoy had made proposals to James for a double marriage between their children, and Anne of Denmark was suspected of secretly intriguing with Spain for a marriage between the young King of Spain and her daughter Elizabeth. Whilst these matrimonial schemes were hatching, a treaty was taking place in Germany which was to lead to a very important event.

In March, 1612, an alliance was concluded at Wesel, between James I. and the Protestant Princes of the Union,[4]

---

[1] *Sign Man.* iii. No. 4.—*S. P. Dom.*
[2] Ranke's *History of England.*   i. p. 424.
[3] *Ibid.*
[4] In 1608 the Protestant Princes of Germany entered into an alliance for their mutual defence in case of oppression by the Roman Catholic Princes This alliance they called the *Evangelical Union.* In opposition to this Union was the *Roman Catholic League,* based on the same defensive clauses as the *Evangelical Union,* and having for its head Maximilian, the powerful Elector of Bavaria.

among whom were the Princes of Brandenburg, Hesse, Palatinate, Baden, Anhalt, and Wurtemburg :—

" Both contracting parties," says a German historian, " promised one another mutual support against all who should attack them on account of the Union, or of the aid they had given in settling and maintaining the tenure of Cleves and Juliers." [1]

In order to cement the alliance between James and the Protestant Princes, the latter were most anxious that the Princess Elizabeth should be given in marriage to a prince of the Union.   It so happened that Maurice of Nassau was uncle, by blood, to the young Elector Palatine, and that the Duke of Bouillon was uncle to the Elector by marriage.[2] The Duke of Bouillon was the head of the Protestant cause in France, and was quite as inimical to the House of Austria as Prince Maurice.   After the Wesel conference was over, the Duke of Bouillon and Count Hanau, who had married another daughter of William the Silent, visited London, and made proposals to the King for a marriage between their young nephew and the Princess Elizabeth.[3] Prince Henry, who was devoted to his sister, was strongly in favour of this match, notwithstanding the Elector's inferior rank.   It was mainly due to the Prince's influence with his mother that the Queen withdrew her opposition to what she considered an unequal and poor marriage. The King followed suit, and, on May 16th, the marriage contract was signed by the members of the Privy Council.

Frederick, Elector Palatine, arrived in London the middle of October, 1612, and received a most hearty welcome

---

[1] Ranke, i. p. 424.

[2] The late Elector Palatine had married a daughter of William the Silent, who was mother of Frederick V., Elector Palatine.   The Duke of Bouillon had also married a daughter of William the Silent.

[3] Ranke, i. p. 427.

from the people, to whom the marriage gave great satisfaction. Prince Henry welcomed him as a brother, and
declared his intention of escorting his sister to her new
German home after the marriage. The marriage was fixed
for early in November, but before the King could claim
the Elector as a son, death had robbed James of his first
born son, and the whole royal family were plunged into
the lowest depths of misery by this cruel blow. A low
fever, caught in a peculiarly unhealthy season, had carried
off this hopeful young prince in the eighteenth year of his
age, on November 6th. Owing to the fear of contagion,
Elizabeth was not allowed to visit her brother, but tender
messages passed between them, and his last audible words
were, "where is my dear sister."[1]

"To tell you," says the Earl of Dorset in a letter to Sir T.
Edmonds, "that our rising sun is set ere scarcely he had shone, and
that with him all our glory lies buried ; you know and do lament
as well as we and better than some do and more truly, or else you
were not a man and sensible of this kingdom's loss." [2]

England had not sustained such a loss since the death
of the youthful Edward VI., and she did not sustain such
another till the untimely decease of Princess Charlotte, on
November 6th (the anniversary of Prince Henry's death),
1817.

The marriage of the Elector Palatine and Princess
Elizabeth took place on February 14th (St. Valentine's
day), 1613, having been postponed three months in consequence of Prince Henry's death.

Never was a royal marriage performed with greater
splendour, and never did a more united couple plight their

---

[1] Chamberlain to Carleton, Nov. 12, 1612.—*S. P. Dom.*
[2] Nov. 23, 1612. Quoted in *Letters to King James VI. from the Queen,
Princess Elizabeth*, &c., published 1835.

vows to each other before God's altar than did this youthful pair in the chapel of Whitehall Palace. Many writers have given an account of this wedding, and a very brief mention of it, extracted from one of Chamberlain's letters, will suffice:—

" The bridegroom and bride were both in a suit of cloth of silver, richly embroidered with silver, her train carried up by thirteen young ladies or lords' daughters, at least, besides five or six more that could not come near it. These were all in the same livery with the bride, though not so rich. The bride was married in her hair, that hung down long, with an exceeding rich coronet on her head, which the king valued the next day at a million of crowns. Her two bride's-men were the young prince and the Earl of Northampton. The king and queen both followed, the queen all in white, but not very rich saving in jewels. The king, methought, was somewhat strangely attired in a cap and feather, with a Spanish cape and a long stocking. The chapel was very strictly kept, none suffered to enter under the degree of a baron but the three lords chief justices. In the midst there was a handsome stage or scaffolding made on the one side, whereof sat the King, Prince, Count Palatine, and Count Henry of Nassau. On the other side the Queen, with the bride, and one or two more. Upon this stage they were married by the Archbishop of Canterbury, assisted by the Bishop of Bath and Wells, who made the sermon. It was done all in English, and the Prince Palatine had learned as much as concerned his part reasonably perfectly. The French, Venetian, and States' ambassadors dined that day with the bride. The Spanish ambassador was sick, and the archduke's was invited for the next day, but would not come." [1]

Masques, feasts, tournaments, and revelries of all kinds made the next two months fly very quickly for the happy young couple, who were soon to leave England for their German home. It had been settled that certain British noblemen should accompany Elizabeth to the Palatinate as

[1] Chamberlain to Alice Carleton, Feb. 18th.—*S. P. Dom.*

commissioners. The Duke of Lennox,[1] Lord Arundel, Lord Harington,[2] and Lord L'Isle, were chosen for this duty ; and Lady Arundel, Lady Harington and Lady Cecil, with divers other ladies, were selected as ladies in attendance on the Electress during her journey. James was determined that his daughter should travel in all comfort and royal magnificence. No expense was spared, and Elizabeth's first start in life was a golden one in all respects. As she and her whole suite were to travel as far as the Palatinate at the king's expense, it was necessary that she should have a treasurer to defray all the expenses incidental to the journey, which were many and varied. The somewhat arduous, though honourable, post of treasurer to the Princess was bestowed on Sir Edward Cecil.[3] It does not appear whether he had applied for this post or whether it had been offered him on account of his affection to the service of the late Prince of Wales. Sir Henry Wotton rather sneers at a general accepting such an appointment.

"Sir Edward Cecil goeth as Treasurer to keep up that office in the name," wrote Wotton to Sir Edmund Bacon, "though it be otherwise perhaps from a General rather a fall than an ascent."[4]

There was unfortunately no military employment for a general at this time, so Edward Cecil was glad of

---

[1] Ludovic Stuart, 2nd Duke of Lennox, in Scotland, born 1574, and died, without legitimate issue, 1624.

[2] Sir John Harington, created Baron Harington of Exton in 1603. He was tutor to Princess Elizabeth until her marriage in 1613, and she resided for some years with him and Lady Harington at Combe Abbey, near Coventry. Lord Harington died at Worms, a few weeks after his arrival at Heidelberg in 1613.

[3] "A Warrant to Sir Edward Cecil, Knt., to be Treasurer for the disbursement and payment of all such somes of money as shalbe paid in forraine parts, by appointment of his Majesty's commissioners of the jorney of the Lady Elizabeth, besides 2000 li. delivered them out of the Exchequer, April 5th, 1613." Signet Office, Docquetts.—*S. P. Dom.*

[4] Wotton's *Reliquiæ*, p. 407.

a temporary civil appointment. Like everyone else he was devoted to the charming Princess Elizabeth, and a soldier's instinct would doubtless tell him that sooner or later the Palatinate would be involved in a war, when generals would be more valued than they were in this time of peace, and that it might be of future advantage to him his having served the Princess. The suite of the Duke of Lennox consisted of forty-one persons; the Earl of Arundel's company was not less numerous; that of General Cecil amounted but to half the number.[1] Lady Cecil accompanied her husband, as one of the ladies in attendance on the Electress Palatine, and two officers of the board of green cloth were appointed to attend Sir Edward Cecil as deputy treasurers.[2]

On the evening of April 25th, the Royal party and their numerous train departed from Margate. The Elector and his bride sailed in the *Prince Royal*.[3] Most of the train were accommodated on board other vessels.[4] The fleet arrived off Ostend on the evening of the 27th, and the next day anchored off Flushing. The arrival of the fleet was made known by salvoes of artillery, and Prince Maurice, his brother, Prince Henry, and the Prince of Portugal, came on Board the *Prince Royal* and welcomed the royal pair to Holland.

"The next day being the 29th of Aprill," says the author of the *Journal* of Princess Elizabeth's journey to Heidelberg, "they went to land, honourably accompanied with Grave Maurice, the

---

[1] Miss Benger's *Memoirs of the Queen of Bohemia*, i. Appendix. This authoress, in giving the names of Lord and Lady Arundel who attended Elizabeth on her journey, says :—"The brave General, Sir Edward Cecil, was still more acceptable to Elizabeth." p. 161.

[2] Green's *Princesses of England.* v. p. 231 note.

[3] Built by Phineas Pett, the shipbuilder whom Prince Henry patronised.

[4] The *Royal Anne*, the *Repulse*, and the *Red Lion*. Benger, p. 160.

Duke of Lennox, the Earle of Arundell, the Lord Viscount Lisle, the Lord Harington, the Lord Effingham, General Cicill, besides divers Knights and Gentlemen; the Princess having attending on her the Countess of Arundell, the Lady Harington, the Lady Cicill, Mᵐ Anne Dudley, Mᵐ Elizabeth Dudley, &c." [1]

From the time of her arrival at Flushing to her entry into Heidelberg six weeks after, Elizabeth's journey was a continual triumphant progress—a series of gorgeous pageants and splendid entertainments. Gifts of great value were presented to her by princes, nobles, and civic authorities, who showed herself, her husband, and their suite, every possible honour and respect. It is quite needless to give a detailed account of this Royal Progress, suffice it to say that the Princess and her retinue stayed at Middleburg, Dort, Rotterdam, the Hague (here the Elector took leave of his bride, taking his way to Heidelberg, to make all due preparations for her coming), Leyden, Harlem, Amsterdam, and Utrecht. At Utrecht were stationed seventeen foot companies and two troops of horse,[2] who at the coming of Princess Elizabeth marched out to meet her, and conducted her to her lodging.[3] From Utrecht the Princess proceeded to Arnhem, Emerich, Wesel, Does-burgh, Cologne and Bonn. At the last-named place she was sumptuously entertained by the Prince of Brandenburg. Maurice of Nassau, his brother Henry, and Emanuel of Portugal, who had accompanied Elizabeth thus far on her journey, now took their leave. The road was now ex-changed for the river—the beautiful Rhine. The monotony of the river was forgotten when such beautiful places as

---

[1] From a contemporary journal of Princess Elizabeth's journey to Heidel-berg, quoted in Nichols' *Progresses of James I.* ii. p. 613.

[2] Sir Edward Cecil's regiment was stationed at Utrecht, and comprised part of this force.

[3] Nichols, as above, p. 615.

Andernach and St. Goar were reached, and short stoppages made there.   Soon after leaving the latter place Gaulstein was reached, and Elizabeth (who had now been joined by her husband) set foot for the first time on the territory of the Palatinate.   The object of the British commissioners was now over, and they informed the Electress of their intention to return home.   Elizabeth gave a special invitation to the Duke of Lennox, Lords Arundel, Harington and L'Isle, to accompany her to Heidelberg, which they gladly accepted.[1] Sir Edward and Lady Cecil returned to Utrecht, where Cecil's regiment was quartered.   On Cecil's departure, an inconvenience, unforeseen and unprovided for, transpired. Presents had been given in all the towns through which Elizabeth passed, and these presents had been furnished by Cecil, her treasurer.[2]   On his departure she was to travel at the Elector's expense.   Being unwilling to ask her husband for money at this early stage of their marriage, and not liking, in her generosity, to forego these customary presents, she was forced to ask her jeweller to lend her a sum of money on one of her own jewels.[3]   A few days after this the Elector and his bride made their entry into Heidelberg, where they received a most enthusiastic reception.   And here, for the present, we must leave them to their happiness, which was as complete and as great as it was possible for human happiness to be.

Leaving Sir Edward Cecil at the dull garrison town of Utrecht, whither he had gone after leaving the Electress, we must return, for a short time, to the English court and see how the downfall of Robert Carr, Viscount Rochester, the

---

[1] Green's *Princesses of England*, v. p. 238.

[2] " Cecil was punctual in refunding to the civic authorities of the different towns all charges for the diet of her train, and at the Hague alone he spent £491 in provisions and in presents to the servants of Counts Maurice and Henry." *Ibid.* p. 231.

[3] Green, p. 238, as before.

royal favourite, made way for the rise of a new favourite—
a much greater and more fortunate star than his predecessor and the future patron of Sir Edward Cecil.
The downfall of monarchs, governments, and individuals
in public and private life, can generally be traced to one
particular false step in their careers. Mary Queen of Scots
completely estranged herself from her subjects by her
marriage with Bothwell—one of the suspected murderers of
her former husband. James the Second's irreparable false
step was the sending the seven bishops to the Tower. The
invasion of Russia by Napoleon the First was one of the
greatest of that great man's false moves. In our own days
we have seen that Napoleon the Third's interference in
the affairs of Mexico was the turning point in his career—
the first step downwards, which was never recovered. And
Robert Carr, Viscount Rochester, owed his downfall to his
iniquitous marriage with Lady Frances Howard, Countess
of Essex, who had waded knee-deep in crime to obtain a
divorce from her unoffending husband, in order that she
might gratify her adulterous passion for Rochester. Every
history of the reign of James I. mentions this disgraceful
affair, which was one of the worst scandals of a reign replete
with scandals. The less said about this affair the better,
and only as much will now be said as will make incidental
mention of this affair, hereafter, intelligible.

Robert Devereux, Earl of Essex, and the Lady Frances
Howard, daughter of the Earl of Suffolk, were married in
1606, when the Earl was only 15 and the lady 13.
Lord Essex was sent abroad directly after his marriage,[1]

---

[1] This marriage is said to have been arranged and brought about by the Earl
of Salisbury, who had been the bitter enemy of the late Earl of Essex, and
wishing to be on good terms with the son, married him into a family which he
(Cecil) was nearly allied to, his son, Lord Cranbourne, having married Lady
Catherine Howard, sister to Lady Frances.

and did not return to London till 1610. He found his
young wife one of the greatest beauties at court and
became deeply enamoured of her. She not only did not
return his ardent affection, but openly refused to live with
him, and when forced to do so by her father, she shut
herself up in her own room and became very melancholy.
The reason for all this strange conduct was that she had
set her affections on the King's handsome favourite, Robert
Carr. Lord Essex finding it impossible to win his lady's
affection, and growing tired of an apparently useless contest,
left his wife to go her own way, and troubled himself no
more about her. The Countess, having returned to court,
was not long in letting Rochester know for whose sake she
had repudiated her husband. To do him justice he had had
no hand so far in her strange behaviour to her husband, but
being flattered by the preference of this young beauty for
him, he became an easy conquest to her charms. The *liaison*
between Rochester and the Countess soon became noto-
rious, but as Lord Essex showed no disposition to divorce
her, she determined to divorce him, in order to marry the
object of her passion. Knowing the King's great partiality
for his favourite, Lady Essex saw small difficulty in the
way of a divorce. The guilty pair got the Earl of Northampton (uncle to Lady Essex) to present a petition to the
King begging that the Countess might be divorced from
her husband. This petition contained a gross libel against
the Earl, which was the ground the Countess chose for the
better obtaining of her divorce. It is believed that James
was well aware of his favourite's passion for the lovely
Countess, as he is said to have loved hearing of his courtier's
intrigues.[1] Whether he suspected or not, he commissioned
the Archbishop of Canterbury, the Bishops of Worcester,

---

[1] Wilson's *History of James I.* (in Kennett's *History of England*, ii. p. 692).

Ely, Lichfield, Rochester, and some laymen, to hear and determine this affair. While the enquiry was proceeding, Rochester confided to his friend, Sir Thomas Overbury, that he intended to marry the Countess as soon as she had obtained her divorce. This knight, with true and disinterested motives, advised Rochester against marrying a woman with a disgraced name, who would probably mar all his future life. The Viscount resented this advice, and was weak enough to tell Lady Essex what Overbury had said. Fearing she might after all lose the prize she had sinned to acquire, this lost beauty determined on Overbury's downfall. Working on her lover's weak mind she gained him over to her views. Rochester undertook to get Overbury disgraced in the King's eyes, and he managed this so well that his quondam friend was sent to the Tower. Having once got him there the lovers determined he should never quit it alive, and by their instruments he was poisoned and immediately buried, it being given out that he had died of small-pox.[1] In June, 1613, to the eternal disgrace of the bishops who had a hand in it, the Countess of Essex was divorced from her husband.[2] Rochester now openly paid his addresses to her, and the King gave his permission for the marriage. In order that the lady might not lose rank by marrying Rochester, James created him, on November 4th, Earl of Somerset. On December 23rd, the sentence annulling the marriage between the Earl of Essex and Lady Frances Howard was confirmed.[3] Three days after this Somerset married the Lady Frances. There were such extraordinary rejoicings on the occasion that a writer of those times says: "Had the King's own son been

---

[1] Chamberlain to Carleton, Oct. 14, 1613.—*S. P. Dom.*
[2] The Archbishop of Canterbury was opposed to a divorce being granted, and protested against the decree granting it.
[3] *Grant Book*, p. 11.—*S. P. Dom.*

married there could not have been greater." Chamberlain, in a letter to Alice Carleton, giving details of the marriage, says : " The presents, indeed, were more in value and number than ever I think were given to any subject in this land."[1] Thus did guilt triumph for a season, but only for a season, as will be seen hereafter.

Towards the close of 1613, it was announced to the King that his daughter was shortly to become a mother. James was very anxious that a married lady of good position should be despatched at once to Heidelberg, to be with his daughter at her *accouchement.* Orders were given to the Privy Council to select a lady for this employment. Lady Burgh[2] was chosen with the King's approval. On November 20th, we find Lord Suffolk, the Lord Chamberlain,[3] writing to Chief Secretary Sir Thomas Lake, and sending for the King's choice the names of four ladies, any one of whom he considered suitable to supply the place of Lady Burgh, who was prevented by illness from going to Heidelberg. These are the ladies, with their qualifications:—

" Sir Edward Cecill's lady alreadie in the Lowe Countries, and may be with my Ladies Grase in foure daies, which in my opynion may serve for thys tyme of my ladies Grase lyinge in—afterward it may be further considered of.

" Lady Warburton, widow to Sir Richard Warburton, &c.

" Lady Howard, wife to Lord Admiral's brother, &c.

" M^n Goring, a widow, sister to my Lord Denny, &c."[4]

Lady Cecil was now chosen, and in all respects she was a good person to be sent to the Electress, having had four children of her own, and being already known to Elizabeth.

---

[1] Dec. 26, 1613.—*S. P. Dom.*
[2] Probably widow of Thomas, 5th Lord Burgh.
[3] The Earl of Suffolk was made Lord Treasurer of England, July, 1614, and at the same time the Earl of Somerset was made Lord Chamberlain.
[4] *S. P. Dom.*

On November 24th Suffolk wrote to Lake, informing him that Sir Edward Cecil had been ordered to request his lady to attend the Electress at Heidelberg.[1] At the last moment, however, Lady Cecil was countermanded, Lady Burgh having recovered sufficiently to travel to Heidelberg. "Lady Burgh is to go to reside with the Electress Palatine, with an allowance of £500 per annum," wrote Chamberlain to Carleton on November 25th.[2] Mrs. Mercer, a skilled midwife, was also sent to Heidelberg early in December.[3] Owing to their tardy arrival at Heidelberg, Elizabeth had not the comfort of their presence in her hour of trial, as she gave birth to a son on January 2nd, 1614, some days before Lady Burgh and Mrs. Mercer arrived.[4]

The birth of a son and heir caused great rejoicings all through the Palatinate, and still greater in Great Britain. James, in the plenitude of his joy and gratitude for his dear child's happy deliverance, settled £2,000 a year on her for life, and the child was declared heir to the throne after his mother.[5] The child was christened Frederick Henry. Colonel Schomberg, the Comptroller of the Elector's household, sent glowing accounts of the young Prince to King James; but the happy grandfather wishing to have the testimony of English eye-witnesses to the health of Elizabeth and her infant, sent Sir Edward and Lady Cecil to .Heidelberg, to report on the health of the Electress and her child. They brought back a very

---

[1] Suffolk to Lake.—*S. P. Dom.*

[2] *Court and Times of James I.*, i. p. 230 The date of Chamberlain's letter is doubtless Nov. 25, *old style*, i.e., Dec. 5, *new style*, so that Lady Burgh's journey must have occupied a month at least.

[3] Suffolk to Lake, Dec. 8.—*S. P. Dom.*

[4] Green's *Princesses*, &c., v. p. 259.

[5] Prince Charles, Elizabeth's brother, was of such a weak constitution that it was not thought probable he would live to be king.

favourable report.[1]   Sir Edward Cecil received £500 for this journey to Heidelberg.[2]

Early in 1614, it was found necessary to call a Parliament. James was in sore need of money, and his ministry had come to the end of their resources for raising it. The expenses of his daughter's marriage, the extravagance of his court, and his lavish prodigality to his favourite, Somerset, had completely drained the exchequer, which had of late been kept pretty well filled by the sale of titles. A baronetcy cost £1,000, and two hundred patents of this newly-invented title had already been sold.   The dignities of baron, viscount, and earl, were respectively sold at ten, fifteen, and twenty thousand pounds, and benevolences had been exacted to a large amount. A Parliament having been summoned to meet on April 1st, for the purpose of granting the King a large subsidy, James opened the session in person, and in his speech compared himself to a mirror which discovered his true intentions, and assured the members that his integrity was like the whiteness of his robe, his purity like the gold in his crown, his firmness and clearness like the precious stones he wore, and his affections like the redness of his heart.[3]   A speedy supply having been demanded by the King, the Commons refused to grant it, until their grievances had first been discussed

---

[1] Green's *Princesses of England*, v. p. 261n.

[2] "Whereas by our expres order and appointment Sir Edward Cecill, knight, did undertake a voyage togither with the Ladie Cecill his wife out of the Low Countries unto Heidlbergh to oᵉ dearest daughter the Princess Palatine, we are wylling to defray, &c. Thes are to will and command yᵉ to pay out of yᵒʳ Treasurie, &c., or cause to be paid unto the said Sir Edward Cecill, or to Peter Chapman on his behalf, the full some of five hundred pounds, to be taken unto him as of our free gift, without account, imprest, or other charge to be set upon them, or any of them. Given under oᵉ private seal at oᵉ palace of Westminster the xxxᵗʰ daie of June, in the xiᵗʰ yeare of oᵉ raigne." *Privy Seals Books*, 11–17 *James I.*

[3] *Parliamentary Hist.*, iv. p. 273.

and redressed. Their obstinacy caused James to dissolve Parliament on June 6th, before one statute was enacted, and several leading members were thrown into prison for their contumacy.[1]

Sir Edward Cecil was elected member for Chichester[2] in this Parliament, but as his name is not mentioned as being present at any of the debates, it is to be concluded that he was absent from England during this two months' session.

Hardly a third part of the twelve years' truce between the United Provinces and Spain had passed, before a fresh war cloud arose, which made both belligerents fly to arms and take the field, notwithstanding the solemn compact they had both entered into scarce four years before. The threatened violation of the Treaty was caused by a rupture between the two rulers over the duchies of Juliers and Cleves, &c. It was only to be expected that the two kings of Sparta would fall out sooner or later ; and when the Prince of Neuburg married a Roman Catholic princess,[3] and soon afterwards announced his conversion to the ancient church, the foregone conclusion as to the expected rupture between Brandenburg and Neuburg became a reality. A sudden rising on the part of the Brandenburgers resulted in the Neuburgers being turned out of Juliers, and

---

[1] These were Chutts, —— Nevill, Lord Abergavenny's son, Wentworth, and John Hoskins. Camden's *Annals.* " This," says Coke, " was the greatest violation of the Privileges of Parliament that ever was done by any King of England before." p. 79.

[2] Chichester returned two members—Adrian Stoughton and Sir Edward Cecil. *Notitia Parliamentorum*, by Browne Willis.

[3] Schiller tells us in his *Thirty Years' War* that the young Prince of Neuburg was to have married the daughter of the Elector of Brandenburg, which would have settled for ever, probably, the differences between these two princes and made their interests one, but " a box on the ear, which Brandenburg had the misfortune to bestow on his future son-in-law in a fit of drunkenness, caused Neuburg to break off the engagement, declare for the Roman Catholics, and ally himself to a Bavarian princess."

the strongest fortress in the duchies remained in sole possession of the Elector of Brandenburg.

"The States-General," says Motley, "not concealing their predilection for Brandenburg, but under pretext of guarding the peace which they had done so much to establish, placed a garrison of 1,000 infantry and a troop or two of horse in the citadel of Jülich. Dire was the anger, not unjustly excited, in Spain when the news of this violation of neutrality reached that government. . . . The German gate of the Spanish Netherlands was literally in the hands of its most formidable foe."[1]

The peace establishment of the States' army amounted to 20,000 foot, 3,000 horse, and the English and French regiments. Archduke Albert's army had been reduced to less than half that number. A large subsidy was, however, speedily sent to Brussels by Spain, and levies of Germans and Walloons forthwith raised, so that by the end of July there was an army of 21,000 men ready for active service.[2] Early in August the Marquis Spinola took the field, and on August 22nd encamped on some plains midway between Maestricht and Aix-la-Chapelle. The States-General had taken the precaution of increasing the garrison of Juliers with three thousand infantry and a regiment of horse. All the British officers on leave in England, who belonged to the States' army, were recalled.[3] Maurice of Nassau having collected an army of 14,000 foot and 3,000 horse, followed the trail of the wily Genoese captain. War had not been declared, and the commanders of both armies had strict orders to abstain from all hostility towards each other.

---

[1] Motley's *John of Barneveld*, i. pp. 340–1.
[2] *Ibid*, p. 343.
[3] Rev. Thos. Lorkin to Sir Thos. Puckering, July 21, 1614. *Court and Times*, i. pp. 336–7.

"It was a phantom campaign," says Motley, "the prophetic rehearsal of dreadful marches and tragic histories yet to be, and which were to be enacted on that very stage and on still wider ones during a whole generation of mankind."[1]

Yet this campaign of 1614 was productive of great results, as will presently appear.

Spinola soon unfolded his plan of campaign. Swooping down on the neutral town of Aix-la-Chapelle, he soon reduced that important place, whose inhabitants had committed the unpardonable sin of showing a preponderating Protestant tendency. Turning out the German Protestant garrison, Spinola substituted a stronger garrison of German Roman Catholics, to protect the inhabitants who adhered to the old faith, and to whom the municipal government was now confided. Several other small but important places on the Rhine were seized by Spinola and treated in the same fashion, but by the Archduke's express commands his forces abstained from all pillage and carnage. Continuing his rapid march, the great Genoese captain crossed the Rhine at Rhineberg and laid siege to Wesel on September 7th. This important place was called the Geneva of the Rhine, owing to the attachment of its inhabitants to the reformed faith. Aware of the importance of Wesel to the Protestant cause, the States-General had offered, a short time previously, to send a strong garrison there to protect the town. The authorities declined the offer.

"Had they complied," says Motley, "the city would have been saved, because it was the rule in this extraordinary campaign, that the belligerents made war not upon each other, nor in each other's territory, but against neutrals, and upon neutral soil."[2]

---

[1] Motley, p. 343. [2] *Ibid*, p. 345.

Wesel surrendered within three days and was occupied by the States' forces.

In the meantime Maurice had not been idle. Following in the steps of his old enemy, he seized the towns of Emerich and Rees, and placed garrisons within them. Nothing, however, could compensate the United Provinces for the seizure of Wesel by their enemy, and the whole Protestant world was aflame with indignation at its loss.

The two rival armies now lay strongly intrenched within two hours' march of each other. The States' army had been increased by the arrival of the Prince of Brandenburg with 800 cavalry and an infantry regiment. The Duke of Neuburg had joined Spinola with an army of 4,000 foot and 400 horse. A pitched battle between the rival armies might have satisfactorily settled the Cleves question, but, to the great disappointment of the commanders on both sides, the truce was respected. Sir Edward Herbert, in his autobiography, tells us in his quaint way how Spinola had sent word to Maurice that if he intended taking Rees, he would give him battle before the town ; and how the States' army marched to Rees prepared for battle, but found no enemy to oppose them when they arrived there. Among the officers named by Sir Edward Herbert as being present at the taking of Rees, were Sir Edward Cecil, Sir Horace Vere, and the Earl of Southampton.[1]

War being denied to the belligerents, diplomacy stepped in to settle the question. It was agreed by both sides to hold a conference at Xanten, in the Duchy of Cleves. James I. sent Sir Henry Wotton and Sir Dudley Carleton there as his ambassadors. The Protestant Princes, the Archdukes, France, and the United Provinces, were all

---

[1] *Life of Lord Herbert of Cherbury*, p. 99.

represented by their delegates at this conference. The negotiations ended in smoke, after weeks of wrangling. Neither side seemed ready to give up what they had taken in the "amicable campaign." Wesel and Juliers were the rocks that shipwrecked the negotiations for a settlement between Brandenburg and Neuburg.

" Prince Maurice distributed his army," continues Motley, " in various places within the debatable land, and Spinola did the same, leaving a garrison of 3,000 foot and 300 horse in the important city of Wesel. The town and citadel of Jülich were as firmly held by Maurice for the Protestant cause. Thus the duchies were jointly occupied by the forces of Catholicism and Protestantism while nominally possessed and administered by the Princes of Brandenburg and Neuburg. And so they were destined to remain until that Thirty Years' War, now so near its outbreak, should sweep over the earth, and bring its fiery solution at last to all these great debates." [1]

---

[1] Motley, p. 353.

CHAPTER VIII.

1615--1618

LETTERS.

A SOLDIER'S correspondence is generally a more truthful index to character than that of any other professional man. Soldiers generally write to the point and say what they mean. Their letters have not the grace and finish of the statesman, the diplomatist, or the professed man of letters, but they have an especial interest of their own which is not to be found in a civilian's letters ; for between the soldier and the civilian is a great gulf fixed, and the latter cannot compete with the former on his own ground. In the olden days, letter writing was at a much higher pitch of perfection than it is now. Divest the letters of the 17th and 18th centuries of their flowery border of flattery and hyperbole, and you will find clever, courteous, and interesting epistles from people in every rank of life. Bad spelling and bad grammar (as we consider) may characterise these letters, but, with all their defects, how immeasurably superior to the flippant, brusque, and egotistical style of the *average* 19th century letter. Soldiers, as a rule, have been at all times averse to letter writing. Sir Francis Vere, the greatest captain of his time, never wrote more than he could possibly help. So difficult was his hand to decipher, that Sir Robert Cecil, when Secretary of State, and in the habit of receiving letters in every style of handwriting under the sun, told Vere how difficult he found it to decipher his letters, and we find Sir Francis employing an amanuensis

when writing to the Secretary of State, "because he hears
Cecil cannot read his hand readily."[1] Sir Horace Vere
wrote a still worse hand, and the few letters of his still
extant, plainly show what an uncongenial employment
letter writing was to him. Sir Edward Cecil, on the contrary, wrote a good straight hand, and has left many of his
letters behind him, which, though not conspicuous for talent
or surpassing interest, afford us curious and interesting
information, both as regards Cecil's career and the profession to which he was so ardently devoted.

Sir Edward Cecil spent the year 1615, and most of the
year 1616, at Utrecht, where his regiment had its head-
quarters. In the spring of 1615, we find him writing to
William Camden, the great antiquary :—

SIR E. CECIL TO MR. W. CAMDEN.

" SIR,

" I am bold to trouble you with a request, wherein I presume
no man can so certainlly satisfie mee, unlesse it bee Sir Robert
Cotton, whose understanding of antiquities and yours, are imparted one to the other. My request is to have the knowledge
from you, or by your meanes from Sir Robert Cotton,[2] who was
the first cause of instituting the English march now in use with us,
upon what reasons the old one was lost, and this found and received ; and what other circumstances of persons, time, and place,
you shall think pertinent to my satisfaccion herein.

" You have power to command your owne recompense of mee
any way I can be usefull to you in ; which you may doe as much
for my respect of your worth as for the benefitt I desire to make
of you, so I rest

" Your assured loving friend,
" ED. CECYLL.

" Utrecht, 17th of Apr., 1615."[3]

---

[1] Vere to Cecil, Feb. 6, 1602–3.—*S. P. Holland*.

[2] Sir Robert Cotton, the famous antiquary, was born 1570, and died at his
house in Westminster, 1631.

[3] *Cottonian MSS.*, Julius. c. v.

Camden returned the following answer :—

" HONOURABLE SIR,

" The proposition you make is out of the reach of my profession, and not of antiquity, but of late memory. By reason of Sir Robert Cotton's absence, I can impart nothing from him as yet, and for my own observation, it is very slender. Only, I remember that after Captain Morgan, in the year 1572, had first carried to Flushing 300 English, and had procured Sir Humfrey Gilbert to bring over more and to be colonel of the English there, a new military discipline was shortly after brought in ; and the new march, by some that had served the Duke of Alva, and entertained especially by the important instance of Sir Roger Williams ;[1] although strong opposition was then against it by captain Pykeman, and after by captain Read, ancient leaders, and Sir William Pelham, who were scornfully termed, by the contrary party, Saint George's Souldados ; and Sir John Smith, who had served under the constable Momorency, yea, and under d'Alva, encountred with his pen against the new discipline, and did write much which was never published.

" This in haste, untill I may happen upon Sir R. Cotton, I thought good to impart to your lordship, whom I wish all happy success to the encrease and complement of your honour."[2]

It was entirely owing to Sir Edward Cecil's representations to King Charles I., many years after the two foregoing letters were written, that the old English march, which had fallen into disuse, was revived. Walpole, in his memoir of Sir Edward Cecil, Viscount Wimbledon, thus refers to this military march :—

" As we have few memoirs of this lord, I shall be excused for inserting a curious piece in which he was concerned. It is a warrant of Charles I. directing the revival of the old English march as it is still in use with the foot. The manuscript was found by the present Earl of Huntingdon in an old chest, and as the parchment

---

[1] Sir Roger Williams, a gallant soldier of fortune, distinguished himself in the Low Countries and in France. Biron, Marshal of France, once saying, "That he did not like the march of the English drum, because it was so slow ; " Sir Roger, hearing him, sharply replied, "As slow as it is, yet it hath gone through all France." Quoted in Grose's *Military Antiquities*, ii. p. 44.

[2] *Camden's Epistolæ*, p. 351.

has at one corner the arms of his lordship's predecessor, then living, the order was probably sent to all lords-lieutenants of counties.[1]
" (Signed) CHARLES REX.

" Whereas the ancient custome of nations hath ever bene to use one certaine and constant forme of march in the warres, whereby to be distinguished one from another.   And the march of this our English nation, so famous in all the honourable atchievements and glorious warres of this our kingdome in forraigne parts (being, by the approbation of strangers themselves, confessed and acknowledged the best of all marches) was, through the negligence and carlessness of drummers, and by long discontinuance, so altered and changed from the ancient gravitie and majestie thereof, as it was in danger utterly to have bene lost and forgotten.   It pleased our late deare brother Prince Henry to revive and rectifie the same, by ordayning an establishment of one certaine measure which was beaten in his presence at Greenwich, anno 1610.   In confirmation whereof, wee are graciously pleased, at the instance and humble sute of our right trusty and right well beloved cousin and counsellor, Edward viscount Wimbledon, to set down and ordaine this present establishment hereunder expressed.   Willing and commanding all drummers within our kingdome of England and principalitie of Wales, exactly and precisely to observe the same, as well in this our kingdome as abroad in the service of any forraigne 'prince or state, without any addition or alteration whatsoever.   To the end that so ancient, famous and commendable a custome may be preserved as a patterne and precedent to all posteritie.

" Given at our palace of Westminster, the seventh day of February, in the seventh yeare of our raigne of England, Scotland, France and Ireland." [2]

Walpole does not give the march itself, which is a very necessary adjunct to the preceding warrant, but Sir John Hawkins, in his *History of Music*, gives the measure in full, as follows :—

---

[1] A digest of this warrant is given in the " Analytical Index to the series of Records known as the *Remembrancia*, preserved among the Archives of the City of London, A.D. 1579–1664." p. 254 and note.

[2] *Royal and Noble Authors*, ii. pp. 302–4.

VOLUNTARY BEFORE THE MARCH.

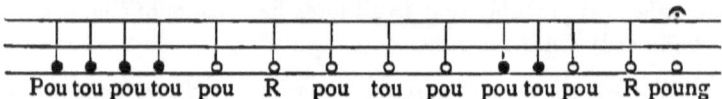

Pou tou pou tou pou   R   pou   tou   pou   pou tou pou   R poung

THE MARCH.

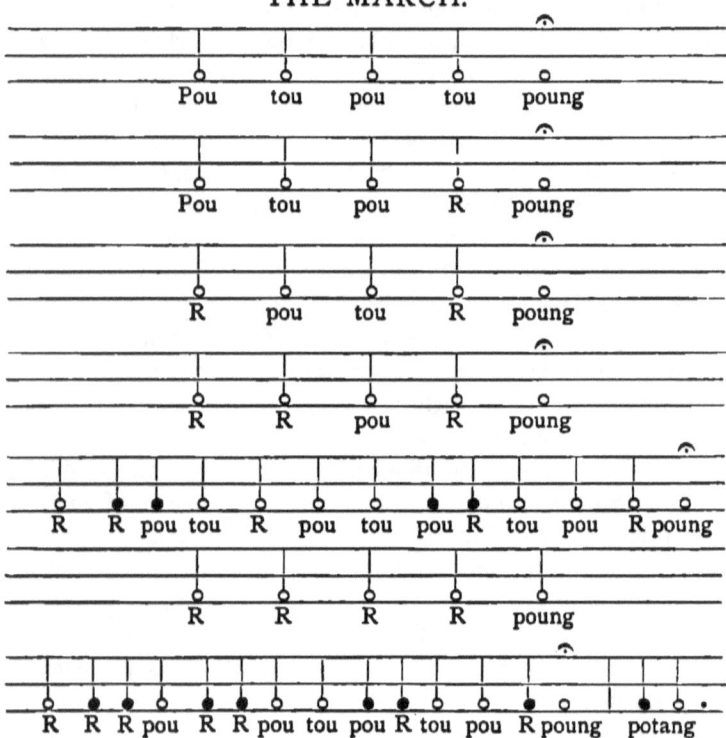

Pou   tou   pou   tou   poung

Pou   tou   pou   R   poung

R   pou   tou   R   poung

R   R   pou   R   poung

R   R pou tou   R   pou   tou   pou R   tou   pou   R poung

R   R   R   R   poung

R   R   R pou   R   R pou tou pou R tou pou R poung   potang

" Subscribed, Arundel and Surrey.
" This is a true copie of the original, signed by his Majestie.
                              " ED. NORGATE, Windsor." [1]

SIR EDWARD CECIL TO MR. THOMAS MURRAY.[2]

" SIR,

" I have by acquaintance observed a disposition in you worthie to make me of an opinion that yo' desire is, the Prince

---

[1] i. p. 229, note.
[2] Thomas Murray, tutor to Prince Charles, was afterwards made provost of Eton. He died 1623.

shall inherit the hono[r] of vertue w[ch] his brother did possesse as well as he doth his other honors, and the devotion I did beare to the service of the late Prince, hath continually applyed me (according to my dutie) to the study of what may be profitable to this. Therefore both of yo[r] in clynation and myne owne having mett wth a worthie occasion, I thought it not unfitt to recomend it to you and by you to his highnes. It rises out of mine owne occupation, and therefore the more fitt for me to present; wherein among other observatons, I have found in the hands of an officer of this Army (whoe is very cunning) certayne modells of all Instruments and Engines necessarie to an Armye, espetiallie concerning all manner of Artillerie that Prince Morys hath by long experience found fittest, and of everie part of everie Instrument (w[ch] come to be many in number) w[th] their right formes, just measures and due proportions, W[ch] in my opynion would be a fitt object for his highnes to bestowe some of his [time] uppon. First, because a peace cannot be well assured w[th]out a . . . understanding, and by reason they are the instruments of use in the exactest warres of the worlde, and made out of soe great an industrie and sense of judgement that any workman may make in great such instruments that noe prince in the world hath the like for use, without any contradiction, soe that they may be accounted as jewells of the crowne to all posteritie. No manner of Theorie upon this subject can be so profitable or satisfie so well. In theis Modells a mann shall have before his eye not onlie the demonstration of reason, but even the verie practise of everie thinge either defensive or offensive, without confusion or crowdinge more neare his apprehension, w[ch] as it will furnish his Judgment wth the possabilities that are cheiflie proper to a prince, for that will likewise impart the fame of his honor to the world, and help to render his highnes an opynion worthie the greatnes of his qualitie w[ch] his brother by his affection to such exercise had, for there is noe occupation to a king but to understand truly a warre (?). They are of some worth, for they are valued at a thousand pounds by him that made them, what hath been offered oftentymes seaven hundred pounds.

" I thought it not unfitt to propose this unto you, for that if you shall think goode likewise to comend it to yo[r] owne likeinge you

may by some convenient meanes present the knowledge of it to
the Prince whome I understand to be apt inough. . . . .

"and soe I rest yor affectionat friend,

" ED. CECYLL.

" Utrecht, the 21 October " [1615].

End.

" Sir Ed. Cecil's l^{re}
touching the models of armes
to be provided for the Prince." [1]

SIR EDWARD CECIL TO SIR DUDLEY CARLETON.

" MY LORD,

" I have receaved from y^r lo. a full assurance of y^r affection
and y^r Lades in the condoling my losse. I must confesse it
inflicted a very strong sorrowe upon mee, for she was a deare
and good wife to mee. But it hath pleased God to allow me
patience wth my afflictions, and accordinge to y^r good counsell I
doe humbly submitt myselfe to his pleasure. Y^r lo. well wishing
unto mee hath deserved my respecte and servis, and y^o shall ever
find me faithfullie readie to make myselfe worthy of y^r good
opinion. The report of y^r arrivalle heere was most wellcome to
mee ; [2] and had not this unfortunate trouble beene so heavie uppon
mee, I would have visited y^r lo. and have presented you wth
my gladenes at the Hage uppon my first hearing of y^r beeing
come.[3] That will not bee long before I purpose to performe that
office of my respect unto y^o, and then I shall be carefull to

---

[1] This letter has been wrongly placed among the *Domestic State Papers* for
1612. It was evidently written in October, 1615. The endorsement is in Sir
Dudley Carleton's hand, which is easily accounted for, as Carleton having
been chosen to succeed Sir R. Winwood at the Hague, was chosen by the
Prince and his guardians as an umpire in the matter of the purchase of these
warlike models. See letter from Carleton to Murray dated May $\frac{7}{17}$, 1616.—*S. P.
Dom.*

[2] Sir Dudley Carleton succeeded Sir Ralph Winwood as Envoy to the
States early in 1616.

[3] Carleton, in a letter to his friend Chamberlain, from the Hague, April 8,
1616, says, "Sir Ed. Conway came hither this day from the Brill ; we expect
Sir Ed. Cecill the next weeke now he hath pformed the ceremonie of his
wife's funerals at Utrecht."—*S. P. Holland.*

acquante y^r lo. with such things as the Prince doth desire as raretes belonging to our professione.   In the mean tyme I hope y^r lo. will give the necessitie yet of my staye heere, leave to excuse mee ; I desier to have my humble servis affectionately recommended y^o and y^r worthy lady, desiring y^o to beleeve that I am y^r lo. most humble servant,

" ED. CECYLL.

" Utrecht, the
20 of Marche " [1616].[1]

Add.
" To the Rig. honorable S^r
Dudley Carleton, lor. Ambassadore for his Matie of
Great Britany, resident at
the Hage."

End.
" From Sr Edward Cecyl, the 20th March, st. vet."

Theodosia, Lady Cecil, who died in March, 1616, at the early age of 32, was buried in Utrecht cathedral.   She left four surviving daughters, viz., Dorothy, Albinia, Elizabeth, and Frances, of whom hereafter.   It is to be regretted that we know so very little of Lady Cecil's life, but her loss seems to have been a great blow to her husband.

The following extracts from letters refer to the "rarities" which Sir E. Cecil was so anxious the Prince should purchase :—

SIR DUDLEY CARLETON TO MR. T. MURRAY.

" There is nothing but the price wch makes me suspend my advice, otherwise I should judge them fitt for a Prince, and wish them rather wth his High^s then wth any whosoever, because he may reade in them a soldiers lesson, *en petit volume*, and make him selfe perfect in his chamber against he come into the field.

---

[1] S. P. Holland, 1616.

If his High* will please to comand any farther service in the busines, I pray you wth the soonest lett me understand his pleasure, because S^r Ed. Cecill and myself have staied the disposing of these things otherwise untill we receave your answear." [1]

MURRAY TO CARLETON.

" The Prince leaves the decision as to the purchase of the models of warlike engines to the opinion of Sir Horace Vere and Sir Edward Cecil." [2]

The models were finally purchased by the Prince, and they were sent to London in custody of a Dutchman, who understood how to arrange them.

EDWARD SHERBURN [3] TO CARLETON.

" Sept. 21st., 1616.   Has carried the models to St. James', where the Prince will give instructions to the Dutchman for setting them up." [4]

SIR HORACE VERE TO CARLETON.

" Oct. 4th, 1616, Thistleworth.   The Prince has not yet had time to view the models." [4]

SHERBURN TO CARLETON.

" Oct. 12th, 1616.   The Prince has paid the carriage of the models and diet of the Dutchman, whom he keeps for a month." [4]

VERE TO CARLETON.

" Oct. 22nd, Thistleworth.   The Prince is delighted with the models." [4]

MURRAY TO CARLETON.

" June 27th, 1617.   The Prince is grateful to him for sending the models." [4]

---

[1] May $\frac{7}{17}$, 1616.—*S. P. Holland.*
[2] Greenwich, May 23, 1616.—*S. P. Dom.*
[3] Agent for Sir Dudley Carleton in London.
[4] *S. P. Dom.*

This last reference to the models seems to imply that some more models belonging to the original set had been forwarded by Carleton in June. If this was the case it was doubtless owing to the Prince's tardy payment for the models, occasioned by the low state of the Exchequer.[1] As will presently appear by a letter of Sir Edward Cecil's, the Prince had not been fairly dealt with by the Dutch vendor of the " warlike engines."[2]

Several notable events occurred in England and the United Provinces in the year 1616.

In the spring of this year, James, being hard pressed for money, offered to restore the Cautionary towns to the States, if they paid off the debt which had been owing since the days of Elizabeth. The debt amounted to eight millions of florins, besides eighteen years' interest. Barneveld, the Advocate of Holland, who had for long been patiently waiting for a favourable opportunity to pay off the English mortgage, and who had instructed Noel de Caron, the Dutch ambassador, to whisper a suggestion into the Royal ear as to how a large sum of money might be obtained, managed the affair so well that James consented to take £250,000 as payment in full. This unworthy transaction on the part of James I. only finds a parallel in the sale of Dunkirk by Charles II. to the French. The surrender of the towns of Brill, Flushing, and Rammekins, broke up the British garrisons there, and deprived the governors of those places of their lucrative posts. To reconcile the latter, James bestowed a pension of £1,200 per annum on Lord L'Isle, the governor of Flushing, and a pension of £800 per annum was given to Sir Horace Vere, governor of Brill, with the promise of

---

[1] "The payment is to be arranged within a year, lest by stipulating for delay, the wants of the Exchequer should appear." Murray to Carleton, May 23, 1616.—*S. P. Dom.*　　[2] Sir Edward Cecil to Carleton, Nov. 1617.

an additional £200 on the death of Lady Burgh, and the reversion of the mastership of the ordnance.[1]

The attention of the British public was partly withdrawn from the surrender of the Cautionary towns by an event in England which had been long impending, and which caused the deepest interest. This was no less an affair than the downfall of Robert Carr, Earl of Somerset, the king's once powerful favourite. Half the story of this wretched man's life has already been told—the sequel is now to follow. "The desire dieth when it is obtained," said that learned philosopher, Sir Walter Raleigh, and never was a saying more truly verified than in the case of the Earl of Somerset. He had obtained the hand of the lady on whom he had cast his unholy affections. He had desired revenge on his quondam friend, who had advised him against marrying a disgraced woman. He had obtained his revenge. Titles, honours and riches had been showered upon him, and he was the king's lord high favourite. What could he desire more? Yet he was not happy. His spirits forsook him; he became moody and unsociable. His very beauty of features seemed to deteriorate, and consequent on this change of temper and looks his royal master began to weary of him. A waning friendship, like a waning passion, can seldom, or never, be whipped back into its former state of pristine ardour when once the affection of one of the parties concerned has begun to flag. And the affection of James for his favourite was of that shallow nature that required a constant supply of fuel to keep it alive. Somerset's enemies, who were many, were quick to read the signs of the times, and taking advantage of the favourite's gloomy and absent state of mind, determined to turn the king's affections into a new channel—a channel which they could

---

[1] Chamberlain to Carleton, April 30, 1616.—*S. P. Dom.*

make use of for their own advancement. Knowing the
King's weakness for handsome youths with good figures, the
Earls of Pembroke and Bedford, the heads of the anti-
Somerset faction at Court, made choice of young George
Villiers, second son of the late Sir George Villiers, of
Brokesby, Leicestershire, as a likely person to supplant
Somerset, and do them a good turn when he had acquired
the King's favour. Their efforts to throw him in the way of
James were eminently successful. Struck with the youth's
face and figure, James caused him to be appointed one of
his cup-bearers. Somerset's enemies had now got the
narrow end of the wedge in, and it only required expert
hands to drive it home.

An unexpected accident, which Somerset had long
dreaded, placed him at the mercy of his enemies. This
accident was the discovery, by Sir W. Trumbull, of the
murder of Sir Thomas Overbury in the Tower. The information was sent to Sir Ralph Winwood, then Secretary
of State, who presently revealed it to the King. James
showed no wish to bring his favourite to trial, and, it has
been thought, would have let the matter drop entirely, if
Somerset had made friends with Villiers and not opposed
his advancement. By the King's advice, Villiers, who had
now been knighted, and made a Gentleman of the Bedchamber, threw himself on Somerset's protection, and said :
" My lord, I desire to be your servant and your creature,
and shall desire you to take my court preferment under
your favour, and your lordship shall find me as faithful a
servant unto you as ever did serve you." Somerset
returned this quick and short answer : " I will none of your
service, and you shall none of my favour ; I will, if I can,
break your neck, and of that be confident." [1] This ill-

[1] *Court and Character of James I.*, by Sir Anthony Weldon, in Francis
Osborne's *Memoirs*, i. p. 98.

judged reply was repeated to James, who, like many another monarch, before and since, found how impossible it was to make two rival favourites agree. After a time James summoned up courage to break the fetters that had so long galled him. He sent a private message from Royston to Sir Edward Coke, the Lord Chief Justice, desiring him to issue warrants for the apprehension of the Earl and Countess of Somerset, the lieutenant of the Tower, and the persons concerned in the death of Sir Thomas Overbury. Somerset was arrested in the King's presence, who pretended the most utter ignorance of the whole affair, and took a most affectionate farewell of his favourite, kissing him repeatedly, though it is said, the door had hardly closed on Somerset before James exclaimed : " Now the deil go with thee ; I will never see thy face more." [1] And he never did.

On Somerset's arrival in London from the court at Royston he was sent to the Tower, whither his Countess, and their guilty minions in this horrible affair, had already been taken. The same day, Chief Justice Coke, going to Royston, was informed by James of all he had been told by Trumbull, and Coke was enjoined to search strictly into the whole affair without partiality or respect of persons.

Most of the parties accused were tried in October and November, 1615, and, being found guilty, were condemned, and executed. The trial of the Earl and Countess of Somerset was postponed until May in the following year.

SIR EDWARD CECIL TO SIR DUDLEY CARLETON.

" My Lord,

" 'This bearer commeth to attend y^r plesure in his busines wth Cap. Sprye,[2] and I cannot but request y^r lo^e in his behaulfe,

---

[1] Weldon, p. 100.

[2] Captain, afterwards Colonel Spry, was reported to have been killed at the Siege of Rochelle, in 1627. *Court and Times of Charles I.*, i. p. 284.

now that onlie in regard of my respecte to y^r lo. the satisfaction hath been thus long forborne. And I doe the rather desier this favore for the wagin master at this present, bycause hee is now going for England and shall have neede of the money wch is dewe to him to furnish his iourneie wth all.[1]

"I have receaved letters from Toby Mathue,[2] that say our Embassadeur at Paris motion there for the peace was so reiected by villeroy; as he sed he would rather declare himselfe directlie a gainst the pease, then see the English Ambassidores subscription to it, wch was much pressed by him.[3]

"I know not whether y^r lo. may have heard of the Earl of Shrowsburie's death, who (they say) hath left his Countess 20,000£ a yeare iointure, and 7000£ of heneritance to dispose of,[4] m^r secriraty winwood [5] and young Candishe[6] being the executers, and my lo. Cooke oversier.[7]

"Wee heare the Arranemente is a gaine put of for all that there were scaffolds fully made at westminster, if it be put of a gaine it will be for Domesday as I thincke.[8]

"I heare the cause that they [the] Artikells of france doe not appeare is because theyre wisist of that kindom is a shamed of them.

---

[1] See letter from Cecil to Carleton, Feb. 12, 1617-8.

[2] Toby Mathew was son of Dr. Toby Mathew, Archbishop of York. He was born 1578, and having become a convert to the church of Rome about 1604, and refusing to take the new oath in 1607, was obliged to leave England. He was afterwards recalled.

[3] Villeroy was the aged minister to Louis XIII. of France. That kingdom was at this time rent in two by civil war—Roman Catholics *versus* Huguenots.

[4] Gilbert Talbot, 7th Earl of Shrewsbury, died May 7, 1616. He had married Mary Cavendish, daughter to his stepmother, the Dowager Countess of Shrewsbury (Bess of Hardwicke), by Sir Wm. Cavendish. Leaving no male issue, the earldom passed to Lord Shrewsbury's brother, Edward Talbot, who succeeded as 8th Earl.

[5] Sir Ralph Winwood.

[6] Sir Wm. Cavendish, afterwards Duke of Newcastle, son of Sir Charles Cavendish.

[7] Lord Chief Justice Coke.

[8] "The Lord Treasurer [Suffolk] and his Lady had gone to Audley End, for shame at the arraignment of their daughter and son-in-law, the Earl and Countess of Somerset, but this is postponed because the Countess is unwell." Sherburn to Carleton, May, 1617.—*S .P. Dom.*

"I humble beseche y^r lo. if y^o heare of any certantye of my lo. Hayes setting forwards that y^o will oblige me to know it.[1]

"I commend my least (*sic*) respect to y^r lo. and to y^r Noble ladie; both whose affections and favours to mee I will ever gratefullie answere, so farr as I shall be able, by beeying

"y^r lo.

"humble and affectionat servant,

"ED. CECYLL.

"Utr^l, this 24 of Maye.[2]"

Add.

"To the Rig.-honorable S Dudley Carleton, Knight; lo. Ambassidore for his Matie wth the united provinces at the

Hage."

Frances, Countess of Somerset, was tried on May 24, and the Earl the following day, both in Westminster Hall ; Lord Chancellor Ellesmere being appointed High Steward on that occasion. Fancy prices were paid for seats at this trial, so great was the interest it excited.[3]

"The Countess of Somerset," wrote Sherburn to Carleton, "confessed herself guilty on her trial. Her noble carriage, and yet deep penitence commended her to all."[4] The great

---

[1] Lord Hay was sent as Ambassador to Paris in the summer of 1616, ostensibly to congratulate Louis XIII. on his marriage with Anne of Austria. "This was one of the most magnificent Embassies recorded in History. Among other things, the Lord Hay at his public entry into Paris, had his horse shod with silver shoes slightly tacked on, and when he came over against houses or balconies, where persons or beauties of eminency were, his horse prancing in humble reverence, flung his shoes away, which the surrounding mob scrambled for, then one of his train took others out of a velvet bag, and tacked them on." Wilson, p. 704.

[2] This letter has been erroneously placed among the letters for 1617. See *S. P. Holland.*

[3] Chamberlain to Carleton, May 18.—*S. P. Dom.*

[4] May, 25.

beauty of this wretched woman seemed to have fascinated all beholders. " Her behaviour was noble, graceful and modest," wrote another eye-witness to Carleton. " Her confession shortened the trial ; and the Lord High Steward pronounced the sentence so gently that she knew not she was condemned."[1] The Earl was found guilty the following day, and was likewise sentenced to death. Little more need be said of this unhappy couple. James, from motives of affection and mercy, pardoned Lord Somerset and his wife, but they were kept in close confinement for many years in Viscount Wallingford's house. Their love was turned into the most deadly hate, and though they dwelt in the same house they were as strangers to each other.[2]

Sir George Villiers had now no rival to check his onward career, and he was shortly after made Master of the Horse, Knight of the Garter, and on August 27, 1616, was created Baron of Whaddon and Viscount Villiers.[3]

SIR EDWARD CECIL TO SIR D. CARLETON.

" MY LORDE,

" By my last letters I understande my lo. Cooke hath blone awaye the greate stormes of his foule weather that did so much threaton him,[4] for dining in Corte wth my lord Caro,[5] her Ma[tie] sent him a Venison Pasty and bid him drink to his Ma[tie] health

---

[1] Edward Palavicini to Carleton, May 29, 1616.—*S. P. Dom.*

[2] The Countess died, in 1632, at Lord Wallingford's house. The Earl died 1645. The only child of this union, Lady Ann Carr, who was distinguished for her purity and goodness, married the 5th Duke of Bedford, and was mother of the unfortunate Lord William Russell.

[3] *Grant Book*, p. 191.

[4] " Lord Coke has received great disgrace by his stout carriage in the business of the commendams." Sherburn to D. Carleton, June 12, 1616.— *S. P. Dom.* Lord Chief Justice Coke, for his judgments given in King's Bench, 13th James I. was accused of high treason.

[5] George Lord Carew, Vice-Chamberlain to Queen Anne.

and all would be well,[1] but I can heare nothing of my sisters business, wch I k'owe y^r lo. wishes well to.

"I am sory this yeare faleth out so ill, that the Spaye (*sic*) water can not be so profitable to y^r lo. as a hott and drie sommer might have made it.[2]   Therefore we iudge heare that y^r returne will be so much the sooner, and the shortenings of the dayes and the coulde wether maketh mee to prepare so much the sooner for my iurney towards England; and bycause I would be loth to parte w^{th}out the hon of seeing y^r lo. and my la. I shoulde be glade to know when y° thincke to be at Brussels or Anwerpe, that I might cast my iourney to wayght upon y° there.   And so I doe humbly take my leave, remembring my servis to y° and y^r worthy lady, reasting

"y^r lo.
"most affectionat to serv y°,
"ED. CECYLL.

"Utrecht, this
27 of July."[3]

Sir Edward Cecil returned to England from Holland September 11, 1616.[4]   His sojourn in England lasted until the summer of 1619, when he returned to Utrecht. Some of his letters written during his stay in England we have thought fit to give, as they partly serve to carry on the thread of this narrative.   The casual allusions to the *Arminians* in one or two of the following letters, refer to a religious dispute which had done more to divide the people of the Netherlands than even the Inquisition had done.   Hardly had the longed-for truce been signed, and the blessed calm of peace been felt and appreciated by

---

[1] There is a letter from Sir Edward Coke to Queen Anne, dated "June," (?) "begging her and the blessed Prince again to intercede for him."— *S. P. Dom.*

[2] Sir D. Carleton went to Spa early in July, 1616, to take the waters. Alex^r Williams to Carleton, July 3, 1616.—*S. P. Dom.*

[3] This letter is erroneously put among the *S. P. Holland* for July, 1619.

[4] Thos. Carew to Carleton, London, Sept. 11, 1616.—*S. P. Dom.*

the Protestant Netherlanders, than a fierce theological dispute arose which set fathers against their sons and daughters against their mothers—which, in short, caused endless tumults, schism and hatred. *Arminians* versus *Gomarites.* Two sects as diametrically opposite to each other as it is possible to conceive. We would gladly have avoided referring to this theological dispute, which turned Holland upside down, and caused much sorrow as well as bloodshed, and shall satisfy ourselves with merely giving the origin of the quarrel in the first instance, and the vital point of difference between the two sects.

Jacob Arminius,[1] professor of theology at Leyden University, gave his name to the doctrine which is opposed to the idea—the Calvinistic idea—of pre-destination. Arminius preached that, "God has from eternity made this distinction in the fallen human race, that he pardons those who desist from their sins and put their faith in Christ, and will give them eternal life, but will punish those who remain impenitent. Moreover, it is pleasanter to God that all men should repent, and, coming to knowledge of truth, remain therein ; but he compels none."[2] Gomarus also a professor of theology, denounced this doctrine as heresy of the worst kind. He preached that, "by an eternal decree of God, it has been fixed who are to be saved and who damned. By his decree some are drawn to faith and godliness, and, being drawn, can never fall away. God leaves all the rest in the general corruption of human nature and their own misdeeds."[3] The dangerous doctrine of predestination had for long been the prevailing one in the Reformed Church of the United Provinces, as in those of Scotland, France, Geneva

---

[1] Appointed professor at Leyden, 1603.
[2] Arminii *Opera*, p. 283, &c., quoted by Motley.
[3] Gomari *Opera*, p. 428, &c., quoted by do.

and the Palatinate.[1]   We can understand, therefore, what
division and secession the preaching of Arminius caused,
and allowances can be made for James I., who, having
been brought up in the Calvinistic faith, took such an
active part in the religious struggle in the Netherlands
from 1609, when he preached a crusade against Conrad
Vorstius, who succeeded Arminius in the professorship
at Leyden, down to the National Synod held at Dort
in 1619, when Arminians were pronounced heretics, schismatics and teachers of false doctrines.[2]

SIR EDWARD CECIL TO SIR DUDLEY CARLETON.

" MY LORD,

    " Y[r] lo. last letters have towlde mee how exceedingly I am
beholding (I even beyonde expectation) for the sence y° have had
of my honor, and the laboures y° have taken to defend it, w[ch] I
did read in y[r] letters to M[r] Secritary, and receaved as much from
his Ma[s] owne mouth, for w[ch] as it hath obliged mee, y° shall find
y° have not directed y[r] favore to one that will make y° a looser
by it.[3]

    " Touching the busines itselfe.   For S[r] John Ogell part I am

---

[1] Motley's *John of Barneveld.* i. p. 47.

[2] *Ibid.* ii. p. 354.

[3] The above refers to a matter which justly excited General Cecil's wrath.
It seems that in his absence from Utrecht, that State had bestowed a vacant
company in Cecil's regiment on a young nephew of Sir John Ogle, then
Governor of the city of Utrecht, without consulting Cecil in the matter, who,
as Colonel of the regiment, had the privilege of selecting his own officers.
Carleton, in a letter to Winwood, Secretary of State, dated Oct. 30, 1617,
says : "The English company lately void by the death of Sir Barnaby Dewhurst, and given on first news to a young gentleman, nephew to Sir J. Ogle,
was much disputed in the assembly of the States-General and Council of
State ; but in the end the commission was given him upon the understanding
of the State of Utrecht that they knew Sir Edward Cecil would be well contented with what they had done." And in another letter to Winwood he
writes : "This is a matter of much consequence in that it will serve as a
precedent to other provinces to cast companies upon particular favourites, and
thereby weaken the authority of his Excellency, and the respect of the colonel,
whose recommendation will have no more place." See account of this affair in
Letters from and to Sir Dudley Carleton, p. 197.

not much deseaved; for I never harde any man make great
accounte eyther of his frienshipe or his honesty, or to thincke
stronglie of the newes in respecte of him, but would I could have
as good satisfaction from the Arminion States as I will from the
Arminion Governer,[1] for theye have rather showne there free will
to doe mee ronge then reason, yet if I lease [lose] in this I will
thincke it rather my destiny then my deserte, for if ever a
perticular man deserved well of that State for his thankefullness
and affection it was I. All that greeveth mee is that I have
beeyne so conny cached (*sic*) by them to have lost so much tyme,
spent so much mony and leafte my deare wife among them. But
I protest if this there Basse liberality goe forward, I will ask
leave to unbury my wife and laye her in some other plase to
make there unworthynes more famus. For there ronge to mee is
not only, but to his Ex., to the discipline of the warr, to the
generall unite of the State, whereof there is no presedent.

"It hath pleased his Ma^y to be scenceble of the ronge done
mee ; and he is an ernest speaker for Ensine Cromwell that he
may be recommended to the companie. I did excuse myselfe
upon his Ma^s letters, but can not excuse his commandments wch I
receaved from his mouth. He [Cromwell] should have brought
these letters, but he is hindered by the unfortunat chance of M^r
Scecritary winwods most dangerus sicknes, of a pestolent feaver
of whose recovery there is but littell hope, wch maketh mee as
sorofull a mann as any having but latly receaved such signes of
his good affection to mee, that I shall be agreat leaser. But S^r
how some ever my Ensigne shall bring his Mat^s letters to ye his
Ex. and the Generall States,[2] wherefore I beseache y^o lo. to

---

[1] Sir John Ogle had given great offence to Prince Maurice and King James
by favouring the Arminians. Sir George Villiers (who had been created
Jan. 5, 1617, Earl of Buckingham), wrote by the King's desire to Carleton as
follows : "Concerning Sir John Ogle his Majesty is sorry he should be the
first of his subjects there that should favour the Arminians, and hath written
me to assure you that whatsoever hopes he may frame to himself there, he hath
no hopes at all here, neither in his Majesty nor any other." Letter dated from
"Whitehall, Oct. 31." *Letters from and to Sir Dudley Carleton.* For further
notice of Sir John Ogle see subsequent letter from Cecil to Carleton, dated
"26 March, 1617-18."

[2] See following letter from the King to Carleton.

continue y⁰ staye of the company if it be possible. One reason I can give a gainst the Province of Utrecke, that is that they have noe other power but to paye the companie, for that it was rased and armed at the Charge of the Generall States, and receaved a commiti'n from them for they [the] rasing of it, wᵗʰ an intente not to humore or streangthen faction of any province a parte, but to serve them all united.

" Touching my sister Hattons business, whoes wellfare I am assured will be welcom to y⁰ and my la., I have beeyne wᵗʰ the king and my lo. of Buckingham. And y⁰ will shortlye heare that shee is brought home wᵗʰ honor and put into a condition better then before to make her able to doe for her friends.[1]

" For Lieftenant Turner, there is no man that can recommende him to mee for eyther a worthy officer, or my friende, for never Coronell hath beeyne more vily used of a lieftenant then I have beeyne of him, yet for yʳ sake I will not revenge any thing against him, but rather for yʳ sake procure Ensigne Cromwell to give him a 100£ sterling if he obtayne the company. Thus wᵗʰ my desier to have my servis remembered to yʳ Noble lady, I reast

" yʳ lo.

" most affectionatt loving

" friend to serve y⁰,

" ED. CECYLL.

" London, this 27 of Oc." [2]

End.

" General Cecyl, the 27 of Octob., 1617."

---

[1] Frances Cecil, widow of Sir Wm. Newport, *alias* Hatton, married secondly, in 1598, Lord Chief Justice Sir Edward Coke, by whom she had an only daughter—Frances. This young lady, being a prospective heiress, was sought in marriage by Sir John Villiers, elder brother to Buckingham ; her mother, who was very averse to the match, carried off her daughter to Sir Edmund Withipole's house near Oatlands. But Sir Edward Coke, having been deprived of his Justiceship by the means of the now all-powerful Buckingham, saw no way of regaining his lost position except by truckling to the favourite. He accordingly followed his daughter to her safe retreat, forced his way into the house, and carried off his beautiful and ill-used child to her former home.

---

[2] *S. P. Holland.*

KING JAMES TO SIR D. CARLETON.

Complaining that the States of Utrecht had, contrary to the course heretofore practised, bestowed a company in General Cecil's regiment without his consent upon a young man of Sir John Ogle's name and kindred, "which," says his Majesty, "we find very strange; and therefore we are pleased that you inform yourself by this draught of a letter which we send you herewith of the reasons of that course; and thereupon insist and press them in our name to revoke that which, contrary to order, they have done herein, and to give Sir Edward Cecil satisfaction."[1]

SIR EDWARD CECIL TO SIR D. CARLETON.

"MY LORDE,

"These are only to accompanie this bearer, my Lieftenant Coronell,[2] wth the continuance of my thancke for your favore lattly received. I heare his Ex. hath givene the younge childe[3] his acte where upon he hath received his commition, but I will beleave nothing till I heare from y^r lo.

"I doute not but it was dollefull nwes to y° to heare of M^r secritares death,[4] he never begane to be greate till his begining to

---

Shortly after this, Frances Coke, "having been first tied to the bed-post and whipped into consenting to marry the half-imbecile Sir John Villiers," was married to that gentleman, Sept. 29, 1617. As may be supposed, this cruel outrage ended in misery and crime. Lady Purbeck (Sir John Villiers had been created Viscount Purbeck in 1619) left her husband and lived with Sir Robert Howard, for which she and Sir Robert were prosecuted in the Court of High Commission, convicted, and sentenced to do public penance.

[1] From "Newmarket, Nov. 19, 1617."

[2] Lieut-Colonel Sir Philip Pakenham, knighted by James I. in March, 1617.

[3] Meaning young Ogle, about whose appointment all this lamentation.

[4] Sir Ralph Winwood was son of Richard Winwood, and grandson of Lewis Winwood, secretary to Charles Brandon, Duke of Suffolk. He was educated at St. John's College, Oxford, and spent some years in foreign travel. He attended Sir H. Neville in his Embassy to France as secretary. Was afterwards resident at Paris, from whence he was sent as Envoy to the States, which latter post he held for many years. His last appointment was Secretary of State. He died Oct. 27, 1617, and was buried in the church of St. Bartholomew the Less, London.

be sicke—if he had lived he had beeyne powerfull and my assured
goode friende—his death hath stagered my sister Hattons good
hopes to have made a goode eande, for all thoughe I wryte to
y° of hope yet I can not doe so now, yet the wind may turne;
but they sayles and taclings ar in tangled wth my lo. Cooke his
pride of the favoritts countinance.[1]

"If y° will heare who are nomenated for secritary, ar these,
Edmonds,[2] Foukgrivell[3] (*sic*), May[4] and Nanton.[5] If y° will
know my voyse I have givened to the worlde, it is for y^rselfe.
Edmonds I know is not in the favorits good opineon in disputing
to hottly for his name to be agente before Beacher,[6] whoe is now
to be. And there is noe man more likly than Nanton, he is my lo.
of Buckinghams kinsman, his creature, healde and (*sic*) honest man
and a sufficient of all the Corte. This I had from a good hande
and one that knoweth much of my lo. of Buckingham his minde.

"If y^r lo. speake wth the States of Utricke, I beseage y^r lo.
know of them whether it was for pollicy or faction they bestoed
the companie so ill for the servis of the lande, or what it shall
please y° to speake in my behaulfe, for never was gentleman more
undeservedly ronged than I have bee (*sic*) that have heare [here]
wth the greatest disputed there actions, wch there Ambassidore can
be wittnes of. Y^r lo. will pardon my passion, for there is nothing
that goeth so nighe mee as unkines of those that I honor and love.

---

[1] Chamberlain in a letter to Carleton, dated October 11, thus speaks of
Lady Hatton. "She lies still at Sir W. Craven's, crazy in body and sick in
mind. There is a commission to the Lord Keeper, the Lord Archbishop,
Secretary Winwood, and I know not who else, to examine her of conspiracy,
disobedience, and many other misdemeanours, and to proceed against her
according as they find cause. But her sickness stands her in some stead for
the time, and if she come again to herself, it may be in that space there will
grow grace. But she is in a wrong way now, and so animated towards her
husband, that it is thought she would not care to ruin herself to overthrow
him."—*S. P. Dom.*

[2] Sir Thomas Edmonds.

[3] Sir Fulke Greville.

[4] Sir Humphrey May, made Chancellor of the Duchy of Lancaster early in
1618.

[5] Sir Robert Naunton, the Under Secretary of State, was appointed
Secretary in the place of Winwood, Jan., 1618.

[6] Wm Beecher, British Agent in France.

"I will be noe longer to truble y° but with my servis to y^r noble lady and assurance that I am

"y^r lo.
"most affectionat loving friend
"to serve y°,

"ED. CECYLL.

"London this last of October."[1]

Add.
"To the Rig.-honorable S^r
Dudley Carlton, Knighte, Loord
Ambassidore for his Ma^{te}
to the United States
leger at the
Hage."

End.
"General Cecill, the
last of 8ber 1617, rec^d
y° 10th of 9^{ber} by Liuet^t
Coronell Pagnom."

SIR EDWARD CECIL TO SIR D. CARLETON.

"MY LORD,

"Did I not assure myselfe y^r lo. understands me well inough and my affection towards y°, I should feare my long silence and my plane dealing might have caused y° by this time to have conceived a lesse good opineon of mee. But for one I can not leave, and for the other, having beeyne long from heance and bending to mariage (though not susdenly) proves the occatione of more busines; wch hath hindered mee from observing that often expressing of my respect, as well to y^r lo. as to many other of my noble friends . . . . The modell seller hath dealte dishonestly wth y^r lo. as well as wth mee. For I fiend there are a mongste the Artilery that ar faltie both in shape and mesure; and differ much from those I saw there. Therefore it must bee that

---

[1] *S. P. Holland.*

hee hath reserved of the best and put theise in the places. And so wth my servis remembered to y° and y^r worthy lady I reast

"y^r lo.

" most affectionat to doe y°

"servis,

" ED. CECYLL.

" Londone, this 19 of November." [1]

Sir Edward Cecil truly states that he was not entering on a second marriage hastily, as it was rumoured in November, 1616, that he was going to marry Diana Drury, third daughter and co-heir of Sir Wm Drury of Hawsted, Suffolk.[2] This lady, who was born about the year 1580, was of equally high birth on her father's and mother's side. The family of Drury came into England at the Conquest, and the name is to be found on the "Battle Abbey Roll."[3] Sir Wm Drury (Diana's father), married Elizabeth Stafford,[4] eldest daughter of Sir Wm Stafford, of Chebsey, Co. Stafford, by Dorothy Stafford his wife (lady of the bedchamber to Queen Elizabeth for forty years), daughter of Henry Lord Stafford, and granddaughter of Edward Stafford, last Duke of Buckingham.

On the death of Sir Robert Drury, only surviving son of Sir Wm Drury, in 1615, his estates passed to his three surviving sisters, who were his co-heirs. The eldest sister, Frances,[5] was married to Sir Wm Wray of Glentworth,

---

[1] This letter, which is unaddressed, is endorsed "19th Nov. 1617."— *S. P. Holland.*

[2] Sir Edward Cecil shall shortly marry Mrs. Diana Drury, who, since the death of her brother, is become a good marriage, with £10,000 or £12,000. Chamberlain to Carleton, Nov. 23, 1616.—*S. P. Dom.*

[3] See Drury pedigree, in Cullum's *Hawsted*, p. 128.

[4] This lady married 2ndly, Sir John Scott, of Nettlested, Kent.

[5] Frances Drury, born 1576, died 1637; buried in Ashby Church, near Grimsby, with her second husband, Sir Wm Wray. Her first husband was Sir Nicholas Clifford, who died before 1600.

Bart., by whom she had issue. The second sister, Elizabeth,[1] had married about 1598, Wm Cecil, Lord Burghley, by whom she had three surviving daughters, and the third sister, Diana, was about to marry Sir E. Cecil, her brother-in-law's younger brother.

SIR EDWARD CECIL TO SIR D. CARLETON.

" MY LORDE,

" The staye of the passage, and my Ensigne's purpose thereupon to goe over, have occasioned this other letter to y^r lo. the rather to let you know that this is the gentleman the King spoke to mee for, to have beene recommended to the companie. But as the dispache his Ma^{le} intended about it, was making; y^r advertisement came that it was determined beyonde the recovery, so as then his Ma^{le} did please in such generale termes onlie, as ar now directed to y^r lo., to insist wth them for the repairing of my honour, wthout the continuing of his former intent to Mr. Cromwell. [2]

＊　　＊　　＊　　＊　　＊　　＊　　＊

" I have a great desier (as it is fitt I should have) to have my companie removed out of Utricke and (if it may bee) some whether into Holland, as Bealse (*sic*) or Harlom. I pray y° (S^r) let this be another suite of mine to y^r lo. when I shall need y^r mediation, wth his Ex., who (I hope for the love and respecte I beare him) will understand how unfitt it is it should tarrye there. And wthout more trouble to y° I will reast

" y^r lo.
" most affectionat to be
" commanded
" ED. CECYLL."

---

[1] Born Jan. 4, 1578, and died Feb. 26, 1654. Gage's *Suffolk*, p. 429.

[2] This was probably the brave John Cromwell, who was made captain in one of the regiments sent to Holland by James I., in 1624, and who eventually succeeded to the command of an English regiment in Holland, and saw much active service.

Add.

" To the Rig-honorable Sr Dud.
Carleton, Ambasidor for his
Ma^{ie} wth the United States at
the
                    Hage."
End.
" Fro S^r Ed. Cecill by
Mr Crumwell rec^d
the —— of 10^{ber} 1617."[1]

SIR EDWARD CECIL TO SIR D. CARLETON.

" MY LORD,

" I have received from y^r lo. the knowledge of the favour y^o
did mee in delivering my humble servis to his Ex. and the satisfaction y^o obtained for mee upon it. I shall intreate your lo. to
lett mee bee excused for having no returned my thanckes unto y^o
sooner, for that I have had many occations to hinder mee, concerning my la. of Exetere [2] her busines, wee having such malitius
and active Enimes.

" For Mr Hewes, I am sorrie that neither my creditt wth the
States nor the fitnes and iustnes of his suite can geate him the
contentment I desiered for him, and that my regiment hath not
as much neede of salvatione as a nother. He hath done the country more honor and servis then all the other have, for he hath
prayed for them in many churches in this kingdom, wch others have
not done, but they have given him cause to leave it. But I shall
be patient in this as I have beeyne in other things. And so wth
servis remembered to y^r lo. and y^r noble lady, I reast

" y^r lo.

" most affectionat servant,

" ED. CECYLL.

_____

[1] _S. P. Holland._
[2] Frances, Countess of Exeter, second wife of Thomas, 1st Earl of Exeter.
Sir Edward Cecil's father had married, in 1615, Frances, daughter of W^m
Brydges, 4th Lord Chandos, and widow of Sir Thomas Smith, who died 1609,
Master of Requests to James I. By this marriage the Earl of Exeter had an
only child, Georgiana, to whom Queen Anne of Denmark stood sponsor. An
account of the libel against the Countess of Exeter, referred to by Sir E. Cecil
in above letters, is given in the next chapter.

" This 4 of December "[1] [1617].

Add.

" To the Rig-honorable
S[r] Dudley Carleton, lord
Ambasidore for his
Ma[le] wth the United
provinces at the
Hage."

SIR EDWARD CECIL TO SIR D. CARLETON.

" MY LORDE,

" I have receaved y[r] letters touching my busines (and so by consequence theye generall good of our nation) wth the States of Utricke, and wth all a copie of y[r] letters to his Ma[le], for w[ch] I am much beholding to y[r] lo. . . . . . to excuse those defects that y[o] find have given y[r] lo. cause to delay the proceeding ; the letters were sent from Newmarket, and M[r] Secretary was only to adde the seales, and they were sealed wth such hast w[ch] was the cause of the errour. The copye of that from his Ma[le] to those of Utricke I sende heare w[th], and the same instructions signed by M[r] Secretary, who promiseth mee he will send his Ma[les] order for y[r] lo. going to Utricke and for y[r] treaty wth theye Generall States ;[2] my humble sute to y[r] lo. is that in case y[o] receave noe satisfaction for mee (as I can not see how theye can very well give me any) that y[o] will be pleased to demand of them and his Ex. leave that I may transporte my commande there upon some mann of quality for the recompense of my 19 years servis, w[ch] to confess to y[r] lo. is not wth an absolute mind to leave there servis if I might wth honour serve them, w[ch] I feare they as littel regard as the may ; my confidence of y[r] integrity maketh mee thus boulde wth y[r] lo. . . . .

" y[r] lo.
" most affectionat to doe
" y[o] servis,
" ED. CECYLL.

---

[1] S. P. Holland.

[2] Carleton, in a letter to Secretary Lake, said it was not *pro dignitate* for an Ambassador to go to Utrecht, and as the Company was given away, it could not be given back. King James saw the matter in the same light, and in a

"Nautone howlde as yet to be the other secritary and mileme [1] (*sic*) shall be M[r]. of the Juell howse, S[r]. Hary Carry, Controler, Edmons, Treasurer, and my Lord Wotton [2] shall have honor and money.

" London this 23 of December." [3]

There is more in this postscript than meets the eye. General Cecil had for some time been a candidate for the Comptrollership, which was vacant by the resignation of Lord Wotton. Cecil makes no mention in his letters of his efforts to get the White Staff, but other writers refer to the contest. " General Cecil tries hard for the Comptrollership, and has got the Duke's [4] favour," writes Brent to Carleton on January 2, 1618.[5]   And the same writer mentions, in a letter written eight days after, that " Sir E. Cecil, Sir Henry Carew (*sic*), and Lord Knollys are rivals for the Controllership."[6]   The contest between Sir Edward Cecil and Sir Henry Cary was very close, both having influential friends to press their claims on the King, who seems to have got very tired of their importunity. The witty Chamberlain gives an amusing account of this contest in one of his letters :—

letter to Carleton, dated December 22, he says :—"We like well that you forbear further to press the removing of him which is possessed ; because it is like to be without effect."   Carleton sent a remonstrance to the Assembly of the States-General in the King's name, which closed this affair as far as James was concerned.   *Letters from and to Sir D. Carleton* (London, 1780, 4°).

   [1] Sir Henry Mildmay, Master of the Jewel House, *tempo* James I. and Charles I., was younger son of Sir Humphrey Mildmay, Knt., of Danbury Place, Essex.

   [2] Thomas, 2nd and last Lord Wotton, born 1588; died 1630.   Burke's *Extinct Peerage.*

   [3] *S. P. Holland.*

   [4] Ludovic Stuart, 2nd Duke of Lennox, Lord High Steward.

   [5] *S. P. Dom.*

   [6] Brent to Carleton, January 10.—*S. P. Dom.*

"Sir Henry Cary hath not yet got the White Staff, unless it was given him yesterday at Theobalds, whither he followed the king, but I verily believe he hath or shall have it, for all the difficulties that are cast in the way by the duke in favour of Sir Edward Cecil; and now lastly by the Lord Holles,[1] supported by the Countess of Suffolk [2] and the Lady Hatton; who, besides all other causes, had won the Lord Wotton,[3] though he had taken earnest to keep aloof till the king was even in his coach to be gone, and being willed to follow to Theobalds pretended indisposition and sickness; but the king answered, 'It all is one, for his staff is not sick.'"[4]

The contest was decided in March, 1618, in favour of Sir Henry Cary.[5]

There are two letters of Sir Edward Cecil's to Carleton, written in February, 1618, which are not worth giving *in extenso*. The first, dated February 11, contains Sir Edward's expressions of gratitude to Carleton for the latter's "paynes and judgement" in the business with the State of Utrecht, which had not been of much avail.

"Neither in deede," says Cecil, "was I ever of the opinion that I should receive any materiall satisfaction from so rusticke poletitions, that are governed rather by there climat than by any reason, for as that province, rather that Towne, hath beeyne observed to

---

[1] John Holles, Baron Houghton; elevated to the Peerage by James I. in 1616, through Buckingham's interest, to whom he is said to have paid £10,000 for the barony. Burke's *Extinct Peerage*.

[2] Catherine, Countess of Suffolk, wife of the Lord Treasurer, who was deprived of his high office, in 1618, for taking bribes and embezzling the public money. "The Countess had rendered herself very odious by her rapacity in extorting money from all persons who had any matters to be dispatched at the Treasury. They were both confined in the Tower for a short time, and fined £70,000, which was reduced by King James to £7,000." Carte's *Hist. of England*, iv. p. 47.

[3] "Lord Wotton keeps his place, because his successor is not agreed on." Brent to Carleton, January 10—*S.P. Dom.*

[4] Chamberlain to Carleton, January 10.—*S. P. Dom.*

[5] Sir H. Cary to Carleton, March 25.—*S. P. Dom.*

be mutinus, so now that the people ar kepte under, the Magistrates ar in the same humores that the people were when the[y] governed." [1]

More will be said later on concerning the mutinous state of the Utrecht citizens, as a crisis was rapidly approaching in the capital city of the province of Utrecht.

The second letter of Edward Cecil's is dated February 12, and recommends " the bearer, John Waymouth [2] the waggon m^r of my Regiment," to Carleton's favour. [3]

A fortnight after this latter letter was written Edward Cecil married Diana Drury.

---

[1] *S. P. Holland.*

[2] John Waymouth was author of a military tract which is preserved among the MSS. in the British Museum, and is entitled :—

" The true order of a March togither with a direction how a company should be exercised according to that exact manner lately perfected by the great and famous Generall of these tymes, His Excellencie Prince Maurice. *Gathered from the Practise of Generall Cecill's Companie,* into these plaine geometricall signes, by John Waymouth, Gent." *Add. MSS.,* 26051 fo. 24.

[3] " London this 12th February, 1618."—*S. P. Holland.* The seal on this letter bears this device—on a wreath, two lions rampant, supporting a wheat sheaf, charged with a mullet.

CHAPTER IX.

1618.

Announcement of Edward Cecil's second marriage—The Bill of Fare at the Wedding Dinner—Troubles in the United Provinces—Remonstrants and Contra-Remonstrants—The story of Barneveld's downfall—The Governor of Utrecht—His difficult position—The Prince of Orange's political triumphs—Revolutionising the States—Imprisonment, trial and execution of Barneveld—Edward Cecil's petition—The feud between the families of Cecil and Lake—Story of a great scandal—The way it ended—A vindictive letter—Uytenbogaert's request to Edward Cecil—Sir Edward and Lady Cecil lose their infant daughter.

"February 1617–8. The 27th of this monethe, Sir Edward Cecill was maried to Diana Drewrye, sister to the Ladye Burghlie and coheyre unto Sir Robert Drewrye."

This announcement occurs in a letter from George Lord Carew to Sir Thomas Roe.[1]   It would seem that Edward Cecil's second marriage was one of ambition more than affection.   Money was the golden key to honours and pre-ferments in the reign of James Stuart.   Merit was wont to be passed over unless backed up by gold.   It is recorded that when the Earl of Somerset reproached Sir Ralph Winwood for his ingratitude in helping to pull him from his high estate after he (Somerset) had procured the post of Chief Secretary for Sir Ralph, that the Chief Secretary coolly replied, that for his Secretary's place he might thank £7,000 which he gave him.[2]

---

[1] *Letters from George Lord Carew to Sir Thomas Roe*, p. 91.   Published by the Camden Society.

[2] *Court and Times of James I.*, i. p. 375.

A curious record of Edward Cecil's marriage has survived to the present day. It is the bill of fare at the wedding dinner of Edward Cecil and Diana his wife. This interesting *menu*, which has never before been printed, is preserved among the manuscripts at Alnwick Castle.[1]

Thursday.—M^{rs}. Drury weding dynner
ffebruary 27, 1616 (*sic*).

" first course

Capons
Chickens
Chines of mutton
Pigeons   }boyld meats
Woodcocks
Larkes
Marrow puddings
Two forced meates

" A leg of mutton soused
A grand Sallet
A corne Sallet
Small Sallets
Sweete Lemons
" Rost mutton or venison
Tongues
Capons
Henns
Fesant

" Veale pies
Oyster pies
Chickens pie

" Second course

Rost kid Larded
Rabbetts
Partridges
Pigeons
Plovers
Larkes
Woodcocks
Chickens
Suites
Soused pigg
Soused Capon
West fallia bacon
Dryed tongues
Chestnut pie
Pippen pie wth ovengado
Potato pie
Two made dishes
Pickled oysters
A Layd tarte
xx dishes "

---

[1] This manuscript, for a copy of which I am indebted to the kindness of the Duke of Northumberland, K.G., is referred to in the "Report of the Commission on Historical MSS. (Appendix to 3rd report), belonging to the Duke of Northumberland." Vol. x., 1612–17, and is thus endorsed :—"Feb. 27th, 1617. Bill of fare at the wedding of Lady Sisil, specifying 24 separate dishes at the first course, and 20 at the second course."

Venison pie
A made dishe
Another dish of creame
xxiiij dishes."

A month after his marriage we find Sir Edward Cecil writing to Sir Dudley Carleton about the injuries put on his company at Utrecht, which injuries were not imaginary, as will shortly appear.

SIR EDWARD CECIL TO SIR D. CARLETON.

" MY LORDE,

" I did expect upon the advertisements I had from y^r lo. that the States of Utrecht would have wryton to the King in answere to his Ma^u tes ; but I heare of none, where in I doe wonder they shoulde so barberusly forget themselves. And I am sorrie y^r lo. was employed in the trouble since y^o can not helpe it.

" I doe heare of more iniuries putt upon my Companie there ; and of some wherein the commander of the Garison is the first man that breakes the law ; booth of that corte of warr, and of the order of the Generall States, wherefore I wounder his Ex. should be so carlas in a nother mans reputatione and let my honor suffer so much, as to have my perticular companie commanded by so unworthy so uniuste a commander wch every particular Cap. is relived in. I understand all the reason his Ex. givethe is that he is more suer of my companie then any other, so that hee useth mee wth less courtesy than he doth others. This is as an Einglis ill custome wch is to sett ons [one's] kinsman at the lower eande of his table.

" Therefore since I cannot serve his Ex. by my companis being in prison there, and that I receave every day one disgrase or other by the staye ; I doe humbly desire that it will please him to consider the ronges I suffer, and for the love and honore I beare him to give me a patente for Breada, against the coming over of Cap. Pine, wherein y^r lo. shall biende mee very muche, for I shall never be contente till I be freed out of that cursed are [air] of Utricke.

" Touching the entertainments of the Preacher, and Wagon M^r., whereas I find by some that there is exseptions takene that the 'Preacher is not in the Country, lett me request y^r lo. to understand that there is noe preacher that useth to go from Garrison to Garrison, but doth eyther live at the Hage or at the Coroneles Garrison, for that he is reserved most for the fealde. For wch eand I have healde him wth mee; making such an increase of meanes to him oute of mine owne allowance as might yeald him that contentment in the place wch the bare entertainment from the Regiment can not give him; and I can assuer y^r lo. that there are none of his country or cotte [coat] for his profession that deserveth better then he doth, yet all the Regiments have allowance from the state for a Preacher but mine, for that Sr Jhon Ogell had none before I turned over to him that which he hath now.   But if any of my Cap. or officers will fiend meanes for the Preacher to live there, I shall be most glade to have him continue there, or that it will please y^r lo. to gitt him an intertaynement as other preachers have of our natione there.   I shall besides thincke my selfe much bounde to y^o, for the only reasone why he is wth mee, is that the Regiment upon the occation of going into the fielde may not want a Preacher as wee have done heere to fore.

" Y^r lo. shall doe mee a great favour to lett me know if there be any liklihoude of our going into the fealde, that I might the better settell my business heare to come over, and so I reast,

"y^r lo.
" much affectionat to
" serve y^o,

" ED. CECYLL."

" For y^r lo.
" This 26 of Marche.[1]

End.
" Sr Edward Cecyll.
26th Marche, 1617." [1618].

The religious controversies which for some time past had convulsed the United Provinces were at fever heat in the spring of 1618.

---

[1] *S. P. Holland.*

The whole country was divided into two factions—
Remonstrant and Contra-Remonstrant. The former were
those who upheld the Arminian doctrines, and the latter
were Gomarists, upholders of the doctrine of predestination.
So fierce had the contention become between these two
opposite factions, that it was quite impossible for any man,
whether of low or high degree, to keep himself aloof from
the struggle. Willing or not, everyone was insensibly
drawn into the rapids, and carried along by the strong
current of popular feeling. Among those who had for
long troubled themselves but little about this religious
dispute was Maurice of Nassau, who professed to be no
theologian, and showed evident disinclination to take the
field in matters theological. The time arrived, however,
when it was necessary for the military dictator to declare
his views, as no one knew better than he did, that those
who follow never lead the way. The head-centre of the
Arminian party was Barneveld, the veteran Advocate of
Holland—a man who had devoted a long life to his
country's welfare, and who had, by his consummate ability
and political capacity, raised his fatherland to the high
rank it now held amongst European nations. The name
of Barneveld has been often mentioned in these pages, but
only casually, being a civilian. Yet was he as much distinguished in a civil, as Maurice of Nassau was in a military
capacity. It had been well for the United Provinces if
these two great men could have gone hand in hand, as they
once had done in bygone days of gloom and danger, until
death claimed one or other of them for his own. But this
was not to be. For full ten years a breach had been
widening between Maurice of Nassau and John of Barneveld,
which was never to be closed. The soldier prince had
never forgiven the statesman for his share in bringing
about the twelve years' truce with Spain. Maurice had

hoped to have gained better terms for his country by the sword than by what diplomacy could effect. It was a never ending source of annoyance to him to see himself virtually a secondary person in the councils of his country. Barneveld had seen too much of the uncertainty of war not to welcome with avidity an advantageous peace. A true patriot at heart, and favourable to the house of Nassau, he yet considered a popular commonwealth the best form of government for his country, and suspecting, rightly or wrongly, that the Stadtholder aimed at sovereign power,[1] he eyed the prince's conduct with suspicion, and thwarted whatever measures he considered unconstitutional and likely to infringe on the privileges of the people. Thus it was that these two chieftains became antagonistic and distasteful to each other. Both were too rooted in their own opinions, and of too unbending a nature, to give way to the other, so that when their interests clashed, and they each became involuntarily or not, it matters not which, the head of a bitter faction, it became an open struggle between the stateman and the soldier—a struggle which could only end in the downfall of one of them.

Barneveld having openly declared himself the protector and favourer of the Arminian sect, Maurice took the opposite course. Not suddenly or without reason, but with due deliberation. Apart from his growing enmity to the advocate, Maurice had taken a violent dislike to John Uytenbogaert, a famous Arminian divine. This preacher had long enjoyed the prince's favour, and had earned for himself the name of the "Court Trumpeter." It is to Uytenbogaert's credit that he is said to have incurred Maurice's displeasure by having boldly expostulated with

---

[1] Prince Maurice became Prince of Orange in 1617, by the death of his elder brother, Philip William, Prince of Orange, who had been kidnapped early in life by the Spaniards and *Hispaniolised*.

him on his immoral life.[1] Maurice never forgave him for
this, and when this preacher denounced the National Synod
from the pulpit of the great church at the Hague, the
prince forsook the church, and on the following Sunday
openly went at the head of a splendid train to the Contra-
Remonstrant church at the Hague. Maurice, having cast
in his lot with the Contra-Remonstrants, many others, who
had no special religion of any kind, followed suit, wishing
to be on the popular and stronger side. Out of the seven
states four were Contra-Remonstrant and three Remonstrant—the latter being the States of Holland, Overyssel,
and Utrecht. It was quite impossible that two forms of the
Protestant faith could both hold sway in a small country
like the United Provinces, when the contention between the
two sects was so violent. The stronger party loudly called
for a National Synod to decide what the established faith
of the United Provinces was to be, well knowing that James
of England and other Protestant rulers were bitterly
opposed to the Arminian doctrine. The three States in
the minority were violently opposed to a National Synod,
and through their mouth-pieces, Barneveld, Hugo Grotius,
and Uytenbogaert, demanded a Provincial Synod to settle
the vexed question. We have already seen how Uytenbogaert incurred Maurice's anger when he denounced the
National Synod so boldly from the pulpit. Barneveld did
more than denounce it. He persuaded the States of
Holland, in an assembly of their body which met on
August 4, 1617, to pass a resolution to the effect that the
National Synod was in opposition to the rights and
sovereignty of Holland, and therefore to be rejected. It
was further resolved, that seeing the insecurity of life and

---

[1] The authority for this statement is the annotator to the second edition of
G. Brandt's "Hist. v. d. Regtspleging," p. 315, Note R, (Rotterdam, 1610.)
See Motley's *John of Barneveld*, ii. p. 61, note.

property in many of the towns, the magistrates and governors of cities were empowered to levy men-at-arms for their security and the prevention of violence. To make a long story short, the States of Holland were declared sovereign and supreme, and their resolutions the laws of the land. In accordance with the resolution passed on August 4, "Waardgelders," or mercenary soldiers, were levied in the principal towns of Holland, Utrecht, &c., to preserve order, and to protect the Remonstrants from the attacks of their enemies. "The right of the municipal governments to raise Waardgelders for the defence and protection of the towns when occasion required, was," says Davies, "indubitable."[1] Yet this levying of troops without the consent of the States-General was the cause of Barneveld's downfall. The State of Utrecht, which was wholly Arminian, and devoted to Barneveld, levied six companies of Waardgelders in the city of Utrecht, who were sworn to obey in all things the States of Utrecht and to take orders from no one else.

Sir John Ogle, the Governor of Utrecht, being a strong supporter of the Arminian cause, was placed in a very awkward position. His commander-in-chief, whom he was bound to obey, had declared in the Council of the States-General that the levying of Waardgelders was unnecessary and unlawful, and the States-General had written to Sir John Ogle, ordering him to look to the repose and quiet of the town, and to admit of no *novelties* without first informing the States-General and his Excellency.[2] On the other hand his inclination and conscience prompted him to favour and obey the civic authorities of Utrecht. We have already seen how the States of Utrecht bestowed a

---

[1] ii. p. 478.
[2] *Letters from and to Sir D. Carleton*, p. 185.

company in General Cecil's regiment, on a young nephew
of Ogle's, without ever consulting Prince Maurice or
General Cecil. There is no doubt that insults and slights
were put on Cecil's regiment by the Utrecht authorities
because these soldiers were sworn to obey Prince Maurice,
and forbidden to take any part against the Contra-Remonstrants. Cecil was only speaking the truth when he
said "his company was in prison at Utrecht," as to all
intents and purposes it was powerless to act in opposition
to the civic authorities of Utrecht. Prince Maurice
intended to pay General Cecil a great compliment when he
said "he was more sure of General Cecil's company than
of any other."[1] One cannot but sympathise with Sir John
Ogle in the difficult game he was called on to take a part
in. He was a thoroughly good and conscientious man, a
brave soldier and a true gentleman. "You shall never see
any bad action in me,"[2] he wrote to Carleton, a few months
before these new soldiers were levied. And it is very
certain Sir John Ogle tried to do what was right, but
human nature is weak, and for one brief space of time he
let his religious convictions overcome him so far as to
reveal the contents of the Earl of Buckingham's and Sir
D. Carleton's letters to the head of the Contra-Remonstrant
faction at Utrecht, for which act he afterwards bitterly
repented.[3] His treachery however was but short lived, and
more in thought than in deed, as when the avenging Prince

---

[1] See Cecil's letter to Carleton of March 26, 1618.

[2] Ogle to Carleton, March 12, 1617.—*S. P. Holland.*

[3] This statement is proved by a letter from Sir John Ogle to the Duke of
Buckingham, (given in *Cabala*), dated from Exeter, June 3, 1625, in which
he says :—" If I had wilfully sinned against you (when I was wickedly beguiled
and insnared by that wretch at Utrecht, to whom I gave some extracts out of.
your letters, as also out of the Lord Embassadour's), or did yet with obstinacie
maintain such indiscreet proceeding, your Grace might in justice reject me as
unworthy."

The " wretch at Utrecht," was doubtless Gillis van Ledenberg.

of Orange, with supreme authority from the Lords the States-General, determined to revolutionise the disaffected states and towns and bring them back by force of arms to their true allegiance, appeared before the gates of Utrecht with a small force of cavalry and infantry, Ledenberg, Secretary of the Utrecht assembly, asked Sir John Ogle if he would stand at the head of the new troops against the Prince of Orange, if need should require. Ogle flatly refused to do so, declaring he was bound in honour to obey his rightful masters the Prince and the States-General. Maurice entered the city, and with · characteristic firmness and composure, ordered the Waardgelders, over 1,000 in number, to assemble in the principal square of the city and lay down their arms. They obeyed to a man, silently and respectfully, recognising their true lord and master. Four days after this *coup d'état* the soldier prince entered the town hall at the head of his body guard, and informed the assembled magistrates that he intended changing their board *in toto*.[1] This was done with the same ease that Cromwell turned the Rump Parliament out of doors in later days—nay, more easily, as none of the Utrecht magistrates seem to have had the spirit of a Sir Harry Vane to make any remonstrance at this summary proceeding. Thus ended the " insurrection " at Utrecht, just a year after Barneveld's decided action in favour of his party. Leaving Sir Horace Vere in temporary command at Utrecht,[2] the Prince proceeded to other Remonstrant

---

[1] Secretary Ledenberg and other members had escaped out of Utrecht the night that Maurice arrived there. Motley's *Barneveld*, ii. p. 268.

[2] Sir John Ogle was deprived of the Governorship of Utrecht a few weeks after this, having offended by " 1. Permitting the levying of the six companies, 2. Suffering said companies to enter into guard and their captains and officers to assist at the Court of War. Lastly, permitting the burghers to guard the Stadt house, &c., which was heretofore the duty of the garrison." Carleton's

towns, and changed the government of each of them in the same quiet manner that he had done at Utrecht, proving the all-powerful influence of a popular military commander who has the army at his back. The Arminian States were thus Orangeised, if one may use the expression, and Barneveld was at the mercy of his rival Maurice.

Little remains to be told of Barneveld's story, as his fate is a matter of history, and his death is an indelible stain on the fame of the first soldier of his time. Arrested on August 29, 1618, by the prince's instrumentality, he was thrust into prison, where he languished for months. The National Synod, which Barneveld had opposed as an unconstitutional measure, was convoked and met at Dordrecht or Dort, where, after innumerable sittings and much fiery eloquence, religious intolerance, and unchristian hatred and ill will, the Synod ended by declaring "the Arminians to be arch heretics, schismatics, and teachers of false doctrines, and they were declared incapable of filling any clerical or academical post."[1] Before this foregone conclusion had been arrived at, Barneveld had been put on his trial, if trial it could be called, as he had to defend himself, unaided, against a host of bitter enemies, who accused him of plotting his country's ruin and accepting Spanish bribes! This trial was also a foregone conclusion, as his enemies had decreed his death. He was sentenced to death, and was publicly beheaded at the Hague on May 13, 1619, in the 73rd year of his age. "Never statesman more upright, never patriot purer, fell a victim," says Davies,

---

Letters, p. 189. Carleton also mentions in a letter to King James, dated 19th August, that Sir John Ogle had secret meetings at night with Grotius (one of the most able of the Arminian faction, and a great author) when at Utrecht. Colonel Fama, a States' officer, was appointed Governor of Utrecht in November, 1618, in place of Sir John Ogle.

[1] Carleton, p. 361.

" to the fury of party rage and the machinations of unprincipled ambition."[1]

SIR EDWARD CECIL TO SIR D. CARLETON.

"MY LORDE,

" I made more hast from the Coste then other wayes I woulde
have done, by cause of the hope I had to have beeyne present
to have visited (*sic*) y° and my la. a good journey before y^r
going from heance. But I missed of the happines to find y° heere
upon my returne, yet I am the less sorrye, by reason of the
welcome newes I have receaved of y^r arrival there in so good a
tyme, to find contentment in succes of a worke wherein y° have
had an honorable parte.[2] A mann would littell have thoughte
such stubborne soveranes as those of Utricke would have ever
come to have beene cashered servants. But now that there
authority is found fault wth all ; amonge the rest of these ruinst
proceeding, meethinkes the giving awaye that companie of my
Regiment, should wth very good reason bee annihilated. It is a
thing that, now y^r lo. is there, having considered how matters doe
stand, it is to be accounted as much an Arminione companie as any ;
I have a great miende to be a suiter for it once againe. And if I
might be bounde to y^r lo. for y^r incouragement in it and y^r
medation to his Ex. for his assistance, I could fiend in my
herte to gitt his Ma^i letters to that purpose, itt being gotte frome
mee by a lie, and to be the messenger of them myselfe. I recommende it to y^r lo. favore. . . . If I may heere be of any

---

[1] p. 519. Secretary Ledenberg and Hugo Grotius had both been arrested
and imprisoned soon after Barneveld's arrest. Ledenberg committed suicide
in prison, and the able Grotius, thanks to his clever and devoted wife,
escaped from prison, concealed in a large trunk, and made his way to
Antwerp.

[2] Sir D. Carleton was bitterly opposed to the noble Barneveld. Had
he not been so, he would have been recalled by his royal master, who was full
of theological spite against the aged advocate. Davies, in speaking of
Barneveld's arrest, says :—" It was supposed by many persons that the Ambassador Carleton was a party to this transaction, from the circumstance of
his having arrived at the Hague the evening before, from England, and having
continued till a late hour of the night in consultation with the Prince of
Orange," p. 491.

servis to y^r lo. I beseech y^r lo. command me confidently, for y^n shall ever finde mee both faithfull and willing in serving y^o. I hope it is sence my beying at Corte that Sr Tho. Lake his hope consumeth more and more, for wee still fiend out one foule thing after another, and lately, as it is suspected, discovered that he and my la. Rosse by the practis of Irishe menn have poisoned my lo. Rosse at Naples, wee having beeyne advised by many and divers letters from Naple to that purpose. And so with my servis to y^o and y^r Noble lady I reast,   "y^r affectiate servant,

"This 22 of August" ^{1} [1618].   "ED. CECYLL.
Add.
"To the Rig honourable
Sr Dudly Carleton, K—,
lo. Ambassidore for his Ma^{tt}
with the united states."

End.
"My Lord General Cecill
the 22th of August,
1618."

The paragraph about Sir Thomas Lake, in Edward Cecil's letter, refers to one of the many scandals which broke forth like sudden plagues in the reign of James I. The scandal has already been hinted at in a former letter of Edward Cecil's, and as he was active in bringing to light a dark and malicious libel made against his young stepmother, the Countess of Exeter, we have no hesitation in giving a short account of the affair, as the honour of an illustrious family shone more brightly than ever when the guilty parties were brought to justice and confessed their crime.

Thomas Cecil, Earl of Exeter, had taken to himself in his lonely old age a second wife. This lady was Frances Brydges, daughter of Wm. Lord Chandos, and the widow of Sir Thomas Smith. Notwithstanding the discrepancy

---

^{1} *S. P. Holland.*

in their age, the Earl being thirty-eight years older than his bride, the marriage was a very happy one, and was blessed by the birth, in July 1616, of a daughter.[1] A grown-up family generally resents a parent's second marriage, and when it happens that the new step-mother is younger than all her step-children, she is sure to be regarded with a jealous eye, how carefully soever she may play her cards. She is looked upon as an unwelcome intruder, and her children are often regarded by their half-brothers and half-sisters as robbers of their patrimony. In Lady Exeter's case, however, it was not her step-children, or her step-grand-children, who gave her the cold shoulder or evinced jealousy of her position. It was the wife of her step-grandson, Wm. Cecil, Lord Roos, a lady of sweet seventeen, who, stirred up by her mother Jezebel, set an infernal machine in motion (speaking allegorically) which, before it could be stopped, brought ruin on her, her husband, and her whole family.

Wm. Cecil, Lord Roos, son of Wm. Cecil, 2nd Earl of Exeter, had married, early in 1616, Elizabeth Lake, daughter of Sir Thomas Lake, the Chief Secretary. This marriage, even in its early days, was a very unhappy one ; why, does not appear, but so it was, and the quarrels of Lord and Lady Roos were events of public comment.[2] His was a strange character, made up of extravagance,

---

[1] In the registers of St. Mary's Church, Wimbledon, is the following entry : " The thirteenth day of Julie, being Satterday, in the yeare of our Lord, 1616, about half an hour before 10 of the clocke in the forenoon of the same day at Wimbledon, in the Countie of Surrie, was born the Lady Georgi-Anna, daughter to the right honourable Thomas Earl of Exeter, and the honourable Lady Frances Countess of Exeter ; and the same Lady Georgi-Anna was baptized the thirtieth day of the same moneth of Julie, in the saide yeare, 1616, being Tuesdaie in the afternoone of the same daie ; Queen Anne and Lord Worcester, Lord Privie Seal, being witnesses ; and the Lord Bishop of London administered the baptism."

[2] Gerrard to Dudley Carleton, June 4, 1617.—S. P. Dom.

recklessness and laxity of morals. Not that these three qualities are at all strange, as they very often go hand in hand, but when coupled with such strong religious feelings as inclined him to turn Roman Catholic,[1] and live abroad, one cannot but be a little surprised. Soon after his marriage, Lord Roos was sent Ambassador into Spain on a special mission.[2] On his return home he is said to have fallen into some neglect of his young wife, which is very likely, as he seems to have been of an unstable and erratic nature, changeable as the wind. When coldness springs up between a young married couple, and they become estranged, there is often cause to believe that the heart of one of them, at least, has been transferred elsewhere. So thought Lady Roos in trying to account for her husband's conduct towards her. So also thought Lady Lake, her mother. When jealousy and hatred once take possession of women's hearts they become utterly bereft of reason, and are hardly accountable for their actions. For reasons best known to themselves, Lady Lake and her neglected daughter owed a grudge to young Lady Exeter. There were only a few years' difference in age between Lord Roos and his step-grandmother, who, it is probable, felt an unusual interest in this extravagant young nobleman, and had perhaps interceded on his behalf with the old Earl, when he was asked to pay his grandson's debts, which were by no means small. Owing a grudge to the young Countess, and being prompted by jealousy to cast a lifelong slur on her name, Lady Lake persuaded herself and her daughter into

---

[1] Note in Birch's *Court and Times of James I.* i. p. 474.

[2] "The Lord Roos is gone for Spain very gallant, having 6 footmen whose apparelling stood him in £50 a man ; 8 pages at £80 a piece ; 12 gentlemen, to each of whom he gave £100 to provide themselves ; some 20 ordinary servants, who were likewise very well appointed, and 12 sumpter cloths that stood him in better than £1500." Chamberlain to Carleton, October 12, 1616.

the belief that Lord Roos was on improper terms of intimacy with his step-grandmother. A story was concocted that Lord Roos had fallen in love with his step-grandmother, and that she had reciprocated his unholy and incestuous passion. A charge like this was of course as fatal to the good name of Lord Roos as it was to his step-grandmother and her aged husband. In order to sow dissension between husband and wife, Lady Lake industriously circulated a report that Lady Exeter had been engaged to marry Sir Francis Crane, and on her breaking her engagement with him, to marry Lord Exeter, had been obliged to give Sir Francis £4,000 damages.[1] Nothing short of the wholesale disgrace of a noble family would satisfy the vengeance of a neglected wife and her enraged mother. Lord Roos, having been accused of this great crime, took the worst possible course he could have done under the circumstances. He left England quite suddenly, without saying where he was going, and disappeared from the scene.[2] What could be a more conclusive proof of guilt, said Lady Lake, than this sudden flight. Lady Lake had scored a point in the game she was playing. Following up her advantage, she spread the story of her daughter's wrongs, and of her son-in-law's guilt, far and wide. The aged earl awoke from his dream of married happiness to hear his young wife's fair name, and his honour, vilified in the most shameful manner.

In this hour of his need his family stood by him, and the aged earl, in company with Grey Brydges, Lord Chandos, his wife's brother, went to Court and craved justice from the King on their knees.[3] The great Burghley's son and Salisbury's brother had not to sue for justice in vain.

---

[1] John Levingston to Carleton, February 28, 1618.—*S. P. Dom.*
[2] Winwood to Lake, August 4, 1617.—*S. P. Dom.*
[3] Gerard Herbert to Carleton, February 23, 1618.—*S. P. Dom.*

Lady Roos was committed to prison[1] for her slanders against Lady Exeter, and James, like a true Solomon, declared he would sift the matter to the very bottom, and mete out justice to the injured parties. To this end the King examined each of the accusers and accused separately. But the person most concerned—Lord Roos—was absent from England, which made matters infinitely worse. His presence was particularly desirable, as Lady Lake and her daughter had produced a paper purporting to be a confession signed by Lady Exeter, acknowledging her guilt and craving pardon for her attempt to poison Lady Roos and her mother. This confession was said to have been written in the dining-hall at Wimbledon House, in presence of Lord Roos and his servant Diego, whose signatures were attached to it. On being shown this damning proof of guilt James sent Mr. Dendy, one of his serjeants-at-arms, to Rome, to interrogate Lord Roos and his servant. Dendy speedily returned with letters from Lord Roos and Diego, stating the confession and their signatures to be forgeries.[2] One of Lord Roos's letters to the King about this unhappy affair is still extant. It is dated from Rome, and begins by begging the King's pardon for leaving England without a licence, and for going to Rome. Lord Roos says despair was the cause of his sudden departure, and he goes on to ask for leave to remain abroad "to digest his wrongs." He also begs that his estate may be managed during his absence by his grandfather (Lord Exeter), and not by Sir Thomas Lake. The letter concludes by requesting his Majesty not to allow Lady Roos's title to save her from any severity, " she being a base creature, a dishonour to his grandfather's house, and not worthy to wipe the shoes of

---

[1] Gerard Herbert to Carleton, February 23, 1618.—*S. P. Dom.*

[2] See account of this libel case in Francis Osborne's *Memoirs of the reign of Queen Elizabeth, James I., &c.*

the Countess of Exeter, whom she has wronged."[1]   This
letter is of importance, as scarcely a month after,[2] Lord
Roos died very suddenly near Naples, not without strong
suspicion of having been poisoned.   Sir Edward Cecil's
charge, in his letter to Carleton, against Sir Thomas Lake
and his family, merely proceeded from idle rumour, and
had no foundation in it to confirm it, but the death of this
unfortunate young nobleman was doubtless a welcome
event to Lady Lake and her daughter.

Sir Thomas Lake, the Chief Secretary[3]—husband of one
defendant in this case and father of another—had been
dragged into this quarrel entirely against his will and
better judgment, but the honour of his family left him no
other course than to take up the cudgels in his wife's and
daughter's cause.   He was in great favour with James,
and was on the point of being made a baron when this
scandal burst out and delayed matters.   James, having
received an emphatic denial from Lord Roos and his
servant that they had ever witnessed a deed purporting to
be the confession of Lady Exeter, made in their presence
at Wimbledon House, informed the Lakes that he required
further proofs of the validity of this confession.   Lady
Lake lost no time in producing a witness in the person of
Sarah Swarton, a waiting-maid, who swore she had been
present in the dining-room at Wimbledon House when

---

[1] Lord Roos to King James, June 1, 1618.—*S. P. Dom*.

[2] It is stated in the Cecil pedigree, given in Blore's *Rutlandshire*, that W^m
Cecil, Lord Roos (De Ros) 16th Baron, died on June 27, 1618.   Dying
without issue, the title passed to his cousin, Francis Manners, 6th Earl of
Rutland, as 17th Baron.   This nobleman had previously contested the title
with the late Lord, and on the day that it had been confirmed to Wm Cecil,
the Earl of Rutland had been created Baron Ross of Hamlake, but dying
without male issue, in 1632, the new barony became extinct.

[3] For some years past there had been two Secretaries of State.   On the
death of Sir R. Winwood, Sir R. Naunton was made co-Secretary of State,
with Sir F. Lake.

Lady Exeter made her confession, and, having been hid behind the window-curtains, had overheard all that passed on that occasion. This seemed a very plausible and likely tale, eavesdropping coming quite natural to servants. Lady Lake also produced a written confession signed by one Luke Hatton, in which he acknowledged that the Countess of Exeter had hired him for the purpose of poisoning Lady Roos and her mother, for which he was to have received an annuity of £40 per annum.[1] James deserves the highest praise for the pains he took to unravel this foul plot, and for the impartiality he displayed throughout the whole affair. He had a difficult part to play, as he was strongly attached to his Chief Secretary, but he did not allow his feelings to stand in the way of justice. It was mainly owing to the King's perspicuity that the damning evidence of Sarah Swarton was proved to be a tissue of lies. He went himself to Wimbledon House and inspected the dining-hall, from the window of which room, behind the curtains, the waiting-maid had sworn she had overheard Lady Exeter make her confession in the presence of Lord Roos and others. James convinced himself, from the immense size of the hall, that it would be impossible for any one behind the window-curtains to have heard a conversation which was said to have taken place at the dinner-table. He also made the astonishing discovery that the window curtains did not reach within two feet of the ground, so that any one hiding behind them must have been plainly visible to all the occupants of the room, and it was indisputably proved that these same curtains had been there for many years.[2] So much for the testimony of Sarah Swarton. The King wisely kept this discovery to himself, and caused search to be made for Luke Hatton,

---

[1] Francis Osborne's *Memoirs*, as before.   [2] *Ibid.*

whose confession had yet to be proved a genuine document. This individual, who was in a humble rank of life,
as may be supposed, was happily found, and, on being
shown his written confession, declared the whole deed to be
a forgery and a lie from beginning to end. The case was
now got ready for the Star Chamber. " The cause between
Lady Exeter and Sir Thomas Lake fills 17,000 sheets of
paper," wrote Sir Wm. Smithe to Carleton.[1] It must be
recorded in Sir Thomas Lake's honour that when the King,
who saw very well how the trial would end, advised the
Chief Secretary to leave his wife and daughter to the law,
and not put his name to the cross-bill, Sir Thomas nobly
replied that he could not refuse to be a father and a
husband, so he cast in his lot with his worthless family and
awaited the results. The Countess of Exeter *versus* Lady
Lake and Lady Roos ; Sir T. Lake and family *versus* the
Countess of Exeter, and Luke Hatton *versus* Lake and
Roos. Luke Hatton had filed a bill against the Lake
family for forgery and false swearing. " Coronell Citcill
(*sic*) was yesterday with the King about Luke Hatton's
bill," wrote Philip Mainwaring to Lord Arundell,[2] which
proves that Edward Cecil took an active part in the
prosecution of his family's slanderers.

This mighty cause came on for trial early in February,
1619, in the Star Chamber, the King being present. The
Countess of Exeter was accompanied to the Star Chamber
by thirty coaches filled with ladies, so great was the
sympathy felt for her. The trial was a foregone conclusion,
and though it lasted five days, there was no doubt as to the
ultimate result. Lady Lake and Lady Roos were proved
to have forged Lady Exeter's hand to a counterfeit

---

[1] October 2, 1618.—*S. P. Dom.*
[2] November 22, 1618. See Lodge's *Illustrations of British History*, iii.
p. 293.

document. Sarah Swarton was proved to have perjured herself, and Luke Hatton proved that at the time he was stated to have been employed by Lady Exeter to poison the Lakes, he was in Somersetshire. The whole plot was laid bare to public view, and the King passed sentence on the guilty parties, comparing Lady Lake to the serpent, Lady Roos to Eve, and Sir Thomas Lake to Adam.[1] Sir Thomas Lake and his wife were each fined £5,000 and a sum of £4,000 to the Countess, as damages ; £500 also to Luke Hatton for compensation. The Chief Secretary was deprived of his office and sent to the Tower with Lady Lake and Lady Roos, until they pleaded guilty and made their submission to Lady Exeter, craving her pardon. Sarah Swarton was ordered to be whipped, branded with the letters F.A., signifying " False Accusation," and to be imprisoned in Bridewell for life.[2]

As is very often the case the least guilty suffered most. Sir Thomas Lake was mulcted altogether of nearly £30,000. He lost his good post and suffered a long imprisonment in the Tower. Lady Roos, the primary cause of all this trouble, got off very easily. She is said to have confessed her share in the plot before the trial was over, whereby she escaped severe punishment, and though imprisoned in the Tower with her parents, it was not for long, as she laid open the whole villainy to the King a few weeks after, and, having made her submission to the Countess and craved her pardon, was set at liberty. " Lady Roos is detested for betraying her parents," wrote Chamberlain to Carleton.[3] Yet she was but a girl of nineteen, it must be remembered,

---

[1] Sir T. Wynne to Carleton, February 14, 1618-19.—*S. P. Dom.*

[2] Sarah Swarton made a full disclosure of her share in the plot, and declared Lady Exeter to be innocent. Chamberlain to Carleton, February 27, 1618-9.—*S. P. Dom.*

[3] Chamberlain to Carleton, June 26, 1619.—*S. P. Dom.*

and was under the influence of a bad mother. Whatever her conduct had been she found no difficulty in finding a gentleman to take her for better for worse two years after.[1] Her mother preferred imprisonment to making her submission to her enemy, and her worthy husband was kept in prison in consequence. He is said to have employed his spare time in sawing wood.[2] Falling into bad health, he was at length released from the Tower, and, on making his submission to the Countess in the Star Chamber, was pardoned. This was in January, 1620. Lady Lake was let out of prison on bail some months after, but refusing to make her submission to the Countess and confess her guilt, was sent back to the Tower. The following letter from Lady Lake to the Countess, shows us what an undying hatred the former bore to the latter, and how she still adhered to her wicked libel :—

LADY LAKE TO THE COUNTESS OF EXETER.

" MADAM, now after all this busines in which you have had to much glorye, cast your eyes upon the *134. Psalme, there you shall finde what God is, no place nor thought hid from him, hee can looke where mens iudgments can not looke, and his records must remaine vpon the fyle for ever, his lawyers will not receave bribes nor bee corrupted, these exhibits cannot be stolen in boxes; to conclude, for this time I wish my submission coulde make you an innocent woman, and wish you as white as a swan, but it must be your own submission unto God, and many prayers and teares and afflictions, wch seeinge you have none outwardly examine your harte, and thinke on tymes past, and remember what I have written you heretofore. The same I do now againe, for I yet nothinge doubt, but that although the lo. Roos was sent away and is dead, yet truth lives and Gods glory will appeare in his good time, and if you

---

[1] Lady Roos married secondly, in 1621, George Rodney, Esqre, and died, in 1630, aged 30. She was buried at Stoke, in Somersetshire. Cecil pedigree, Blore's *Rutlandshire.*

[2] Chamberlain to Carleton, July 15, 1619.—*S. P. Dom.*

flatter your sealfe other, it will fayle you, and this businesse will never have end till you and I meete in the presence of the King's Majestie wch hath byn often my humble suite. Although I can not yet obtaine it, yet I hope ere you and I parte this worlde I shall, yf not I will leave that testimony as shall make all the worlde to see that I die Gods servant, to whose Justice I comend my selfe ;

" MARY LAKE.

" 9 November, 1620.

" To the Countesse of Exeter."[1]

End. " The Lady Lake's letter to the Countesse of Exeter conceminge her submission, wch shee refusinge in michaelmas terme last, beinge brought in to the Star Chamber, was sent agen to the Tower.

" Returne this by the next bearer, or by new years daye at furthest, if ould bicknor comes up."

It was not until May, 1621, that Lady Lake brought her haughty spirit to make submission to the Countess of Exeter, whom she had so deeply wronged. " Lady Lake, after many shifts, is at last driven to a complete sub-mission,"[2] wrote Chamberlain to Carleton, and the next and last notice we have of this obdurate woman is that she was released and pardoned.[3] Thus ends the story of one of the most scandalous libels of a scandalous age. It only remains to add, that though Sir Thomas Lake was deprived of his Secretaryship, being succeeded by Sir George Calvert,[4] he was restored to the King's favour, which he

---

[1] *Harl. MSS.*, 4762. f. 115.
[2] Chamberlain to Carleton, May 2, 1621.—*S. P. Dom.*
[3] Locke to Carleton, May 5.—*S. P. Dom.*
[4] Sir George Calvert was born at Kipling, in Yorkshire, and was educated at Trinity College, Oxford. Having served as Under Secretary to Sir Robert Cecil for some years, was made by him one of the Clerks of the Council. Knighted in 1617. Succeeded Sir Thomas Lake as Chief Secretary, February 15, 1619, which post he held until latter end of 1624, when he was obliged to resign, being too much devoted to Spanish interests. He was, however,

never really had lost, and his family became a very distinguished one in after generations.

SIR EDWARD CECIL TO SIR D. CARLETON.

" MY LORDE.

" As there is not any servant his Ex^{cie} hath that more hartily
congratultes his successe against the enemies of that state, then my
selfe, so for my faithfull respect and service both to his Ex^{cie} and
the state, I must never give way to anything that is thus opposite
either to him or it. Therefore I can not but let y^r lo. know
that I have received a letter from Utenbogaert,[1] dated the 30th of
Septem. but not from any plase named (and never any before),
wherein he desiers mee to bee a suiter to his Ma^{ie} for his safe
conduct hither into England, and for the protection of his aboade
heere wthout being subiect to pursuite ; it is somewhat strange to
mee, considering what disgrase I have received from that faction.
And beside this were to doe a good office for one of the confederacy, booth against the Person of his Ex^{cie}, the union of the
provinces, and the Peace of the Church, anie of wch three, shall
all wayes bee sufficient to make mee account no mann my friend
that should goe about to seeke such an office at my handes. And
I have reiected it as an unworthy motion, wch I intreat y^r lo. to lett

---

allowed to dispose of his place to Sir Albert Morton for £3,000. Created
Baron Baltimore, February 16, 1624–5. Obtained a grant of Maryland in
America, from Charles I., for him and his heirs for ever. Lord Baltimore
died April 15, 1632, and was succeeded by his son, Cecil, as 2nd Baron
Baltimore. The title became extinct, in 1771, on the death of Frederick, 7th
Baron.

[1] Uytenbogaert was for some years the most popular preacher at the Hague,
and on very friendly terms with Prince Maurice and his stepmother, Louise de
Coligny, widow of William the Silent. When he fell into disfavour, he was
accused, as well as his friend Barneveld, of accepting Spanish bribes and
plotting his country's downfall. A number of his letters have been published
by the Historical Society of Utrecht—(*Historisch Gezelschap gevestigd te
Utrecht*—1863, &c., 8°). From a letter of Archbishop Abbot's to Carleton
from Croydon, July 29, 1619, it is evident the Primate of England shared in
the anti-Arminian feeling, as he says :—" The magistrates must be severe with
the Arminians, who are pertinacious and exasperated . . . . Utenbogardt has
secret conferences with the Jesuits. He always sought the applause of men
rather than that of God."—*S. P. Dom.*

his Ex. understand and to assuer him in my behaulfe that I am so willingly and so faithfullie his, that no affaires of mine owne, how urgent soever, shall wth hold me from the attendance I owe his Ex. in person when it shall please him to command it of mee. But if there bee no needfull occation to require my comming over before the spring, unlesse his Ex. call for mee, my humble suite is that he will be pleased to grant me his favour for my staye heere till then ; whe in [wherein] I request y^r lo. mediation. And if in the time of my remaining heere I may doe his Ex. or y^r lo. any service, lett mee receive y^r instruction, and I will not neglect to follow them, nor any other commandements wherein y° will employe

> " y^r lo.
> " most affectionat to be commanded,
>   " ED. CECYLL.

End.
" Fro S^r Ed. Cecill,
without date,
rec^d the 6th of 8^ber
1618." [1]

This chapter commenced with the announcement of a marriage, and it must now end with the announcement of a death.

" Sr Edward Cecill hath lost his little daughter he had by his Lady Diana Drury," wrote John Chamberlain to Dudley Carleton, in December, 1618, " but the best is, she is said to be quick with child again, and so not out of hope of an heir male." [2]

This little child, Anne Cecil, was buried on December 14, in the church (or churchyard) of St. Martin's-in-the-Fields.[3]

---

[1] *S. P. Holland.*

[2] Chamberlain to Carleton, December 19, 1618. *Birch's MSS.*, 4174, Brit. Museum.

[3] " 1618, Dec. 14. *Sepult fuit* Anna Cecill." Parish registers, St.-Martin's-in-the-Fields, London.

CHAPTER X.

1619–1620.

A review of the chief historical events which caused the outbreak of the Thirty Years' War—The King of Great Britain's foreign policy—Perilous situation of the Winter King—Expected invasion of the Palatinate—A small British force to be sent there—Sir Horace Vere is appointed to the command—Sir Edward Cecil's disappointment—His quarrel with the Bohemian ambassador.

MATTHIAS, Emperor of Germany and King of Bohemia, died in March, 1619, without issue, and the attention of the whole of Europe was concentrated on the German Empire, from which kingdom was to emanate the up-holder, or persecutor, of the Reformed Church, throughout a farspreading and mighty nation. Who this man was, who was to hold such great destinies in his Imperial hands, will presently appear, but to show what important issues were at stake on the eve of election of a new Emperor, it is necessary to give a hasty glance at some of the most notable events which had taken place during the reigns of the last two Emperors—Rudolph and Matthias.

The little that has already been said, in a previous chapter, concerning Rudolph II., will not have impressed the reader with a high idea of that monarch's strength of character or fitness to rule over a large portion of the European continent, embracing within its limits so many contending elements of hostile races, and holding religious views diametrically opposite the one to the other. Yet was the reign of Rudolph II. an epoch of glory and prosperity when contrasted with that of his brother Matthias.[1]

Rudolph II., eldest of the six sons of the Emperor Maximilian II., had succeeded to the Empire and the Crowns of Bohemia and Hungary, in 1576. This prince has been severely handled by Motley, whose natural antipathy to crowned heads in general made him a relentless judge in passing sentence on royal autocrats.[2] Schiller's view of Rudolph's character is more merciful, and he tells us that this monarch was not wanting in virtue, and would have been cherished and revered if fate had caused him to be born in a less elevated position.[3] He was an astronomer, a geologist, an antiquarian, a numismatist, a chemist, a philosopher, and a searcher after the philosopher's stone. But such pursuits, when indulged in to the exclusion of public business, were more baneful than advantageous. The ruler of a mighty empire, made up of mixed races and hostile factions, shut himself up with his arts, sciences, and collections, in the palace of the Hradschin at Prague, where he gave audiences to Tycho Brahe, the Danish astronomer, and men of that stamp, but often flatly refused to receive his ministers, or transact the most necessary public business. Is it to be wondered at that Hungary freed herself from Rudolphian misrule, and that other states prepared to follow suit. Hungary, Austria, and Moravia, rising in revolt against their lawful master, cast in their lot with the Archduke Matthias, younger brother to Rudolph, who, foreseeing that his indolent brother was in a fair way to lose all his crowns, from his utter incapacity to keep them, thought it high time to look

---

[1] *Histoire de La Guerre De Trente Ans*, par Schiller, p. 60.
[2] See Motley's *John of Barneveld*, i. pp. 65–67, ii. pp. 294, 295, 300.
[3] Schiller, p. 24.

after his own interests. Having won over Hungary
Austria, and Moravia, to espouse his cause, Matthias,
emboldened by his success, determined to strip the
Bohemian Crown from his incapable brother's head.

Of all the Imperial Crowns, those of Hungary and
Bohemia were the most insecure, the former from political,
and the latter from religious causes. The Reformation
may be said to have begun in Bohemia a hundred years
before Luther's time. The preachings of John Huss, the
famous reformer, laid the foundation of the reformed faith
in Bohemia, and his martyrdom materially strengthened
the Hussite sect. The Hussites closely followed the
religious reforms which later on convulsed Germany and
Switzerland, and under the tolerant rule of Ferdinand I.,
and Maximilian II., Protestantism made such rapid strides
in Bohemia, that at the beginning of the seventeenth
century, the Reformers outnumbered the Romanists. Had
Rudolph II. adhered to his father's and grandfather's
policy, and been wisely tolerant of a faith that had clearly
won the hearts of the Bohemian nation, he might have
worn the Bohemian Crown to his dying day. But
Rudolph's Spanish education had imbued him with a
strong aversion to heresy and heretics, and he doubtless
only followed the dictates of conscience when he issued an
Imperial edict against the Bohemian reformers. The
result of this impolitic act is well known. The States of
Bohemia, taking advantage of the critical moment when
Matthias was marching against Prague at the head of a
large force, informed the Emperor in so many words, that
unless their civil and religious liberties were restored to
them on a firm and lasting basis, they would not take up
arms in his defence. There was no time to hesitate, and
for once Rudolph acted with decision. For the first time
for many years, Schiller tells us, the Emperor showed

himself in public to the citizens of Prague, who doubted his existence, and being present at the assembly of the Bohemian States, solemnly promised to grant his people the civil rights they demanded ; but in granting them the civil rights they demanded, he found means to postpone, till the next session, the most delicate points concerning their religious privileges.[1] Notwithstanding this half concession, the Bohemian States took up arms for their Emperor, and there was every prospect of an unnatural war between the two rival brothers. But it was averted at the last moment by Rudolph opening negotiations with his brother. He purchased a hollow peace by ceding to Matthias what he had already gained, and declaring him heir to the throne of Bohemia. Hardly had the peace-loving monarch settled down again to his old life, before he was again rudely roused from his star-gazing by the States of Bohemia, clamouring, in full assembly, for their religious rights. Rudolph, thinking he was safe from the invasion that had threatened him, when he agreed to take into consideration the religious rights of his Protestant subjects at an early session, now obstinately refused to make any concessions to them. Nothing remained now but for the States to take the law into their own hands. They were the stronger party, and they knew it. A new session was convoked, and the free exercise of the Protestant religion was declared lawful, and all subsidies of money and men were refused the Emperor until he had sanctioned this measure. To ensure this, the States levied an army, of which the Count of Thurn, an ardent Protestant, took the command. Once more driven into a corner, Rudolph, who had sworn never to yield, yielded. He signed the famous *Imperial Letter*, which granted

---

[1] Schiller, p. 33.

immense privileges to the Bohemian Reformers—Hussites, Lutherans and Calvinists—and the free exercise of their religion. The signing of this *Bill of Rights* took place in 1609, and it aroused the spirit of religious independence throughout the German Empire.

The reign of Rudolph II. was now rapidly drawing to a close, and what a miserable evening of life was his. Ignored by his subjects, despised for his weakness, deprived of part of his possessions and threatened to be deprived of the remainder by his ambitious brother Matthias, who hovered near, ready to turn him off his shaking throne at the first opportunity, the unhappy wearer of the Imperial purple knew not where to turn, or whom to trust. In this dark hour he hearkened to the ambitious schemes of his cousin, the Archduke Leopold—Archbishop of Passau and Bishop of Strasburg. We have already seen how Archduke Leopold was sent to take possession of the disputed duchies of Juliers and Cleves, and what bad success he had in that adventure, but it remains to be told how Rudolph II. conceived the idea of making Archduke Leopold heir to the throne of Bohemia, in opposition to his own brother Matthias, whom he hated, and how, with a view to this scheme, an army-corps was raised in the territory of Passau, ready to take the field when a fitting opportunity presented itself. These troops, being kept inactive and without pay, made raids into Bohemia on their own account. This exasperated the Bohemians against their Emperor, whom they naturally held answerable for the conduct of these lawless troops. Fearing his object was to revoke the *Imperial Letter* by force of arms, the States of Bohemia levied an army, and invited Matthias to come to their aid. Matthias, who had been biding his time, joyfully responded to their cry for help, and marched to Prague at the head of a large force. The Passau troops took flight, and Rudolph was left in the Hradschin at the complete mercy of his victorious brother.

Matthias was crowned King of Bohemia in the Cathedral[1] at Prague, May 23, 1611, and he solemnly swore, at his coronation, to maintain the laws and privileges of Bohemia, and to respect and uphold the rights granted to the Protestants by his brother. As there could not be two kings of Bohemia, the deposed Rudolph was forced to sign his abdication, and to release the Bohemians from their oath of fidelity. This last insult was the straw that broke the patient camel's back. " After signing the fatal deed, he threw his hat violently on the ground, and broke between his teeth the pen which had just served him for putting the finishing stroke to his own shame."[2]

A year after this event, Rudolph II. died in the Hradschin, and was buried with his fathers in the Imperial vault in the cathedral of Prague.[3]

After an interregnum of some months, the Electors of Germany bestowed the Empire on Matthias, who had won the confidence of the Protestants. But he no sooner found himself securely seated on the Imperial throne than he laid aside the mask, and denounced the reformed religion. The internal troubles that ensued in various parts of the Emperor's dominions, in consequence of his anti-Protestant

---

[1] The ancient church of St. Veit is within the enclosure of the Hradschin. Matthias was crowned King in the chapel of St. Wenzel (the patron saint of Bohemia), the walls of which are inlaid with Bohemian amethysts, jaspers, and other rare stones. The Crown room, containing the royal regalia, is just above St. Wenzel's Chapel.

[2] Schiller, p. 37.

[3] A splendid white marble monument by Colin of Mechlin, and erected by Rudolph II. in 1589, over the royal vault, is one of the chief objects of attraction as you enter the cathedral. Ferdinand I., Maximilian II., and Rudolph II., besides several earlier Bohemian monarchs, are buried in the vault below this monument.

form of government, were manifold, but it is only those which occurred in Bohemia that concern us at present. " The tranquillity which Bohemia enjoyed thanks to the *Imperial Letter*," says Schiller, " was maintained under the reign of Matthias, until the moment that he imposed on this kingdom a new pretender in the person of his nephew (*sic*) Ferdinand of Gratz."[1]

Matthias having no issue, and the issue male of Maximilian (son of Ferdinand I. brother to Charles V.) ending in him, the Emperor's advisers persuaded him for the sake of religion, as well as for weighty family reasons, to declare his cousin Ferdinand heir to the thrones of Hungary and Bohemia. " For, admitting the succession were hereditary," says Coke, " then by the laws of inheritance these Crowns would devolve upon the King of Spain, Philip the Third, whose mother, Anna, was daughter to Maximilian the Second, and therefore to be preferred before Ferdinand, Archduke of Austria, descended from Charles, Maximilian's younger brother. To prevent this, the Popish party, jealous of the consequences, prevailed upon, or rather forced, the Emperor Matthias to surrender his title to the kingdom of Bohemia to his cousin Ferdinand, a zealous asserter of the supremacy of the Church of Rome."[2]

Archduke Ferdinand, by hereditary right Lord of Styria, Carinthia and Carniola, was a man of firm and unyielding temper. His indomitable will, cool courage, and strength of character, enabled him to overcome the greatest reverses of fortune, and to finally achieve the most surprising successes. Ferdinand made no secret of his strong aversion to the reformed faith, and his rule in Styria

---

[1] Schiller, p. 65.
[2] Roger Coke's *Detection of the Courts of James I. and Charles I.*, i. p. 103.

plainly indicated what his line of conduct would be, if he ever succeeded to the throne of the childless Matthias. It must therefore always be a matter of astonishment that when the Emperor proposed Ferdinand to the States of Bohemia in 1617, they should have accepted him for their king. "Knowing what Ferdinand was," says Naylor, "they threw away their chance and elected him, only demanding a general promise to maintain their privileges and preserve the Royal Charter."[1]

After being elected King of Bohemia, Ferdinand retired to Gratz.[2] But it is not to be supposed that he remained a passive spectator of what was taking place around him. A weak man in weak health, Matthias could not fail to be influenced by his adopted son, and when the Imperial policy to the Bohemian reformers became openly hostile— when Protestant churches were closed and even demolished by order of the Archbishop of Prague, then did Utraquists[3] and Lutherans awake as from a dream, and it suddenly dawned on their minds that the reign of terror which had depopulated Styria of her Protestant population, was about to commence in Bohemia, despite the safeguard of a *Royal Charter.* Roused to action and vengeance by the martial Count Thurn, who, alone of all the Bohemian deputies, is said to have raised his voice against Ferdinand's election, and whose influence was very great on account of the share he had taken in forcing Rudolph II. to grant the famous *Royal Charter,* the representatives of the States of Bohemia having met at Prague, sent a remonstrance to

---

[1] *The Civil and Military History of Germany,* by F. H. Naylor, i. p. 65.

[2] Hungary, following the example of Bohemia, had also chosen Ferdinand for their prospective King. *Ibid.* p. 68.

[3] Utraquists were so called because they received the cup as well as the bread in the holy sacrament. The proclamations and official documents of the Bohemian Protestants were at one time headed, " The Estates of Bohemia, *sub utraque.*"

the Emperor, then at Vienna. This remonstrance was termed by the Emperor a revolutionary act, and so far from promising to redress the grievances of the Protestants, he appeared to approve of the acts of violence perpetrated by the Roman Catholics against the reformed churches. It was this refusal on the part of Matthias that caused the enraged Bohemian Deputies to visit their wrath upon the Emperor's two Councillors—Slawata and Martinitz—then residing in the Hradschin at Prague, and who were credited with being the real authors of the Imperial letters refusing to redress the grievances of the Protestants.

These two nobles had long been obnoxious to the Bohemians by their fierce and relentless persecutions of the Protestants. Late events had roused the anger of the Bohemian Deputies to fever heat, and on May 23, 1618, they proceeded to the Hradschin, and forcing their way into the Council Chamber, demanded of the Councillors then present, if the tyrannical and intolerant edicts against the Protestants issued in the Emperor's name, had been drawn up by them? Not receiving a satisfactory answer, the Protestant Deputies ejected Slawata and Martinitz in Bohemian fashion, by throwing them out of the window, and tossing their secretary, Fabricius, after them. Curious to say, none of the three were much the worse for their fall of eighty feet, as they fell on a dung hill, which graced the castle terrace. Two small stone obelisks now mark the spot where this historic fall took place, and the Council Chamber above remains in much the same state as when the avenging nobles forced their way in. The entrance door still bears the marks of bullets, and near the large window from which the trio were flung, hang the original portraits of Rudolph II. and his brother Matthias—the giver and the revoker of the famous *Royal Charter.* As one gazes from this historical window, over as fair a scene as can be found in Europe, one cannot help feeling a thrill of emotion when one considers that this "Window Tumble," as historians term it, was the first act of violence in the great struggle of thirty years, which began in 1618 in this Chamber, and ended in 1648 with the unsuccessful siege of Prague.

Bohemia was now in open revolt. Matthias was obliged to arm in self defence. The rebellion must be crushed before it spread to the Austrian provinces. Spanish troops under the Count of Bucquoy were put at the Emperor's disposal, and in conjunction with some Austrian troops were sent to Bohemia. But a popular cause had made the Bohemian people rise *en masse*, and soon there only remained three cities in Bohemia which stood firm for the Emperor—Budweis, Krumau and Pilsen. While the Count of Thurn sat down before Budweis, a large force under the Count of Mansfeld, sent thither by the Protestant Princes of Germany—who saw in the Bohemian rebellion a cause that concerned them very nearly—laid siege to the strongly fortified town of Pilsen.[1] At the height of the rebellion, and while revolt was quickly spreading through all the Imperial States, Matthias died.[2] "With his latest breath," says Naylor, "he recommended moderation ; but it is rarely the lot of such exhortations to produce a lasting impression, particularly when the admonition has been uniformly contradicted by the former practices of the expiring penitent ; and unfortunately for the world, neither the example of Matthias, nor the disposition of Ferdinand, was calculated to give them a better chance of success."[3]

The death of Matthias was the signal for increased

---

[1] Mansfeld came from the Duke of Savoy's service in Piedmont.
[2] March 20, 1619.   [3] Naylor, i. p. 94.

anarchy and rebellion throughout Bohemia, Moravia, Silesia and Upper Austria, for the Protestants knew well that the heir of Matthias would chastise them with scorpions. Had not the Protestant refugees from Styria, Carinthia, and Carniola, who had found an asylum in Bohemia, proclaimed the persecutions they had undergone at the hands of the man who called himself King of Bohemia. We say " called himself " because Ferdinand had never entered into actual possession of the kingdom, and was only known to the Bohemians by acts of hostility. Ignoring his very existence, the States of Bohemia declared the throne vacant, and prepared for a new election.

The situation that Ferdinand found himself in at this crisis of his life has few, if any, parallels in history. Bohemia in open revolt; Hungary threatened by Bethlem Gabor the Mithridates of the North; Moravia invaded by a Bohemian army under Count Thurn and in the hands of the Protestants; the Styrian provinces rising against him; Mansfeld, the Attila of Christendom, with a lawless German army, had occupied the town of Pilsen;[1] half Germany approving of the Protestant rebellion, and the other half awaiting the result of the struggle to range herself on the side of the strongest, as Schiller so well puts it;[2] alone in Vienna, with but a handful of troops, mostly Spaniards, to defend him, and surrounded by Austrian Protestants, who were in secret accord with the insurgents marching to besiege the city. In such a position as this did Ferdinand find himself, and no one was better aware of his danger than he was himself. He had sent his family to the heart of the Tyrol for safety, while he waited to face the coming storm. Had he been a Rudolph or a

---

[1] *Ernest de Mansfeldt*, par Le Comte de Villermont, i. p. 105.
[2] Schiller, p. 81.

Matthias, he would have fled, or made a dishonourable peace with the rebels, but Styrian Ferdinand was made of sterner stuff. Bigoted, crafty, heartless, tyrannical, and cruel, he might be, and undoubtedly was, yet was there much to admire and respect in the calm way this descendant of a line of kings awaited his fate, determined to conquer or die. Fortune proverbially, and most invariably, favours the brave. At the very moment when all seemed lost—when the Bohemian army was thundering at the city gates, and their bullets crashing through the windows of the royal palace, where the upholder and hope of the Roman Catholic religion remained, though almost deserted by his friends—sixteen Austrian barons forced their way into the royal apartment, overwhelmed Ferdinand with reproaches, and commanded him, with many threats, to agree to a confederacy of the Austrian Protestants with those of Bohemia. One of the barons went still further. He presented the Archduke with a deed, authorising this confederacy, and seizing him by a button of his coat ordered him in a voice of fury to sign. Historians seem all agreed in saying that Ferdinand did not waver for a single moment, and that he steadily refused to sign. His life hung on a thread, but he was saved-as if by a miracle. The noise of trumpets was suddenly heard. A report ran through the palace that a regiment of cavalry, sent to the assistance of Vienna by one of Ferdinand's generals, had just arrived, and that a force of infantry was not far off. Alarmed by this intelligence the sixteen Austrian barons disappeared, the Viennese Protestants fled for protection to the Bohemian camp, and the Roman Catholics took up arms. Ferdinand was saved.

Good luck, like bad luck, sometimes comes with a rush and one unexpected success is often followed by another

equally sudden.   Thus it was in Ferdinand's case.   Hardly
had he digested the good news of the arrival of succours
before news reached him of the total defeat of Count
Mansfeld near Budweis, by Bucquoy, who was preparing
to besiege Prague.[1]   The Count of Thurn was now compelled to raise the siege of Vienna and depart with his
troops.   The enemy being gone, the roads were free for
Ferdinand to proceed to Frankfort, where a Diet was
shortly to be held by the Germanic Princes, for the election
of an Emperor.   There was no time to be lost, so, nomi-
nating his brother, Archduke Leopold—our fiery Bishop of
old acquaintance—regent during his absence, Ferdinand
departed for Frankfort, July 11, with an escort of 200
cavalry.[2]

The war cloud that spread over the German horizon on
the death of Matthias was watched with keen interest by
the United States of the Netherlands.   The twelve years'
truce with Spain was nearly spent, and there was every
prospect of the war being renewed when the truce expired.
Knowing this, the Dutch fanned the flame of discord in
the Empire, calculating that all embarrassment created for
the House of Hapsburg was the best guarantee for them

---

[1] Mansfeld was defeated by Bucquoy on June 10.   The fight lasted from
nine in the morning until four in the afternoon.   The Mansfeldians were
routed with great loss, and all the artillery, baggage, and several colours fell
into the hands of the Imperialists.   It is said that Mansfeld had sent for
succours on the morning of the 10th to the two Protestant generals, Fels and
Hohenloe, who were quartered with their forces only a few miles distant.
The jealousy and hatred which these two generals entertained for Mansfeld
made them refuse to march to his assistance.   Count Kinsky, colonel of a
cavalry regiment in the service of the States of Bohemia, a surprised witness
of his general's inaction when a battle was taking place only a few miles off,
asked leave to lead his cuirassiers to Mansfeld's assistance.   "Sir," replied
Fels, "know that you are under my orders and not under those of Monsieur
de Mansfeld."   Upon which Kinsky, bursting with rage, broke the pistol he
held in his hand, and said, "And you, sir, know that when you order me to
mount my horse I shall not obey you."

[2] E. *de Mansfeldt*, pp. 151-2.

against interference in their struggle against Spain.[1] On the borders of Germany, with one foot already firmly planted on German soil, it seemed as if the United Provinces must be drawn into the great religious struggle which was marching from east to west with such rapid strides. The rumour of distant war reached even to the British Isles, floating in the air like thunder, sometimes appearing quite close, and then rolling away in the distance. At the first signs of an approaching storm, those British officers in the service of the States, who had been fretting and fuming in England on account of their idle and peaceful career, were filled with hope at the prospect of active service. " If the alarme had continued I had beeyne wth my Regiment long before this," wrote Sir Edward Cecil to the English Ambassador at the Hague, " but since the noise of warre cam to nothing, and my busines many, I have imployed that time heer for my selfe ; yet my resolution is strong to come over, and if it only be to kisse y^r lo. hand and his Ex^y, for I purpose to make my staye but shorte." [2] This was written after one of those repeated lulls in the storm, which were so depressing to a soldier anxious for active service in the field.

Cecil's departure from England was somewhat delayed by his going to Wimbledon, in the latter part of June, to help his father to entertain the Dutch Commissioners (then in England on business connected with the rival British and Dutch East India Companies) who had been invited to Wimbledon House. " The King, on Monday next, is to be feasted at Wimbledon, where the States are entertained this day by the Earl of Exeter and General Cecil," wrote an unknown writer to Mr. Trumbull on June 25.[3]

---

[1] *E. de Mansfeldt*, i. p. 181.

[2] Cecil to Carleton, " London, June 14."—*S.P. Holland*, 1619.

[3] The date of this letter has been wrongly given in *The Court and Times of*

Edward Cecil departed for Holland on or about June 26,[1] in company with his cousin, Mr. Wingfield,[2] having previously notified his lieutenant-colonel, Sir Philip Pakenham, of his coming over.[3] From the following letter to Secretary Calvert, it is very evident that when Cecil was at the Hague he heard various warlike reports, which gave him hopes that the German Protestant Princes were going to take up arms and apply to England for succours, in which case he determined to be an early suitor for employment.

SIR EDWARD CECIL TO SIR GEORGE CALVERT.

" RIG.-HONOURABLE,

" The Princes of Germany (as the reporte is here) will seeke to his Ma[lt] for his ayde for the command of forces. I know there will be many Suitors, and I must looke for great oppositione, yet thus much I have to incourage mee wth all, that I have beeyn his Ma[t] first generall, and for the German service (as not unknown to y[r] H.) w[h] I hope I performed to his good liking; and in that servis spent of my owne purse for the better husbanding of his Ma[t], w[h] by the interposing of enemies I am yet unrecompensed for ; therfor I hope this commande shall not fall to any other. I have written to my lo. Admiralle,[4] and, in his letter, to his Ma[t] for

---

James I. (ii. p. 177) as "June 28." This is manifestly wrong, as King James *went* to Wimbledon on June 28. See *Birch's MSS.* 4176, fo. 257 (Brit. Mus.), also Nichols' *Progresses*, iii. p. 554, where correct date of above letter is given.

[1] Chamberlain to Carleton, June 26. See *Court and Times of James I.*, ii. p. 175.

[2] This was Sir John Wingfield of Tickencote, eldest son of John Wingfield, M.P. for Grantham, son of Robert Wingfield of Upton, M.P. for Peterborough, by Elizabeth Cecil, daughter of Richard Cecil, and sister of the great Lord Burghley. Sir John Wingfield was twice married, and by his second wife (dau. of 3rd Lord Cromwell) left at his decease, in 1631, a large family.—See *Landed Gentry*, art. "Wingfield of Tickencote."

[3] See two curious letters from Sir P. Pakenham to Carleton about "Arminian practises," dated from "Skinkscone, July 7" and "July 14." In former letter Pakenham refers to his "Coronell's" coming over, and sends a complimentary message from Cecil to Carleton.—*S. P. Holland*, 1619.

[4] The Marquis of Buckingham, Lord High Admiral of England.

this purpose. If y^r H. shall at any tyme apprehend an occation to bee my friend in this suite, y° will make one behouldinge to y° that shall no way showe himselfe unworthy of y^r courtesie.

"For the busines of the Arminians, this Gentellman, Eninse Williams, can let you know as much as it is. If it will please y^r H. to make a dispache by this bearer y° shall make us booth behoulding to y°.

> "And so I reast
> "y^r H.
> "most faithfull friend
> "to serve y°,
> "Ed Cecyll.

"My coosin Winkfilde remembers his humble servis to y°.[1]
"Hage this 17 day of July."[2]

"For Mr. Secretary."

This letter may be said to have answered itself, as the Princes of the Union did not apply to James for succours, until long after this, and when they did apply their request was refused.

Sir Edward Cecil seems to have contented himself with visiting his regiment at Utrecht, paying his respects to Sir Dudley Carleton at the Hague, and showing his cousin, John Wingfield, as much as he could of Holland and the Dutch, in a limited space of time. Carleton, in mentioning Wingfield to Chamberlain, in a letter at this time, says :—

"He hath since his arrival made a pettie progresse to Utrecht and Amsterdam wth my Ld Genl Cecill, wth whom he makes account to returne wth in a few dayes by the way

---

[1] Chamberlain, in a letter to Carleton, dated June 26, mentions that Wingfield "was very familiar with Secy. Calvert," which proves, I think, that Cecil's letter was for Calvert, and not for the other Secretary—Naunton.— *Court and Times of James I.*, ii. p. 175.

[2] *S. P. Holland*, 1619.

of Antwerp."[1] And in a later letter Carleton thus indirectly refers to Cecil's return to England :—" Now for a few dayes I doubt not but Mr. Wingfield will have store enough for you ; whose observacons here have bin as particul[r] as any mans I know, and he hath had the opportunitie of seeing much by my L[d] Generall Cecill's companie, but they have changed theyr resolution of going to Anwerp."[2]

A month after this, we find Edward Cecil present at the interesting ceremony in the chapel of Dulwich College when Edward Alleyn, the founder of this College, publicly read and subscribed the Deed of Foundation before a distinguished company, whom he afterwards entertained at dinner. The opening of the College is referred to in the Founder's own diary :—

13 Sept. [1619] This daye wase the fowndacion off the Colledge finish and ther wear present : the Lord Chancellore ; the Lo. of Arondell ; Lo. Coronell Cicell ; S[r] Jo Howland, High Shreve ; S[r] Ed. Bowyare ; S[r] Tho. Grymes ; S[r] Jo. Bodley ; S[r] Jo. Tunstall ; Inigo Jones, the Kinges Surveyer ; Jo. Finch, Counceller, &c. They first herd a sermond, and after the instrument of creacion wase by me read, and after an anthem, they went to dinner."[3]

---

[1] Carleton to Chamberlain, Hague, July 16, 1619.—*S. P. Holland.*
[2] *Ibid.* Aug. 10, 1619.—*S. P. Holland.*
[3] MS. no. ix., *Diary and Account Book of Edward Alleyn,* Dulwich College. See also Warner's *Catalogue of the MS. and Muniments of Dulwich College,* p. 181-2. Alleyn gives the bill of fare at this foundation dinner, as follows—

" Two messe of meat
Capons in white broth
Boyld pigions
Forc't boyld meat
Could rost
Gran salade
A chine of beef
Rost shoulder of mutton with
  oysters
Bak'd venson
Rost neates tongues
A florintyne
Rost capons
Rost ducks, Rost eeles
Westfalyan bacon
Custards."

2nd Course.

" Jellies
Rost godwits
Artychoke pye
Rost partridge
Wett leche
Rost quayles
Codlyng tart
House pigions
Amber leche
Rost rabbit
Dry neates tongues
Pickle oysters
Anchovies."

Cecil's presence at the public opening of Dulwich College (Alleyn's College of God's gift) was probably due to his being one of the Deputy-Lieutenants for Surrey. His signature is to be seen on the Deed of Foundation, with those of the above named persons.

In the early days of August, 1619, the needle of the political compass kept steadily pointing to Frankfort on the Main. And it was there that, on August 20, the Archduke Ferdinand, styling himself King of Bohemia, was elected Emperor of Germany by the electoral vote. This extraordinary man had once again swept aside the obstacles cast in his path by the Protestant Princes. How he did this is not for us to relate now, suffice it to say his iron will carried him safely to the goal, on which he had set his heart from the days of his youth upward. We are told that Ferdinand II. had hardly been proclaimed Emperor before news reached Frankfort of his having been declared in the Bohemian Diet, three days before, to be an enemy to their religion and liberties, and to have forfeited all claim to their kingdom. This news arrived too late to influence the election, but it was a trumpet call to the Protestant Princes to awaken from their apparent lethargy and make a final effort against the persecutor of their religion.

We must again return to Prague, and follow the course of events consequent on the deposition of Ferdinand by the Bohemian Diet.

The Crown of Bohemia being elective, and Ferdinand being declared to have forfeited all claims to the throne, the Bohemians fixed on August 26 for the election of a new monarch. They had already made choice of four candidates to select from, viz.: the King of Denmark, the Duke of Savoy, the Elector of Saxony, and the Elector Palatine. Of these four princes the last named was the favourite—Frederick V. Elector Palatine, head of the German Evangelical Union, and a strong Calvinist. Previous to the eventful day of election, Baron Dohua envoy from the Elector Palatine to the States of Bohemia, produced a strong feeling in favour of his master among the electors, by his diplomacy in vaunting Frederick's character and his fitness for the crown, at the same time that he decried the character of the Duke of Saxony and the other candidates.[1] Frederick also had a strong partisan in the person of Rappowa, Deputy for Lusatia, who, being a Calvinist, was very anxious that the new monarch should belong to that form of religion which was in the minority among the Bohemians, most of whom were Lutherans.[2] As nephew by blood to Maurice of Nassau, head of the Protestant party in the United Provinces, and nearly related to the powerful Maximilian, Duke of Bavaria, the Elector Palatine, if elected king, would have the support of these two powerful and rival champions, as well as that of his father-in-law James of England. At least so thought the Bohemian electors, and carefully weighing these and other considerations in favour of Frederick, they chose him for their sovereign.

The apparent consternation, and evident indecision, with which the young Elector Palatine received the news of his election to the throne of Bohemia, must always lead us to think that he had not sought for, or expected, this honour. As head of the German Protestants, Frederick had taken an active part in opposing Ferdinand's election to the empire,[3] but when all opposition proved fruitless, the

---

[1] *E. de Mansfeldt*, p. 198.

[2] *Ibid.*

[3] The German Protestant princes, thinking that Ferdinand was going to make the whole Germanic body hereditary in his own family, had offered the Imperial Crown to the Duke of Bavaria, and afterwards to the Duke of Savoy, who both declined it, and the remaining claimant, Archduke Albert

Elector Palatine, in common with other electors, acknowledged Ferdinand without hesitation.[1] Writing to his
wife only a week before the Imperial election at Frankfort,
Frederick says : " I have heard nothing from Bohemia this
week, but there is a likelihood that instead of Ferdinand
acquiring a Crown at Frankfort he may very likely lose
two . . . he is a very happy prince, for he has the happiness of being hated by everyone." [2] It is very certain that
many of Frederick's advisers were anxious to hoist him on
to the Bohemian throne, never stopping to consider what
difficulty they would have in keeping him there. Maurice of
Nassau and the Duke of Bouillon, Frederick's two uncles—
the heads and wire-pullers (to use a modern political term)
of the Protestant cause in Holland and France—are said
to have been the first movers in the plan for raising
Frederick to the Bohemian throne.[3] It is impossible not
to feel sympathy for the youthful Elector Palatine in his
state of miserable uncertainty as to how he ought to act
in this crisis of his life. He asked advice all round, and, in
common with everyone who does that, he got the most
conflicting counsels. His old preceptor—Bouillon—was
for his accepting the Crown at once.[4] Louise Juliane,
Dowager Electress Palatine, daughter of William the
Silent, and mother of Frederick V., pointed out to him with
prophetic wisdom the terrible dangers and difficulties that
would beset his path if he left his substance to grasp at a
shadow. The deep love of a mother gave this wise and
pious woman an almost miraculous second sight, as she

---

of Austria, resigned his claims in favour of Ferdinand.—Schiller, pp. 77
and 84.
  [1] Ranke, p. 489.
  [2] "d'Amberg, Aout 13, 1619." Given by Sir G. Bromley in his *Collection
of Royal Letters.*
  [3] Bunnett's *Louise Juliane, Electress Palatine, and her Times,* p. 142.
  [4] *Histoire d'Angleterre, &c.,* par M. de Larrey, iii. p. 738.

foretold, one by one, the dire events that would follow on her son's accepting the Bohemian crown.[1] On the other hand, Maurice of Nassau, who had long planned the scheme of ambition, could not understand Frederick's hesitation in the matter, and saw nothing but glory to Frederick and the cause of liberty, in the Bohemian crown. It is related that Maurice was so angry at his sister Juliane's anticipations of evil, that he asked her hastily if there was any green baize to be had in Heidelberg. "Certainly," she replied, little conscious of his meaning. "What do you want it for?" "To make a fool's cap for him who might be a king, and will not," was the sarcastic reply.[2]

The Bohemian electors were naturally impatient for an answer from Frederick, and Baron Dohna was despatched to Heidelberg. This active diplomatist warned Frederick that the Bohemians already murmured at the delay, and spoke of offering the crown to Bethlem Gabor.[3] The undecided Elector had taken the opinion of his cousin Maximilian of Bavaria, the Duke of Saxony, and other German princes, as to what line of conduct he should pursue, and had he been older and wiser, he would have clearly perceived that the coldness of Maximilian, and the scarcely veiled jealousy of John George, boded him no good if he ever had to seek help from them in the future. Baron Christopher Dohna [4] had been sent to England by Frederick, to sound King James on the Bohemian question. The Elector delayed accepting or refusing the Bohemian crown, until he heard what his royal father-in-law advised in the matter. But it was not James's policy to give a direct opinion one way or the other. Declaring that he

---

[1] *Mémoires de Louise Juliane, Électrice Palatine*, par F. Spanheim, p. 142.
[2] Bunnett, as before, pp. 151-2.
[3] *E. de Mansfeldt*, i. p. 209.
[4] Brother to Baron Achatius Dohna.

must have more information regarding the validity of the deposition of Ferdinand by the Bohemian Diet, and their right to elect a new king, James put off giving his consent, or declaring himself for or against his son-in-law's acceptance of the crown offered him.[1] The English people were unanimous in favour of Frederick being King of Bohemia, and would have gone through fire and water to support him.[2] The Privy Council also were anxious to recognise Frederick as King of Bohemia ; but their King's coldness in the matter prevented any decisive action on their part.[3] Christopher Dohna, taking his cue from the almost universal state of feeling in England concerning his master's affairs, sent letters to Frederick informing him that he believed James would not object when once he (Frederick) had the crown of Bohemia on his head.[4]

Schiller tells us that Frederick was greatly influenced by his young wife ; and that in his state of indecision, she said, "dry bread at a royal table would be more to her taste than the most sumptuous banquets he could offer her in his electoral dwelling."[5] There seems no foundation for this story, which is one of the many speeches put into the mouths of celebrities, that they never uttered, or even imagined. Elizabeth was far too devoted a wife to have let mere ambition incite her to counsel her husband to adopt a

[1] Von Ranke's *History of England*, ii. pp. 489-490. *E. de Mansfeldt*, i. p. 210.

[2] "And it is a great heart's grief to many, 'wrote————to———— on Sept. 16, " that so glorious and brave an occasion should be no better entertained by us, and this noble prince no better seconded in his generous proceeding."—*Court and Times of James I.*, ii. p. 189.

[3] " The zeal of the Council will prevail against those who are too much nourished with Spanish milk," wrote the Earl of Pembroke to Carleton on Sept. 24.—*S. P. Dom.*

[4] *E. de Mansfeldt*, i. p. 210. Ranke, i. p. 492.

[5] Schiller, p. 87. Soeltl, in his *Religions Krieg* (i. p. 153), says this speech was invented by Frederick's enemies.

course productive of so much danger to them both, and, as
she knew, there was but one life, and that not a strong one,
between her and the heirdom to the British crown. It is
quite certain that Frederick took his young wife into his
counsels, and asked her advice in his dilemma. How
could he have done otherwise when he asked the advice
of every one else connected with him by blood or friendship? Who was there—always excepting his mother—
who had his interests more at heart? As a politician
Elizabeth of course was a mere child; both she and
her husband were of that age which looks at all difficult
questions with rose-coloured spectacles, and hopefulness of a
happy issue to the most doubtful speculations. There are
few men in the prime of life, if indeed any, who can throw
away the chances of present power because the future is
veiled to them. And a girl of twenty-one was not likely
to think of consequences. By all trustworthy accounts,
Elizabeth tried only to debate the weighty matter, not
from a worldly, but from a religious view. "Elizabeth persuaded herself that the interest she took in
Bohemia was purely for the sake of religion,"[1] says a
talented biographer of this princess. She accordingly told
her husband that if God had made choice of him as an
instrument to uphold the Protestant cause in Bohemia, it
was his duty to accept the crown.[2] Several writers have
interpreted Elizabeth's religious view of the situation as
merely put on to work on Frederick's feelings.

"We must not regard as hypocrisy the prominence
which the prince and the princess alike gave to religious
considerations," says Ranke; "such was the fashion of
the times generally, and especially of the party to which
they belonged."[3]

---

[1] Benger's *Life*, i. p. 280.   [2] *Ibid.*   [3] Ranke, i. p. 492.

The time had now arrived when Frederick's decisive answer must be sent to the States of Bohemia, and he made up his mind—if a weak character can ever be said to do so—to accept the Bohemian crown. Historians seem very divided in their opinion as to whether Frederick accepted the crown before he heard from his envoy in England what King James advised in the matter. Ranke assures us, that though Frederick was inclined to accept the crown, "he had not yet uttered the final words when Dohna's report came in."[1] On the other hand we find Sir Edward Harwood writing to Carleton on Sept. 14 (old style), to the effect that Baron Dohna had told James that his master awaited his (the King's) advice about accepting the crown, and that the decision must be speedy ; but before the council assembled to consider the matter, news came that Frederick had accepted it.[2] Knowing as we do James's after policy in the Bohemian question, it is easy to conceive that he would not commit himself to giving any direct answer, and it was not possible for Frederick to keep a whole kingdom waiting for an answer any longer.

Early in October, Frederick and his fair young wife departed for Prague, where they were crowned on October 25 (November 4), amidst the acclamations of an impulsive people, with all the magnificent display and unusual ceremonies of a semi-barbaric and wholly simple nation. The youthful Frederick must have forgotten on that one day of universal homage and dazzling pageants, of which he and Elizabeth were the centre of attraction, his mother's wailing cry as he left Heidelberg on that bright

---

[1] Ranke, quoting from secret report in Moser, vii. p. 51.

[2] Harwood to Carleton, Sept. 14, *S. P. Dom.* "However I may decide, there is no peace for me or my country," the unfortunate Elector is said to have exclaimed in his miserable indecision. See also Howell's *Letters*, pp. 72-3.

October morning for his new kingdom: "Alas! the Palatinate is lost in Bohemia!"[1]

Early in the year 1619, James had renewed his treaty with the Princes of the German Union on the same terms as before. The treaty of 1612, being only for six years, had expired. This treaty gave great hopes to the Protestant Princes that if there was to be a war between them and the Roman Catholic League, they would be able to count on the alliance of the King of Great Britain. But in this they were as much mistaken as the Bohemian deputies had been, when they thought that in placing Frederick on their throne they had entrapped James into espousing their cause. The Bohemians showed their hand at a very early stage of the game, by writing to Elizabeth, and begging her to use her influence with her father in procuring for them his alliance and succours, either in the shape of money or troops.[2]

A man of Ferdinand's calibre was not likely to acquiesce in his deposition by the Bohemian Diet, or allow a Protestant usurper to occupy the Bohemian throne. Having once attained the Imperial Crown, he had time to direct his attention to the growing state of anarchy in his Austrian dominions, which threatened to rob him of some of his fairest possessions. Bethlem Gabor, Prince of Transylvania, having espoused the Bohemian cause, invaded Hungary in

---

[1] "Ach! nun geht die Pfalz in Böhmen!" Soeltl *Der Religions Krieg*, i. p. 157.

[2] "Et parce que vostre Ma^{te} nous peut par son Intercession obtenir de Monsr son pere le Roy de la Grande Bretagne beaucoup de Grace et de faveurs, nous supplions pareillement vostre Ma^{te} qu'il luy plaise, pour l'advancement du bien et conservation de la Religion Evangelique, tenir la bonne main envers mon dict Seig^{r} son pere, à ce qu'il plaise à sa Ma^{te} nous tendre la main, et son assistance, soit pour Argent ou par gens de guerre, or en ce faisant conjoinctement avec mon dict Seigneur son Ma a soigner benignement pour ce Royaume."—Extract from a letter to Elizabeth from the Bohemian Deputies, dated Sept. 7, 1619.—*S. P. Germany.*

August, at the head of 60,000 men. By the middle of October, Gabor had reached Presburg, which capitulated after a short resistance, and the modern Mithridates lost no time in laying his hands on the historic crown of St. Stephen,[1] which he valued as much for its intrinsic value as its other sacred properties.[2] The Hungarian nobility, either from choice or necessity, flocked to Presburg to pay homage to the conqueror. Troops from the revolted provinces of Moravia and Lower Austria joined Bethlem's standard, and the Bohemian army, under the Count of Thurn, marched to Presburg to co-operate with Gabor in his coming campaign against Ferdinand. Having secured the neutrality of the Turks,[3] and made a treaty of alliance

---

[1] *Ernest de Mansfeldt*, p. 252.

[2] Bethlem Gabor, whose real name was Gabriel Bethlem, was born of a noble Transylvanian family. He had revolted in 1612 against his sovereign, Gabriel Bathory, whom he caused to be assassinated, and with the assistance of the Turks made himself master of the kingdom. Villermont describes him as a most ambitious and unscrupulous character, whose only aim in life was to aggrandise himself. "For that end all means seemed good to him. Lying was so familiar, falseness so habitual, that no one dared trust to his words, and his contemporaries surnamed him the new Mithridates. . . . A slave to his own interests, he deceived his friends with as few scruples as he did his enemies. He was a perfect master in the art of intrigue, cajoling in turn Christians and Turks, according to the advantages of the moment." *E. de Mansfeldt*, p. 229. "His first wife Carola, tho' well descended," says Harte, "proved the best economist then in Europe, for she was his head cook, and kept the key of his Tokay ; inasmuch as he had negotiated himself with the House of Austria into the possession of that vintage. On Carola's decease he married in his advanced age a young, beautiful princess, sister to the Queen of Gustavus (Adolphus), to whom he assigned three signories on his decease, as likewise 100,000 ducats, as many rix dollars, and as many florins ; which made in all 77,000 pounds sterling. He died in the 59th year of his age, having passed the whole time of his existence in one continued storm of his own making." Harte's *Gustavus Adolphus*, i, p. 171.

[3] The following extract from the treaty made by "Sultan Solyman, Emperor of Turkey, acknowledging Bethlem Gabor as King of Hungary, and promising never to forsake him in his hour of need, and to protect and further his designs whatsoever they shall be," is somewhat curious and novel :

"If I forfeit this pledge let the wrath of God alight on my head ; let me be utterly destroyed and blotted out ; let the Eternal transmute this body to

with Frederick, the wily Transylvanian prince set out for
Vienna on November 24, at the head of a powerful army,
which included Count Thurn's Bohemian army-corps.   The
time seemed admirably chosen for an invasion of Austria.
The Imperialist general, Dampierre, had sustained a serious
defeat a few weeks previously at the hands of Thurn.
Bucquoy had been obliged to seek safety under the walls
of Vienna, where a more formidable general than Thurn
awaited him.   This was the plague, which had caused a
general stampede of the citizens and inhabitants all
round the capital of Austria.   Leopold, the Archduke-
Bishop, who had been left Regent in Ferdinand's enforced
absence, had his hands so full in issuing precautionary
proclamations against the spread of the epidemic, and in
checking the licentiousness of Bucquoy's brutalised soldiery,
that he was ill prepared to undergo a siege ; but such an
old campaigner as he was is seldom taken unawares, and
though short of men, he had the advantage of Wallenstein's
presence and counsel, who alone was worth a thousand
soldiers.[1]   It also appears that Ferdinand had just returned
to his plague-stricken capital,[2] and his master mind was
equal to any contingency.   For three days Bethlem Gabor
beleaguered Vienna, and on the fourth, having received
intelligence of the defeat of his lieutenants in Hungary by
a royalist noble, assisted by the Poles, he suddenly raised
the siege and departed.[3]   The famine and pestilence which
reigned in Austria, also obliged the Bohemian army to depart

stone ; let the earth open wide its jaws to swallow me up from sight, so as
that there shall be neither vestige nor record of me or my armies among the
sons of men.   *From our Imperial Court at Constantinople, November*, 1619."
—Benger, i. p. 366 Ap.
   [1] Wallenstein needs no biographical notice.   His name is a history in
itself.   Suffice it to say that he distinguished himself during this short siege
in repelling the attacks of the assailants.—Naylor, i. p. 113.
   [2] *E. de Mansfeldt*, i. p. 255.
   [3] *Ibid.* p. 256.

with their allies, and their pride being wounded at having a second time to turn their backs on Vienna, they vented their ill-humour and ill-success on their allies. Sanguinary encounters took place between Bohemian and Hungarian soldiers on their line of march, and the two armies were compelled to separate the one from the other.[1] Thus again did Ferdinand's fortunate star appear when all seemed gloomy and dark. Taking advantage of Bethlem's disorganised army, he made a truce with him, which gave Ferdinand time to take fresh steps against his enemies. A treaty was speedily concluded with the three German ecclesiastical electors,[2] by which they engaged to support the Emperor. Maximilian of Bavaria also declared for Ferdinand, the Pope sent him money, and the King of Spain ordered his forces at Naples and in the Milanese to march to the Emperor's assistance.[3] While the Princes of the League were arming to uphold the Imperialist cause, Ferdinand had, by adroit negotiations, decided the King of Denmark to remain neutral, and he had drawn Sweden into a war against Poland. Holland needed all her forces to resist Spain; Venice and Savoy remained neutral, and James of England became the plaything of Spanish perfidy.[4] The Princes of the Union who supported Frederick, seeing what a head was being made against their party, also flew to arms. Each side now tried to engage the Duke of Saxony for their cause. While John George remains undecided as to what line of action to pursue, we must mark the course which James of England, the so-called champion of Protestantism, the father of the

---

[1] See extract from letter of Ferdinand to Maximilian, dated Dec. 5, 1619, quoted in Mansfeldt's *Life*, i. p. 256, note.
[2] The Archbishops of Meintz, Triers, and Cologne.
[3] Rapin's *History of England*, ii. p. 199.
[4] Schiller, p. 93.

Queen of Bohemia, and the ally of the Princes of the Union, thought fit to pursue.

The policy which James pursued on and after the acceptance of the crown of Bohemia by his son-in-law, has been almost universally condemned. But in this, the latter part of the nineteenth century, a change seems to have come over the face of history. Characters that we have been led to despise, policies that we have been taught to condemn by historians we read and believe in, are put before us now in an entirely new light. Authors adopting the same views of certain historical characters that historians have adopted for centuries, are held guilty of " old, partial, prejudiced views," and if they repeat even in a modified form, and free from all Whig or Tory bias, their own opinions on these historical characters, which coincide with the views of ninety-nine out of every hundred writers on the subject, they are declared guilty by the remaining unit of " commonplace repetition " of prejudiced statements.[1] In these days of universal authorship, history, like every other subject, is worn to rags. A work throwing no new light on the subject it treats of, is a useless and ephemeral contribution to literature. And by the same token a work that strikes out an entirely new line of argument attracts attention. But it by no means follows that the latter gives the truest picture of the persons and things it treats of. It is one of the transparent fallacies of this century, that we think we can improve on everything that has gone before, that we can read characters, construe motives, and account for actions, much better than the contemporary writers who were acquainted with the persons of whom they wrote, or those writers who lived soon after those persons had passed away.

---

[1] See article in *Quarterly Review* (Vol. cxxxix.) for July, 1875, on the reign of James I.

The writer of the present day, in commenting on past events, has the great and inestimable advantage of not being much influenced by the politics of that time, which doubtless swayed the contemporary writer, and helped to colour the picture he drew for future generations. No writer can be quite free from Whig or Tory principles. Even supposing a modern historian to be the largest-minded, most impartial and unprejudiced writer ever known, who steers clear of all books, and founds his work on the letters and documents in plain black and white, left by the persons of whom he writes, it must still be borne in mind that the very writers of these letters and state papers are by no means always more impartial, more truthful, or more free from all party spirit and political bias than the contemporary historian who has left us his views in print. It is for this reason that we have, as it were, to read between the lines in studying history, and we, who see the after bad effects of some impolitic measure, should not be too hard on the original cause of it, as could he have seen the results of his policy in the same way that we do, he would have taken a different line of action from the first. When it was too late, James I. saw how mistaken his policy in regard to the Palatinate had been. We have it on the authority of an honest—though interested—writer, that James confessed on his death-bed how mistaken he had been in seeking for the restitution of the Palatinate in Spain, and begged his son to pursue a very different policy.[1] Whether this is true, or not, it is very certain that James was partly answerable for the loss of Frederick's hereditary dominions. Let it be granted that James had from the very first advised Frederick not to accept the Crown of Bohemia ; that he was the one man in England who foresaw the miseries that would ensue from this

---

[1] Rusdorf's *Vindiciæ Causæ Palatinæ.*

imprudent act ; that he was true to his principles of a peacemaker, and an upholder of a sovereign's sacred rights ; that
he did his best to allay the storm by representations and
protestations at every Court in Europe ; that he employed
the most able diplomatists in these negotiations ;[1] that he
was right for the sake of his subjects not to rush into a long
and expensive war ; that Great Britain was ill prepared for
war ; that it was a worldly-wise policy to be on friendly
terms with the strongest power.   Let these and many other
kindred arguments in favour of James's policy be granted, it
must still be deemed a cowardly and despicable policy to
allow a man who had stepped into the breach at the most
critical moment of the quarrel between Protestanism and
Roman Catholicism, and was the instrument, willing or
unwilling it matters not, of the party which James was
bound to uphold, to be robbed of his hereditary dominions, be
outlawed and proclaimed a traitor, without his nearest ally,
his wife's own father, showing a bold front to the enemy,
and making the first invasion of the Palatinate a *casus belli*.
It would be unreasonable to blame James for not supporting
Frederick on his tottering Bohemian throne, and for not
asking the citizens of London for a large loan to bolster up
a hopeless cause ; but when Frederick was compelled to
flee from Bohemia, leaving his crown behind him for good
and all, he ought to have found his hereditary dominions—
which he had ostensibly quitted in the interests of the
Protestant cause—secured to him by the Princes of the
Union and their allies.   And it was chiefly owing to the
obstruction, and benign neutrality of James, whom the
Princes of the Union regarded as their most powerful
ally, and who, of all persons concerned, was bound to help
in preserving the Palatinate intact, if not for the sake of his

---

[1] " We doubt whether any British sovereign was ever served by abler
diplomatists."—*Quarterly Review*, as before, p. 13.

children and grandchildren, at least for the sake of that
religion of which he considered himself a supporter, that
Spain dared to lay waste and sequestrate the Palatinate.
No one ever had so many warnings of what was coming, or
so many opportunities of averting the catastrophe, as James
had, yet he threw them all away, one after the other, and
contented himself with lowering the *prestige* of Great Britain
by the abject remonstrances made by his ambassadors
abroad, who must have often blushed for their master's lack
of manly spirit.[1]

In February, 1620, the Princes of the Union sent an
ambassador to James asking for troops and succours to help
them in resisting the League, and in defending the Palatinate. Here was a grand opening for James, who, if conscientiously convinced that Ferdinand had been illegally
deposed by the Bohemians, might now have drawn his
sword in a really just cause—in the defence of the Palatinate.
Unfortunately, he was not far-sighted enough to adopt this
policy. James informed the ambassador (Buwinckhausen)
that he was only bound to assist the princes, by the terms
of the late treaty, in a defensive war for religion, and as
they had not been attacked, he must decline to assist them.[2]
With this "cold comfort," as Chamberlain calls it, the
princes' ambassador was sent back to Germany with a
present of silver plate which he was too high-spirited to
accept.[3] Spain was in great fear of an Anglo-Dutch force
being sent to defend the Palatinate, and co-operate with the
Union army, and there is every reason to believe that had

---

[1] "Les Ambassadeurs désavouaient bassement à Vienne, à Madrid, à
Bruxelles, l'entreprise de Frederick. Dans ces trois cours on amusait Jacques
de belles paroles : disons mieux on le jouait de la manière du monde la plus
grossière et la plus méprisante."—*Histoire du règne de Louis XIII.*, par
Le Vassor, iii. p. 625.

[2] Chamberlain to Carleton, Feb. 26.—*S. P. Dom.*

[3] Dr. S. R. Gardiner's *History of England*, 1603-1642, iii. p. 341.

James shown a bold front on this occasion, and despatched troops to Germany, the Palatinate would have been saved.[1]

There is no analogy between the usurpation of Bohemia and the invasion of the Palatinate. The Bohemians had of their own free-will deposed Ferdinand, elected Frederick for their king, and invited him to their country. The inhabitants of the Palatinate had not deposed Frederick, or sent for the Spaniards to conquer their country, and give it to Maximilian of Bavaria. Had not then the Protestants of the Palatinate a right to the assistance of the Princes of the Union, and those who were allied with them?

The Union was in danger of dissolution from the schism among its members. John George, Duke of Saxony, the most powerful Protestant prince in Germany, declined to join with the other Princes of the Union in their struggle against the House of Austria. James, their trusted ally, refused to support them. They were in great straits. They made a final effort to induce James to declare for them in the middle of May, but again met with a rude repulse.[2] Were they so much to blame when, two months later, Louis XIII. of France mediated a peace between the Princes of the Union and the League, at the very moment when hostilities were about to commence between the two rival factions, they consented to an honourable peace, as they considered it? This was the Treaty of Ulm, and never was a treaty more foully broken by one of the parties to it. The Princes of the League and Union engaged not to make war one on the other in Germany.[3] Bohemia was

---

[1] See extract from letter of Philip III. to the Archduke Albert (March ⁴⁄₅), quoted in Dr. S. R. Gardiner's *History of England*, iii. p. 335.

[2] R. Woodward to F. Windebank, May 22.—*S. P. Dom.*

[3] "The two armies which lay near Ulme (Catholic League and Union), have turned tail the one to the other, one going to the Emperor's aid against

excepted, but the hereditary estates of Frederick were included, in this convention.[1] Hardly was the ink of the signatures to the treaty dry, than Philip III. sent secret orders to Spinola, who for some time had been concentrating his troops and making his preparations, to invade the Palatinate.[2]

By diplomatic scheming on the part of the League, Archduke Albert had not been included in the treaty signed at Ulm, and was therefore free to order Spinola to invade Germany. Albert was a mere puppet in the hands of the King of Spain, and, as was well known, Spinola received his orders direct from Philip III., and not from Archduke Albert. Philip had belonged to the League since 1610,[3] so that in reality he had broken the Treaty of Ulm, but by a miserable subterfuge, the prince who had been excluded from the treaty was now put forward as the real scene-shifter. Louis XIII. ought to have resented as an insult the flagrant violation of the Treaty of Ulm,[4] but his was not a nature to openly resent any insult.

At the commencement of 1620, Baron Achatius Dohna had been sent to London by Frederick, to obtain from James recognition of his master's title as King of Bohemia, and at the same time to raise a loan from the City of London of £100,000, for carrying on the war in Bohemia. Not only could Dohna get no open recognition from James of his master's title, but he could not get him to ask the City to contribute to the loan.[5] So cautious was James

---

the King of Bohemia, and the Union to defend the Palatinate against Spinola." Carleton to Chamberlain, July 20.—*S. P. Holland.*

[1] Spanheim, as before, p. 159.
[2] *Ibid.*   [3] Spanheim, p. 166.   [4] Naylor, i. p. 136.
[5] The City of London said they would gladly contribute to the loan if certain the King and Council would not blame them.—Nethersole to Carleton, March 21.—*S. P. Dom.*

and fearful of giving offence to the House of Austria by appearing to support Frederick, that he went so far as to forbid the clergy to pray for Frederick as King of Bohemia.[1]

For some months now there had been a strong war party in England, which included most of the nobility, military, and clergy. Frederick had hardly accepted the crown of Bohemia before James was inundated with applications for command of the troops to be sent to Bohemia.[2] But James had no intention of sending any. It was not until the spring of 1620, that Colonel Andrew Gray, a Scotch officer in Frederick's service, obtained a tardy consent to raise a regiment for his master's service.[3] This regiment was to be partly raised in Scotland, and partly in London, James being in no way answerable for their pay. Later on, when Spinola's preparations for war became more and more patent to everyone, excepting James, who was blinded by the dust thrown in his eyes by Gondomar, the Spanish ambassador, Dohna and the war party in England prevailed on James to allow a regiment to be raised and sent to the Palatinate for its defence.[4] Dohna hoped to have been able to send a body of 4,000 British soldiers to the Palatinate to co-operate with the Union army, under the command of the Margrave of Anspach, but owing to James's do-nothing policy, the hoped-for loan of £100,000 from the City had fallen through, and private subscriptions came in but slowly, so

---

[1] His Majesty rebuked Bishop Bayly for praying for the King of Bohemia.— Nethersole to Carleton, January 8.—*S. P. Dom.*

[2] Sir H. Vere to Carleton, October 2.—*S. P. Dom.*

[3] Chamberlain to Carleton, March 11.—*S. P. Dom.*

[4] " It hath pleased his Majesty to consent to the raisinge of 4000 foote under command of General Vere for the defence of the Palatinate." Sir Thomas Roe to Elizabeth, June $\frac{7}{17}$.—*S. P. Germany.* Edward Lisle to Zouch, June 11. —*S. P. Dom.* Vere to Carleton, June 14.—*S. P. Holland.*

that little over half the number of men intended had been raised by the end of July, 1620.

If the Palatinate was to be saved from invasion and confiscation now was the time. Spinola, with 20,000 men, was preparing to march to the Rhine, giving out that he was going to Bohemia, but everyone knew his course would be changed directly he crossed the German frontier. Maximilian of Bavaria was on his way to Upper Austria, at the head of a large force. John George had been won over to the Imperial cause by being offered Upper Lusatia, by Ferdinand, on condition that he conquered it, and he could not withstand the temptation of acquiring a country so near his own kingdom.[1] Such was the ominous state of foreign affairs at the close of July, 1620, and still James believed in Spain and in Spanish honour. Why he trusted to such a broken reed will be made fully apparent hereafter.

It seems that James had held out hopes to Sir Edward Cecil that in the event of troops being sent to the Palatinate, that he (Cecil) should have the command of them.[2] The

---

[1] John George had long meditated defection, and he had never forgiven Frederick for having been the successful candidate for the Bohemian crown. The following extract from a letter of Sir Francis Nethersole's (who had been sent to Dresden to sound the Elector and report thereon) to Secretary Calvert, showed pretty clearly what side John George was likely to choose :—" But being now at last I thanke God gotten safe out that Duke his dominions, and finding in the first town of Bohemia on the Elve (*sic*) an unsuspected cover for my letter to pass Dresden, I will rather give y^r Hon. a blinde accompt in time than a more perfect to late . . . And now concerning the Duke his desseign . . . he holds some towns from the crown of Bohemia . . . and must before a year is over do homage for them . . . is not likely to pay homage to present King as it would be equivalent to recognising his election . . . he receives into his country all refugees from Bohemia . . . admits them to his Court and even to his Councils, &c." " From Teitshen [Tetschen] in the frontiere of Bohemia, this 30th of July, st vet."— *S. P. Germany.*

[2] Cecil to Buckingham, June 25 (?) *S. P. Holland.* " And it was once resolved that Generall Cecill should be generall of them, but that is now altered for Sir Horatio Vere is generall." Young to Zouch, June 14, 1620.—*S. P. Dom.*

Marquis of Buckingham had also promised Cecil his all
powerful support in this matter.[1] But the choice of a
commander was no longer in the hands of the King.[2] It
rested alone with the King of Bohemia, and Baron Dohna,
acting for his master, naturally made choice of the most
experienced English officer he knew. This was Sir Horace
Vere, commander of the English forces in the service of
the United Provinces, and Cecil's senior officer. Dohna
had been greatly importuned by many persons of high
rank for the coveted command. Sir Thomas Roe, writing
to the Queen of Bohemia from London at this time says :—
" I desier y^r Matie should knowe the generall affection for y^r
service hath even in this begotten great emulation ; for
there was almost none worthy of any hope but hath declared
and stoode up for himselfe,—the Earl of Southampton
first, S^r Ed. Cecill, and some others." [3] Sir Horace Vere's
retiring disposition, and modest opinion of himself, made
him refrain from applying for a command which he was
so eminently fitted for, as Baron Dohna was quite well
aware of.[4]

If, as we are led to suppose, Edward Cecil had been
promised the command of troops which ought to have
been sent in the name and in the pay of the King of Great
Britain, but were in reality raised and supported by private
contributions, it was not unnatural that a man of his
ambitious and war-loving disposition should feel hurt at
being passed over. That he was deeply mortified is
certain. " S^r Ed. Cecyl hath received a terrible digrace,"
wrote R. Woodward to Fras. Windebank, " whoe a great
while made full account to goe. And whether the K.

---

[1] Dr. S. R. Gardiner's *History of England*, iii. p. 358.
[2] *Ibid.*
[3] Roe to Elizabeth, June 7.—*S. P. Germany*.
[4] R. Woodward to F. Windebank, July 1 (?). —*S. P. Dom*.

and my L. of Buck. intertaynd him with promises of going,
I know not ; but surely he made great promises to himselfe
and his frends."[1] It is hinted by an able modern historian
that Cecil had in some way or other offended the Queen of
Bohemia—hence Dohna's reasons for passing him over.[2]
Baron Dohna's own words to Cecil, given in his statement
of what passed between Cecil and himself, negative the
idea that Cecil had given offence to Elizabeth.[3] But then,
ambassadors, according to the description given of them by
one of themselves, do not always tell the truth :—"An
ambassador is a good man sent to tell lies for the sake of
his country."[4]

As the unfortunate quarrel between Baron Dohna and
Sir Edward Cecil has been fully detailed by the historian
above referred to, and a jumbled account of it has even
found its way into a French biography,[5] it cannot be
omitted here, however unpleasant it may be to discuss an
affair in which Cecil cut a bad figure. The best method
of arriving at a truthful solution of what passed between
Dohna and Cecil, is to give an account of the affair in the
words of both plaintiff and defendant, and leave the reader
to form his own judgment thereon.

---

[1] Woodward to Windebank, July 1.— *S. P. Dom.*

[2] Dr. Gardiner's *History of England*, iii. p. 358. It appears that there was
some misunderstanding between Elizabeth and Sir Edward *Sackville*, who
was to have been employed in her service : "Here hath been some difference
about Sir Ed. Sackville's attendance on y' Matie and some distaste, I will
not meddle with the relation, only I assuer y' May his own affection, and his
brothers are the same to y' service however the conclusion wil be, and the
Baron Dona is excuseable for he is driven to many straights by importunitye
for privat ends, and it is impossible to content all." Roe to Elizabeth,
June 30.—*S. P. Germany.*

[3] See Dohna's account of his conversation with Cecil, given in this chapter.

[4] Sir Henry Wotton, an ambassador of many years' experience, made this
epigram, which so displeased James I. that Wotton was for some time in dire
disgrace and lost his chance of being appointed Chief Secretary. Chamberlain
to Carleton, November 4, 1612.—*S. P. Dom.*

[5] *E. de. Mansfeldt*, p. 238.

Y 2

"BARON DOHNA'S ACCOUNT OF WHAT PASSED BETWEEN HIM
AND GENERAL CECIL : [1]—

"The Bohemian Ambassador, goïng from Greenwich to Westminster on Saturday 24 June, passed General Cecil's house [2] at 7
in the evening. Seeing the door open he sent his servant to see if
General Cecil was at home, and finding he was then at supper, the
Ambassador passed on, leaving a message to say that having heard
General Cecil was going into Holland, he desired to kiss his
hand, and if convenient would do it next day on his way to
church. Cecil's answer was that it would not be inconvenient,
provided it was before 9 o'clock, because he also desired to go
to church. The Ambassador came before 9 o'clock, and was
received at the head of the staircase, and conducted to the gallery.
Cecil said he had not expected to see the Ambassador there.
The Ambassador replied that it was his duty to come, as he had heard
General Cecil was on the eve of departure. They talked together
about the affairs of the States and Spinola, and then General
Cecil began to complain loudly and accuse the Ambassador of
having been the cause of the ill-treatment he pretented he had
received in these occurrences, and said he did not know how
he had deserved such treatment from the King and Queen of
Bohemia, and the Prince of Anhalt. He said he would complain
to their Majesties, and would ask if it had been their wish that
things should be managed in this fashion. The Ambassador
replied he had always comported himself as a faithful servant of
his Majesty's, and humbly and gently begged General Cecil not to
take that to heart, assuring him their Majesties of Bohemia were
always very affectionately inclined towards him, and that it was
in no way to his dishonour his not having obtained the command
which he had desired ;[3] that there were always many applicants
for the same one appointment, and only one could get it, but it
was no prejudice to the honour and reputation of the unsuccessful

---

[1] This account is translated from Baron Dohna's statement, which is in
French. July—(?), 1620.—*S. P. Holland*.
[2] Cecil House, in the Strand.
[3] "Se pouvant assurer que leurs M. M[tes] de Boheme luy estoient toujours
tres affectionnés et que ce n'estoit aucunement à son deshonneur de n'avoir
peu obtenir la charge qu'il auroit desiré."—Dohna's report.—*S. P. Holland*.

ones. The Ambassador went on to say, he did not think Cecil would have accepted such a small command. Cecil replied that he might not,[1] but would the Ambassador have acted differently if he had known the contrary? He then went on to say that he knew the respect due to Ambassadors, but that Baron Dohna would not always be an Ambassador. On which Dohna said, his ambition had never led him to expect that.

" *Cecil*—' If I ever meet you in another place or in another rank, I shall speak to you in a different manner.'

" *Dohna*—' Alas ! Sir, what do these threats mean ? '

" *Cecil*—' What threats ? I have only too much right on my side for what I say, and I tell you again, If I ever meet you in another rank, &c. (repeating the same words as before).'

" *Dohna*—' If you ever meet me or speak to me in another manner you shall find a man ready to respond to you. Otherwise I am your friend and servant always.'

" Cecil descended the staircase with the Ambassador, who begged him not to trouble himself, but Cecil said he did it for the Ambassador's rank. At the foot of the staircase he bowed to the baron, who returned the bow ; then Cecil mounted the stairs again, the Ambassador got into his coach, and drove off to church."

"SIR EDWARD CECIL'S ACCOUNT OF THE SPEECH THAT PASSED BETWEEN THE BOHEMIAN EMBASSADOUR AND HIM ; THE EMBASSADOUR COMING TO VISITTE HIM AT HIS HOUSE THE 25TH JUNE, 1620 :—[2]

" The Embassadour told me that hearing I was to goe out of England, hee came to wish mee a good journey. I answered that I did much wonder to see him take the paines to come to

---

[1] If Cecil ever said this it must have been from wounded vanity, as he had long been a suitor for the command.

[2] *S. P. Holland.* The MS. is in a clerk's handwriting. See also copy of letter from Cecil to Buckingham in same handwriting, dated June 28 (old style ?), in which he says :—" I have received from his Ma[ties] Ambassadour [at the Hague] here that the Baron of Dona hath so incensed his Ma against me, as I am required to ask pardon for the fault which he pretends I have committed against him . . . I have seen a relation of it written by himselfe wherein he hath either mistaken or putt my wordes into another form for his advantage. For in much of it there is a great deal of aggravation used, taking [out] and leaving and adding as it might best serve for his own construction." —*S. P. Holland.*

my house; the world taking notice what disgrace hee had cast upon mee, and myselfe finding that when I expected well for the divers times of my service in person to the King and Queen of Bohemia, with mine own danger and the losse of my wife, I had at his hand received wrong. He asked me in what. I said, in this, that notwithstanding my former [services], and that I was nominated by his Majestie for the present employment, and that the world tooke notice of it, and hee in particular; yet he would never declare himselfe till I was so farre engaged as hee knew it might prove a dishonour to mee, and then did nominate one who had never done the King of Bohemia service, though he confessed (besides) he had no instruction for it. This, I told him, I tooke for a disgrace that he did purposely meane unto mee; and I could not but be sensible of it. His answer was, hee thought it no disgrace to mee to choose another, the rather because he supposed the command was so small as I would not have accepted of it. I returned him this: that it was not the choice that troubled mee, but the fashion of his proceeding, when having been so often with him, and having directlie expressed my affection to his Maties service, hee would not deale clearlie with mee, nor shew himselfe against mee till he saw mee engaged to the uttermost of my Lord Admirall's promise. But considering him as an Embassadour (I told him), I would saie no more, hoping hee should not alwaise be an Embassadour, and then I would make no doubt but with the Baron of Dona, I might meete, and come to speake of the business upon more equal terms, in some indifferent place.

" Hee said hee hoped I would not threaten him.

" I replied he mistook mee. I did not threaten him; for I hoped when he should be no Embassadour, it would be no strange thing to anie man to hear that I did speake with him upon equall terms. But what did belong to Embassadours I was not ignorant of, and as the King of Bohemia's Embassadour I would give him all respect; whereupon I waited on him down to his coach, and so left him, without anie wrong (in my opinion) either to him or myselfe.

" ED. CECYLL."

Soon after his arrival at the Hague, Edward Cecil sent
the following letter of thanks to his cousin, William Cecil,
Earl of Salisbury, who appears to have stood his friend
when Cecil's back was turned.

SIR E. CECIL TO THE EARL OF SALISBURY.

"MY LORD,

"I never found any thing of pleasure where with I have
beene so much taken, as the injoying of his affection whom a man
honours. Nor have I ever been more sensible of it then now, that
I, by many of my friends, heare how much I am behowlding to y^r
lo. for beying sensible of mulitius offices done mee in my absence,
for the wch I give y^r lo. many humble thankes, and with all I
humble beseach y^r lo. to thincke that I will be as carefull to doe
noe unworthy acte againes my enimes, as I will be carefull to
deserve my friends' good opineon. My lo., y^r beleafe of my
great affection towards y^o, is not one of the least obligation I
howld from y^o wch I beseeach y^o continue, for I will be most
presise to increase it, and continue it so longe as I live.

"For Baron Dona, by the inclosed y^o will find I had more
respect of an Ambassadour than hee of his integritie, and might
justlie have beene the plainteffe my selfe. We looke to Reste
with our army one the 17, if the enime keepe his promis. They
had marched before now, but that some diference that did falle
out betwixte Spinola and the Spaniards, whoe are troubld that an
Italian shall commande so glorius an army as this will be, where
there is the King of Spane's Royall standard to flige (*sic*) which
was never heare (*sic*) before. Spinola's designe is thought to be
the taking in of all the great Townes ajoyning to the Palitenat,
thoughe they be Free townes, as Franforte, Ullemes, Spiers, and
such like. If he gitt them he will wante noe munnye, and
besides lett his army feade of the spoyle of the Palitenat.

"I will howld y^r lo. noe longer but to wishe for some better
occation to show how much I am

"y^r lo. faithfull and affectionat
"kinsman and servant,
"ED. CECYLL.

"Honor me so much that my servis may be remembered to y^r noble lady, for whose hapyines and your and all yⁿ, I will all wayes pray for.

"Hage this 8 of July, ould stile" [1620].[1]

Add. "For my lo. of Salbury
"For y^r lordshipe."

End. "S^r Ed. Cecyll to me."

---

[1] *Cecil Papers, Hatfield*, 128/72.

CHAPTER XI.

1620–1621.

"Some say Sir Edward Cecil can
Do as much as any man ;
But I say no—for Sir Horace Vere
Hath carried the Earl of Oxford where
He neither shall have wine nor cheer.
Now Hercules himself could do no more."

Military Rhyme.[1]

As the last chapter ended with the relation of a quarrel, so must this one begin with the relation of another, of long standing, which Sir Dudley Carleton had the gratification of adjusting.

For many years there had been a difference between Sir Horace Vere and Sir Edward Cecil about the extent of their commands, and to such an extent had this coolness grown, that when the States' army had last taken the field in 1614, Vere and Cecil marched and lodged their troops in separate bodies and quarters, entirely apart the one from the other. This caused both scandal and inconvenience, and all efforts to reconcile the two rival commanders had failed, "by reason of some ill instruments who wrought upon both their discontent, to set them further asunder." [2] Before the States' army took the field in 1620, the Prince of Orange begged Sir Dudley Carleton to try and bring about a reconciliation between Vere and Cecil, before they returned to

---

[1] Quoted by Chamberlain in a letter to Carleton, August 4, 1620.—*S. P. Dom.*

[2] Carleton to Buckingham, June 10, 1620.—*S. P. Holland.*

Holland from England. With this intent Carleton wrote to Buckingham, who, as the King's favourite and Cecil's patron, was the one man likely to succeed in a difficult task. "It were a worke worthy of your Lordship to make them understand one another better," wrote Carleton, "and what they will not yeeld to of themselves, to over rule by His Majestie's authoritie."[1] Before Buckingham had time to take any steps in the matter, the unfortunate disagreement with the Bohemian ambassador had taken place, and directly after that *contretemps*, Cecil left England for Holland to assume command of his regiment, which was about to proceed to the German frontier with the States' forces.

Hardly had Cecil arrived at the Hague before the English ambassador there received a despatch from Sir Robert Naunton, Secretary of State, directing him to send for Sir Edward Cecil, and request him to give an account of the passages that passed between him and Baron Dohna. Naunton enclosed Dohna's account of the affair, and said the ambassador had complained to His Majesty of Cecil's conduct, and the King had at once sent for Sir Edward Cecil, but found he had already gone to Holland.

"Tell him from his Majesty," wrote Naunton to Carleton, "that he will have him acknowledge his fault, and ask forgiveness both of his Majesty and Baron Dohna, or to expect condign punishment from his Majesty whenever he shall return hither."[2] It was in consequence of this letter of Sir R. Naunton's, that Cecil wrote the statement, already given, of what passed between himself and the Bohemian ambassador, and he furnished Sir D. Carleton with a copy thereof. In spite, however, of the contents of this statement, which was more an accusation than an apology, Cecil was obliged to humble himself to the king, as we find by Carleton's reply to Naunton. "General Cecill doth ingeniously[3]

---

[1] Carleton to Buckingham, June 10, 1620.—*S. P. Holland.*
[2] Sir R. Naunton to Carleton, July 20/30, 1620.—*S. P. Holland.*
[3] Doubtless this is meant for "ingenuously."

confesse it," wrote Carleton of Dohna's complaint, " but for the circumstance saith it is much aggravated in the narration, and greatly to his prejudice . . . . Sir Edward Cecill doth humbly ask pardon of his Ma⁽ⁱⁱ⁾, and of the Ambassador, for having forgotten what belonged to his qualitie." [1]

James had no real sympathy with Baron Dohna's feelings, and having himself led Sir Edward Cecil to believe that he should command any body of British troops that might be sent to the Palatinate, he must have felt some sympathy for Cecil's resentment against Dohna. James was quite satisfied by Cecil's apology sent through Sir D. Carleton, and we find him sending a message to Cecil by Sir Edward Sackville early in August, that he was "well satisfied." [2] Naunton also wrote to Carleton informing him James was satisfied with Cecil's apology. [3] The Queen of Bohemia was not so easily satisfied, but her good judgment made her decide to have no more words about it. [4] Thus ended an unpleasant business, all brought about by a hot-headed soldier's restless ambition and desire for command.

At this very same time, Sir Dudley Carleton happily brought about a reconciliation between Sir Horace Vere and Sir Edward Cecil.

" I have the contentment of having done a good worke the day before his Ex⁽ᶜⁱᵉˢ⁾ departure," wrote Carleton to Chamberlain, " in making friendship, after long and many differences, betwixt S⁽ʳ⁾ Horace Vere and S⁽ʳ⁾ Ed. Cecyll, S⁽ʳ⁾ Ed. Cecyll and S⁽ʳ⁾ John Ogle, S⁽ʳ⁾ John Ogle and S⁽ʳ⁾ Charles Morgan, which was a troublesome peece of worke, and of many dayes continuance, but ended happily, and they all dined with me, and dranke one to an other kindly, whereuppon is followed a reconiunction of our English,

---

[1] Carleton to Naunton, July 27.—*S. P. Holland.*
[2] "His Majestie hath lett General Cecyll understand by S⁽ʳ⁾ Ed. Sackvile that he is well satisfied." Carleton to —— August (?).—*S. P. Holland.*
[3] Naunton to Carleton, August 10.—*S. P. Holland.*
[4] Carleton to —— August (?).—*S. P. Holland.*

wch by theyr falling out were separated before Rhees; and thereby they will have more reputation, both here and in the field, as it proved by a joinet request signed by the three Coronels the same day, whereby they have gotten payment of great arrerage owing the whole troopes, and when they come before the Enemie, I doubt not but they will find as good effects of theyr agreement." [1]

On July 22, Sir Horace Vere, with his splendid regiment of 2,250 men arrived at Dordrecht from England, and marched to Delft and other places, where they remained a fortnight. An English writer of the period thus refers to the appearance of this regiment before it left England.

"There never went such a Regiment forth of any kingdome as this which is now preparing—the other is to followe soone after this is gone. The Captaines are all, or the most part, lords, and the Companyes will be filled with gentlemen.[2] The Erles of Oxford and Essex, the ll. Lisle, Cromwell, Garret, Graye, and S^r Ed. Sackvill.[3] They speake now also of the Erle of Warwick, and my l. Chandois. The Erle of Oxford hath a Company of the first Regiment, and is to be Coronel of the next. Sr Thomas Hutton is to be his Lieutenant Coronel, and Sr John Barlacy, that to Sr H. Vere. The griefe is, that old and experienced Captaines, whoe are out of imployment, are now disappoynted by the forwardness of the youthfull nobility. But the preparations are much greater in the Archdukes State, in which there is this particular, that whosoever is owner of 3 horses must depart [part?]

---

[1] Carleton to Chamberlain, August 8. See also Harwood to Nethersole, August 10, and Carleton to Buckingham, August 1.—*S. P. Holland.*

[2] "Sir George Smith is come to a fair preferment for a man of his rank to trail a pike in my Lord of Oxford's company." Chamberlain to Carleton, August, 4.—*S. P. Dom.*

[3] These five last named persons did not go with Sir Horace Vere, whose commission, dated 1st July, 1620, is given in *S. P. Germany*, with a list of his companies, as follows :—"General Vere, 200; Earl of Oxford, 250; Earl of Essex, 200; Sir John Borlase, 150, Lieut.-Col.; Sergt.-Major John Burroughs, 150; Sir Chas. Rich, 150; Sir John Wentworth, Bt., 200; Sir Gerard Herbert, 150; Captain Stafford Willmot, 150; Captain Fras Bucke, 150; Capt. J. Bonygthon, 150; Capt. Wil. Fairfax, 150; Capt. Thos. Thorn-hurst, 150."

with one at a reasonable price for this service, whether it be for
Cleve or the Palatinate ; wherein I pray God oᵣ slownesse and
credulity doe not the like harme as at Wesell. The States have
sent in great hast for all their Captaines here, and wilbe redy
with their Army to wayte upon the Marquis Spinola." [1]

Early in July, James had despatched Sir Henry Wotton,
Sir Edward Conway, and Sir Richard Weston, to Germany,
Brussels, &c., to exhort to peace all the princes engaged in
the quarrel between Ferdinand and Frederick, and to induce
Archduke Albert not to invade the Palatinate.[2] These
embassies of course resulted in nothing, and one cannot
but agree with Sir Anthony Weldon in his remark, "that if
James had spent half as much on swords as he spent in
words, for which he was but scorned, it had kept his son-in-
law in his own inheritance, and saved much Christian blood
since shed." · Christian IV. of Denmark, James's drunken
brother-in-law, though not a character to be generally
esteemed, had the courage to let John George know how
much he despised him for deserting the Protestant cause,
and espousing the side of the Emperor Ferdinand. "I hope
to get the copie of a braving letter from the K. of Denmark
to the D. of Saxony," wrote an English politician, "wherein
he stiles him the reproach and scandal of religion, with
a great deale of vinegar and tartnesse, enough to make him
an enemy, if he weare not so resolved." [3]

Up to the very moment of marching for the Rhine,
Spinola had kept his instructions secret. He informed Sir
Thomas Edmonds, the British envoy at Brussels, that he
had sealed orders, and could not open them till he had
crossed the Rhine. Spinola was good enough to invite
Edmonds to accompany the army if he wanted further

---

[1] Woodward to Windebank, July 1.—*S. P. Dom.*
[2] Woodward to Windebank, as before.
[3] *Ibid.*

intelligence. The Spaniards set out on their march on August 8, and Edmonds accompanied Spinola as far as Coblentz. Here the Spanish commander opened his sealed orders in the presence of the British envoy, and informed him he had orders to make war on all who should declare for the Elector Palatine. This was all Edmonds could gather from the wily Italian. Spinola's next move left no room for any further doubts, even to the sanguine temperament of James, as to where he was bound. "Suddenly wheeling round, he recrossed the Rhine, and when Conway and Weston entered Mentz on August 19, they found the town full of Spanish troops."[1]

The Union army lay near Oppenheim, in the Palatinate, in strength about 12,000 foot, and 4,000 horse.[2] "All good men, and of good courage, as they seem before they come to blows," wrote Sir D. Carleton (doubtful of the way these troops would acquit themselves) to Sir Francis Nethersole.[3] And here we must perforce leave both the Spanish and German armies—the one to invade the Palatinate, and the other to defend that doomed Electorate —while we return to the States' army, and the brave little band of the "new English," as Vere's force was generally termed.

"The Prince of Orange is yet at Arnhem," wrote Carleton to Nethersole early in August, "from whence his next remove will be to Skink sconce, where his troops meet him, not above 2,000 horse and 10,000 foot, but such men as he may trust upon for a good piece of service . . . . General Vere's troops set forward to-morrow from their general garrisons at Delph, Rotterdam and Dort."[4]

In the absence of Sir Horace Vere, the command of the

---

[1] Dr. Gardiner's *History of England*, iii. p. 368.
[2] Carleton to Nethersole, August 7.—*S. P. Germany*.
[3] *Ibid.*
[4] *Ibid.*

British troops in the States' army was bestowed on Sir Edward Cecil, as next senior officer. It would appear from one of General Vere's letters to the British ambassador at the Hague, that the Prince of Orange was inclined to grant more favour and authority to General Cecil than had previously been granted to Vere himself.

"Hee hath bin very earnest with me about Sr Edward Cecill and his command in my absence," wrote Vere to Carleton, " I am (as I tould y^r Lordship), willing that hee should have as much as was exersysed by me, and to have more is more than hee in reason can expect; but for anything I can perceave his Ex^{cie} is desyrous that sutch a kinde of autoritie should be practised by him, as was never yealded unto me." [1]

The States' army conducted the "new English" as far as Wesel, where they arrived the end of August. Since the landing of Vere's regiment in Holland, great pains had been taken by General Vere and his officers to drill the men, and teach them military discipline. Sir Dudley Carleton, who saw two companies of this regiment being drilled at Delft, early in August, by their captains, the Earls of Oxford and Essex, thus criticises them :—

" I saw the two companies there (at Delph) in armes ; and though I liked the men well for new leavies, yet nothing pleased me so much as to see those two great persons take contentment in commanding thyr little troopes, and in obeying their little general." [2]

It being thought unsafe for such a small body of men to march to the Palatinate alone, it was determined by the Prince of Orange that they should have a strong cavalry escort. Accordingly, nearly all the States' cavalry, with a few men from each company of foot, under the supreme command of Prince Henry of Nassau, left Wesel on

---

[1] Vere to Carleton, August 12.—*S. P. Holland.*
[2] Carleton to Chamberlain, August 8.—*S. P. Holland.*

August 31,[1] and crossed the Rhine by a bridge of boats, in company with Vere's regiment, *en route* to join the Union army, under the German princes.

And so departed Sir Horace Vere, with his gallant little British force, who were gone on a forlorn hope. Well might Count Gondomar jest at the smallness of the force James sent to defend the Palatinate, saying, "the English must be a very brave nation, as they sent 2,000 men to encounter 10,000!"[2] Before Sir Horace Vere drifts away from our sight into the whirlpool of the Thirty Years' War, in which, for a brief space of time he was to play a distinguished part, let us express our admiration of his character, which stands out in bold relief in the annals of those times as being pre-eminently grand. Every inch a soldier, and a thorough gentleman. Possessing at all times a calm courage, a cool temper, and a warm heart, he was beloved by his soldiers, who followed him to battle confident of victory. "Had one seen him returning from a victory," says Dr. Fuller, in his article on Vere, "he would, by his silence, have suspected that he had lost the day; and had he beheld him in a retreat, he would have collected him a Conqueror by the cheerfulness of his spirit."[3]

Between Rhinberg and Wesel lay a Spanish force of 6,000 men, commanded by Don Louis de Velasco. These troops, which were in close proximity to the States' army, though somewhat higher up the river, had strict orders not to renew hostilities with the Dutch, but to respect the truce which had not yet expired.

In like manner the Prince of Orange gave his troops

---

[1] Prince Henry was accompanied by Marquette, lieut.-general of horse, Prince Christian of Brunswick, a son of the Landgrave of Hesse and the Lord of Brederode. Grimston's *Netherlands*, p. 1405.

[2] Chamberlain to Carleton, July 8.—*S. P. Dom.*

[3] Dr. Fuller's *Worthies of England*, p. 331.

strict orders to observe the truce, so that the two armies lay side by side in perfect security, each watching the other, and each keeping guard over the frontier towns and forts they severally possessed. During this strange state of affairs the officers of both armies met together on the most friendly terms. A visit of some British officers to the Spanish camp is thus recorded :—

"Certain English volontaries, as my Lord Garratt, and Sr Edward Sackfield [Sackville], who took wth them S^r Ed. Cecill for companie, went to visit about a week since Don Loys de Velasco in his camp, where it was theyr hap to arrive uppon a day of muster, by wch meanes they did see a good part of the armie and make a most contemptible report of it, as not exceeding 6000 foote and 1000 horse; the whole disposition of those troopes being (to use one of theyr words who can judge) poore, disordered, fearfull, sad, and in such ill case both General and soldiers, that they would never have believed it had they not seene it."[1]

Three letters written by Sir Edward Cecil at this period give us some information regarding the small doings of the armies gathered together along the German frontier.

SIR E. CECIL TO THE EARL OF SALISBURY.

"MY VERYE GOOD LORDE,

"I have noe commandment of y^r lordshipe to employ my selfe in at this tyme, nor anie great matter find I heare to make a letter of; yet my affection and servis wch I owe y^o shall ever put mee in minde of this respect, when the meanes, as it now doth, offers it selfe unto mee.

"The new Englishe marched from heance upwards on wedensday last; prepared for their journey, and accompained and convayed with all our horse, rather as an assistance to the Princes then other wayes (for they ar not to come these 3 monthes) who hath seene Spinola with his Armie in there faces

---

[1] Carleton to Chamberlain, (?), Sept. 11.—*S. P. Holland.*

ranged in Battalia 24 houers together and (wee thincke) must fight with him ; which in all reason (if hee resolve upon it) he will force them unto, before this secours come to joyne with them. So as y° may (in likelyhood), by the nexte, heare of a battall fought. Howe soe ever his first designe, which was for Frankford, is interrupted, and for this yeare (I thincke) lost, our Army in the meane time sittes still heere, as Don Lewis de velasquo with his troopes does by Riuskerke, so that wee goe one to anothers Army, till our 6 monthes of truce bee eanded. I was there the other day with my lo. Garratt[1] and Sir Ed. Saxfilde, but wee found a great diference betwixte our Army and thers, for ours is full of discipline and glory, theres full of disorder, poverty and dednes. Wee looke within these 6 weakes to returne out of the fealde, and I hope then to have the honor to see y[r] lo. at london. And so I reast y[r] lo. and y[r] Noble Lades

" moste faithfull servant,

" Ed. Cecyll.

" at our campe before westell
    this 4 of September "[2] [162c].

Add. " Lo. of Salbury."

End. (by 2nd Earl of S.)   " S[r] Ed. Cecyll to me."

SIR E. CECIL TO SIR GEORGE CALVERT.

" RIG. HONORABLE,

    " As I never deserved ill of y° in my hart, so I have nowe assuredly found the successe belonging to an uncorrupted, w[ch] y° have expressed in wryting to mee ; confermed it in my beliefe by the friendly office y° have done mee among the adverse dispositions that I have of late found in the Corte.[3]

    " Wee heare out of Germany that Spinola stood 24 hours in

---

[1] Gilbert Gerard, 2nd Baron Gerard of Gerard's Bromley, co. Stafford, who died 1622.

[2] *Cecil Papers, Hatfield,* 128/71.

[3] Sir George Calvert had stood Cecil's friend in the Baron Dohna quarrel and its results. As far back as July 22, 1620, we find one of Cecil's officers writing to Calvert, and informing him that he had forwarded the Chief Secretary's love to Sir E. Cecil, who sent many thanks for his kind remembrances. Couldwell to Calvert.—*S. P. Holland.*

Battalia to invite the Princes (who have so much threatned what the would doe to him if he came into the Palatinat), but they show noe affection to it (whether it be that they desire that the States assistance [were] joined wth them or not) yet it is like they will come to blowes by compulsion. For it is Spinola[s] advantage to fight with them before theyr ayde come up to them, wch consisteth of almost all the States forces of horse (a brave ayde), besides the 2000 foote carried in wagines of the new Englishe, so as it is probable Spinola is the hotter upon them, and thus y^r next may tell y^o of a Battaille.

" Wee have little heare to doe but to expect the coming backe of our wagines, but not of our horse, wch we expect some 3 weeks hence, and then we looke to returne into Garison, in the mean tyme we are putting our whole Army in to Battalia, to give a triumph to an Extraordinary Ambassadore from Venice, that is passing to the Hage.

" What I can lay hold of to let y^o know from hence I will, as readilie as I can, give y^o an account of it, so I rest,

" y^r H.

" most unfaned friend and servant,

" ED. CECYLL.

" From the
camp this 4 of Sep."[1]

Endorsed in Calvert's hand :—
" 4 Septemb. 1620.
Sr Edw. Cecill to me."

SIR E. CECIL TO SIR GEORGE CALVERT.

" RIG. HONORABLE,

" The newest relations I have received from the Armies above ar these, Spinola hath taken 4 townes, places of no strength, but full of provition for victuall, booth of wines and all sorts of corne, in a quantity esteemed sufficient for the wintering of his whole Army. The Princes ar by all the world censured for leaving them to him ; espetially Oppenheim, and the rather bycause they left the provition for him wch might have beeyn

---

[1] *S. P. Germany*, 1620.

ether transported or destroyed—one thing I must remember to tell you that is over all, as the nwes cam that these townes were taken, the Prince of Orange would seeke to mee to know whether any of those Townes were the ioynter of the Queene of Bohemia, that was as much as to say his Ma^y must looke of necessity to that.

"For the loss of thes provitions, the counsell of Hedelberbe [Heidelberg] ar blamed bycause the[y] would not sell these thinges to the Princes at ieasonable rates. Howesoever, between them booth there is a great oversight committed, wch cannot be otherwise, seeing the Army is commanded by so many Princes, for if it be hard to serve 2 maisters, how can an Army serve many. For there are some that would fight and others will not, and some that will nether resolve to fight or not to fight ; so farr as the souldiers ar ashamed of there [their] commanders. The people of the country are full of feare, the ould Electrice flead wth the children,[1] so that if the States forces wth the new English doe not ioyne in some convenient tyme, wch went from heare some 14 dayes agoe, the[y] are in danger to loose the country for nothing.

"The Prince of Orange is sending from hence some more forces to make a sconce about Bund [Bonn ?] to give some countinance to the 2000 troopes and the new English that ar to pass the mosell, wch as yet we heare is not yet passed, for that Spinola doth seeke by all meanes to hinder them, fearing them more than all the Princes.

"The Prince of Epenay, of Spinola's side, is taken prisoner going from his quarter to meete the reast of his Regiment at the Randevous.

"Heare passed an Extraordinary Ambassidore of venise [Venice] to the Hage, whoe is to returne shortly againe ; he was entertaynd by his Ex^y wth as much honor as our Army could afford any Prince, and I thincke to his good satisfaction as rather to his admiratione.

"The States are in good hopes to make an alliance wth the Kinge of Denmarke, wch will avalle them much booth, and espetially the cause of Bohemia.

---

[1] Two of Frederick's children, who were at Heidelberg, were taken away by their grandmother and placed under the care of the Duke of Wurtemberg.

"I beseeche y° to give this enclosed leave to have yʳ convoye to come to my lo. Admirall, for that it is to thanck him for his favor (in my diference wᵗʰ the Ambassidore), wᵒʰ I receaved by yʳ hands, and if there be any occation to serve y° heare, I will doe it as hartily as if it were for my lo. of Saliburie himselfe, and so I reast,

"Yʳ H°

" most affectionat to serve y°,

" ED. CECYLL.

" From the army before westell
This 14/24 of September."[1]

End.
" 14 Septemb. 1620.

S' Edw. Cecill
    to my master."

The Prince of Orange broke up his camp near Wesel the end of October, and retired his troops into their wonted garrisons for the winter season.

Sir Edward Cecil journeyed back to the Hague in company with Sir Edward Sackville, with whom he seems to have struck up a friendship.[2] Sackville was one of those daring, fiery spirits who were constantly in hot water. One of the handsomest men of his day, and possessing undoubted great talent, he ought to have left a brighter name in history, but his natural profligacy of life out-

---

[1] *S. P. Germany.*
[2] Carleton to ——— (?) October 30, 1620, *S. P. Holland.* Edward Sackville was second son of Robert Sackville, 2nd Earl of Dorset (son of Lord Treasurer Buckhurst) and was born in 1590. His duel with Lord Bruce under the walls of Antwerp, which ended so fatally for the latter, has left a stain on his reputation which time has never obliterated. For Sackville's own account of this duel see his letters published in *The Guardian,* numbers 129 and 133. He succeeded to the earldom on the death of his elder brother in 1624, and on the breaking out of the rebellion espoused the Royal cause, and was appointed Lord Privy Seal and President of the Council. He died in 1652. His younger son, Edward, who predeceased him, had married Bridget Wray, Baroness Norreys, niece of Sir Christopher Wray who married Albinia . Cecil, second daughter of Sir Edward Cecil.

balanced all his fine qualities, and was as a very millstone hung round his neck. A mutual friend of Cecil and Sackville was Sir Edward Herbert of Cherbury, another daring, fiery spirit, whose well known chivalry was carried to such an extent that it bordered on quixotism. Herbert, who had served under Cecil at Juliers, seems always to have entertained a strong feeling of friendship for his first general, and in his letters from Paris at this time to Sir Dudley Carleton, Herbert makes friendly enquiries after both Cecil and Sackville.[1]

Cecil still clung to the delusive hope that James would send troops in his own name and pay to the Palatinate, and that his Majesty would give him (Cecil) the command over them.[2] How little James thought of sending any succours to the Palatinate will be speedily gathered from the details of what passed in the Parliament which James was, at the close of 1620, obliged to summon.

The King had issued a proclamation on November 6, wherein he ordered, "that the knights and burgesses should be chosen of the gravest, ablest, and best affected minds that could be found,—persons approved for their sincerity in religion and not noted, either for superstitious blindness or turbulent humours." [3] Edward Cecil was elected member for Chichester, and took his seat in the Parliament which assembled at Westminster, January 30, 1621.

On November 8, 1620, was fought, outside the walls of Prague, the fatal battle of the " White Hill," in which the Bohemian army was defeated by Maximilian of Bavaria

---

[1] Sir E. Herbert to Carleton, Paris, Sept. 15/25, 1620 ; Oct. 13/23, 1620 ; and July 28, 1623.—*S. P. Holland.* Lord Herbert of Cherbury lies buried in the church of St. Giles-in-the-Fields, in which church Albinia Cecil (Lady Wray) and some of her children were buried.

[2] Carleton to ——— (?) October 30.—*S. P. Holland.*

[3] Rymer's *Fœdera*, xvii. p. 270.

and Count Bucquoy. This defeat decided the fate of the
"Winter King," who had to seek safety in immediate flight,
with his wife and children, leaving his crown and baggage
behind him.

The day after the battle, Prague surrendered to the
Imperialists and Bavarians. When this evil news first
reached England, the nation would hardly credit it, and
awaited in feverish anxiety for a contradiction of the
report. But that contradiction never came, and when full
details of Frederick's crushing defeat arrived in London,
an almost universal gloom spread over the metropolis.
James seemed to be the only man who had expected this
sudden termination of Frederick's reign over Bohemia, and
never having assisted in the smallest way to put the
Bohemian crown on his son-in-law's head, or to try and
keep it on when it was once placed there, he could not be
expected to show much grief at the news. He had been,
however, very sensibly affected by Spinola's successes in
the Palatinate, and had striven by means of a Benevo-
lence to raise a large sum for the defence of his son-in-law's
inheritance. The well known misappropriation and misuse
of these loans was doubtless why the English nation subscribed such a comparatively small sum, notwithstanding
the strong war feeling which animated the greater portion.
Mistrusting the King's foreign policy, the nation clamoured
for a Parliament, and other means of "raising the wind"
having failed, James was obliged, as we have already said,
to issue a proclamation on November 16, summoning a
Parliament to meet on January 16.[1]

Early in this winter (1620–1) the Earls of Oxford and
Essex returned to London from the Palatinate, and having
made a full narration of the precarious state of affairs in

---

[1] The meeting of Parliament was postponed until January 30.

those parts, the King called a Council of War on January 13, to consider and report on the best course to be pursued for the preservation of the Palatinate. The names of the members of this Council were :—the Earls of Oxford,[1] Essex, and Leicester, Lords Wilmot,[2] Danvers and Caulfield,[3] Sir Edward Cecil and Sir Richard Morrison, Knights, and Captain Bingham.[4]

The King opened Parliament in person, and in a long preamble told both Houses what the duty of a Parliament consisted in. He then touched slightly on religion, and held out vague hopes that the Protestant religion would never suffer through him. After this he turned to subsidies and the importance of granting him a speedy supply, declaring how much he had spent on embassies in hopes of saving the Palatinate, and in putting an end to the war in Bohemia. " Now I shall labour to preserve the rest of the Palatinate," continued James, "wherein I declare, that if by fair means I cannot get it, my crown, my blood and all shall be spent, with my son's blood also, but I will get it for him ; and this is the cause of all, that the cause of religion is involved in it, for they will alter religion where they conquer, and so perhaps my grandchild may suffer who hath committed no fault at all. But this is nothing without a speedy supply, *Bis dat qui cito dat.*"[5]

The business of the House of Commons commenced on February 5. Under this date is calendared amongst the Domestic State Papers, a speech of Sir Edward Cecil on

---

[1] Henry de Vere, 18th Earl of Oxford, and Lord High Chamberlain of England. He married Lady Diana Cecil, the beautiful daughter of Will. Cecil, 2nd Earl of Exeter. Lord Oxford died of fever caught at the siege of Breda, in May 1625, where he greatly distinguished himself.

[2] Sir Charles Wilmot, Lord President of Connaught, created Viscount Wilmot of Athlone, in January 1620, for his services in Ireland.

[3] Sir Toby Caulfield, Lord Caulfield and Baron Charlemont, a distinguished Irish soldier.   [4] January 13, 1621.—*S. F. Dom.*

[5] Nalson's *Collections of Affairs of State*, i. p. 13.

the importance of granting an immediate supply to the Palatinate. This " speech " was printed, and many copies of it distributed at the time, as it was both clever and un-common.[1] Unfortunately, there is conclusive proof that it was never uttered in Parliament, either on February 5 or any other day. No mention is made of it in the Parliamentary Journals, and it was certainly not a speech that would have been lightly passed over. The first notice we have of it is in a letter from the Rev. Joseph Meade, to Sir Martin Stutteville, dated April 28, 1621 : " And they say that Colonel Cecil made a brave speech in Parliament concern-ing the want of warlike provisions in the kingdom, and the means to redress it ; they say with much approbation." The next notice we have of it is in a letter of Chamberlain's dated November 16, 1622 :—

" There is a speech of Sir Edward Cecil in the last parle-ment come in print, I know not how, and bycause y^t is not very common, I thought goode to imparte it to you."[2] Carleton expresses his suspicion of the speech in a letter to Chamberlain dated December 3, 1622,[3] and on December 21, Chamberlain replies : " Upon inquiry, I am fully of your opinion touching Sir Edward Cecil's speech, that he was not guilty of it ; but that one Turner about him was the true father."[4] This is all that is known, apparently, about this speech, and for very obvious reasons we are com-pelled to refrain from quoting it or giving Sir E. Cecil the credit of it.[5] " Whoever was the author," says one well

---

[1] *A Speech made in the Lower House of Parliament, anno* 1621, *by Sir Edward Cicill, Colonell, printed in* 1621 (4° Brit. Mus.)

[2] Chamberlain to Carleton, November 16, 1622.— *S. P. Dom.*

[3] Carleton to Chamberlain, December 3, 1622.— *S. P. Holland.*

[4] Chamberlain to Carleton, December 21, 1622.— *S. P. Dom.*

[5] Dr. S. R. Gardiner in referring to this mysterious " speech " in his *History of England* (iv. p. 29, note) says :—" Nothing in the course of writing this work, has been more painful than the act of drawing my pen, in obedience to

able to judge, "the speech does him great credit. There is a fine ring in its language from beginning to end."[1] There was undoubtedly some good reason—political reason—for printing this speech, which every member of Parliament must have well known had not been uttered in the House of Commons. It was an age of pamphleteering, and Sir Edward Cecil doubtless lent his name, as a prominent military man, to promote a good cause, and arouse the nation to a warlike feeling. We are told all is fair in love or war.

The Council of War, of which Sir E. Cecil was a member, delivered its report on February 13. An army of 25,000 foot and 5,000 horse would be necessary to defend the Palatinate. To levy such an army, support it and provide artillery, warlike stores and field equipments, etc., a sum of £250,000 would be needed immediately, and an expenditure of £900,000 a year while the army was in the field.[2]

Secretary Calvert, by the King's orders, informed the House of Commons that an army of 30,000 men would be needed, and that at least £500,000 would be required for their support.[3]

The Commons, not having been told that if they voted the very large sum necessary to support an army of 30,000 men, the King would at once despatch an army to the Palatinate, and being very doubtful of the use the money would be put to, contented themselves with granting the

---

the laws of historical veracity, through the extracts which I had credulously inserted in the text."

I may go still further and say that I had long regarded this speech as one of my firmest stepping-stones in crossing a troubled stream.

[1] Dr. Gardiner, as before.

[2] Report of the Council of War, February 12.—*S. P. Dom;* Grose's *Military Antiquities*, ii. pp. 149–51 ; Dr. Gardiner's *History of England*, iv. p. 31.

[3] Dr. Gardiner, as before, p. 32.

King two subsidies—a sum equal to about £150,000.[1] This was, in the days we write of, a very large grant. " I hear that the parliament have at length concluded to grant his Majesty two subsidies freely and without condition," wrote an Oxonian to a friend, " thereby hoping to find him the more favourable and gracious to grant what they desire."[2] One of the favours greatly desired was that the King should not allow English ordnance to be exported to Spain.[3] It seems that, notwithstanding the exportation of English ordnance was forbidden, James had given leave to the Spanish ambassador to purchase a hundred guns and send them out of the kingdom. This gave great offence to the nation at large, who naturally did not wish to furnish Spain with ordnance to be used against the Protestants. This grievance was brought to the notice of the House, who debated the matter, and sent a petition to the King requesting him to stay the ordnance ready to go to the King of Spain. James refused to withdraw his consent, which he said had been given two years previously.[4]

There were few people more interested in the grievance about the ordnance than the British officers in the service of the United Provinces, as they heartily mistrusted the Spanish ambassador's assertion, and James's reassurance, that these guns were only wanted for Portugal.[5] Sir Edward Harwood, a gallant Low Country officer, engaged to have the House moved about the ordnance,[6] and Sir

---

[1] It is said that the readiness with which Parliament granted these subsidies was a good deal owing to the fact of the King showing what large sums he had expended in the cause of the Elector Palatine.
[2] Rev. J. Meade to Sir M. Stutteville, February 25, 1621.—*Court and Times of James I.*, ii. p. 229.
[3] *Ibid.*
[4] Chamberlain to Carleton, February 17.—*S. P. Dom.*; *Journals of the House of Commons*, i. p. 520.
[5] *Ibid.*
[6] Locke to Carleton, February 24.—*S. P. Dom.*

Edward Cecil was doubtless one of those members who petitioned the King against its exportation. Cecil's interest in ordnance was a well known fact, and as far back as 1613 we find him named for the post of Lieutenant of the Ordnance.[1]

After granting the King two entire subsidies, the Commons proceeded to the examination of grievances, of which there were many. The abuse of patents first attracted their attention. Amongst these monopolies, which had increased to an alarming extent since the accession of James I., three were especially complained of, viz.: the patents for licensing inns and alehouses, and the patent for the sole manufacture and sale of gold and silver lace. Of the last patent a contemporary historian condemns it in these words:—"The lace [manufactured and sold] was made of copper and other sophisticated materials, which were of so poisonous a nature that they rotted the hands and arms, and brought lameness and blindness upon those that wrought this composition."[2] By this iniquitous trade, Sir Giles Mompesson had amassed considerable sums, as any person making any other gold lace was imprisoned and heavily fined. This grievance being brought into the Lower House, a select committee was formed to investigate and report on the case to the House. Sir Edward Cecil was one of this committee, which included such well known names as Sir Dudley Digges, Sir Edwin Sandys, Sir Edward Sackville, Sir Robert Philips, and Messrs. Noy, Pym, Crewe and Glanville.[3] An investigation of Mompesson's transactions, both as regarded his patent for

---

[1] "I hear that Sir Edward Cecil is the Lieutenant of the Ordnance." Chamberlain to Carleton, March 25, 1613.—*S. P. Dom.* Sir Richard Morrison, a distinguished Irish soldier, was appointed to that post.

[2] Arthur Wilson's *Life and Reign of James I.*, p. 731.

[3] *Commons' Journals*, i. p. 530.

licensing alehouses, and his monopoly for gold lace, opened out a long course of corrupt practices. The Commons were not long in impeaching him, and had already agreed as to his punishment, but in their eagerness to punish they had forgotten that they must have the concurrence of the House of Lords. A conference was demanded, and both Houses were unanimous in their verdict and sentence. But Mompesson had made his plans in case of things coming to the worst, and when the Parliamentary officers came to arrest him, he cleverly managed to make his escape, and was soon safe on the other side of the channel. He was declared an outlaw, and his estate confiscated. His partner in guilt, Sir Francis Michel, was degraded of his knighthood, fined a thousand pounds, imprisoned for life, and carried on horseback, with his face to the horse's tail, through the streets of London.[1]

The Commons were so much encouraged by this success, that they determined to correct abuses in a still higher quarter, and sent up an impeachment to the Lords against the learned Sir Francis Bacon (Viscount St. Albans), the Lord Chancellor. With the ignominious fall, and terrible punishment, of "the wisest, greatest, and meanest of mankind," we have nothing to do beyond echoing Horace Walpole's words: "Alas! that he who could command immortal fame should have stooped to the little ambition of power."[2]

About this time a Bill was brought into the Lower House, "for making the arms of this kingdom more serviceable in time to come."[3] This bill, which was a most important and necessary one, has been but little noticed in the various accounts of the Acts brought forward

---

[1] Rushworth's *Historical Collections*, i. p. 27.
[2] *Royal and Noble Authors*, ii. p. 208.
[3] *Commons' Journals*, pp. 542-3.

in this Parliament. Sir Edward Cecil supported the Bill very energetically in the House, and said " he aimed at nothing in this Bill but the good of the Commonwealth, and did not wish to change the arms then in use, but only to order the armourers to keep to the [regulation] size of swords," etc.[1] Cecil was one of the committee selected to draw up a Bill for " finding of arms and muster masters,"[2] and four days before the adjournment of Parliament, we find him again supporting the " Arms Bill,"[3] of which we shall hear more hereafter.[4]

The Commons found time in their zeal to correct grievances, to turn their attention to Ireland, which kingdom was still in its infancy of civilisation. Their good intentions with regard to the sister island were, however, frustrated by James, who desired the Commons to leave Ireland alone, as he considered he was doing all that was necessary for the reformation of that kingdom. The Commons were by no means pleased with this damper to their legislative ardour, and in the debate that ensued on the King's message about Ireland to the House, some of the members freely expressed their discontent. Sir Edward Cecil said : " We desire herein only to assist the King by our information, and such I take to be the sole and whole intent and desire of the House, and not to share in the honour of the reformation."[5] Another member (Mr. Malet) spoke still stronger. " He said there was a great difference in the information received by the King, and that received by the House. The King thought Ireland had never been in a more flourishing state, and the information Parliament

---

[1] *Commons' Journals* p. 543.
[2] *Ibid.*
[3] *Ibid.* On May 31, p. 631.
[4] See letter from Sir E. Cecil to Sir E. Conway regarding small arms, given at the end of Chapter I. in Vol. II.
[5] *Proceedings and Debates of the Commons*, 1620–1., i. p. 358.

received was, that the religion and the state of Ireland were never in a worse state than now, especially for matters of religion ; and he therefore would have them beg his Majesty to give them leave to take further information herein, and then proceed to certify it to his Majesty."[1] As James had positively declined the offer of the Commons to co-operate with him in his management of Irish affairs, the subject had to be definitely dropped. It is only fair by James to say that Ireland made a rapid stride in civilisation and colonisation during his reign, and that the steps he took to reform the Irish were judicious as well as conciliatory.

The crusade against grievances still went on in Parliament, and there was no lack of work for the committee appointed to investigate the crying abuse of monopolies. On April 30, Sir Edward Cecil, who was on the committee concerning grievances, informed the House "that he knew that a nobleman of this kingdom, having a chest of glasses brought over hither from beyond sea, for his own use, the patentees, by virtue of their patent, seized the same, and kept them away from the same Lord."[2] Sir Thomas Puckering said, "that he, being beyond sea, and sending home a small chest of glass before him, the patentees seized them, and detained them still."[3] The patentees were nine in number, and had been granted, for the space of twenty-one years, the sole monopoly in England for making glass. The price of glass, under these nine monopolists, had risen to an exorbitant sum, and the committee, who had investigated this grievance, produced petitions from the glaziers of Lancashire, Gloucestershire, Staffordshire, and Hereford, etc., showing how much they were oppressed

---

[1] *Proceedings and Debates*, i. p. 360.
[2] *Ibid.*
[3] *Ibid.*

by the excessive prices charged for glass.[1] Further
investigation into the complaints lodged against the glass
patentees revealed many acts of injustice to the manu-
facturers and sellers of this article. Accordingly, before
the session closed, "it was resolved, by question of the
committee, that the patent of glasses is a grievance, both
in the creation and execution."[2]

We now come to what is known in the annals of this
Parliament as the "Floyd case." This was certainly one of
the most extraordinary and most disgraceful affairs ever
recorded. A Roman Catholic gentleman, Edward Floyd
by name,[3] a barrister by profession, but at this time suffering
imprisonment in the Fleet for some offence against the
Lords of the Council, was accused of speaking scornfully
of the King and Queen of Bohemia, and of rejoicing at
Frederick's defeat in the late battle before Prague. His
words being reported to the House of Commons, that body
took on itself to condemn and pass judgment on a man
who denied the words imputed to him, and who, not having
been tried, had no means of proving his innocence. The
temper of the House, and the feeling against Floyd, may
be judged of by the different modes of torture proposed by
the members to be inflicted on a man who had not offended
against them. Sir Robert Philips said "that he would
have him [Floyd] ride with his face to a horse's tail from
Westminster to the Tower, with a paper in his hat wherein
should be written 'a popish wretch that hath maliciously
scandalised his Majesty's children,' and that at the Tower
he should be lodged in Little Ease [dungeon] with as
much pain as he shall be able to endure without loss or
danger of his life." Sir Thomas Roe moved "that since

---

[1] *Proceedings and Debates*, pp. 361-2.
[2] *Ibid.* ii. p. 73.
[3] Some writers call him *Lloyd*.

he was committed to the Fleet by the Lords of the Council, he would have them send to the Lords and confer with them touching his punishment." Sir Dudley Digges "would have them first acquaint the Lords and make them sharers in the honour of punishing so vile a subject." Sir George Moore "would have Floyd whipped from hence to the place from whence he came, and then left to the Lords." Sir Francis Seymour "would have him go to the Tower at a cart's tail with his doublet off, his beads about his neck, and that he should have as many lashes as beads." Sir Edward Giles condemned him "to stand in the pillory at Westminster two or three hours, then to be whipped with as many lashes as he had beads, and to be so likewise whipped at Court Gate, the Temple, and then recommitted to the Fleet, for he would not wish any man to come into a worse prison." Sir Francis Darcy wished "a hole to be burnt through his tongue." Sir Jeremy Horsey thought "slitting his tongue" a fitting punishment. Sir Edward Cecil said "they should make a difference between the scandalising of a Prince, and the scandalising of a subject ; he therefore considered boring through the tongue and branding on the forehead a good punishment." Sir George Goring "would have his nose, ears, and tongue cut off, to be whipped at as many stages as he had beads, and to ride to every stage with his face to the horse's tail, and the tail in his hand, and at every stage to swallow a bead ; thus to be whipped to the Tower, and then to be hanged."[1] "Alone among the popular party, Sandys, the veteran champion of liberty, showed some glimmerings of sense," says Dr. Gardiner in his graphic account of this strange and mad scene. "The real cause of Floyd's offence, he

---

[1] For an account of Floyd's case, see *Commons' Journals*, i. p. 601 ; *Proceedings and Debates*, i. pp. 370-1.

observed, was the difference in religion. If in his punishment his religion were touched he would be looked upon
as a martyr. Nor was it proper to whip a gentleman." [1]
Floyd was thereupon sentenced by the House "to be
pilloried three times, to ride from station to station on a
bare backed horse with his face to the tail, and a paper on
his hat explaining the nature of his offence. Lastly, he was
to pay a fine of £1,000 " [2] It must be said in extenuation
of this undue and uncalled for severity, that the members
of the House of Commons were " chafing under the self-
imposed silence which had for many weeks restrained their
tongues from even mentioning the name of the Palatinate,"
and that they " were in a temper to catch eagerly at the first
opportunity which offered itself to give vent to the thoughts
which were burning within." [3] Had the Commons been
obeyed, the sentence against Floyd would have been carried
out to the very letter, but James, who viewed the matter
from a dispassionate point of view, interposed before the
sentence could be carried out. James had justice on his
side, and he only spoke the truth when he told the House
tney had not the power to punish a man who had not committed any fault against them. James also sent the House
a record showing that in the reign of Henry IV. the
Commons had acknowledged that they had nothing to
do with sentencing offenders. [4] The Commons were very
unwilling to accept this ancient record as a precedent, and
determined to make a stand for what they considered their
privilege. " The Lower House attended the King to plead
their privilege to punish Floyd," wrote a contemporary
chronicler to a friend. " His Majesty said they could not

---

[1] See Dr. Gardiner's account in his *History of England*, iv. pp. 119-124.
[2] *Commons' Journals*, as before.
[3] Dr. Gardiner's account.
[4] *Ibid*. p. 122.

condemn a man judicially whose guilt was unproved, but as Floyd had confessed to him, he would take care he should not go unpunished. The House retired dissatisfied ; bold speech of Sir Edward Cecil thereon."[1] The bold speech referred to was evidently Cecil's speech regarding a precedent for the punishment of Floyd by the House, in which he made the bold assertion that the King ought to be respectful of his subjects.[2] Sir Edward Sackville spoke at the same time just as strongly regarding the right of the House to punish Floyd,[3] and as he, like Cecil, was devoted to the cause and person of the Queen of Bohemia, they must both be partly absolved of wishing to raise an unconstitutional precedent.

Meanwhile, the House of Lords judged the proceedings of the Commons to be a great infringement of the Lords' rights, and they demanded a conference with the Commons to consider of Floyd's case and punishment. In the debate which this demand produced in the Lower House, we find Sir Edward Cecil upholding the right of the Commons to proceed against delinquents, and he voted " that we do not go to the Lords to move them to patch up our faults."[4] The King having denied the right of the Commons to punish Floyd, they were obliged to leave the matter in his hands. James turned Floyd over to the Lords, who investigated his case, and condemned him for :—

" 1. Rejoicing at losses happened to the King's daughter and children.

" 2. For discouraging of others, who bear good affection to them.

" 3. For speaking basely of them.

---

[1] Chamberlain to Carleton, May 5.—*S. P. Dom.*
[2] *Commons' Journals*, report for May 2, 1621, p. 604.
[3] *Ibid.* ·
[4] *Commons' Journals*, i. p. 608.

"4. For taking upon him to judge of the rights of kingdoms."[1]

Their judgment was more harsh even than that of the Commons. His fine was raised from £1,000 to £5,000 ; he was condemned to perpetual imprisonment, and sentenced to be branded and whipped.[2]   A small part of his sentence was remitted by the King, but the greater part of the sentence was, to the everlasting disgrace of King, Lords, and Commons, carried out.[3]   Robert Harley, Earl of Oxford, who made a collection of facts relating to the Floyd case, says, " They show how far a zeal against Popery, and for one branch of the Royal family which was supposed to be neglected by King James, and consequently in opposition to him, will carry people against common justice and humanity." [4]

The reformation of abuses, however agreeable it was to the nation at large, was viewed in a different manner by those who had so greatly benefited by the practice of these abuses, amongst whom were to be counted some of the highest personages at Court. These worthies influenced the King against the Parliament, and he, being very jealous of his prerogative, and all that appertained thereto, was ready enough to believe that Parliament was taking too much on itself, and touching his prerogative too closely, if not altogether overstepping the limits assigned to them in his kingly mind. Being imbued with this idea, James adjourned the Parliament at the very time when the Commons were striking at the roots of several hoary abuses.[5]   In the debate which ensued in the Commons, on

---

[1] *Lords' Journals*, iii. p. 133.
[2] *Ibid.* p. 134.
[3] Chamberlain to Carleton, June 2, 1621.—*S. P. Dom.*
[4] *Harl. MSS.* 6274 ; Appendix to *Proceedings and Debates*, ii.
[5] On May 7, a grievance was brought into the House against the Com-

the House receiving notice to adjourn on June 4, Sir
Edward Cecil spoke. " He observed " he said " the House
was divided into three sorts of speakers ; free, silent, and
reserved speakers ; that it had been a good testimony of
the worthiness of the House that at the first they went on so
well, and were so well approved of. It is true, he had
heard, and did believe, there had been ill offices done to
this House by some members of this House ; for, at first
sitting, while the King's ear was open to them, there was a
good harmony between his Majesty and them ; but, by the
carriage of some ill messages, the King hath been mis-
informed.[1] He desired they might have a conference with
the Lords to join with them in going to the King, and to
let his Majesty understand the hearts of this House." [2] It
was on this motion resolved that a message should go to
the Lords to desire a free conference, which message was
accordingly delivered to the Lords by Sir Edward Cecil.
The Lords appointed a meeting for a free conference the
same day. " In vain the Commons appealed to the Peers
to aid them in obtaining a change in the King's intentions." [3]
The day of adjournment was fixed for June 4. Much
dissatisfaction was felt. Many speeches were made, which
savoured more of truth than prudence, in that age when
free speech, even in Parliament, was held to be one of the
seven deadly sins, and punished as such. The boldest,
truest, and most needful speech of the whole session, was
made on June 4, the day of adjournment. This speech was

---

pany of Merchant Adventurers. Sir Edward Cecil spoke against some of the
Company's practices in a short but pithy speech. *Proceedings and Debates*, ii.
p. 35.
  [1] Sir Edwin Sandys in a speech on this occasion spoke of " the many misin-
formations his Majesty had touching the business of this House." *Proceedings
and Debates*, i. p. 365.
  [2] *Parliamentary History*, i. p. 1279.
  [3] Dr. Gardiner's *History*, iv. p. 127.

made by Sir John Perrot, who for long had wished to bring the House to discuss a matter more important even than abuses, and the trade of the country. Taking advantage of a discussion in the House upon the mode of levying customs at the ports, Perrot rose and said :—

"The House had shown itself careful of the ports, but there was something still more necessary, namely, to provide for that port which would be the surest resting-place, and which would procure for them a perpetual rest when the merchandise, trade, and traffic of this life would have an end. True religion must be maintained. Abroad it was in sad case. At home it was in danger. At the beginning of the Parliament the King had declared that if the Palatinate could not be recovered by treaty, he would adventure his blood and life in the cause. Let them, therefore, before they separated, make a public declaration that, if the treaty failed, they would, upon their return, be ready to adventure their lives and estates for the maintenance of the cause of God, and of his Majesty's royal issue."[1] Hardly had Perrot sat down, before Sir Edward Cecil rose and said, "This declaration comes from Heaven. It will do more for us than if we had ten thousand soldiers on the march."[2] Perrot's speech and Cecil's addendum were received with "much joy, and a general consent of the whole House," the members "lifting up their hats in their hands as high as they could hold them, as a visible testimony of their unanimous consent in such sort that the like had scarce ever been seen in Parliament."[3]

Cecil[4] and a few other members were appointed to draw up this resolution of the House. This was at once done.

---

[1] Dr. Gardiner's *History*, iv. pp. 128-9.
[2] *Parliamentary History*, i. p. 1293.
[3] *Proceedings and Debates*, ii. p. 170.
[4] *Commons' Journals*, i. p. 631.

"Again, when the declaration had been read, the hats were waved high in the air. Again the shouts of acclamation rang out cheerily."[1] Thus ended the session. Parliament was adjourned until November 14 ; excepting the subsidy bills, and some naturalisation bills,[2] no bills whatever had been passed. But a blow had been struck against monopolies, bribery and corrupt practices in high places, which did incalculable good, and which must ever make the first session of this Parliament a memorable and happy one to the end of time.

In January, 1621, six Commissioners were sent over to England by the States-General to sound James as to his intentions regarding an alliance with the United Provinces, in view of hostilities recommencing between the States and Spain this spring. It was characteristic of James to answer a question by asking another in return. When the Dutch Commissioners asked him in plain language what he meant to do for the upholders of the Protestant cause, he answered by demanding the intentions of the States regarding the herring trade and other irrelevant matters. The Commissioners made a prolonged stay in England, but met with little civility from the King, beyond being invited, in common with the Dutch, Polish, Venetian, French, and other ambassadors, to a tournament in the tilt-yard on March 24, the day of the King's accession to the crown of England. On that day we read that, "Sir Noel Caron and the six Commissioners from the States were conducted by Sir Edward Cecill to the chamber next the gate at the lower end of the tilt-yard,

---

[1] Dr. Gardiner, as before.
[2] A bill to naturalise "Mrs. Albinia Cecill, daughter of Sir Edward Cecill, Knt., born in Holland" was brought into the Lower House on May 2, and passed on the bill being read a third time. *Commons' Journals*, i. p. 625. This bill was read a third time and passed by the Lords on May 29. *Lords' Journals*, iii. p. 139.

and thus with his company saw the tylting."[1] It appears that James had given the States some cause to believe he intended co-operating with them against Spain as far as the preservation of the Palatinate was concerned, as the British Ambassador at the Hague had been told to make preparations for 10 or 12,000 men.[2] This may have been as a blind to Parliament, and as a consequence of what James had declared in his speech to both Houses. Whatever motive the sudden warlike order had proceeded from, it soon appeared that it meant nothing, and the States had to face the coming storm alone.

Early in March, Pecquius, the Chancellor of Brabant, arrived at the Hague. He was the bearer of important propositions from the Archdukes, on the acceptance or rejection of which depended peace or war. Pecquius, finding the populace " much stirred against him," and in fear of his life, demanded the protection of a guard. This favour the Prince of Orange granted. No one was allowed, on pain of heavy punishment, to visit the Chancellor at his lodging, for fear of corruption and collusion.[3] The day after his arrival the Chancellor was summoned to the Assembly of the States-General. In the names of the Archdukes the ambassador demanded that the revolted Provinces should return to their former allegiance. The gauntlet had been thrown down, and once more the brave little Republic picked it up and accepted the challenge. The twelve years' truce was virtually at an end.

In the phraseology of that time Pecquius was sent " packing home." He was so apprehensive of the rage of the people that he departed from the Hague at four in the

---

[1] *Finetti Philoxensis*, p. 77.
[2] Carleton to Calvert, March 15.—*S. P. Holland.*
[3] *Ibid.*, March 20.—*S. P. Holland.*

morning with twelve musketeers to guard him.[1] He took ship as soon as possible, but met with the grossest incivility at Rotterdam.[2]

Hardly had Pecquius left the Hague before news came that the King and Queen of Bohemia were journeying thither from the frontier, and preparations were made to receive and house them.

Meanwhile letters passed backwards and forwards between Secretary Calvert and the British Ambassador at the Hague. Calvert informed the latter, as a great secret, some weeks before the arrival of Frederick and his family, that the Prince Palatine (as he termed him) had resigned his will and put himself entirely into King James's hands.[3] Frederick was in a state to put himself into any one's hands just then. Deprived of his patrimony and his Bohemian Crown, a fugitive and an outcast from Germany, whose Emperor had just proclaimed Frederick and his partisans to be traitors, in an imperial ban,[4] the ex-King of Bohemia had come in a forlorn state to a strange country which was from henceforth to be his home. Warm-hearted and impulsive, Elizabeth had openly declared her intention of paying her father a visit. In her adversity she yearned for her native land, her father, and only brother. Her mother had died two years previously, and her remaining parent she had not seen since her marriage, eight years previously. As we have said before, James was an affectionate and kind-hearted father, but political difficulties had sprung up like weeds in his garden of love, and sooner than take energetic means to eradicate them, he allowed them to grow before his eyes until they finally hid the

---

[1] Carleton to Calvert, as before.
[2] *Ibid.*, March 22.—*S. P. Holland.*
[3] Calvert to Carleton, March 1.—*S. P. Holland.*
[4] In January, 1620-1.

natural products of the ground from his view. We have it on good authority that James secretly instructed his ambassador in Holland to throw cold water on Elizabeth's plan of coming to England.[1] The ambassador promised to do this,[2] and we may be sure he conscientiously did his duty, as Elizabeth gave up the idea, and father and child never again met on earth.

Although the truce virtually expired in April, neither belligerent took the field until July.[3] The death of Archduke Albert, governor of the Netherlands, in this month, made no difference in the state of affairs. The Spaniards were the first to take the field, and they opened the campaign by attacking Juliers, which was garrisoned by six companies of English, and eight of Dutch and French foot, and one troop of cuirassiers. Count Henry Van den Berg commanded the Spanish army, which consisted of 14,000 men and a battering train. The Prince of Orange assembled the States' forces at Schenkenschaus early in August, and having made a bridge across the Rhine, transported his army into the Duchy of Cleves, and marched straight to Dornick, a village close to Emerich.

"The difficulties of this day's march," says an old historian, in describing the march of the States' troops from Schenkenschaus to Dornick, "were something great by reason of wind and rain, whose storms being violent did beat directly in our soldiers' faces, and besides, the sands grew plashie (*sic*) with the raine, and did much incomodate the marching of our army. Yet labour surmounting these impediments, they arrived at Dornicke about the shutting in of the evening, some few straglers being left behind. Here they lodged that night in the boores' houses, where they were afterwards billeted by order from his Excellency ; who lay

---

[1] See Carleton's letter to Calvert, April 4.—*S. P. Holland.*
[2] *Ibid.*
[3] Sir Horace Vere to Calvert, July 7.—*S. P. Holland.*

to the eastwards of our quarters in a younker's or gentleman's house not far from the old Rhine. His brother Henricke lay near to the parish church, and close by the quarters of the Lord Lisle and Colonel Ogle."[1]

The same historian tells us that the enemy had three armies in the field — one besieging Sluys in Flanders, another hovering about Xanten, watching the movements of the States' army, and a third army, under Van den Berg, besieging Juliers.[2]

Amongst the many notable persons in the States' camp, were the ex-King of Bohemia, Christian Duke of Brunswick, the Earl of Essex, and Sir Henry Rich (afterwards Earl of Holland). "His Matie of Bohemey (*sic*) is every daye in our quarter, but lodges at Emerick" wrote a gallant English captain to Secretary Calvert.[3] The same officer also informs the ambassador in this letter from the camp that, "Generall Cecyll, by order from his Ex^y, commands our Nation this year."[4] Cecil had every reason to be proud of the troops he commanded. Sir Dudley Carleton, in a letter home at this time, thus refers to the army at Dornick :—

"The King [of Bohemia] is now at the camp wth his Ex^y to gayne the experience of this country discipline of which he found the want at Prague. His Ex^y lodgeth in villages betwixt Emerick and Rees, strong 20^m foote and 4000 horse. The Marquis Spinola, on the other side of the Rhyn wth 30,000 foote and 6000 horse, having layde a bridge over that river nere wesell. Nether of the armies are intrenched, nor have hetherto made huttes for the soldiers, so as there is no likelyhood of theyr long abode where they are. There were never fairer troopes of our

---

[1] Grimston's *Netherlands* (continued by W. Crosse), pp. 1412-3.
[2] *Ibid.*
[3] Captain T. Couldwell to Calvert, September 3/13.—*S. P. Germany.*
[4] *Ibid.*

nation in this service, nor never more adventurers of qualitie. My L⁴ of Essex remaines in this armie without returning into the Palatinite. Sʳ Hen Rich came this way the last week and is gon to the armie wᵗʰ six good horse and other solderly equipage, for wᶜʰ I can not but comend him, the comon fault of our countrimen of the best ranke, having bin heretofore to come over to these warres rather like spectators then actors." [1]

Two letters written by Sir Edward Cecil from the camp near Emerich are extant.

Sir E. Cecil to the Earl of Salisbury.

" My Very Good Lord,

" The servis yʳ lo. favours have bound mee unto, will con-tinuallie bee yʳ Agent to call upon mee wheresoever I am, when I may have the meanes of presenting yᵒ wᵗʰ it, not to forgett yᵒ.

" Though wee are in the field, wee have littell to wryt of, not-withstanding the great preparations of the Enemie, three Armies they have on fote ; one of them our neighbours, a second in the land of Juliers, and the thirde in flanders, where it hath had a repulce. What the Enime might have done had hee beene sooner in action, wee dispute not, but the wonderfull deale of raine that fell, is supposed his excuse for marching so late, and the same weather is not yet ceased. So that water is the thing the states have continuallie beene beholding to. If any nwe occatione come to my hand to employ the next messenger wᵗʰ all, I shall bee glade of the occation to tell yᵒ againe that I am
" yʳ lo.
" yʳ faithful servant and kinsman
" to be commanded,
" Ed. Cecyll.

" I can not forgitt my humble servis to yʳ Noble lady, and my servis to Sʳ Arter Capell,[2] whoe I can nether forgitt, when I looke upon his handsome and vallante brother heare, whoe hath hade

---

[1] Carleton to Chamberlain, September 5, 1621.—S. P. Holland.

[2] Doubtless one of the eleven sons of Sir Arthur Capel, of Hertfordshire, whose grandson and successor, Sir Arthur Capel, was created Lord Capel of Hadlam, and perished on the scaffold, March 9, 1648-9.

as bitter a marche as ever I have seene thes 20 years w^{th}out shrinkine.

" by Embricke, this 13 of September. " [1] [1621]

Add. " To the Rig. Honorable and his very good lorde the Earle of Salbury."

End. " S^r Ed. Cecyll to me."

SIR E. CECIL TO SIR GEORGE CALVERT.

" RIGHT HONORABLE,

" Y° are one of those true friends in whome I have found a good interest. My employments in the world have not beene such as were able to bring me much nearer unto y° in y^r courtesies, then only the acknowledging and the hopes I have to become worthy of them. I know not y^r H°. desier, how farr it reaches, to know of any prociding here, yet I cannot chuse but wryte something to lett y° know that in time of warr there never was so little done, yet the preparations of o^r enemie made us look for some great matter this sommer wth his 3 Armies and a great expense. We are loged between Emrik and Rees for the defence of Rees, which one of these Armies points at in all probabilitie to no purpose, the 2. army lootes and pilfers, the 3. at Sluse, where they have received a Repulce. The element of water hath beene alwayes the States' friend; this yeare in ill weather it hath exceeded in frendship to them, having made the defendant side stronger than the assailant, and is gathered for the reason why our enemy hath done nothing. If the weather may excuse them, I am sure it will us, and myselfe likewise, that I have no more to wryt.

    *   *   *   *   *

" If y° have any occatione to imploy any one here, change not my servis for any others, if I may be accounted as able to performe it, so I remaine,

" most affectionitly to doe y° servis,

" ED. CECYLL.

---

[1] *Cecil Papers, Hatfield,* 129/73.

" By Emrick, this 13
of September [1621]."
" For Mr. Seecritary." [1]
End.   " 13 Sept. 1621,
S[r] Edward Cecyll to me,
brought by M[r]. Pringle,
rec[d] in St. Martin's lane,
13 Octob., 1621."

The rain, dirt, want of forage and proper accommodation, bred great sickness in the States' army.[2] The British troops suffered more than any, as they were principally employed by the Prince of Orange in the construction of new works at Rees and in manning the forts when con- structed.[3] Most of the 4,000 men employed in guarding these works perished [4] ; not by the hand of the enemy, as, excepting a cavalry skirmish in which Prince Henry and the Duke of Brunswick were surprised and nearly captured by the enemy, the two armies never appear to have been engaged, but by sickness and disease, which proved a much worse enemy than Spinola and his legions.   The Prince of Orange took great precautions in guarding the Dutch frontier against the enemy.   In this he was eminently suc- cessful, but it obliged him to keep to a defensive, and not an offensive, strategy, and he was unable to march to the relief of Juliers.   Thus the autumn drifted away, and the rigours of winter obliged both armies to retire into winter quarters early in December.[5]   The British, Dutch and French troops returned to their wonted garrisons much

---

[1] *S. P. Germany*, 1621.
[2] Grimston's *Netherlands*, p. 1414.
[3] *Ibid. ;* see also Captain Couldwell's letter to Calvert from the camp, September 3/13.—*S. P. Germany.*
[4] Grimston, as before.
[5] *Ibid.* p. 1415.

reduced in numbers and dispirited by the hardships they had undergone in a fruitless campaign.

Parliament had reassembled on November 20, and there was every prospect of a stormy session, as indeed proved to be the case.

During the recess Sir Edwin Sandys had been arrested and imprisoned by the King's order, for his activity and energy in promoting certain affairs in Parliament which were displeasing to his Majesty. This was the real cause of his arrest, though other causes were hinted at. The Earls of Southampton and Oxford were also put under restraint. The former had committed the grievous fault in the King's eyes of furthering the cause of Frederick. It was said " he had encouraged the Palsgrave in his wars." [1] Oxford had been heard to denounce the intended match between the Prince of Wales and the Infanta of Spain, which was regarded as high treason by the prime mover in this ill-judged scheme. These arrests had greatly irritated both Houses, added to which the complete breakdown of the King's foreign policy, the growing power of the Roman Catholics, the low estate of Protestantism, and the perilous state of the Palatinate, had roused both Lords and Commons, as representing the pulse of the whole nation, to a higher state of resistance against their sovereign's actions than they had ever yet dared to display. Before detailing the measures proposed by Parliament to remedy the state of affairs at home and abroad, it is necessary to give a short summary of the transactions abroad during the last six months, as they were to some extent consequent on the peaceable demonstrations of James and the warlike measures of Frederick and his party.

In May of this year the Princes of the Union disbanded

---

[1] *The Diary of Walter Yonge* (Camden Soc. pub.), p. 41.

their army. The cause of Protestantism, when coupled
with, and one may say saddled with, the cause of the
ex-King of Bohemia, seemed utterly hopeless. An old
historian speaks of these Princes of the Union as " spun-
geous, hollow hearted Princes," [1] but had they met with the
support they had every reason to expect from England,
Denmark and Saxony, they might have acted very
differently. Deprived of his supporters in Germany,
Frederick, in an evil hour, entered into negotiations with
Count Mansfeld, and put his cause into that most reckless
and most unprincipled commander's hands. This hasty
act was one of the greatest difficulties James and his
ambassadors had to contend with in their strenuous efforts
to bring about a peace between Ferdinand and Frederick.
A stone had been set rolling which no one could stop,
and which carried misfortune and devastation in its wake.
The enraged Ferdinand hurled a second ban at Mansfeld
more terrible than the first.[2] It was not fear of the consequences that made Mansfeld swerve from his allegiance
to Frederick and enter into negotiations with the Duke of
Bavaria and the Archduchess Isabella. Fear had no place
in that bold warrior's breast, and he never gave consequences
a thought, but as a soldier of fortune, without any religious
principles to keep him straight, he was at all times ready
to sell his services to the highest bidder. His army was
composed of men who only looked forward to plunder and
rapine, and not to the triumph of the cause they fought for.
Such a leader, and such an army, in a religious war were
sure to do more harm than good, in the long run, to the side

---

[1] Crosse (in Grimston's *Netherlands*), p. 1449.
[2] " The Emperor hath again renued the Ban against the lo. of Mansfelt,
who had almost been murthered by a french man. He is taken and confesseth
it to have been at the instigation of the Jesuits." Extract of a letter from
Frankfort, the 4/14 August, 1621.—*S. P. Germany.*

they fought for. Yet so great was Mansfeld's power in raising large armies to follow him whithersoever he listed, that both Roman Catholics and Protestants tried to come to terms with him. From Bohemia, Mansfeld marched to the Upper Palatinate, where he soon had a force of 20,000 men at his back, the remnant of the Union army. Maximilian of Bavaria, as Ferdinand's lieutenant, had invaded the Upper Palatinate, and with the promise of acquiring that territory from the Emperor, when conquered, he had thrown every possible obstacle in the way of a peace between Frederick and Ferdinand. The sudden arrival of Mansfeld with his army was a serious check to the Bavarian army. Maximilian, knowing the kind of man he had to deal with, made an offer to Mansfeld which was ultimately accepted.[1] The offer was, that for certain pecuniary benefits to be received, Mansfeld should disband his army and not serve against the Emperor. A treaty was drawn up accordingly and sent to Mansfeld to sign. To do Mansfeld justice, we must remember what a precarious position he was in. Serving a master who could give him little or no pay for himself and his soldiers, placed between two hostile armies (the Bavarian and Austrian), and with no succours to fall back upon, his was no agreeable position, and though it cannot excuse his treachery, which by all accounts had been long premeditated, still it must be allowed that the difficulties of his situation had something to do with his acceptance of a dishonourable proposal. We are told he signed the treaty and withdrew his troops to the vicinity of Nuremberg.[2] At this critical moment Lord Digby appeared at Nuremberg and changed the whole aspect of affairs.

---

[1] *E. de Mansfeldt*, i. pp. 514-6.
[2] *Ibid.*

Digby, the most able and the most far-seeing of all James's ambassadors, had been sent in the summer of this year to Vienna, to mediate a peace between Ferdinand and Frederick. The latter had consented to put himself entirely into James's hands, and if he had kept his word, and made due submission to Ferdinand, renouncing at the same time all pretensions to the Crown of Bohemia, he might have been restored to his electorate, or a part of it. Such pressure was put on Ferdinand, and his affairs were in so unsatisfactory a state in the summer of 1621, that if Frederick had remained perfectly passive, there is good reason to believe Lord Digby's mission to Vienna would not have been in vain. The Archduchess Isabella had been persuaded by Sir George Chaworth, envoy from James, to intercede with Ferdinand on Frederick's behalf,[1] and even Spain, for real or pretended reasons, raised her voice in the Elector Palatine's behalf.[2] The auspicious moment, however, for effecting a peace and reconciliation, was lost, never to return. The same events which depressed the Emperor, raised new hopes in Frederick's youthful breast. His conduct reminds one of the old adage :—

" The devil when ill a monk would be ;
  The devil when well, the devil a monk was he."

The very fact of Frederick joining the States' army, and proceeding with it to Emerich irritated the Emperor, and Mansfeld's invasion of the Palatinate in the name of the ex-King of Bohemia destroyed the chance of peace. It is true that Mansfeld agreed to disband his army, but before

---

[1] Sir George Chaworth's *Journal* in the *Loseley MSS.* edited by A. J. Kempe, p. 464, *et seq.*

[2] It was said that Count Mansfeld intercepted a letter from the Emperor to the King of Spain, in which he much blamed him for soliciting him to give up the Palatinate and to trust the King of England with it, being a heretic.— Walter Yonge's *Diary*, p. 47.

the treaty was duly carried out, Lord Digby had appeared on the scene, and so remonstrated with the versatile Count, that once more Mansfeld turned round, and to the utter surprise of friends and enemies alike, marched with his whole army to the Lower Palatinate, after tearing up the Duke of Bavaria's treaty, and sending him a message of defiance.[1]

Mansfeld's arrival in the Lower Palatinate was hailed with joy by Horace Vere's little band of troops, who were garrisoning the important towns of Heidelberg, Frankenthal and Mannheim. The Spanish general, Cordova, was at that time laying siege to Frankenthal, of which place Captain John Burroughs was governor. Mansfeld's arrival compelled Cordova to raise the siege and retire. With the exception of the three towns named above, all the Lower Palatinate was in the hands of the Spaniards, and the Upper Palatinate was overrun by the victorious Bavarian troops. Lord Digby hastened his return to London, and on his arrival made James acquainted with all these important facts. Parliament, which had been prorogued, was summoned to meet on Nov. 20. James wrote once more to Ferdinand on behalf of Frederick, who had been induced some time before to leave the Dutch camp and return to the Hague. The pith of the King's letter was, that if Ferdinand would reinstate Frederick, in the Palatinate, James would guarantee that Frederick should renounce for himself and his son all pretence of right and claim to the Crown of Bohemia, and crave the Emperor's pardon upon his knee. If Ferdinand declined to do this, James gave him to understand there must be war between them.[2]

---

[1] *E. de Mansfeldt*, i. p. 516.
[2] James I. to the Emperor Ferdinand, November 12, 1621. *Cabala*, Pt. ii., p. 113.

Parliament was opened (in consequence of the King's being detained at Newmarket by illness) by the Lord Chancellor—Williams.[1] The Lord Keeper, after declaring all that his Majesty had done for the nation, by issuing proclamations against no less than thirty-seven grievances complained of by the people, and by doing all in his power to bring about a peace on the continent, and the restitution of the Palatinate, informed the Commons that the King had sent £40,000[2] to support the army in the Lower Palatinate. He finished by demanding a supply. Lord Digby, who had been commissioned by James to inform Parliament of the results of his mission to Vienna, next spoke. After detailing what had happened abroad, Digby informed both Houses that he had discovered it was the Emperor's intention to bestow the Upper Palatinate on the Duke of Bavaria. It was therefore absolutely necessary, he added, both to keep Count Mansfeld's army together, and to send a strong supply of British troops to the Palatinate.[3]

The Lord Treasurer (Lord Cranfield) said his Majesty's coffers were empty, having been exhausted by the sums employed in the defence of the Palatinate, and a liberal supply was therefore needed.

The Commons met to debate the King's message on

---

[1] John Williams, Dean of Westminster, Bishop of Lincoln, had been advanced to the dignity of Lord Chancellor of England, on July 20, 1621.

[2] Rushworth, i. p. 39. £30,000 appears to have been the sum sent by James early in November. See a letter from Sir D. Carleton to J. Chamberlain, dated March 9, 1621-2, in which he complains of "a troublesome office of receiving and disbursing 30^m£ sent about three months since to the King and Queen of Bohemia out of England, which was putt upon me by his Maj. commandment, and I leave it to you to imagine that this sum being wholly expected on one side by Count Mansfeld for his troops in the field, on the other by my Lord General Vere for his garrisons, there be many gaping after it for payment of debts, how hard it was to feed so many pigeons with one beane." *S. P. Holland,* 1622.

[3] Rushworth, p. 40.

Nov. 26. After some very animated debates concerning the alarming decline of the Protestant religion, the growing power of the Roman Catholics (both which occurrences were justly laid to the intended marriage of the Prince to a Spanish Princess), and likewise the necessity for a more decided policy as regarded the Palatinate, the Commons drew up a remonstrance against the growth of popery, and the Spanish match, advising the King to take his sword into his hand for the speedy and effectual reconquest of the Palatinate.[1] James no sooner heard of the intended remonstrance of the Commons, than he wrote to the Speaker, and sharply rebuked the House for debating on matters which he asserted were far above their reach and capacity ; forbidding them to meddle with anything that regarded his government or deep matters of state, and not to concern themselves about his son's marriage with the daughter of Spain.[2] This remonstrance, and the answer it met with, form a good illustration of the distrust and ill-feeling which had unhappily crept up between the King and Parliament, and which were to bear such bitter fruit in the subsequent reign. From a letter of Prince Charles to the Marquis of Buckingham, written at this time, it would appear that the Prince shared his father's low estimate of what the duty of a Parliament consisted in.

PRINCE CHARLES TO THE MARQUIS OF BUCKINGHAM.

" STEENIE,

" This day the Lower House has given the King a subsidy, and are likewise resolved to send a message humbly to entreat him to end this session before Christmas. I confess that this they have done is not so great a matter, that the King need to be indulgent over them for it ; yet, on the other side (for his reputation abroad

---

[1] Rushworth p. 41.   [2] *Ibid.* p. 43.

at this time), I would not wholly discontent them ; therefore my opinion is, that the King should grant them a session at this time ; but withal I should have him command them not to speak any more of Spain, whether it be of that war, or my marriage.[1]

" This, in my opinion, does neither suffer them to encroach upon the King's authority, nor give them just cause of discontentment.   I think you will find that all those of the council that the King trusts most, are likewise of this mind.   Sir Edward Cecil wrote me a letter from the army, of much stuff, but it was of fashion ; the most of the letter was of reasons why the King should enter into a war for the defence of the palatinate, and trust no more treaties.   But the end of it was that he might be employed in it.   Now, in earnest, I wish the gentleman well, but yet I would not have Sir Horace Vere (who has both endured so much misery, and so good service there) either to be discouraged or disgraced ; therefore I think the King shall do well to employ Cecil, but I would not have him come over other's head.   So, praying you commend my humble service to the King, I rest,

" yours more than can be expressed, and

" as much as can be thought,

" CHARLES P." [2]

This letter explains Sir Edward Cecil's absence from the Parliament.   He did not return to England until the middle of December, and after the Commons had addressed a second remonstrance to the King, which sufficiently

---

[1] " It was strangely reported also at this time that the Spaniards had promised a restitution of the Palatinate to the Prince Elector, which gave the King great content.   It is possible that he [Philip] hearing of the successful proceedings of the later parliament, and how much the English desired war, fearing a greater danger, meant really to have performed that promise ; but, hearing that it was dissolved, to the great grief and discontent of the whole kingdom, they grew secure of any great action to be attempted from hence, and so altered their former resolution, for to this day they could never be drawn to any such restitution."—*Harleian MSS.*

[2] Halliwell's *Letters of the Kings of England*, ii. pp. 161-2.   See also *Harl. MSS.* 6987, art. 96.   This letter is undated, but it was evidently written on November 28, as Chamberlain in a letter to Carleton dated December 1, says, the Commons agreed to grant the King a subsidy on the previous Wednesday, which was the 28th of November.—*S. P. Dom.,* 1621.

showed that they knew their own strength and dignity.[1] The second remonstrance was couched in still stronger language than the first, and contained this plain-spoken bit of advice, viz : "that the voice of Bellona must be now heard, and not the voice of a turtle ; that there was no hope of peace, and his Majesty must either abandon his children or else declare war."[2] James sent a copious reply to the second remonstrance, again advising the Commons to keep to their proper sphere, and plainly telling them they had no title to interpose with their advice except when he was pleased to ask for it. Their privileges, he said, were derived from the grace and permission of his ancestors, and if they wished him to maintain and preserve their privileges they must contain themselves within the limits of their duty.[3] Hardly had the Commons recovered from their consternation at this reply, before another letter of the King's, on the same subject, addressed to Secretary Calvert, was made known to them. This letter was of a very conciliatory nature, and modified, though it did not retract some of the pretensions he had arbitrarily laid claim to. In the debate that ensued on the reading of the King's letter in the House, on Monday December 17, Sir E. Cecil took a part, and in a short speech, said, "he would have them go on with the bills and business of the House, if it be but to show their thankfulness to his Majesty for his gracious message ; but he would principally have them appoint a committee to consider of their privileges. He was glad to see by a precedent even now showed by Sir Edward Coke, that it had been an ancient use that on discontent the House hath use to be silent, and it was now no new thing."[4]

---

[1] Rushworth, i. p. 45.
[2] *Ibid.*
[3] *Ibid.*, pp. 50-2.
[4] *Parliamentary History*, i. p. 1353.

Sir Thomas Wentworth, Sir E. Coke, and other members had moved that the privileges of the House should be set down in writing by way of protestation. Their advice was followed, and a committee was formed to draw up the protestation of the House, and enter it in the journals of the House. This memorable protest asserted "that the liberties, franchises, privileges and jurisdictions of parliament are the ancient and undoubted birthright and inheritance of the subjects of England."

When James was informed of this proceeding, he determined to dissolve Parliament. He came to Whitehall on December 30, and having sent for the journals of the House, he tore out the page recording the protestation, in the presence of the Privy Council and Judges. He then prorogued the Parliament, and soon after dissolved it by proclamation. Sir Edward Coke[1] and several leading members of the House were committed to prison, and others were sent to Ireland,[2] ostensibly to act as commissioners, but in reality to get them out of the way for a time.

It would appear from a letter of Sir Edward Cecil's, written in the spring of this year, that he had a house at Chelsea, where he resided when in England. This letter has been reserved for the end of this chapter, as its contents are entirely irrelevant to any subject before treated of, but being a characteristic letter, and referring as it does to one of the most interesting churches in London, it would be a pity to omit it altogether. Space does not allow of the answer to this letter, or of Cecil's second letter on the subject, being given here, but it may be stated that the disputed matter was satisfactorily arranged.

---

[1] Sir E. Coke had been created Chief Justice of the King's Bench in 1613, but having lost the favour of James by his opposition to the illegal exercise of the royal prerogative, he was displaced in 1616, and was returned to Parliament in 1621.

[2] Chamberlain to Carleton, March 9, 1621-2. —*S. P. Dom.*

SIR E. CECIL TO SIR JOHN LAWRENCE.[1]

" SIR,

"I received a letter from you wherein you tel me of exceptions you take at a pue I made in the Church at Chelsea, which I had then answered if your dwelling had beene so well knowne to mee as mine is to you. You pretend a claime of royaltie by inheritance unto it. I send you now an account of my self and my purpose touching your claime. When I came into the Church I found all men accommodated with pues, speciallie you and your house, sufficientlie becoming your person and qualitie. I intruded upon no man, but found out an unhandsome neglected corner, imployed in nothing but for the roome of an old rotten chest. Seeing everie man served, I thought it no iniurie to goe into that poore corner to serve God in. I have been at the charge of the pue in that place, which was never put to this use before. You take a rent for your owne, and make use of my charge. I know not what greatnes belonges unto you that you cannot content yourself with a reasonable proportion in só little a Church, nor what strange kind of malice it is you beare mee that you seeke to keepe mee out of a place in the Church that till my coming into it you never made account of to serve God in, and I believe not now, but to serve yoʳ owne humour in. In such a case there is a simile of a Dogge in a Manger that may not unfitly be applied unto it. Now for your authoritie and inheritance. I cannot understand the iustnes of it. In my minde these are thinges given in generall to the parish, especiallie when they concerne groundes that have not beene used and are to be disposed of by the Churchwardens. For my Grandfather and some other of my frends have made pues in St. Clementes,[2] and St. Martine's,[3] and wee their children can challenge no right but what the parish

---

[1] Sir John Lawrence, Knt., of Chelsea and of Delaford in the parish of Iver, co. Bucks, was created a baronet in 1628. He married Grisel, daughter and one of the co-heirs, of Gervase Gibbons, by whom he had a son, John, afterwards Lord Mayor of London, who succeeded as second Bart. The elder Sir John died November 13, 1638, and was buried in the Lawrence chapel in Chelsea Church, where several members of this ancient family are buried. The title became extinct in 1734.

[2] St. Clement's Danes in the Strand.

[3] St. Martin's-in-the-Fields.

will allow us. Therefore, I would wish you (Sir) to forbeare my pue, and not to valleu yourself at so great a rate, and mee at so little, as to possess it when you know I am in Chelsea, unless you wilbee content, as I shall find it, to take as great an affront as you have done me. I pray you consider with yourself what you have done, and what you will doe.

" Y^r frend

" ED. CECILL.[1]

" Aprill ye 29th, 1621." [2]

Add. " To my Worthie Friend,
      Sir John Laurence
      Knt:, &c., &c."

---

[1] Very few of Sir E. Cecil's letters are signed "Cecill," as he almost invariably spelt his name "Cecyll."

[2] This letter, which is in private hands, is published in *Notes and Queries*, xi. second series (January, 1861), pp. 13-4. Sir John Lawrence's answer, and a counter reply from Sir E. Cecil, will be found in same vol. pp., 14-5.

END OF VOL. I.